HOLLY BOURNE is an author and journalist. Her feminist education began when she read Caitlin Moran's *How to be a Woman*, but it was working at an advice charity for young people and her own experiences of blatant everyday sexism that drove her to write critically acclaimed *Am I Normal Yet?*. Followed by *How Hard Can Love Be?* and now *What's a Girl Gotta Do?*, the trilogy is an incredibly honest and hilarious insight into the complexities and contradictions of being a teen feminist. Holly has appeared at #FeminisminYA panels across the UK and Ireland. She is a 2016 World Book Night author and was shortlisted for the YA Book Prize.

www.hollybourne.co.uk

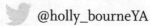 @holly_bourneYA

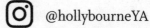 @hollybourneYA

HOLLY BOURNE

WHAT'S A GIRL GOTTA DO?

USBORNE

For every girl who does what is right,
rather than what is easy.

First published in the UK in 2016 by Usborne Publishing Ltd., Usborne House,
83-85 Saffron Hill, London EC1N 8RT, England. www.usborne.com

Text © Holly Bourne, 2016

Author photo © Dannie Price, 2016

The right of Holly Bourne to be identified as the author of this work has been asserted
by her in accordance with the Copyright, Designs and Patents Act, 1988.

The name Usborne and the devices 🏆 🌐 are Trade Marks of Usborne Publishing Ltd.

A CIP catalogue record for this book is available from the British Library.

JFMAMJJ SOND/16

ISBN 9781474915021 03983/8

Printed in the UK.

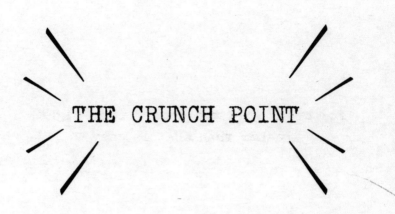

THE CRUNCH POINT

one

I wasn't even wearing a short skirt.

Stupid thought. Totally stupid thought.

But, afterwards, as I stewed and cried fat hot tears of rage, I kept thinking...

...I wasn't even wearing a short skirt.

If you really want to know what I was wearing, so you can reassure yourself that I was the perfect victim in all this, it was just a normal pair of jeans. And my lacy jumper. BUT CALM DOWN – all that erotic lace was FULLY HIDDEN under my duffle coat. So, unless pervy van men have X-ray vision – *and let's all for a minute thank God that they don't* – I was wearing nothing, *nothing*, to trigger what happened that day.

Which was this...

I was running late for college, due to an epic argument with my parents about My Future. This was a regular thing. My Future is their obsession, but this particular spat over

My Future had been pretty nasty. For reasons known to nobody, not even me, the argument ended with me shouting, "Meditate on THIS!" and grabbing my crotch. I'd then slammed the door in their stunned faces and dashed down the road. Almost crying.

It was cold and bright. A nice October day, but one where the golden sunshine has no impact on the temperature. I was half-running, partly because of my lateness, and partly to keep warm.

I saw the van as I turned the corner.

Two builder-types sitting in the front seat noticed me straight away. They stared at me through the windscreen. The way they assessed me sent an instant blodge to my stomach.

That female intuition blodge.

The *there's-going-to-be-trouble* blodge.

No – screw that. It's not female intuition. I'm not psychic – I'm just highly experienced in sexual harassment, like pretty much every other girl on this earth who dares to walk places.

The van was parked on my side of the quiet, residential street. The only side of the road with a pavement. I paused for a second, weighing up my options. I sensed trouble, but I had to walk past the van. Even though I already felt sick from the way they looked at me. Like I should be ashamed...

Maybe I'm wrong about them, I thought. One of them was as old as my dad. Maybe they were just innocently looking out their windscreen. Maybe there wouldn't be any trouble. And because I was exhausted and alone and already upset and all-the-things-I've-just-told-you, I didn't walk past them with my normal confidence.

I instinctively averted my gaze, pretended they weren't staring, pulled my coat further over my totally-concealed chest and walked faster towards them.

I was approaching the van. I could still feel their eyes on me. But I was almost there. And almost there meant almost past them…and…it would be fine…I would be fine…and it was broad daylight anyway and I could always scream but I wouldn't need to scream because it would be okay and I'd imagined these builders being worse than they are, and…and…and…

…and then the van door opened.

I stopped dead. Their open door now blocked the pavement. The younger man was slowly getting out and I looked up, all darting and scared. Because why had they opened the door? I heard a slam and flinched. It was the other van door. Because the other guy had got out too. My head whipped in his direction and I saw him walk around the bonnet, closing me in. He was bald, old, all red in the face like he'd had one too many for too many years.

I had one man in front of me, one behind. I was pinned in. Hardly any space to get around either of them.

The man blocking my way forward spoke first.

"You look very sexy in that red lipstick," he said, his voice so leery I shuddered and recoiled.

Oh yes. I forgot to tell you. I was wearing red lipstick.

IS IT MY FAULT NOW?

He bent over, right in my face, giving me no choice but to look at him. He was younger than the other – with fluff instead of proper facial hair.

The bald man behind me joined in.

"You wore it especially for us, didn't you, love? We like it. We really like it."

My heart beat so fast I thought it would combust. My breath was already short and sharp. There was a man in his garden across the road, deadheading a plant. I looked at him desperately, silently asking for help. But he seemed to be deliberately pretending not to notice.

"What's wrong, love? Why aren't you talking to us?"

"I…" I stammered. "I…"

"Shy, are you? Shy girls don't wear lipstick like that."

The younger man stepped forward again; I had no personal space left. His breath stank of something sweet, like he'd been drinking Red Bull. I looked around frantically, sizing up the gap around him. Calculating if I could fit through.

I saw a chance. I took it.

I barged past, pushing his arms up as I fled down the road as fast as I could. My feet thumping hard on the pavement, my heart going nuts. Were they going to chase me? It was broad daylight.

"PRICK-TEASE," one of them yelled after me.

The insults pelted off my back. I ran and ran – so sure they'd follow me. So sure this wasn't finished yet.

"COME ON, LOVE, IT WAS ONLY A COMPLIMENT."

"RUDE BITCH."

The cold air hurt my lungs, ripping down my throat. My stomach wanted to empty itself. I shook so hard I could hardly run in a straight line.

I couldn't hear their footsteps behind me. When I reached the end of the street, I dared myself to quickly look back.

The two men were leaning up against their van. They were laughing. Leaning over and grabbing their knees, giggling like children.

And, as I struggled to hold back the tears that had bubbled up and lodged in my throat, I thought:

But I wasn't even wearing a short skirt.

two

Steadily, my day got worse.

I got to class just in time and whimpered my way through politics and economics – hardly able to concentrate. My hand shook as I held my biro, scratching down notes that made no sense. I kept replaying the scene in my head. The way they'd looked at me. The way it had felt when they'd blocked my path.

I felt so many emotions at once, as my teacher droned on at the front about the failures of our first-past-the-post voting system.

Shame – like I was to blame. For wearing my stupid lipstick, just because it matched my bag and, until that morning, had always made me feel happy.

Embarrassment – at letting them get to me so much. Though it felt like the builders had ripped off my clothes and exposed me to the whole neighbourhood.

Fear – that they'd be there on my walk home...

And pure, white hot rage. At them – why did they think they could treat me like that? Why didn't that man help me…? But also at myself… Lottie, why the hell didn't you yell back? What sort of weakling are you?

When my lesson finished, I went straight to the college canteen for my philosophy study group. A few of us queued up for chips, as was our custom. By then, I'd stopped shaking, but I still had *all* the emotions.

"Hey, Lottie." Jane joined me in the queue, with a milkshake on her tray. "You okay? You look kind of wiggy."

I smiled back at her. Jane was old friends with Evie, one of my two best friends. We'd been put in the same philosophy class again for our A-level year and I was finally warming up to her after a couple of false friendship starts.

"I'm okay…" I found myself lying. "You ready for all the fun of deontology?"

Jane sighed and ran her hand over the new pink section of her hair.

"I'm ready for you to help me understand it."

I nodded to Mike, and a few others who'd joined the queue behind us as we inched our way towards the hot food section. I stood on my tiptoes to see the state of the chips.

"Ergh," I said loudly, "they're nearing the end of the batch. I hate end-of-the-batch chips – they're always soggy and cold."

"Maybe someone before you in the queue will order them first?" Jane said.

"Let us hope, Jane. Let us hope."

But nobody ordered chips before I got there. I looked down at the measly leftover ones – some crispy, some bent and soggy – and frowned. I turned to the other study group guys in the queue behind me. "So, it's going to be very 'utilitarian' of me if I order these," I joked. "I'm going to take the hit by finishing off this batch of old chips, but then you guys get the good ones."

But no one was really listening and it pissed me off, because now I had a plate full of poo chips and no one laughing at my amazing philosophy joke.

While Mike and the others ordered chips from the lovely new tray that was brought out, I walked towards the table in the corner we always used. It was stuffy and smelled of egg sandwiches. The sunshine flooded through the giant glass windows, making my face hot and the egg-sandwich smell worse. When we'd all assembled, there were seven of us in total – me, Jane, Jane's boyfriend Joel, and four other guys. Mike was running the group today. I'd kissed him when drunk and overexcitable about my five As on AS results day and he hadn't quite forgiven me yet for not letting it turn into anything more than that.

Mike gave me his obligatory evil over the table and began. "So, guys, I talked to Mr Henry and he said that deontology and utilitarianism will definitely be on the exam…"

His words faded to background babble as I picked up a cold chip unenthusiastically and the morning whirred through my head again. It had been SUCH a bad argument with Mum and Dad. Dad still hadn't got over me dropping my fifth A level at the start of term. Even though I only need four to get into Cambridge. And he'd tried, yet again, to change my mind this morning – even though we were a month into the academic year now. Mum had flittered nervously between us, as always. Trying and failing to keep the peace.

"You need to think about your priorities," Dad had said. It was always Dad who started these things. "You only get this one shot, Charlotte."

Mum chipped in. "I know this Spinster Club is very important to you, darling. And we're so proud of you…but don't you think the time is better spent doing that extra A level, just in case?"

Me, Evie and my other best friend, Amber, had formed a feminist discussion group last year called The Spinster Club and it had really taken off. College had even turned it into a proper club – FemSoc – that we ran together. The whole thing made me supremely happy, but Dad wasn't so chuffed.

"Look, Charlotte," Dad added, "aren't you worried how this feminism group will look on your UCAS application? I mean, it's not the most…traditional of extra-curricular activities. Doesn't your college have a debate team or something? It's a bit more Cambridge…"

He was such a hypocrite! All *let's save the world* and *we're all equal* until it came to his ambition for his one and only daughter. Then his obsession with The Prestige And Importance Of Education rendered him all double-standardy.

And Mum, well…she was mostly chanting half the time or just saying what she thought she should say to make us stop fighting.

I shook my head, bringing myself back to Mike's drony voice droning on and on…

"Okay, so the way I see it, utilitarianism is all about the greater good…"

He was so stupid… We'd gone through all this on, like, day one of this module. I hated it when I wasn't allowed to run study group but we all took it in turns. Why had I kissed him again?

"So, if we apply this theory of utilitarianism to…" Drony drone drone… My brain faded out again and I watched Jane play with her pink hair.

Those builders…the way they'd looked at me…

I'd spent the morning arguing with Mum and Dad about feminism – only to walk out my front door and straight into a glaringly obvious reason why we *needed* feminism.

Why didn't I yell back at them?

The way they looked at me…

I shuddered. So noticeably that Jane gave me a small *I'm bored too* smile.

I gave her a half-smile back, and turned my attention to a group of students over at the ancient college jukebox – shoving a pound in and giggling.

There was a pause, and the first song echoed around the cafeteria's speakers. A murmur of laughter rippled through the tables.

They'd chosen Marvin Gaye's "Let's Get It On". It was beginning to become a college-wide joke to constantly play this song on the jukebox.

"And, well, if we look at last year's exam questions..." Mike tried to continue over the shrills of Marvin's voice, but he wasn't getting through. Joel had already turned to Jane and begun his own over-the-top serenade. His ponytail flapped behind him as he dramatically mouthed along with the lyrics. Jane wiggled her shoulders...even my own pen tapped in time. I relaxed into the cheesy music until Mike said loudly...

"So a really easy way of understanding utilitarianism is to think about chips in the canteen."

My pen dropped to the floor, and when I re-emerged from picking it up, Mike was pointing at my plate.

"So, Lottie here sacrificed a nice plate of chips for herself by taking the last of the stale batch, knowing more of us would get better chips after her. A perfect example of utilitarianism, right?" He grinned around at everyone, inviting them to laugh at his point – and they did.

Everyone was smiling, nodding. I shook my head. Too confuzzled to speak.

"That's a good point, Mike."

"Yeah, I never thought it could be as simple as that. But you're right."

"Sorry about your chips, Lottie." Joel saluted, like I was a soldier. Then they all laughed again.

I caught Jane's eye, to see if she'd noticed. She shrugged

and rolled her eyes at Mike, confirming my outrage.

I didn't laugh. I didn't nod. I didn't agree with the others.

I couldn't believe it.

That was *my* point. And *my* joke!

And Mike was shamelessly passing it off as his own.

What was worse was that everyone was listening to him.

Because Mike had said it.

Not me…

Mike.

And the only reason I could see it being better now than when I'd said it was…because Mike was a boy…

three

By the time the bell rang at the end of the day, I was completely het up. I'd worked through lunch, trying to get through all the extra reading I needed to do to get an A* in English lit. In my own company, I let the festering muck of my morning seep into my entire being.

I felt a mixture of numb, furious and helpless.

I don't think that is even psychologically possible.

Why did they take more notice of MY point when Mike said it?

Why hadn't I stood up to those disgusting builders?

Why did stuff like this keep happening?

All I wanted was to go home and reset, but we had a FemSoc meeting. Evie was chairing this one and I knew how nervous she was about talking in front of people. I had to go for moral support. I picked up my books and made my way to the meeting room in the art and photography block. My phone buzzed with another *we're sorry* message from

Mum. She couldn't handle it when we fought. It wasn't in her "ethos" to have "negative energy" with anyone.

Her words...not mine. *So* not mine.

I didn't even know what today's meeting was about. I hadn't had time to look through the agenda Evie had emailed last night. We hadn't expected FemSoc to take off the way it had. Last summer term we'd campaigned to get this offensive song removed from the college jukebox. We won – which was great. Half of college hated us for it – which wasn't so great. But lots of girls expressed an interest in joining and we now had over twenty members. We'd only had two meetings so far this term, but more girls had turned up to each one. And Evie, Amber and I still ran our own private Spinster Club meetings out of college – so we could spend time together, just us.

You can't adequately share cheesy snacks with twenty plus people.

I pushed my way through the heavy double doors and the hubbub of everyone's conversations hit me as I stepped into the meeting room. Some of them waved hi as I walked to the front, and I waved back weakly – hardly able to muster the energy. My emotions still swirled around my body, like a vortex had opened up in my guts. The worst thing was that today had felt so ergh...but really...what had happened that was so extraordinary?

Evie was a jangly mess, her normally sleek blonde hair

all straggly from running her hands through it. Amber had her arm around her, muttering reassuring things.

I made myself smile. Not wanting to worry them. Not at Evie's big moment. I plopped my bag on the chair next to them. "How's the blood pressure?" I asked.

Evie took an exaggerated breath. "Remind me why we decided to make this a public club again?"

Amber wrapped her arm around tighter. "Because it will look good on our uni applications?" she joked.

I shook my head. "Not according to my dad."

They both made *aww shucks* sympathy faces – they'd counselled me through many an argument about this with my father.

"And, anyway, it's public because we want to save the world. And we cannot do that holed up in Evie's unnaturally tidy bedroom, eating cheese on toast and preaching to just each other."

"Stop being so reasonable." Evie's eyes darted out over the crowd. "You know it doesn't work on me."

I smiled sadly. I knew… Evie has OCD – though she's got it pretty under control at the moment. She got really ill last year, before Amber or I knew about it. I felt guilty for asking her to run the meeting. It was tough being Evie's friend sometimes. You had to maintain a delicate balance of not pushing her too hard to do things that scared her as it made her feel crap about herself, versus knowing that sometimes the odd nudge helped her grow.

I put my arm around her, so we were all hugging.

"You're going to be fine. You know that, right?"

She smiled. "I just still can't believe you're letting someone else talk."

"Hey," I said, while she and Amber burst out laughing. "I'm not that bad...hang on...yes, I'm definitely that bad." I had a reputation for being quite...umm...chatty. Though today all I wanted to do was sit in the corner quietly and mull. My mood had got steadily worse.

The last few trickles of girls came in and the room quietened, sensing the meeting was about to start. I pulled out my notebook and pen and started sucking on the end.

Evie rustled some papers and stood up, readying herself. Amber pulled her chair up next to me. "You think she's going to be okay?" she whispered. "I saw her wash her hands beforehand..."

The blodge of guilt blodged blodgier.

"I think she'll be fine," I said, though not entirely convinced. "She does still do that sometimes. Just as long as it's not all the time, I guess."

"You read her agenda?"

I shook my head. "Not had time."

Amber inched forward – a stray bit of her frizzy red hair tickled my cheek.

"Speaking of being okay, are you okay?" she asked. "We missed you at lunch. And, well, you look upset about something."

I sighed again and opened my mouth to tell her – but just as I did, Evie coughed to signal the start of the meeting.

"Hey, everyone." Her voice squeaked with nerves. She coughed and started again. "Hi, everyone."

The girls, all sitting in rows facing us, quietened respectfully.

"Thanks for coming." Evie's hands shook but her voice got stronger with every word. "So, in the last meeting, we decided we wanted to campaign for something. You've all put forward some ideas, and I thought today we could run through them and see if we could get a shortlist to vote on? There's a lot here we could really get our teeth into... Can someone at the back dim the lights, please?"

Someone scuttled to the light switch and plunged us into gloom. Evie clicked a laptop and the big white screen behind her lit up.

"Trust Evie to make it all super-organized," Amber whispered to me. "I bet you ten pounds she gets out a special pointy stick."

I smiled in the darkness. "When I hosted the last meeting, the only prep I did was sing 'Eye of the Tiger' to myself into the mirror," I whispered back.

"Think what would happen if we combined the pointy stick with 'Eye of the Tiger'. I reckon you've just come up with an excellent strategy for taking over the world."

Just as we started laughing, Evie gestured to the screen behind her.

"Okay, girls, here's the first entry. Sonia put this forward." Sonia, a short girl with incredibly long, blonde hair, nodded and smiled. "It's a new aftershave advert that Sonia thinks we should campaign against. Hang on…" Evie fiddled with the mouse to click play. "Right, here it is." She pointed to it with the handle of her umbrella, which was almost a pointy stick. I would've giggled if the video Evie was pointing at wasn't so completely distressing.

Loud edgy music blasted out as a girl and boy – both insanely good-looking – rolled around on a bed with exposed brickwork in the background. Then the boy flipped himself on top and started pinning the girl's arms down as he kissed her more aggressively. She laughed, but tried to fight him off. My heartbeat had already quickened and I felt my insides turn in on themselves. This wasn't good…this so wasn't good. Then the boy reached into his jeans pocket and got out some of the aftershave, sprayed it on, and the girl stopped resisting. She started gasping and groaning as the guy kissed her neck and then it faded to black.

There was a stunned silence. A cough the only thing punctuating it as the room digested what we'd just seen.

"Umm, Sonia?" Evie asked. "Do you want to stand up and explain why you think we should use this as a starting point for a campaign?"

She nodded, and stood, tucking some hair behind her ear.

"Yeah, so…I saw this on TV last night and, well, I think we can all agree it's worrying. I mean it's essentially normalizing force in regards to sex, even romanticizing abuse and rape in relationships…"

And that's all I heard before I saw Megan, a new member, stand up quietly and practically run out of the room. Her face was all red and pinched, like she was trying hard not to cry.

I stood up too. Not many people seemed to have noticed, most were listening to Sonia.

"I mean, I'm sure you all know that statistically, girls are more likely to get raped by someone they know – like a boyfriend or an ex. This advert is practically encouraging that. It's basically saying 'Buy our aftershave and it will help you abuse your girlfriend – she won't even mind! She'll like you pinning her down!'"

Evie had noticed though, and silently nodded at me, encouraging me to follow Megan. So I stood up and pushed my way out to the corridor, looking both ways to see where she'd gone.

I found her in the nearby ladies' toilets, washing her hands under the tap. Crying.

"Oh, hi, Lottie," she said, like nothing had happened. Even though her hands were shaking and tears rolled down her face. She stood upright, hastily wiping the evidence of distress from her cheeks.

"Hey. I just wanted to see if you were all right?"

I didn't know Megan hugely well. It sounds awful, but I knew her more as "Max's girlfriend". She'd gone out all through Year Twelve with this guy, Max, from a band we knew called The Imposters. She was in mine and Amber's art class but never spoke much. She and Max had seemed so in love – I hardly ever saw her without him. So we were all surprised when he'd broken up with her over the summer.

Even more so when she'd joined FemSoc, as she'd never expressed an interest when they were together.

Megan still had her hands under the water, even though all the soap was off them. Her dark hair hung over her face.

I stepped closer, seeing that all of her was shaking – not just her hands.

"I'm fine."

"Megan?" I stepped closer again. "Did something in the meeting upset you? The advert?"

She stood up straight then, looked me right in the eye. Her cheeks were all blotchy and her eyelashes were clumped together with wet mascara. She turned the tap off, shaking her head slightly.

"I'm fine…I'm fine… It's just…well…that advert… Max…it kind of brought something back." Her voice broke on the word "Max", stuttering over his name. "He…he…" She trailed off, shaking harder.

What?!

"Megan, did Max, do someth—"

"Sorry, I didn't mean to cause a fuss," she interrupted suddenly – her voice strong again. "I must be getting my period or something."

She yanked a towel out of the towel dispenser, dabbed at her face, dried her hands and chucked it roughly into the bin. It bounced back out again. What was she saying? What had happened to her?

"Megan? I'm sorry if the meeting triggered something… something that happened between you and Max?"

Megan shook her head. "No, you didn't. It didn't, I mean. I'm fine. Fine." She must've seen the doubt on my face. "Honestly!"

"Megan?" I found all I could do was just repeat her name. "You can tell me…"

"Nobody will ever believe me anyway," she said, almost to herself. Then she looked up at me and smiled. She actually smiled. "I might not come to the rest of the meeting, if that's okay?" she asked, like she needed my permission. "See you in art tomorrow?"

And before I could stop her, or say something, or hug her, or do anything other than stand there feeling confused and sick, she'd breezed out of the toilets – leaving only the sweet smell of the college apple soap behind her.

four

The FemSoc meeting was almost over when I slipped back inside. I'd spent a while sitting on one of the toilets, my face in my hands, trying to digest what had just happened.

Evie was just wrapping things up while Amber scribbled down people's ideas on the whiteboard.

"Thanks for all your great ideas," Evie said. "It sounds like we've narrowed down what we want to do. We can go through a shortlist at next week's meeting and vote then. I'm really excited, guys."

Everyone descended into talking and laughing and there was a fizzing in the air of good ideas.

I stood, still helpless. Amber noticed from across the room and mouthed, "Are you okay?" and I nodded...then shook my head. Amber held up her hand to say *give me a minute* and I gave her a small smile. Part of me felt broken. I'd had hairline fractures inside me all day, and this meeting, and Megan, had suddenly ripped them into chasms.

Normally I would've been the one talking the loudest, getting the most excited, getting everyone else fired up by my enthusiasm. But today, all I could do was picture Megan's shaking hands. The way her voice had stumbled on the name "Max". All I could see was those two guys and the way they'd looked at me, and how I hadn't done anything about it. All I could think was, even if I had stood up to them, it wouldn't have made a difference anyway.

Nothing makes a difference anyway.

Not to people like them…

So what was the point?

Evie flopped over her desk as people started filing out and I gave her a huge hug.

"You were amazing," I managed to say.

"Really? My hands are still shaking."

"Honestly. Totally brilliant. You're a good public speaker, you could definitely be a politician or something."

She broke the hug and smiled up at me, looking worried. She could obviously see something in my face.

"I thought you were the one who wants to be prime minister?"

I did this raw odd laugh I didn't recognize.

"Lottie, are you…?"

Amber bowled over before she could finish, wringing her hands. "Lotts, what's wrong? Why did Megan leave? I was about to follow her, but I saw you go."

I let out a huge deep sigh – not sure what to say.

"She was crying in the loos," I started. "I think that advert was a bit close to home. She mentioned Max. You know? Her ex-boyfriend, in Ethan's band? She…" I inhaled sharply, Megan's words cutting through my insides like shards of ice. "She didn't say exactly, but she implied…she…"

"Go on," Amber prompted, her eyes all wide.

"Well, she implied that maybe Max had done something to her…sexually… Well, I *think* that's what she was implying. She didn't spell it out. But she was shaking… I think that advert definitely triggered something…"

Evie welled up. "Damnit! I'm so stupid! I didn't think to warn anyone beforehand what the advert was about… I'm so dumb!" She thumped the table and we all listened to the noise echo around the silent room.

I was trying to think of everything I knew about Megan and Max. They'd seemed happy…although I did find it weird that she followed him everywhere and didn't talk much. They held hands wherever they went. She wore his hoody all the time. And Max…he seemed nice… He played guitar with this guy we knew called Ethan. He smiled at everyone. He once got up at our college Battle of the Bands and dedicated a song to her. Everyone was shocked when he broke up with her over the summer… I mean…*he* broke up with *her*… But now Megan was implying he'd done something awful to her… Well not exactly implying… She just couldn't stay in the room when Evie played that advert. I was guessing. But I also had a horrible suspicion I couldn't ignore – from the way she ran out of that meeting, from the way she said his name – that he'd done…something to her.

Amber broke the silence and gave Evie a squeeze. "We're all new to this, Evie. I didn't think of warning anyone either. And we don't know for certain anything did happen with Max and Megan."

"It did," I insisted, even though I was practically just saying it to myself. "It must've done. The way she shook, girls… And she said 'no one will believe me anyway'. Surely that must mean something?"

Amber blinked a few times, shook her head, like she was trying to dislodge what I was saying. "Well, we don't know for certain, but, yeah, we've learned we need to warn people next time if we're going to mention abuse in our meetings."

My mind flashed back to that morning – to those men. The way they'd so obviously felt entitled to me. That my body was theirs to comment on.

And even though it seemed petty compared to everything else, I thought of Mike, and how he'd stolen my point. How he maybe hadn't even realized it was mine. How it got more acknowledgement regardless. Was that petty? Or did things like that lead to bad stuff happening too? Was it all linked? Did all the horrid little moments where girls got treated like crap somehow create a society where the horrid big moments could happen – like whatever had made Megan's voice shake in the college toilets?

I closed my eyes and pushed my thumbs into them, liking how the pressure felt.

"Lottie?"

God – if what I'd guessed was true, I couldn't even imagine how Megan felt. For her not to say anything. To just let everyone carry on thinking Max is some nice guy in a band. My head started banging, like a tiny monkey was inside my brain, smashing the sides in with a hammer.

"LOTTIE?"

I looked up.

"Shit! Lottie, what's wrong. Are you crying?"

Was I? I stared down at my hands – they were wet. I touched my face. It was drenched with tears. I heaved a sob. One I didn't even know I'd been holding in.

"Lottie? What is it?" Amber asked. Both of them kicked into supportive-friend mode, their arms around me, cooing and asking and caring. The kindness in Evie's eyes. The strength of Amber's grip on my shoulder. It was the release I needed.

I cried.

There was snot. There was more snot.

"I just...I should have said something... I should have stood up to those builders..." I stuttered as my shoulders rose and fell. "And...I wasn't even wearing a short...skirt... and Megan...and Megan...and that fucking advert...that FUCKING ADVERT."

Evie had printed off the accompanying poster of the advert. I swiped it off the table, trying to rip it in two. But Evie, being Evie, had bloody laminated the thing. So all I did was bend it slightly and hurt my hand.

"You see!" I yelled out. "That just represents EVERYTHING that I'm crying about… I try to rip that FUCKING ADVERT and I'M the one who gets hurt… It's so pointless. Fighting… Trying… It's all so FUCKING POINTLESS unless…unless…you fight all of it. And who has the strength to do that?"

"Woah, Lottie. It's okay. What builders? It's going to be okay," Amber said. I looked up just as she said it though, and she was making frantic eye-movements at Evie. I wasn't usually the emotional one of the group. I think they were shell-shocked.

"Amber's right," Evie soothed. "Just let it out."

They let me cry it out. Because they knew that's what I needed. Because they're awesome like that.

My sisters who aren't my sisters.

My blood who aren't my blood.

My choice, my friends.

They waited until I was done. Until there was copious amounts of snot trailing down my lacy jumper so it looked like the scene of a slug orgy.

Eventually Evie said the words I needed to hear.

"We need cheesy snacks. Come back to mine?"

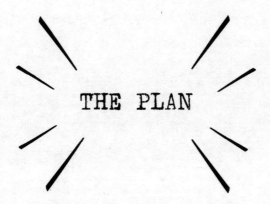

THE PLAN

five

After devouring three bags of Wotsits, I was feeling slightly better.

Amber stared at me in disgust. "You've got an entire beard made out of cheesy neon goo," she said. "If you hadn't been crying uncontrollably for the past hour, I would take many a photo."

I put my hand to my face and it came back covered in orange stickiness. I licked my finger.

"That's disgusting," Evie announced. "You're triggering me by being so gross."

I smiled, then saw her face. "Seriously?"

She nodded. "Seriously."

We both laughed, but I still grabbed a tissue from the box on Evie's bedside and dabbed off my cheese beard. I took extra care to put it in the bin.

"Would you judge me for ever if I eat a fourth bag?"

"Yes," they replied in unison.

"But I'm upset!"

Amber crossed her arms. "You still haven't told us why."

I shrugged, not knowing where to start. I didn't want to relive it. I looked around Evie's room helplessly. It was less sanitized-tidy than it used to be – but still waaaaay neater than mine and Amber's. Evie had explained that you can just be a tidy person without it having anything to do with OCD but we chose to ignore that. Her giant film collection dominated one wall – the shelves of DVDs towering up to the ceiling. Evie was the only person I knew who still bought DVDs. I stared at them vacantly, though I'd already borrowed the ones I wanted to watch.

"How about," Evie started, "you tell us why you've become sadness personified and afterwards I'll reward you with more cheesy snackage?"

I gave a small smile. "It will have to be one hell of a cheesy snack."

She levelled me with her deep blue eyes. "I have Boursin in the fridge."

I chucked one of her pillows in the air. "WELL WHY DIDN'T YOU SAY SO?"

Evie went downstairs and returned with a stinky circle of cheese covered in foil and some posh crackers. My tummy lurched. All the Wotsits in my stomach recoiled at the sight of the Boursin – feeling all ashamed of themselves for not being proper cheese. Not proper stinky garlicky Boursin

– with all its garlic and herbs and garlicky herbs of yummness.

Evie wafted it under my nose, like I was a mouse in a cartoon.

"Okay I'll talk."

Amber gave me a look of utter disgust.

"What?" I protested.

"Never. Ever. Become a spy," she said.

We all laughed.

I told them about the men. I told them about running away instead of fighting back. I told them about the fight with my parents – how annoyed I was at Dad's pressure over Cambridge. His hypocrisy about wanting me to be a strong, educated and powerful woman…but also not wanting me to run FemSoc. I told them about Mike stealing my philosophy point and everyone reacting more when he said it. They already knew about Megan…

"Essentially" – I sprayed more crumbs as I helped myself to my third lump of Boursin – "I hate myself. And I hate the world. I'm just struggling to work out which one I hate the most."

It sounded dramatic, but it was how I felt.

Amber was eating her (respectable) first bag of Wotsits. "Why do you hate yourself?"

I closed my eyes and pictured that morning again – the laughter, how it felt like victory laughter.

"Those men…" I said, my garlic-filled stomach twisting. "I should have said something…"

"Like what?" Amber asked.

"I dunno…anything…I just let them do that to me… I didn't fight back."

Evie laid a hand on my shoulder. "Lottie, it sounded more extreme than them just honking a horn as they drove past. I would've felt scared too."

I nodded. "They seemed…worse than most. I didn't know what they were capable of. I just froze."

"Which is a totally natural response."

"Yes," Amber butted in. "You were just protecting yourself."

"But what they did was wrong." I was sure of that much. "I should have stood up to them. Now they'll just think it's okay to do what they did. They'll do it to other girls."

"That's not your fault."

"It feels like it is."

"How?"

"I dunno. But it does…"

Evie gave my shoulder a squeeze. "Lottie," she said gently. "You don't have to fight back all the time…"

Don't I?

"Sometimes you need to just let things go. To know when it's not worth the trouble. To protect yourself."

But who will protect people weaker than me?

I shrugged again. Knowing I didn't quite know what I felt yet, that I was only on the cusp of it.

"What are we going to do about Megan?" I asked.

Amber's face scrunched up. "How was she?"

"She was…okay. Well, that's what she kept saying. It was clear she didn't want to talk about it. I thought maybe we could try and include her in more stuff? Get to know her better."

Evie nodded. "That's a good idea. To invite her to more things… She doesn't seem to have anyone she really hangs around with since Max. I still can't believe it though. I mean, Max seems so nice!"

"That means nothing though," Amber said. "You never know what goes on in people's relationships behind closed doors. Besides, we can't jump to conclusions about what happened between them. We have to let Megan tell us in her own time, if at all."

"I know something terrible happened." I shook my head. "It was all over her body language, the way she held herself."

We sat there quietly, all of us depressed in our own ways. My brain was on a loop – playing the day over.

Amber stood up.

"Amber, you are standing up," I said.

"That I am."

"Why?"

"Because I'm going to dance to Joan Jett."

"Why?"

"Because we need cheering up."

And, before I had time to compute, she'd put "Bad Reputation" on her phone and started dancing like a maniac.

Amber doesn't dance often. She is just under six foot, and all big of hair, so she's usually too self-conscious. But when she does, it is a sight of a sight to be seen. She flailed her limbs in the air, she attempted to shimmy, she pogoed up and down.

"Are you guys going to join in?" she puffed. "Or just watch me here making a huge tit out of myself?"

Evie and I gave each other a look, then got up and joined her. Evie – all short and curvy – wiggled her shoulders and twisted herself in circles. I waved my hands over my head, grabbing Amber's hands so we could twirl. They laughed and I smiled, and the beat of Joan Jett flowed through me and helped a little. But not as much as I needed it to.

"See!" Amber yelled over the music. "There are some days you can fight, and there are other days when all you can do is pretend none of it is happening and dance and laugh and dance."

I twirled her under my arm again, still smiling, but my unusual bad mood wasn't shifting.

All I could think was, *But, while we're dancing, what unspeakably bad things are happening outside of this bubble?*

six

My parents were waiting for me when I got home. Sitting patiently, the very painting of serene. Though I could see Dad's inner turmoil from a mile off and knew Mum must've given him a talking to.

Mum stood up to hug me. "Lottie, honey. You're home."

I stepped through the annoying beaded curtain and made myself hug her back.

"Hi," I said, preparing for them to kill me with kindness – their favourite trick.

Dad sipped on his herbal tea, his lips all pursed, but he stood and hugged me too when Mum gave him a nod.

We were a family of huggers. Well, Mum was. Dad and I never had much say in the matter.

Dad pointed to a chair next to him. "Come, sit."

It was like we'd never argued – which is how he always played it. Anger and strictness followed by niceness and *we're-only-doing-it-for-your-own-good*.

"You want a cup of tea?"

I nodded. "Do we have any of the special flowering ones of Mum's left?"

Dad pulled one out of the special pot we had for them on the tea tray. He poured hot water from our ancient teapot onto a jasmine flower and I watched it unfurl slowly as the water hit it. I never got bored of this posh flowery tea.

I slowly took a sip…waiting. Mum peered anxiously at me over her glasses. Dad kept running his fingers over the wrinkles around his eyes. He never wanted to fall into the pushy-parenting cliché; I think he thought he was above all that. He wasn't. It's like when it came to my education he couldn't help himself. Even with Mum balancing him out. I guess that's what it's like if you're a professor. Sometimes I wondered if he only wanted me to get into Cambridge and do well in politics because it would sound good in front of his elbow-patch lecturer mates.

"I'm sorry I grabbed my crotch at you and yelled 'Meditate on this'," I opened, taking another small sip. "I'm still not sure what happened there."

They both smiled slightly.

"We all lost control of our tempers," Dad said. "And, yes, I'll grant you. It was original."

"You can see why I was upset though, right?"

They looked at each other, and I could tell then that they'd already planned what they were going to say. They had a script and I didn't. All I had was a roundabout of emotions, and no inclination to let them bully me.

"We're just worried about you…your future," Mum answered.

I crossed my arms. "We went over this. College said four A levels are more than enough to get me into Cambridge."

"Yes. But in your interview, you have to talk about your extra-curricular activities…and we're worried this…Spinster Club may…well…it doesn't seem very Cambridge. Maybe if you just joined a debate team, or…something?" Mum's eyes looked so small behind her thick-rimmed glasses.

I levelled her stare. "I thought you raised me to want to make the world a better place?"

"We did." Dad was talking now. "You know we wholeheartedly support your ambitions. They're our ambitions too… That's why we're having this chat. To try and work together to help you achieve them. And that may mean taking the more…umm…conventional route, so you can really change things later."

The conventional route…

Here's the embarrassing thing… I want to be the prime minister. I know that's about as ridiculous as wanting to become a prima ballerina, or a professional footballer, or an astronaut or whatever – but think about it…*someone* has to be prime minister. Why can't it be me? I am smart enough. I am strong enough. And I really, honestly, want to take this shitty world we live in and use whatever strength, intellect and passion I have to leave it a little bit better off than when I found it. I don't just want to complain about the world, I want to change it.

The problem is…I'm still not sure exactly where to start, what route to take, how to get there. I went to a Labour party meeting and didn't like it. But weirdly my parents totally think I can be PM too – and they've drilled into me since before I can remember that prime ministers go to Cambridge or Oxford.

"Why does the conventional route mean giving things up I believe in?" I asked.

They shared another look. "We're not saying you should give up things you believe in. Just maybe sort out your priorities a bit?"

I stood up. "My priorities are to make the world better."

"Which you're much better placed to do if you stick to doing five A levels to ensure you get a spot at Cambridge," Dad insisted. "We already supported you when you decided to leave Heartly School, giving up an incredible once-in-a-lifetime scholarship, I may add."

I rolled my eyes. *This* again. "I didn't like it there," I said – for what seemed like the eight trillionth time. "Why would I want to carry on going somewhere I didn't fit in?"

Didn't fit in was the biggest understatement ever – I was the squarest of pegs in a school filled with round holes. Especially as I was there on a scholarship and therefore couldn't afford all the right "stuff" or to go on the two thousand pound Year Nine ski trip.

"Because you know they have an excellent track record of getting their students into Oxbridge, for one thing?"

I shook my head – so mad at them. They were such

hypocrites. They drank herbal tea and Mum was a Buddhist, and they both volunteered to help with food banks, and we had freaking *crystals* all over the house…but the moment it came to me, their one and only child, they were willing to let a good few things slide to get me where we wanted me to be.

I wasn't ready to let *anything* slide. Not after today.

"I got sexually harassed today," I said, to try and shock them. "These guys in a van blocked my way into college and shouted abuse at me."

Mum was up, instantly at my side. "Oh, Lottie, honey. I'm sorry. Are you okay?"

I shook my head, shook off her hug.

"No. I'm not okay. And I won't be okay until stuff like that stops happening. That's why I'm in the Spinster Club. That's why I started FemSoc. I can't wait until I've decided which party I want to join, or I'm at Cambridge or whatever, before I change stuff. I have to do it now."

Mum hugged me again; Dad looked unconvinced.

"Lottie, I'm sorry that happened to you, that sounds awful." He paused, always unable to let go of a point once he'd locked down onto it. "But I'm struggling to understand why this is relevant."

"ARGH!" I threw my hands up in the air. The tears from earlier threatening to respill. "Don't you see? It's all relevant! It's all linked."

I pressed my fingers into the pressure points either side of my eyes, taking deep breaths. Despite everything that had happened today, I was still in the same argument as this morning.

I took another deep breath and looked up, fixing Dad with my best ever glare. The one I'd learned from him. "I've told you," I said, my voice so much calmer than I felt. "Four A levels is enough to get into Cambridge, college said so. And, if my FemSoc activities put them off, well then, I don't want to go there anyway. I don't have to get into Cambridge to get into politics…"

Dad opened his mouth to interrupt.

"Yes, I know it helps. But, look, I've not even joined a political party yet. I'm only seventeen. I'm not ready to make my mind up about that – it's an important decision to get right. And I don't want to start compromising what I believe in before I've even properly started."

We argued for another forty minutes, before I pleaded coursework. My magic word which always meant they left me alone. Mum went off to the centre to do her chanting, and it was Dad's night for Professors Down The Pub. That's what they actually called it – his colleagues' Tuesday evening drinks. Though Dad usually drank orange juice and drove everyone home safely at eleven. I wilted up to my bedroom – feeling like today had been much longer than regular days.

I had so much work to do. Four pages of art coursework, all the required reading for philosophy, an essay was coming up in politics and economics. It was almost nine already. It was going to be a long night. Luckily I've always been one of those people who can thrive on hardly any sleep – a secret weapon I'm terrified will disappear one day.

After an hour of gluing in a few collage-y bits for art, I started on philosophy, considering I'd been too out-of-it to concentrate at study group earlier. I flipped open my course book, and looked at a practice exam question.

A runaway train is heading towards a fork in the railway tracks. The tracks are set so that the train will veer left and kill five people stuck on the tracks. You have access to a switch that will cause the train to veer right, killing only one person stuck on that side of the tracks. Do you hit the switch?

Explain what deontologists and utilitarians would decide, based on their methods of thinking.

I stared at it for a long time…

I knew I didn't have to decide what I would do, that wasn't the homework. I knew what to write to pass the exam (well, to do more than pass, to get an A). Deontologists wouldn't hit the switch. They would call it murder; they would say you could never justify letting one person die, even if it saved the lives of five others. Whereas utilitarians would hit the switch in a second – one person dead is a lot better than five people dead. If the overall outcome was better, what's a few moral sacrifices along the way?

What would hitting the switch mean in my life? I started to think.

Like Dad said, getting into Cambridge meant I was statistically more likely to become prime minister, or even just an MP. In theory, I could use Cambridge to become someone who has the power to change things. Make things better in the long run. Is that worth giving up FemSoc for? Flick the switch? Let the train career into people like Megan while I wait to help more people further down the line?

I stood and made my way over to my window ledge, hurling myself up onto it and against the glass – watching the sleepy street under me. After a while Mum came home and barged in, all high from her chanting, to tell me she loved me. Dad got in a little later, knocked gently on my door and sat on my bed briefly.

"Sorry, Lottie. You know I don't like to fight with you. It's just you only get one future. And I only push because I care about you." I gave him a half-smile from my ledge. "I trust you'll make the right decision," he said, with meaning. Undoing all his apology. But it was too late to get mad, so I smiled again until he left me and went to bed.

My stomach hurt, my head throbbed. I knew then, looking out at the orangey glow of my little road, that I was on the cusp of a choice. One of those big choices. One of those choices that makes you.

Maybe most people get to delay a decision like this. But those men today, Megan today, everything today, had made me realize that, for me, I was out of time.

What sort of person do you want to be, Lottie?

What sort of compromises are you willing to make, Lottie?

Are you going to hit the switch, Lottie? Are you going to wait to change things, and accept a few casualties in the meantime? Or are you going to start changing things now?

I was exhausted from being angry. I was angry about being exhausted.

That exhaustion – it had stopped me talking back to those men.

It had stopped me calling Mike out for stealing my point.

And, directly or indirectly, I just knew – somewhere deep inside of me – that those moments, those glimmers of time when you're supposed to shout about something you see that's wrong but you don't... They somehow lead to something like what happened to Megan.

I knew then what I had to do.

The decision ballooned inside me, trickling through my guts. The energy of clarity cascaded through my limbs, filling me up till I felt golden and light.

I got down from the window sill.

With a decision.

With a plan.

I wasn't the sort of person who would flick the switch.

seven

I dressed carefully the next day.

A tiny pair of shorts that had shrunk in the wash, worn over fishnets from a fancy dress party. A cropped jumper I rolled up even higher. My kick-ass knee-high heeled boots that I usually only wore to parties. No coat. Even though it was freezing. I backcombed my dark hair even bigger, and shoved extra eyeliner on around my green eyes.

Just before I left for college, I applied a second coat of red lipstick.

I'd rummaged in Mum's top drawer that morning and nabbed her old mobile phone. We'd bought her a new one for her birthday but she didn't understand how to use it. I'd only receive nonsensical text messages saying things like GARDEN COMING ALONG NICELY and IT WILL BE COLD OUT COAT.

It was colder than yesterday – all grey and cloudy – with no sunshine to even trick you into thinking it was warmer.

My stomach was freezing – and my breakfast hung out below my crop-top, my belly spilling over the top of my shorts.

Would this attract unnecessary attention? Yes.

Did I care?

No. Today I did not.

I strode with purpose, my scarf flapping behind me in the wind. It was a gamble – assuming the builders would be parked in the same place, assuming, if they were, that things wouldn't get out of hand.

I was going to gamble though.

I turned a corner onto the road they were on yesterday, and paused for a second. There, there was the van. And the same two men were in it, sharing a Thermos of tea.

I punched 999 into my mum's phone, and shoved it into my shorts pocket, my thumb hovering over the dial button.

I closed my eyes, took three very deep breaths and started walking towards them. I saw the younger man spot me and nudge his friend through the smudged windscreen. He looked up, surveyed me, my outfit, and they both grinned at the same time.

The van door opened, but I strode straight towards them.

"Look who it is," the younger man said. He blocked my path again, but I didn't care today. My thumb was still poised over 999, while my own phone was in my other hand.

"Red lipstick girl. I like what you've got on today, red lipstick girl."

"You've got lovely curves," the older man said, getting

out and walking around the bonnet. Like it was all okay. Like they hadn't made me run away in sheer terror only the day before.

I held out my phone ostentatiously, and took a picture of them. The loud clicking sound filling the air between us.

"Hey, what you doing?"

I didn't reply. I just punched in the phone number plastered across the van with shaking fingers, and hit *call*. Praying, praying to God even though my parents tried to raise me a Buddhist – praying it wasn't their company…

And thankfully, it wasn't their phone that rang. I felt a small trickle of relief, though my hands still shook.

"*Hello?*" said a gruff voice down the line.

"Hello?" I said, staring the builders down with the stinkiest of stink eyes a stinky eye could muster. "Is that U&T Scaffolding Ltd?"

The whites of both their eyes doubled in size.

"What you doin', lipstick?" the younger one asked.

"*It is,*" the phone echoed.

I took a step forward, even though everything in my body told me to take a step back.

"Can I speak to the manager, please?" I said.

The moment the words were out of my mouth the older man kicked into action, putting his hands up. He yelled "Hey hey hey, come on. Whatcha playin' at?" The hand in my pocket quivered uncontrollably over the 999 button, but my voice didn't break.

"*You're speaking to him.*"

I took one more step forward, so I was almost chest to chest with both men. Our breath mingling in the frosty air. I wanted to talk fast, to get it over with, but I resisted. Speaking as slowly and confidently as I could, I said, "Two members of your staff are sexually harassing me every time I walk past their van."

"Hang on a minute!" the older guy protested.

I ignored him again. "I'm just trying to walk to college," I continued. "But they're blocking my path and pestering me. Now, do I need to call the police or are you going to discipline your staff?"

"You little bitch," the younger man muttered, almost to himself.

I shook my head at him menacingly. "One of them just called me a bitch."

There was a pause on the phone, a sigh… I wasn't safe yet; I was so far from safe.

Then the voice said, *"I think I know who you mean… What's the number plate? Can you see? Are you okay, love? Or are they threatening you?"*

I read off the number plate while they stood there, open-mouthed.

Another pause. Then, *"Tell them they need to come into Head Office this afternoon."*

"No, you tell them," I replied. "And if they ever speak to me again, I *will* call the police."

I hung up and looked at them both squarely. Their faces furrowed. Like they were waking up from a dream, they

shook their heads. Now was the most dangerous time…
right now.

"Come on, love, we were only joking. There's no need to
take it so far."

"It was just a compliment," the older one added. "Ring
'im back and tell him it was just a compliment."

"You can take a compliment, can't you?"

I put my hands on my freezing-cold hips and stood strong.

"It wasn't a compliment," I said. "It was sexual
harassment. I should be allowed to walk down a road
without some men I don't know letting me know whether
they find me attractive or not. I should be allowed to wear
whatever I want and walk wherever I want without being
threatened or objectified, or even just bothered."

"Fucking whore," the younger one muttered.

"Careful," I shouted, holding up the photo of them on my
phone. Just as I did it, the older man's phone started ringing.
"You don't get to make me, or any other girl, feel like I did
yesterday ever again. Gotit?" I said, almost growling.

He looked genuinely scared. It tasted amazing, the
victory on my tongue. He was finally feeling how I felt
yesterday – scared, helpless, confused as to why this was
happening to him. He answered his phone.

"John? John?" He turned away and signalled for his
colleague to do the same. "John, no! She's just some crazy
bitch who can't handle a compliment…"

I dodged past the open van door and walked away, leaving
them behind me.

"Come into the office, why? What? Are you being serious?"

Every part of me wanted to run. To put as much distance between me and their anger as possible.

But I didn't run down the road.

I walked.

And I smiled.

eight

I had philosophy first thing.

I breezed in, two minutes before the bell, and everyone stared. I was too high to care.

I usually sit next to Jane and Joel, but today I scooted in next to Mike.

"Hi, Mike," I said, way too friendly. "How's tricks?"

"Lottie!" He looked up from his textbook. It was open at the page I'd read last night – he'd highlighted the train question in yellow.

I will not be the sort of person who flicks the switch.

"I'm all right," he said. "Though this module is kicking my butt." He ran his hands through his blond Draco-Malfoy hair then clocked my outfit. His eyebrows shot up his face.

Ignoring him, I dumped my stuff out onto my desk.

"Okay, so this is going to sound totally strange, but why did you steal my point yesterday, Mike?" I asked.

His eyebrows danced higher. "What?"

"My analogy about philosophy," I continued. "Yesterday you copied it and pretended it was yours. Everyone laughed and gave you the credit? Remember?"

He looked at me like I was truly nuts. But I wasn't. And even if I was – it was his nuts that had made *me* nuts.

"I honestly have no idea what you're talking about," Mike said, but the confusion had vanished from his face and it was getting red, glowing against his white-blond hair. He knew *exactly* what I was talking about.

"Look, it's not a huge deal," I continued, leaning over the desk and then realizing, in this outfit, that wasn't the best idea. "I just find it strange, that's all. Don't you?"

To be fair to Mike, his eyes stayed level with mine, despite my very low-cut top.

"I don't mean this the wrong way, Lottie," he stammered. "But, well, you sound a little…bonkers."

I threw back my head and laughed. Bonkers. I hadn't heard the word bonkers in ages. Why didn't we all use it more? It's such a bonkersly brilliant word. And, actually, it totally summed up how I felt. I WAS bonkers. I felt bonkers. But in this really special and useful way.

I laughed while Mike stared at me with his mouth open, looking half-intrigued, half-terrified of what I was going to say next. I was done here. I'd made my point. It really wasn't a huge deal, but I couldn't let it go totally unnoticed. Not any more.

I took off my big scarf, and instantly regretted it. The

college central heating hadn't been switched on yet and my tummy turned to a puffy plain of goose pimples.

"Anyway, Mike, you can continue pretending you have no idea what I'm talking about. But next time...next time... don't think I won't call you out on it."

He didn't reply, just kept his eyes determinedly locked on his textbook rather than my cleavage. But, as our teacher came in, I heard him mutter, "Totally, totally bonkers."

Everyone was at lunch. Amber, Evie, Evie's not-quite-boyfriend Oli, Jane, Joel. Two baskets of chips lay in the middle of the table, with a liquidy pile of burger sauce. Joel had the worst habit of mixing mayonnaise with tomato ketchup wherever he went.

"I am here," I announced, instead of a straight hello. "And I have the most excellent of plans."

Everyone but Joel and Jane (who'd seen me in philosophy) stared in shock. An actual chip fell out of Amber's mouth onto the table.

"Umm, Lottie?" Evie asked. "Why are you dressed like Jodie Foster in *Taxi Driver*?"

I looked down at my ensemble. "Not seen the film."

Oli, a fellow film nerd, elaborated. "She's asking why you look like a child prostitute."

"Oh!" I grinned madly and tapped my nose. "It is part of the plan." I pulled up a chair and sat right between Oli and Evie, just for laughs. They'd managed, after a year of nervously looking at each other, to have one whole kiss. Two weeks before, at this girl Anna's house party. But both of them were so shy they were pretending it hadn't happened. I yearned for their innocence. I've kissed soooo many boys. And that's not the half of it.

"I'm scared," Amber said.

"Seconded," Evie said.

"You should have seen how weird she was in philosophy," Joel added.

"HUSH," I said. "I told you…I have a plan."

"Well, what is it then?" Amber asked.

I stood up again, for extra dramatic effect – pulling down my minuscule shorts.

"I'm starting a project. Either for FemSoc, or the Spinster Club, or maybe even just for myself. It's going to run for a month, I think. And, well, for an ENTIRE month I HAVE to call out EVERY SINGLE INCIDENCE of sexism I see."

I waited for applause, but they all just looked at me. Apart from Joel, who'd stopped listening entirely and buried his face into a greasy hamburger.

"WELL?" I demanded.

"Every single sexist thing you see?" Evie was the first to speak.

I nodded. "Everything. Even the sexist stuff against boys too."

Amber put her hand up.

"You don't always have to put your hand up to speak," I said.

"Yes I do," she grinned. I have a habit of…er…dominating conversation when I get overexcited.

"What is it, Amber?"

"Why?"

I pointed at her. "Yes, ten points to Gryffindor. Why would I do such a thing? Why indeed?"

I pulled her out of her chair to dance with me. She was pretty wedged in but got up reluctantly and let me spin her under my arm.

"I decided after yesterday's horribleness that it wasn't so much all the sexual harassment that bothered me. It was the fact I didn't stand up for myself."

"But those men could've been dangerous," Evie pipped in.

"They weren't," I said. "I took them on this morning and reported them to their boss." I spun Amber harder but she broke free and dizzily turned to face me.

"You did what?"

They all stared at me like I was a teeny bit mad.

"I told you, I reported them. I even deliberately lured them in." I pointed to my goose-pimpled body.

"And that explains why she's dressed like a child prostitute," Oli whispered loudly to Evie, who giggled.

"Hush!" I called. "I can dress HOWEVER I like, thank you very much. Yes, I may have frostbite of the entire thigh and stomach area, but that is MY CHOICE."

"Leave Oli alone." Evie gave him a small look then instantly turned red. God, those two were hopeless. "There's having your choices and then there's choosing to dress as BAIT."

"Evie's right," Amber said. "I mean, A, it sounds like you didn't need to dress as bait anyway, they harassed you yesterday when you were all covered up in a winter coat. And, B, Lottie, that was dangerous! There's a difference between finding trouble and trouble finding you."

I pulled a face. "But you know I have a flair for dramatics."

"Oh, we know," Evie said pointedly, with a smile.

"As I was saying," I continued. "I felt bad because I let it slide yesterday. And then I thought of all the other small things I let slide. Then I realized… What if it's all connected?"

"What if all of *what* is connected?" Jane asked. Wow, I even had Jane's attention. Probably because Joel was still totally entranced by his burger.

"Sexism. Well, all just general badness, but I'm focusing mainly on sexism. What if all the tiny shitty sexism things build up to allow the smaller shitty sexism things, and then what if all the small shitty things build up to allow the medium, and what if the medium things build up—"

"We got it," Amber said, smiling. She loved to deliberately interrupt me when I was in full flow.

"Yes, well." I pulled down my shorts again. Why were they so determined to be up my bumhole? I was being sexually assaulted by my own item of clothing. "That's why I've decided that, for a month, I'm not going to let anything slide. You never know – I might even change the world!"

There was silence. Well, apart from Joel's chomping noises.

Evie was the first to speak. "I like it, Lottie. I think you're totally nuts, as always, but I like it."

Amber nodded her freckly face. "I like it too. Though I think you need to think some stuff through."

"Like what?"

"Like the rules. What does 'calling out' sexism mean? How will you identify if something is sexist?" She listed her points on her fingers.

I nodded. "This is useful."

"We could help you," Evie offered. "Maybe make this the FemSoc campaign like you said? See if the other members agree?"

I nodded even more furiously. "Yes, yes, yes, yes, YES!" I punched the air. Then, suddenly exhausted, I flopped down on the chair. "Meeting at mine tonight then?"

Both Evie and Amber nodded. "Though I don't have any cheese left to bring," Evie said. "You ate it all last night."

"I don't think I can handle any more cheese," I said. "Can we get chocolate instead?"

"Seconded," Amber said. "I was doing Boursin burps all night."

"Sexy." I winked.

"Oh, don't I know it. I told Kyle about them. He was suitably appalled."

"He'll still love you anyway. That boy is OBSESSED with you." Kyle was Amber's trans-Atlantic boyfriend. He was worryingly perfect, apart from the fact he lived thousands of miles away.

I looked at the others. Joel had finished his burger but put his headphones in. Jane shared one headphone with him, doing the same half-smile she always did to us when she was only half there. I seriously thought that, after a year of going out together, Jane and Joel would've cooled things down. But, if anything, they seemed even more besotted with each other. Only Oli was still paying any attention, with his shockingly green eyes. I could totally see what Evie saw in him. Though I could never put up with his terminal shyness...even though he had some pretty good explanations for it.

"What do you think, Oli?" I picked up a now-cold chip and ate it. "A guy's opinion would be useful...as long as it's positive." I gave him a mock-evil.

He laughed, and held his hands up in defence. "I think it sounds interesting," he said. "You know what you should do, though?"

"What?"

"Get someone to film it. Make it into an online video campaign. It will reach more people that way."

I was quiet as I digested what a very good idea that was.

"What a very good idea that was," I said.

Oli went bright red. Evie looked at him, then he looked at Evie, then she went bright red too.

"None of us can use a camera though," Amber pointed out.

"We have a few wannabe film-makers in film studies, don't we, Evie?"

She nodded, still red. "We could ask around?"

"That would be amazing!"

I felt all full of love and meaning and fight and cold chips. I was onto something…I could just feel it…

Until Amber muttered. "Uh oh, Teddy alert. Teddy alert."

My tummy squidged up. "Oh bollocks, where?"

"Six o'clock."

I twisted my head around gormlessly. "Amber, where the heck is six o'clock…? Oh…here he is."

Teddy was heading straight over with a lunch tray. His hair flopped in his eyes, but not enough to cover the huge stinky stinkeye he very deliberately gave me when he realized I was there. He didn't have his usual bunch of hyena mates with him, otherwise he'd probably have said something.

My stomach turned again. Teddy was this hairy rugby guy I dated last year who seemed fun at first and then got totally intense super quickly. When he told me he was in love with me, on, like, our third date, I freaked out but ended things as considerately as I could. He didn't take it well though. He still didn't take it well. Him and his rugby team went totally ballistic when the girls and I campaigned for a rape song to get taken off the college jukebox and made our lives hell.

"I've honestly never seen so much hatred in anyone's eyes before," Evie marvelled.

"Shh," I said, before looking up to smile at him.

He saw, he definitely saw. But he just stopped and gave me a very slow and deliberate sneer. Then he stalked off in the opposite direction.

"Wow," Amber said. "Do you think he came over just to sneer at you?"

Evie chuckled. "That's what happens when you take an intense person's virginity and then dump them."

"Hey!" I said, trying not to smile. I'd felt guilty about Teddy for months, but even with all my apologizing, he still went out of his way to make me feel like a slutty she-wolf. "I didn't know he was a virgin. Or a vengeful bell-end. All his chest hair confuzzled me."

Joel, for the first time that lunch, looked vaguely interested in the conversation.

"So virgins don't have chest hair?" Amber asked.

I shrugged. "Well, you never imagine them having it, do you? Gah. Why is he still at college anyway?"

"He's retaking his A levels, isn't he? He failed a few." She smiled. "It's your fault."

I picked up a congealed chip and threw it at her. "It's totally not my fault! He failed his first year before I was even here, because he spent every spare moment playing rugby rather than revising. And don't mess with me today, I have a plan."

"You do indeed, my evil genius."

I grinned back, slumping in my chair, feeling happy – as long as I didn't look in Teddy's direction. I felt strong, I felt unstoppable, I felt ignited. It pulsed through my blood with every heartbeat.

Then I saw Megan leaving her table and carrying her lunch tray to the bin. I stood up quickly.

"Where you off to?" Evie asked.

"I've got to go talk to someone. Meet you both at the gates after last bell?"

Amber and Evie nodded.

I turned to Jane. Amber and I were getting better at not leaving her out – though it was still an effort sometimes. "You want to come, Jane?" I asked her.

"Huh?" She still had one earphone in.

"Mine? Tonight? To plan my supersonic feminist social experiment?"

"Oh." She looked panicked. "Thanks, umm…" She turned to Joel, who'd lost interest the moment we'd stopped discussing virginity. "I'm watching Joel's band practise tonight though."

"Oh, okay then." I resisted the urge to roll my eyes. Joel and his mates were in this heavy metal band called Road of Bones – the very epitome of everything that is bad about local bands. Also, their lead singer, Guy, totally messed Evie around last year – making me hate the band even more. "Right, better go." I dashed off, trying not to lose the back of Megan's head in the smush of the crowd.

I bobbed and weaved around people – just about keeping her long brown hair in sight. Then, once I was out of the bottleneck of the cafeteria doors, I launched into a mini-jog to catch her up.

"Megan!" I called. She stopped and turned around. She carried three bright folders in her arms, and wore a bright red jumper, but her face was…dimmer…than I remembered. Or maybe it had been that way since summer, and I was too uninterested to notice.

She smiled. "Hey, Lottie. What's up?"

"Hey…" Suddenly I wasn't sure what to say. All the words I'd planned last night garbled in my throat. Was this right, what I was doing? Was it my place? But then I couldn't know what I thought I knew and not do anything… "So, about yesterday…" I started.

Megan's face went from dim to dimmer.

"What about it?"

I could tell she'd tried to ask that casually, but it came out all sharp. I chewed on my lip, mulling every word over carefully.

"Umm…well…I was thinking… It's quite an emotive topic…for lots of people…for lots of reasons…and… umm…well…I'm sorry if we didn't organize it properly, so that people didn't know what we were going to bring up… it was stupid."

Megan shrugged. "I didn't mind," she said, in a sing-song voice.

You walked out of the meeting and cried in the toilets…

"Yeah, cool. That's cool." A group of footballer guys barged past us, jolting my shoulder. "But, umm, well, I thought you should know I'm doing a project, maybe for FemSoc. I'm not sure yet. I thought you might be interested?"

"Oh yeah?" Megan shifted her folders from one arm to the other.

"Yeah. It's a campaign where I have to call out every

single incidence of sexism I see, the moment I see it, for an entire month."

Megan's eyebrows furrowed, but she was smiling. Her features a teeny bit brighter now we'd changed the topic of conversation. "Is that even possible?"

"I don't know yet. The point is to try… But, well, you're in my art class, aren't you?"

She nodded.

"I've seen how good you are at graphic drawing, whereas I'm crap. I can only draw real-life stuff, so I could really use your help."

She chewed on her lip. "Like how?"

"I'm not sure yet. I only came up with the idea yesterday. It still needs a name. Amber and Evie are going to help me flesh it all out tonight. But I was thinking I definitely need campaign stickers and badges and stuff. I thought your graphic style would be perfect."

Megan smiled, though I could see eight million defence mechanisms orbiting around her, like anti-aircraft missiles. Everything in me ached for her. Why wasn't she opening up?

"Sounds cool," she said. "I need some extra stuff for my UCAS personal statement. I'm in."

"YAY!" I hugged her without warning. She stiffened but then settled into it. "You're a lifesaver."

She smiled wider. "This campaign sounds totally bonkers, you know that, right?"

"God, I love the word bonkers!" I said. "But sexism is totally bonkers. I'm hoping this campaign's bonkersness will be able to highlight the bonkersness of it. Fight bonkersness with better bonkersness, that's what I say. So, want to meet later this week to discuss plans?"

"Definitely."

"Hooray and hooray." I made her high-five me.

Everything we weren't saying hung heavy in the air between us. But I didn't bring it up because she didn't.

All I said was, "Great, see you in art then."

And all she said was, "Sure…and, umm, Lottie? Why are you dressed like a…erm…child prostitute today?"

nine

I surveyed Amber's creation in marvel. It towered before her mouth, wobbling slightly in the breeze from my bedroom window.

"You are truly the master of cheesy snacks," I told her, in serious seriousness. "You should become a cheesy snack yogi, and start a cheesy snack ashram. I will come and worship there until I find your cheesy enlightenment."

"Let's wait and see how it tastes first," Evie said, always the voice of reason.

We'd stopped at the Co-op on the way home from college to stock up on supplies. Now back at mine, we'd barely said hi to Mum before trundling through all the beaded curtains to my bedroom. Amber had just spent the best part of fifteen minutes using some leftover Dairylea to mould together a tower of Cadbury's cubes.

She hesitated before taking a bite.

"I'm still worried this will ruin two of my favourite

things," she said, eyeballing her creation.

"EAT IT," Evie and I yelled.

Amber did. Getting most of it in her mouth, but still a considerable amount around her face. She chewed, her eyebrows throwing all sorts of eyebrow dance moves.

"And...?" I demanded, getting closer so I could better analyse her face.

"I'm schtill...schewing..." She sprayed some out her mouth and Evie visibly recoiled.

"Hurry up...I want to try it."

She chewed and chewed, her face going red from the exertion. Finally she swallowed.

"Weeeell?"

A pause. Her face neutral. Then she gave a huge thumbs up.

"MYGODGUYS, IT'S AWESOME. YOU HAVE TO TRY IT!"

I didn't need telling twice. I hastily dipped some Fruit and Nut in the leftover cheese spread, and shoved it into my mouth.

I chewed...I grimaced...I grabbed a tissue from my bedside table and spat it out.

"AMBER!"

She laughed manically, pointing with one hand and holding her belly with the other.

"Got you, I totally got you!"

"ARGH! It's disgusting!" I grabbed her Coke bottle, just as she yelled "Oi!" and glugged down half of it to disguise the taste. Evie, meanwhile, stared at my spitwodge with utter horror.

"Shit, sorry, Evie. I'll go put it in the downstairs bin."

Evie shrugged, like it was nothing. But she was still staring at the tissue.

"Blame Amber." I picked it up and ran downstairs. When I thundered back up, Amber was sitting next to Evie, her arm on her shoulder. Oh no. I'd triggered her with my grossness.

"Oh, Evie, are you okay?! I'm really sorry," I said. "I've put it in the bin and washed my hands and everything."

They both looked up, smiling.

"Chill, Lottie," Evie said. "I'm not freaking out. I'm just showing Amber the last message I got from Oli. I don't understand what it means."

"I thought my spitwodge had broken you."

"Maybe last year." She smiled again. "But today I'm more worried about boys…well not boys…Oli." She pointed to her phone. "What does this mean?"

I squatted next to them immediately to try and help.

"Both your breaths reek," Evie complained, showing me the screen of her phone.

"Reek?" Amber answered. "Yet another Evie special, I've not heard that word since 1992. And I wasn't even an embryo then."

I laughed in one short burst. Evie had the most grandma vocabulary ever.

"Shut up." Evie swatted us both. "And help me decipher this ruddy message."

I let the "ruddy" pass, and leaned further over, trying not to breathe on her.

Hey – this film essay is the worst! Last weekend was fun. Oli x

I threw my head back in exasperation. "You two! I can't believe your interactions haven't come on in a whole YEAR."

Amber nodded. "This is a bullshit message. What does it even mean?"

"I don't know! That's why I asked you guys. He's shy, remember?"

I scrunched up my nose. "I thought he was over that?"

Evie turned around and playfully slapped my hand. "Oi. He's recovered mostly from his agoraphobia, that doesn't mean he's not still shy."

"Yeah yeah, whatever. You mental health people and your excuses."

Another slap.

"I definitely deserved that."

To be fair, Evie and Oli had very good reasons for taking it slow. She had her OCD, and last year, we found out that Oli had agoraphobia. They were essentially banned from dating anyone while they focused on getting better. They'd been more like mental health study buddies than boyfriend and girlfriend – chatting through therapy together, going away on some mindfulness weekend. But now they were both in a "good patch", as Evie called it, they were allowed to act on their urges. And Oli does have very green eyes and very cheekbony cheekbones – he definitely makes girls have urges... After last year's shared singledom, my fellow Spinster Club friends were on the verge of coupling up and leaving me behind.

Amber grabbed the phone. "He says he had fun last weekend. Does that mean he's referring to the kiss?"

"Yes," I declared. "Of course he is!"

Evie took the phone back sadly. "But how do we know? He may have gone...I dunno...kayaking on Sunday. And be referring to that."

Amber shook her head. "No. He definitely wouldn't be referring to that. Kayaking is the sport of the devil. Take that from someone who had to do it all summer at an American camp."

We laughed. Amber's emails last summer about getting stuck in a canoe were still a highlight of my life.

"How's it going with Kyle, anyway?" Evie asked. "You missing him?"

Amber went completely red – which I always love. She blushes so badly.

"He may be coming over to visit at Christmas actually..." she admitted and we all squealed.

While Amber was shoving her long body into a canoe, she'd fallen stupid in love with this American HUNK and had run away with him, driving across America. It was the most romantic thing that had ever happened to me...and it wasn't even me it had happened to. I was jealous and happy for her in equal measures.

"I can't wait to meet him," Evie said.

"Can he bring some fit American mates with him?" I asked, and Amber thumped me.

"There's no solid plan yet. I don't want to get my hopes up."

"Or your loins…"

She thumped again.

"ANYWAY," I said, sorting out my hair, which was all messed up by Amber's thumps. "This is supposed to be my supersonic feminism meeting, and all we're doing is talking about boys again."

Evie sighed. "Right you are. Okay. Just give me five more minutes to totally obsess over this message, and then I'll be with you."

To save her time, we all read it again, and came to the conclusion that,

a) Oli was shy (and it wasn't his fault)

b) This was his way of saying he enjoyed kissing Evie at the house party.

And, together, we composed the following reply:

I had a great weekend too. Agreed tho, this essay is the worst x

Then I made Evie send it and turn off her phone for the rest of the evening. "I don't want you checking to see if he's replied when you should be listening to my mono—"

"I'm not going to let you monologue," she interrupted. "You need to learn that every time you get to speak, doesn't mean you get to monologue."

"But I'm so very good at it," I wailed, breaking off another line of chocolate.

"Talk us through this project again." Amber took the bar from me to help herself to another piece. "And mentally prepare for the fact we will stop you to ask questions."

"Am I allowed to at least get up and pace?"

Evie sighed. "If you must..."

I finished my mouthful, then got up, and started pacing the length of my bedroom – telling them about all the thoughts I'd had the day before. About the philosophy train question, and how I didn't want to flick a switch that made a less-bad thing happen if it still allowed bad things to happen. About how maybe sexism was all linked, all the bad stuff. And that by allowing one, seemingly small, sexist thing to pass, you may actually be paving the way for the bigger shittier things to happen.

"Like a patriarchal butterfly effect?" Amber said.

I pointed at her. "Yes! Exactly that! Well I was thinking of it more like a pyramid. A big feminism pyramid. Close your eyes and picture a pyramid now." I closed mine, opened them, and saw that Evie was using this moment to grab a cracker. "Oi, Evie, close your eyes!"

"Okay okay, I'm closing them..." she said, the cracker hanging out of her mouth.

"Now picture a pyramid... Are you...?"

"Yes," she snapped. "I'm picturing a ruddy pyramid. With you impaled on the top."

Amber snorted with laughter with her eyes closed.

I chose to ignore them both. "Now, under the tip of the pyramid is a huge amount of pyramid underbelly, am I right? There's the bottom layer of bricks, and the layer of bricks above that, all building to a point."

Amber opened her eyes. "Lottie, I love you. And I know you're smarter than me. But I do know what a pyramid looks like."

"It's more dramatic this way," I wailed.

Evie opened her eyes too. "Just let her get on with it. It's quicker."

I nodded gratefully. "Well just imagine all the very worst stuff that happens to women is at the top of the pyramid. Like what we think happened to Megan. Like honour killing and FGM and women dying in illegal abortions, and worldwide structural inequality... I know it's difficult to measure harm, but still these awful things...if they're at the tip of the pyramid – what's propping it up? And the more I thought about it, the more I realized it's being propped up by layers and layers of other smaller, 'silly' sexism! These layers of bricks – seemingly minor bricks, like slut-shaming a girl in a short skirt, or, umm, even rap music with misogynistic lyrics... You may think that tackling them isn't as 'worthwhile' as the truly terrible things. That maybe it's minor, or a pointless waste of energy. But, actually, I think it's all these tiny bits of wrong that are building the structure that allows the really bad stuff to happen." I took yet another breath, knowing I was only half making sense. "SO, the plan for my project is this. For one month, I will challenge EVERYTHING. I think if I can show people just how much sexism there is, it will help recruit others to join our cause. And that could mean we achieve more, quicker, and maybe we start to stop bad things happening as a brilliant side-effect."

Both of them were quiet for a moment.

"Well…?" I asked.

"Oh, you're finished?" Evie asked. "I was just checking."

"Yes, I'm finished! But you have to help me shape it."

Amber dragged her college bag over, digging stuff out. "This requires art supplies." She pulled out her sketchpad and loads of coloured pens. "I think you need some rules." She pulled off the top of a marker. "Like I said in the cafeteria, you need to make this more concrete. So what counts as something sexist that you need to object to?"

I thought about it, which required an actual scratching of my head. "Well, I want it to be about equality, so I'm going to holler about sexist stuff that impacts boys too…"

Evie pushed herself up on the bed, watching as Amber wrote it down.

```
Rule no. 1 - Call out anything you see that is
unfair or unequal to one gender
```

"Yeah, that's good," she said. "God, though. You're going to be exploding all over the place. You're going to have, like, incurable feminism hiccups."

I grinned. "That's the point..." I trailed off and frowned. "Will I ever have time to sleep?"

"I know," Amber said. "How about you only have to call something out once? So you're not going over the same stuff again and again?"

"Great idea." I grabbed her pen and wrote it down.

```
Rule no. 2 - Don't call out the same thing
twice, so you can sleep and breathe
```

Evie took the pen and looked at me. "You need to keep it funny though," she said seriously. "I mean it. This could very quickly look like one big whinging feminist rant. People will turn off to that."

I crossed my arms. "They shouldn't..."

"But they will." Amber took Evie's side. "You know they will."

"Okay," I conceded. And Evie wrote down:

```
Rule no. 3 - Always try to keep it funny
```

I scratched my head again. "How do I make this funny?" We were all quiet for a second.

Evie said, with her hand up, "How about you get a giant clown horn, and you honk it whenever you see anything?"

Amber's face lit up. "Oooh, one of those brass ones, with a long neck and a black spongy ball?"

Evie nodded. "Yeah, those ones."

"You have good taste in horns."

"Why thank you."

I nodded. "I like it. And I can yell, 'I'VE GOT THE HORN' too."

"YES!" And we all high-fived.

"And you need merch," Amber suggested. "Make this brandable, darling."

"Yes, yes and yes. I've already asked Megan if she'll help with arty stuff. I thought it was a good way to include her more and get to know her better."

"That will be great! She's so good at graphics."

Evie stretched her arms behind her head, until there was a crack. "Are you just going to focus on gender specifically?" she asked. "Or are you going to try and point out all the different ways you can get double-pooed-on if you're a girl? Like if you're not white? Or straight?"

I pointed at her. "Ten points to Hufflepuff! I HAVE been thinking about that. A lot. And it's HARD. I mean, there are so many different crappy reasons girls get pooed on and they're all so important...but I guess I don't feel I can speak for everyone's individual experiences, you know? So, what I'm hoping is, this campaign will prompt other people to do their own campaigns, highlighting things from *their* experience, and together we can all sew a beautiful duvet made of our different voices and drape it over the world and say, '*LOOK AT THIS FUCKING DUVET, THE WORLD NEEDS TO CHANGE – PRONTO!*'"

"I think you mean quilt," Amber pointed out. "Not duvet."

I flipped her the finger.

"I'm all for this," Evie said. "Maybe I'll start honking a horn whenever anyone misuses the term OCD to describe being tidy, or calls someone mental or a psycho bitch just because they're a female with perfectly valid emotions."

"YES! See, this duvet is already taking shape."

Evie saluted. Then she said what I'd been stuck on all day. "You need a good name for this, Lottie. Something catchy."

"I've been trying all day but I can't think of one."

"Oooh, I know!" Amber's hand shot up, she was so excited by her own idea. "Oh my God, it's good, guys. You're going to love me. You're going to WORSHIP me."

"What? What is it?"

She paused, for added drama. "How about…The Vagilante? Like a vigilante, but with a big honking vagina?"

I stood up. "I LOVE IT."

She waved her hand. "Wait, I'm not finished. Seriously, I think I may be a genius. I think the main reason I was born was for this very moment. I feel overwhelmed by myself, I—"

"Amber," both Evie and I warned. "Get on with it."

"Okay okay. Well, the tagline should be… *Letting the cat lady out of the bag.*"

I launched myself at her, knocking over my bedside table holding all the remaining chocolate.

"That's such a great idea! Oh my God, I love it. I LOVE YOU!" I hugged her again, and then threw my head back to the sky and yelled, "KYLE, CAN YOU HEAR ME OVER THERE IN AMERICA? I'M STEALING YOUR AMAZING GINGER GIRLFRIEND AND HER GINGER BRAIN OF BRILLIANCE."

Amber laughed from underneath me, but also put a lot of physical effort into trying to get me off.

"Oi, Lottie, stop planking on me."

"Never! This is how I show my appreciation." I climbed further on top of her.

"Evie, help!"

And, Evie, who was basically becoming the mum of us, came over and pulled me off. We lay in a heap, our heads all together, laughing ourselves out.

Evie rolled over.

"You seem much happier than yesterday," she said. "I'm glad."

Yesterday seemed like a lifetime ago. The helplessness I felt, the anger…it had all gone now. Maybe all you needed in life was the belief you could change things. Somehow. Some way.

We plotted and planned, until Dad came up and told me I had to do my homework. *"Two week nights seeing your friends in a row, Lottie. Come on."* Like I wasn't almost eighteen or anything. But, in that time, we'd decided to try and recruit someone from Evie's film class to get involved. We planned to propose it as the new FemSoc campaign in

84

the next meeting, hoping they'd be behind it, as we'd technically be highlighting every other injustice put forward for a campaign in this one. And we gave ourselves two weeks before it started – to get everything sorted. When we'd pulled out the calendar I'd bitten my lip. I hadn't heard back from Cambridge yet. And if I got an interview, it would be worryingly near the month of the Vagilante Project.

I almost didn't want to think about it…

Would I keep up the project during the interview?

I'd have to.

My tummy flipped on itself, like it had been scoured down the middle. I mean, surely, if I had to point out sexism, it wouldn't be appreciated? But if I didn't get in, what if Mum and Dad were right, and not going to Cambridge messed up my chances of climbing the political ladder so I could really change things?

Would not speaking up count as flicking the switch?

Slowly, I lowered my head onto the desk.

ten

Evie found me holed up in the library two days later.

"Lottie," she whispered so loudly it could hardly be called a whisper. "I have exciting but not perfect news."

About ten annoyed-looking heads spun around to glare. I was in the silent area, cooped up in one of the weird little cubicles they have, trying to make sense of my economics coursework.

I pointed to the door, Evie nodded, and we both walked out. She was dancing around on her feet even more so than usual – she was obviously excited about something. It's weird she's so curvy, considering how many calories she burns every day with nervous energy. But, as she'd said before, *"Even when I was sectioned because they'd misdiagnosed me with an eating disorder, I still had these bloody boobs."*

The ordinary section of the library seemed extra-noisy after being holed up in silentland for so long. My ears adjusted to the buzzing of students – chatting, comparing homework answers, showing each other videos on their phones.

"What is it, O excitable one?" I asked. "You're making me want to Cossack dance."

"I've found someone to film your project," she said. "They want to meet you later today."

"You have?! Oh my God, that's amazing. Maybe we SHOULD do some Cossack dancing!" I was just in the process of bending down, ready to fly my legs out, when Evie pulled me up again.

"Wait. There's a catch."

"Oh." I readjusted my skirt. It was a tight lacy pencil one – I'm not sure how I would've managed to Cossack in it. "What is it?"

"There's no nice way of saying this…"

"Evie!"

"Okay. Well, he's an arsehole."

"Woah, really?" I stood back with the shock of hearing Evie swear. "If *you're* calling him an arsehole, he must *really* be an arsehole."

She nodded, her blonde hair whooshing around her face. "His name's Will and he really is. Oli and I have asked everyone, but we've got this coursework coming up so people are pretty busy. Will's up for it though. And he's a good film-maker. He's made a few shorts already."

"How is he an arsehole?"

"Well…umm…"

"Evie, spit it out."

"Well, he's quite chauvinistic, I think…"

"What? Seriously?"

She nodded again. "He's VERY arrogant. I think he gets off on starting debates… Oli says he's all right, but I don't like him. And I don't think you will. I'm always getting into arguments with him in class because he says stuff like male directors are better than female directors."

I felt that hot itching feeling of anger spread through my face and tighten my jaw.

"Why the heck is he interested in helping me then?" I asked, pushing my hair off my face. "Does he just want to bait me?"

"I've already asked him that, and he promised me no." She smiled. "I asked him that a lot."

"I don't get it then. Why does he want to do it?"

She shrugged. "He said he genuinely wants to do it as, like, documentary practice. He wants to be the next Werner Herzog, and says he needs experience interviewing people doing stuff he doesn't agree with."

"I have no idea who you're talking about…Herzee Whatnow? Hang on…doesn't agree with? So he doesn't agree with, like, feminism?"

Evie shook her head sadly. "Nope."

I pushed more hair back. "Holy moly, is there no one else?"

"Did you just say 'holy moly'? Even *I* don't say holy moly."

"This is definitely a holy moly kind of moment."

"Why don't you just meet him?" She stepped to one side to let a group of students past. "See how you feel then?"

eleven

I instantly fancied Will.

He was everything a cocky wannabe film director should be. Big black-framed glasses, a slightly-oversized stripy jumper with tighter jeans, the kind of mouth that stayed in a permanent superior type of smirk with a tiny beard thing in the middle of his chin. I couldn't believe I hadn't noticed him around the college campus. Because he was definitely the sort of boy I instantly fancy.

Though, to be fair, I instantly fancy lots of people.

It still surprised me though, as I'd spent the whole walk there already arguing with him in my head – fuelled by Evie. He had two chairs in the college canteen, leaning back in one, his feet up on the other – showing off some posh leather shoes. A coffee from the Italian deli down the road perched in front of him, like the college's instant coffee machine wasn't good enough. Alongside it sat some posh ciabatta bread, with tiny plastic pots of oil and balsamic vinegar. I mean, what?

He raised his eyebrows when I walked over.

"Lottie, I presume?" he said.

I mean who even talks like that? So I said: "Who even talks like that?"

Another raise of his eyebrows. He picked up his coffee cup and slurped it, watching me as I pulled up a chair across from him.

"So, Evie said you want to help me with my project?" I asked, copying his body language. He leaned further back in his chair, crossing his arms, so I mirrored him.

"Yeah, it seems interesting enough." He said it like it was the most boring idea in the world.

"Don't wet yourself with excitement."

He didn't even smile, just smirked.

"I never do."

"I can imagine."

I don't like it when people act all superior with me. I went to a private school on a scholarship; it happened there a lot. I don't like it more when I find myself fancying them. But I'd learned to never let anyone think they were better than me. Because, usually, just the fact they're thinking it means they're not. So I decided to disarm him. I reached out, ripped a piece of bread off, splashed it in the vinegar and ate it.

His cocky eyebrows shot up instantly in shock. Ha, I thought, you weren't expecting that.

"Did you just eat my food?" he asked, in genuine disbelief.

I shrugged. "What seventeen-year-old brings oil and

vinegar dipping pots into college?" I asked. "Now, are you going to help or not?"

His face – ha! – his face. He really, truly, didn't know what to do.

"You can't just go around taking people's food."

"Yes, well. The whole point of this project is me pointing out all the things people shouldn't really be able to go around doing, but they do them anyway."

He opened his mouth, then closed it again.

"So…" I breezed on. "Evie tells me you're not really a feminist?"

His smirk returned instantly. "I'm an equalitist." He said it so smugly that his attractiveness nosedived by at least ten points.

"It's the same thing," I argued.

"Well, I prefer to use the word equalitist." His lip was curling, and I shook my head in disbelief.

"I mean, millions of women all over the world are being oppressed, tortured, undermined and massacred, and you're more worried about *branding*?"

"Well if that's the case, why are you so het up about using the word 'feminist'?"

"BECAUSE…" My fists were clenched. "Because, yes, equality for everyone is important but using the word 'feminist' makes it pretty darn clear that gender is a main offender in the universe-is-bullshit Olympics. The word feminism acknowledges that, since the dawn of time, society historically split humans into two categories – male and female – and one has uncontrollably shat on the other…"

Will looked bored by my rant – actually bored. He stopped me with his hand, and I was so stunned by the rudeness that I let him.

"Since the dawn of time?" He smirked. "So, were, like, male dinosaurs oppressing female dinosaurs?"

I threw my hands up. "Oh, by all means, ignore everything important I just said and focus on the one tiny thing that wasn't perfect. Because that's constructive."

"I was just joking."

"Yeah, well, I was just leaving. The last thing I need right now is help from someone like you." I stood up.

He didn't stop me leaving, so I carried on walking away from him – feeling that anger back in my stomach from those days before I came up with the project, feeling like I was losing, even if I was pretending I was winning.

"Wait," he called, just as I was at the door. I stopped and watched him make his way over. He was shorter than you'd think, standing up. I stood taller.

"What is it?"

"You honestly got that angry, that quickly? How are you going to cope with a month of all this?"

I did a huge big sigh. "You were rude."

"You were ruder."

"You wound me up."

"By politely disagreeing with you? So you storm off? From what Evie said, the point of this project is to stand up for yourself, not storm off."

God, he was cocky. And he knew he'd got to me. His smirk was super strained – from being so wide across his face. His eyes danced all triumphantly behind his glasses.

I smiled a tiny smile. "Yes, well, the project's not started yet."

"Just as well."

"Do you even need those glasses?"

It was his turn to smile. "As a matter of fact I do."

"I'm worried about working with you," I admitted. "I'm not sure if I can do this with someone who doesn't believe in what I'm doing."

We were bashed by a group of students streaming through the doors, soaking wet. I looked through the windows – it had suddenly started pissing down outside. Will grabbed my arm and steered me away and, again, his assertiveness gave me fancying-him vibes. I hated myself for those vibes.

He lowered his voice, so it was calmer, almost soothing. "Don't you think you're going to have to get used to people not agreeing with this pretty quickly?"

I didn't say anything.

"Look…" he continued. "Just because I don't call myself a feminist, doesn't mean I don't think this is an interesting project."

"You're not acting like it's interesting. You're acting all superior."

"Because you are! You didn't even say hello!"

Didn't I? I'd been so prepared to fight him after Evie's briefing that maybe I did go into it in full-on argue mode.

"It's going to take up a lot of your time." I changed the subject, not saying sorry.

"Yeah. But it's just what I need for my portfolio."

"How can I trust you not to edit me all wrong and make me look stupid?"

He actually rolled his eyes. "I'm not going to stitch you up. I'm not a total jerk."

I challenged him with my own eyebrows.

"I'm not..."

"Evie said you argue with her a lot in film studies."

"She argues with me."

That's my girl...

We stood – sizing each other up. He'd emailed me a link to his own video channel earlier that day – it was frustratingly good. I needed him. And, from the sounds of it, he needed me.

I held out my hand. "Promise you'll be completely objective?"

He held out his. "Promise you're not going to be this hard to work with the whole time?"

I smiled. "Promise me you do actually need those glasses?"

"Promise me you're not going to make me film your grown-out bikini line."

"EWW!" I sputtered, and we both started laughing.

Okay – so he was a cocky jerk who used the word "equalitist" rather than feminist. But at least he didn't call himself a "menimist", and he was talented and willing.

My downfall combination.

"You will have to grow out all your body hair, right?" he asked, pushing his glasses up his nose. He put on a squeaky voice. "I mean, isn't, like, being hairless totally a way of oppressing women for a capitalist agenda?"

My mouth fell open. "We've not sorted out the rules on body hair."

"Yeah, well, whatever you decide, you can film those bits on your own."

I laughed again, and we finally shook hands – still sizing each other up as we entwined palms.

Damnit, I thought. I really fancy you...

twelve

The days leading up to the start of the project were pretty frantic. Everyone at the FemSoc meeting agreed to support the campaign. I stood up and talked about the men cat-calling me, and how it had all stemmed from there. The response I got was amazing – everyone clapped and cheered, so much I felt inclined to bow.

"Lottie, stop bowing," Evie whispered through gritted teeth.

Megan and I blew off a whole day to make all the campaign artwork. We hid out in the smaller art room where students could work on their coursework outside of lessons – but we didn't do coursework. And I didn't tell my parents about blowing off a day of lessons for obvious reasons.

Megan had designed this awesome logo of me dressed as a ninja, with loads of cats with ninja eyebands on too. It was totally superb, and I was trying to copy it.

"I'm jealous of your use of black fineliner," I said, my face practically up against the table to make sure I kept the line straight.

"Well, I'm jealous of how good you are with acrylic paints."

We'd put the radio on softly in the corner and coloured in contented silence, which was pretty cool considering I didn't know Megan that well. She was a comfortable person to be around, if I stopped trying to analyse her for signs of emotional trauma. Not always easy. I'd noticed that she only ever wore baggy clothes. The only times I saw her without the sleeves of her hoody pulled down over her hands and her arms crossed were when she was working on her art.

"Could Amber not come?" Megan asked, reaching for the scissors to cut out some more cat shapes.

I shook my head. "She got really bad tonsillitis right at the beginning of term so her attendance is down too much to skive off. She thinks she caught it on the plane back from America."

"Aren't you supposed to be keeping your attendance up? I remember last year you said you were applying for Cambridge."

I didn't look up. I hadn't heard back from them yet, and I was beginning to get nervous. "I am."

"Jeez, you must be smart."

I did look up then, and smiled. "I don't even know if I've got an interview yet… Anyway, even if I do get one, I'm not sure what they'd make of all this…" Our artwork was now covering most of the available table space in the room. "What're you doing next year?"

It was Megan's turn to avoid eye-contact. She looked back down at her poster. "I'm not sure. I kind of messed up my exams last summer because of...stuff."

What stuff? Max stuff?

"Megan..." I started, but she cut me off completely, with, "So, what are you, like, hoping to achieve with this thing?" She met my eye and the way she held her jaw made it clear she knew she was deliberately interrupting me, taking me off topic. I ignored the blodge in my stomach and obliged her.

"What do you mean?"

"Like...what's the ideal outcome? You going to try and change laws? Or is it just about visibility?"

"You know," I smiled, "I should probably know the answer to that..."

Megan smiled too, the ice melting between us once again. I thought about her question as I started to draw another cat. My previous one was so not as good as hers.

"I think it's just about raising awareness," I said. "I feel like people need to know the problem exists before they can want to help get rid of it. My hope is that I'll be behaving like such a thing possessed, because there'll be so much to call out, that it will change people's minds...or open them."

"Well you've certainly got some kick-ass posters to help you along the way."

"I have indeed." There was another long silence between us, but this time it was comfortable again. "I don't know,

Megan," I eventually said. Because I didn't know what else to say. "I just hope it changes something."

A week before it all kicked off, during half term, I came home from the library to find a letter on our Buddha welcome mat. It was in one of those posh stiff envelopes and my breath caught just looking at it.

Cambridge…

I picked it up, turning it over in my hands – savouring the moment of not knowing what was inside. The instant I opened it, I'd step into another part of my life. A part that knew whether or not Cambridge wanted me. I mean, I guess getting in could really change my life.

I peeled back one tiny side of the envelope, sniffing it – I wasn't sure why. Then I sighed and carried it through to the kitchen. Mum and Dad would kill me if I opened it without them. Bugger. And tonight I was going to tell them about the Vagilante Project too. Maybe, if it was good news in the letter, it could help cushion the blow?

There was a note on the oven, scrawled out in Mum's handwriting.

Baked pots inside – turn oven on at 5:30 – home at 6ish

I yanked the knob of the oven out to turn it on, helped myself to a glass of water and went up to my room to do some work. Mum rents a room at the town's natural health centre. She does all sorts – shiatsu massage, reflexology, aromatherapy. I don't think she makes much money, but it makes her very happy – and our house smell pretty weird. I think it's more pocket money to use around Dad's income… He teaches at the local university – thus all the academic pressure. Plus, he's always banging on about the amazing opportunities I have, compared to what he had growing up as a child.

I couldn't work, not with the letter downstairs. I pictured it having a heartbeat, and saw it thumping where I'd left it on the kitchen table – *thump thump thump…*

The front door opened and cold air rattled the beaded curtain.

"Lottie?" Mum called up the stairs. "I'm back. Did you put the potatoes on, darling?"

"I did."

I listened to her getting-in noises – clicking her way into the kitchen to get the kettle boiling for an end-of-day herbal tea. I heard her stop.

"Lottie? Is this letter from…?"

"Cambridge?" I yelled down the stairs. "Yeah, I think so."

A clatter, a thump and a rumble and Mum burst through my open bedroom door – her face red.

"OHOHOHOHOHOHOHMYMYMYMYMY," she gurgled, the letter clutched in her hand. She danced about my room, leaping on and off the bed like a child too excited about going to Disneyland.

I couldn't help but laugh. "Mum, calm down. It may be a rejection letter. It may not be an interview offer."

"It will be, it has to be. Oh, where's your father? I want us to open it NOW. I'll ring him, hang on…" She clattered off and I heard her on the phone in the hall. "There's a letter here from Cambridge…yes…we'll wait…but be quick…" A thunk of her plonking the landline down. "He's on his way," she called. "Now, let's calm our nerves with some nice, fresh tea."

Fifteen minutes later, and I was nursing a mug of fresh peppermint tea when Dad burst through the kitchen door, still wearing his coat and scarf.

"Tea?" Mum offered but he stopped her with his hand. I noticed him do it…

"Lottie, thank you for waiting." He came and kissed my forehead. "Is that it?" His gaze went to the envelope, which had pride of place on the kitchen table, amongst Mum's freaky orchids.

"That's it."

Dad pulled up a chair and Mum dragged hers around, so we were in a huddle. I picked up the waddy envelope, and peeled back the flap, sticking my finger in to rip it open.

"Careful," Dad said. "You don't want to damage what's inside."

I rolled my eyes and yanked the letter out. It was folded in three. I opened it, scanned it, reading it quicker than Dad who was reading it aloud.

"Dear Charlotte Thomas…" he mumbled under his breath. "We are delighted to invite you to come to interview at King's College for Human, Social, and Political Science… Fantastic, you've got an interview, Charlotte! You've done it! You've got an interview!"

My hands shook on the paper… An interview. Despite dropping my extra A level, despite leaving my scholarship at posho school. I'd done it. I allowed myself to smile, and swallowed the lump I didn't even realize was in my throat. It felt strange though… I'd worked towards this moment for so many years – it was surreal having it played out in actual life. Like it was a play I'd forgotten the lines to.

Mum and Dad were hugging me – Mum's squeals doing all sorts of permanent damage to my eardrums. Cambridge…

Hang on, when was the interview date?

With a lurching heart, I scanned the page for the date and time. *Please don't be during my project, please don't be during my project.* I let out a sigh I didn't even know I'd been holding. It was the week *after* my project was due to finish.

"Lottie, I'm so proud. We're both so proud."

"We have to celebrate! Shall we order a curry?"

"Yes, Lottie, would you like a curry?"

"And bubbly. Do we still have that bottle Frank and Anne gave us?"

"I think so, though it's not cold. Lottie, bubbly?"

They'd let go of me and were now milling around, ordering takeout, shoving loads of ice into the sink and putting a bottle of champagne in there. Mum and Dad rarely drank so there was a huge stockpile of bottles under the kitchen sink.

I felt so many emotions all at the same time – relieved, scared…and guilty. What if the dates of the interview *had* overlapped with Vagilante? Would I have still carried on the project during the actual interview?

Dad went out to pick up the takeaway while Mum fussed with laying the table, not letting me help. She gurgled with joy as she laid out forks and took our old jar of mango chutney out of the fridge, and a flash of resentment washed over me all of a sudden. At them. At how big a deal this was to them. Was it my dream? Or theirs? It got blurred sometimes.

"Oh, Lottie. This is so exciting. I mean, there's a lot of hard work, obviously. But college will train you up for the interview, and you'll definitely get the grades you need. No excuse after you dropped history…"

There wouldn't have been any sexism to call Cambridge out on during my interview anyway, would there? I mean, it's Cambridge! It's, well…an old institution steeped in tradition and history…umm…sexism never happens in places like that. And, anyway, I'd applied to King's. That was one of the most progressive colleges. I could make loads of totally kick-ass liberal friends and we'd end up running the world together in a really nice way.

Dad charged back in, an aromatic plastic bag swinging off his wrist, letting the most gorgeous smells into the kitchen.

"The celebration food is here," he announced, decanting

silver containers of red juicy goodness into bowls and shoving some spoons in. We all sat around the table. Mum made me pop the champagne and I got most of it all over the walls, but managed to tip some into three flutes.

"A toast. To Lottie and Cambridge." Dad held up his flute. "Only one more step to go, then watch out House of Commons."

We all clinked.

"There are still a few more steps," I said, even though I knew he was teasing. I grabbed two poppadoms and snapped them into bite-sized pieces. "I have to choose a political party, and then join one, then get elected MP, then win the party leadership…then, well, an entire general election."

Mum shrugged, like it was nothing, smiling at Dad, in on the joke. Like I'd said, *I just need to go upstairs and get a jumper.* "Pah," she said. "That's nothing. I'm so proud of you, Lottie."

"You know, I don't *have* to go to Cambridge to become prime minister."

"That's true." Dad helped himself to some of the chopped onion that came in a small tub. "But it certainly helps. Especially doing Human, Social, and Political Science."

We ate in contented silence – Mum and Dad occasionally looking at me with gooey eyes. The food, as always, was awesome. And even though my tummy was all twisted, I had seconds.

I still hadn't told them about my project. As I ate yet another poppadom, I pondered over telling them now. With their stomachs full, with their moods good, with their worries currently put on hold…

"So, I'm starting an extra-curricular thing next week," I announced, crumbling my poppadom into pieces. "I'm really excited about it."

Mum and Dad looked up.

"What's that?" Mum asked.

I could see Dad looking nervous already, the laugh creases around his eyes no longer there.

I gulped and poured myself more champagne.

"I'm doing this video project called The Vagilante…" I paused for dramatic effect. "Letting the cat lady out of the bag. It's a feminism thing…" My parents shared a look as I explained the concept to them – how FemSoc were helping, how I'd got a professional film-maker (sort of) on board.

Their reaction was to be expected.

"That's, erm…" Dad coughed. "Great, Charlotte. Really great. But, are you sure it's not going to distract you from your studies?"

"Dad's right," Mum said, putting a hand over his. "You've got a lot of prep to do for this interview. Do you need that extra commitment?"

I pushed some uneaten pieces of rice around my otherwise empty plate.

"You say you want me to do great things," I said. "And then you get annoyed when I try to do just that."

They shared another look. Dad sipped from his glass and put it down.

"We're proud of you, Lottie. It's just we know you'll be able to achieve amazing things if you go to Cambridge. Isn't it worth holding on for a bit?"

"Being a hypocrite for a bit, you mean?"

"I'm just struggling to see why you have to start something like this now. At such a key time."

"Can't you just be excited about it? Like everyone else is?"

Dad ignored me. "Have you told college you're doing this?"

I shook my head.

"So, how do you think they're going to react, when you turn up next Monday, honking a giant horn and calling everyone sexist?"

I actually hadn't thought about that. "They'll think, *Aren't we lucky to have such an awesome student?*" I said.

Mum shook her head slowly, all the glow from the letter unglowed in her face. "It's not great timing, sweetie, that's all. It's a great idea though…"

"I know. That's why I'm doing it. Now."

They shared yet another look.

"Is there anything we can do to stop you?"

"Have you ever been able to stop me doing anything?"

And they didn't say anything. Because they hadn't.

thirteen

Two days before the project began, Will messaged me, asking to meet in the photography studio at college. He'd got special permission to film there during half term. An annoying bubble of excitement raced to the top of my stomach when I got it – but I pushed it away. I did not have time to fancy unsuitable boys right now... Especially ones who play the classic *I'm an equalitist, not a feminist* trick.

When I got there, I literally stopped in the doorway in shock. He'd transformed the shabby studio into a white glowing cube of light. There was a professional white backdrop set up, with at least four giant lamps with huge bulbs, and even one of those reflective silver umbrellas. A chair stood on the stark white background, in front of a massive camera.

"Woah," I said, stepping in. "Did you do all this?"

Will was adjusting the setting of his camera, all bent over. I could just about see the tops of his boxers poking out the waistband of his jeans. They were a posh brand. The sight made me all squiffy.

He looked up, acknowledging my arrival, but then squinted back down into the lens.

"Yeah, I did," he said into his camera. His deliberate emotional distance made me like him more. Which I'm sure was the point. Luckily, I was good at this game. Good as in, I don't play it. Ever. I sent my brain extra signals, instructing it not to fancy him any more.

"It's all very fancy." I walked over and deliberately tilted his camera. He threw up his hands as he stood up.

"Oi!"

"Whoops." I smiled and shrugged my shoulders.

"I did all this for you – why are you sabotaging it?"

I smiled again. "Because it's fun." I walked onto the white sheeting, feeling him watching me. "What are we doing here anyway?"

I spun on my heel, and he was back fiddling with the camera. I didn't know for sure he'd been watching. He held his framed eye to the lens.

"Sit on the stool," he answered.

I stayed standing. "Say please."

"Jeez, Lottie. I'm doing you a favour here. Can you please act like it?"

I sighed and sat astride the stool – my legs wide apart.

"Very demure," he sniped, but I saw a hint of a smile.

"I pride myself. Now, why are we here?"

One last twist of a lens and he straightened – looking

right at me. He was SO serious. Serious vibes just radiated off him – along with superiority vibes and cockiness vibes.

"I thought it would be good to film an opening interview," he said. "You know, to capture what you hope you're going to get out of this project? What you think the hardest bits will be. What you're hoping it will achieve, etc. etc. It will be interesting to watch it back when the project's over."

I nodded, and tucked my hair behind my ears. "Okay, cool."

"Hang on; I need to mike you up." He came over with a little clip-on mike and held it out towards my chest. "Normally I'd just clip it on, but if you're a feminazi, you're going to accuse me of sexual assault if I do that, aren't you?"

I snatched the mike off him and clipped it to my blouse. It was my favourite one – white, with little red hearts all over it.

"Do you really think it's appropriate," I said, "to compare wanting equal rights for everybody with a group of people responsible for mass genocide?"

"You'd totally have flipped if I'd touched your boob though."

I shook my head. "That's not the point. And, also, yeah, I would've done, and that doesn't make me any kind of Nazi – it makes me someone who believes she should be the only one who decides who can and can't touch her boobs."

Though – to be fair – I would probably let Will touch my boobs...

Hang on – BAD LOTTIE – NAUGHTY LOTTIE. God, I hated being so attracted to people all the time. It was exhausting being so in touch with one's loins.

"Let's just get this over with," Will said, and he clicked something that made a red light come on.

"Are we filming?"

"Yes."

"I'm not ready. Where's it going to go?"

"On the video channel I've made for you. And you don't need to be ready. You just need to answer questions."

"Hang on, I need to put some lipstick on."

Another smirk. "Now, if you're a feminist, then why is it okay for you to wear lipstick?"

"Because I want to wear lipstick." I made my voice all slow and dumb.

"But isn't that quite hypocritical? You say you don't want to be objectified, but then you put red lipstick on?"

"Is this for the video? Or are you just taunting me for fun?"

"I'm just…" Will fiddled with the lens again. "Trying to figure out your rules for The World, as they don't seem to be very consistent."

I tilted my head at him. "Do you actually want to hear my reasoned argument about why it's okay for feminists to wear lipstick? I have one prepared. Though my hunch is you're just trying to undermine, rather than genuinely listen to me."

Will shrugged. "I guess I could hear it. Though it seems

like an unimportant thing to focus on when there's, like, starving people in the world, and disease and stuff."

I held up my hands. "Hang on…you've attacked my choice to wear lipstick, and now I'm trying to argue back, you're going to make me feel bad for spending time arguing with you when I could be helping orphans?" I blew out a breath in disbelief. "Have you helped any orphans today, Will? Have you given any money to charity today, Will?"

His ears were starting to go red. "No," he admitted.

And most of the first half of his memory card was just a film of us arguing.

WEEK ONE

fourteen

I applied my war paint.

After my usual copious amounts of eyeliner, I got out a purple lipstick I'd once experimented with and vowed to never experiment with again, and dabbed lines across my cheeks.

In my bag was: a giant clown's horn – ordered online, 'cause you know I don't normally need a giant clown's horn – hundreds of badges and posters, some paper plates, two tubes of squirty cream, and countless other mini horns.

I looked at my reflection… I looked nuts. But I also looked fierce. I needed to look fiercer than I felt.

I was ready.

"What have you put on your face?" Mum asked me over breakfast. Dad, fortunately, had already gone to prepare for an early lecture.

"War paint." I poured myself some orange juice. "My project starts today."

"Oh dear," was all Mum had to say about that.

The doorbell rang just as I was finishing my toast. "It's for me." I swung my bag over my shoulder and ran to open the door. It was Amber, Evie and Will – Will had his camera running.

"HAPPY VAGILANTE DAY," the girls cheered, pulling me out the door for a hug.

"Your war paint is awesome," Evie said. "I want some."

"I've got the lipstick in my bag, hang on."

Will shoved his camera in my face just as I was handing over my purple lipstick.

"How does it feel, Lottie?" he asked, all uber-professional. I grinned into the camera lens and pointed to my face.

"This feminist is READY to declare war on patriarchy." Then I dipped into my bag. "Hang on, I've got horns for everyone."

"HORNS!" Amber delved in to grab herself one. I could tell she was already far too excited. "All my life, I've wanted an excuse to toot a horn."

She honked it right in my face, making me wince. "Oww, Amber. We only honk it when we see sexism, remember?"

"Oh sorry." But she honked it again.

Will walked backwards to get us all in shot. "So, you've just left the house, Lottie. Do you see any sexism?"

"Not yet, but it's only been five seconds."

He peered up from his lens and I saw the corners of his eyes twinkle – if that's possible.

"You decided to still wear make-up?" he commented,

just loud enough for us to hear. Instantly three horns honked right into his face.

"FIRST SEXISM OF THE DAY – FIRST SEXISM OF THE DAY!" I yelled, delighted that it was Will himself to give me my first instance. He needed vast amounts of being cut down to size.

"Why is asking that sexist?" he asked, not breaking professionalism, as we all started walking to college.

I threw him major shade. "A," I said, "we had this argument the other day, so God knows why you're bringing it up again. B, just by asking this, you're judging my choices as a woman."

"Woooah, hang on." He put his hand over the lens briefly. "I'm not judging your choices as a woman." He made quotation signs with his fingers when he said "woman", which put my back up a bit. "I'm judging you as a female campaigning against sexism but wearing a faceful of make-up at the same time."

Evie rolled her eyes at him. "Will, just film already. Stop being difficult."

Amber honked the horn right in his ear, and his face scrunched up. "Yes, WILL. IF that's even your real name."

Will rubbed his ear. "What? Why wouldn't it be my real name?"

"I'm just saying." Amber tapped her forehead with her finger, confusing all of us.

I put my hand up to stop everyone. "Guys, come on! The project has only been going two minutes, and we're already attacking a boy."

117

"He started it," both Evie and Amber yelled.

I nodded, then threw Will more shade. "He did, and he knows he did…but no angry ranty feminismy-ness. It puts people off, remember?"

"Thanks, Lottie," Will said. He raised his eyebrows at me – in an almost flirty way. Gah! He was already so annoying!

"Now," I continued, "I'll explain to you *again* why I'm wearing make-up at MY BIG MEETING ABOUT IT this afternoon. If you would just WAIT, I have a whole PUBLIC SPEECH prepared about my frickin' make-up for this afternoon's special FemSoc meeting. So will you quit trying to shame me before I've even started, Mr Cameraman who's supposed to be HELPING me?"

"Okay okay okay."

"Thank you."

I spied my first opportunity just as we approached a bus stop.

"I need the clown horn," I yelled, pulling it out and running towards the stop.

"She's found one, she's found one!" Amber ran after me – excitement radiating off her like a child who'd just run through the entrance to Disneyland. I drew up to the bus stop, where four or so people were waiting, and I started madly honking my horn at the advertisement on the side of it.

"Attention, attention." I raised my voice. "I just have to let you know, this poster is TOTALLY SEXIST."

Will and Evie ran up to me with the camera. I could see

the bus drawing up behind them. I didn't have long to try and win these people over.

I pointed to the advertisement. It was for a new Hollywood film and the movie poster was shot between a woman's legs. You couldn't see her face or any other part of her apart from her perfect legs that most women could never get unless they lunged instead of breathed and then married a Photoshop specialist. The lead male was shot in all his bodily gloriousness and posed between the inanimate legs. He was allowed a face, a head, shoulders, arms, and all other body parts to be included on the poster at the same time.

"This poster is sexist," I repeated, feeling slightly disheartened by the fact that people were ignoring me – instead looking at the arriving bus and fumbling for their bus passes in their pockets. "Why just have a random pair of women's legs? Would you EVER see a film poster like this the other way round? Where the body parts of men were cut into pieces and assembled nicely around a full-bodied woman?" The loud hiss of the arriving bus drowned me out. Everyone got on, pretending I wasn't there. Apart from a very elderly-looking lady who said, "You look just like my son, Michael," before wobbling her way up the steps.

The bus left us in a cloud of exhaust fumes.

Amber slow-clapped. "Wow, Lottie. You really got through to them."

I coughed, feeling my face go red. "The important thing is I pointed it out," I said, half to them, half to the camera

lens. I smirked, remembering what I had with me. "And...
I'm not finished with this poster yet." I kneeled down,
unzipped my bag, and yanked out a paper plate and a can of
squirty cream.

"Umm, what the heck do you have there?" Evie peered
over my shoulder.

"Shh." I pulled out a marker pen and wrote *This is sexist*
on the back of the plate. "I am making a cream pie."

Amber, Will and Evie all crowded around me.

"You're...you're...*Bugsy Malone*-ing the bus shelter?"
Evie asked, wonder in her voice.

I nodded. "You said to make it funny."

Amber put her hand up while Will zoomed in. "Umm,
what's '*Bugsy Malone*-ing' mean?"

As I was too busy determinedly squirting cream onto the
plate to answer, Evie explained.

"Have you not seen the film? They all carry these
things called splurge guns – they're like machine guns, but
filled with cream instead of bullets. And they splurge each
other instead of killing each other, because it's all acted
by kids."

I stood up, brandishing the plate on my palm. "Will?
Make sure you get this." I spun on my feet and hurled the
pie at the poster. It splattered marvellously, right between
the woman's butt cheeks, dripping down onto her airbrushed
legs. The cream stuck the plate there – with *This is sexist*
clear for anyone to see. I cannot adequately describe the
soaring euphoria I felt as I let go of that pie, nor how it

quadrupled when I heard it splatter over that poster – but it's safe to say I felt the happiest I've felt in a long time.

People don't throw enough cream pies – that's what I've decided.

People walk past too many bullshit posters and don't throw cream pies.

Evie, Amber and Will looked on, stunned, as more trickles of melted cream eked their way down the poster. I heard a hiss behind us. Another bus was coming.

"What now?" Will asked, moving the camera from the poster back to my face.

"Now?" I asked, staring right back at him. "Now, we run."

fifteen

A bunch of FemSoc girls waited for us at the college gates. When they saw us running over, lipstick war paint all over our faces, they cheered. I ran straight into them, colliding with about four people, feeling amazing.

"Oomph, hello, Lottie," Megan said.

She'd really outdone herself. She'd handed out balloons and badges that she'd designed and, from the looks of it, even brought a flask of coffee.

"Thanks for doing all this, Megan." I pulled her in for a hug. When I pulled back, I studied her quickly. Her hair hung over most of her face but, from the bits I could see, there was light glowing inside her. "And thanks for coming, everyone." I turned towards the girls around me. "Day one of Project Vagilante has officially BEGUN. The cat lady is out of the bag!"

They cheered again. Evie retrieved my lipstick and began painting their faces.

"We've got a special one-off meeting this afternoon, where I'll explain some stuff. And thanks for being here. Having your support means the world."

More cheering and clapping. I still couldn't believe I was doing this. Nothing felt real. But I was so glad – so glad I'd met Evie and Amber and made the Spinster Club happen, and now FemSoc happen and ALL THE GOOD THINGS happen. Will made us group together for photos, or "campaign collateral" as he called it. I watched him as he arranged us, barking orders with confidence. A piece of hair kept falling over his forehead and he kept shoving it back into place – the only tell that he wasn't as cocky as he seemed.

No one is ever as cocky as they seem.

I wondered again why he was doing this. He kept saying it was just for his portfolio. And from the arguments we'd already had, I was inclined to believe him. But I couldn't help also hoping it was because somewhere, deep inside all that superiority complex, he believed in what I was doing...maybe.

Students gave us funny looks as they walked past. A few of the rugby lads, including Teddy, started nudging each other. Teddy looked at me in particular and yelled "SLUTS!" before all of them burst into hyena laughs and clapped him on the back.

We stopped chatting. Everyone stared at me. Teddy and his mates walked on by, towards the main college building.

Will put his camera right in my face.

"What you going to do, Lottie?" he asked. "You just going to let that one go?"

I rolled my eyes directly into the camera. "What do you think?"

"They would say it was just a joke," he argued, deliberately winding me up.

I squinted into the winter sunshine. They certainly weren't looking back at us.

"Evie!" I barked her name like I was an army general. "Please help me assemble a pie."

She scuttled over and got the cream out, while I pulled out another paper plate. The girls saw, and started cheering harder.

"You sure you want to do this?" Evie whispered under her breath as she squirted the cream. "I mean, Lottie, you'll get into trouble. I'm not sure you're allowed to splurge people outside of *Bugsy Malone*."

She was right, I'd get into massive trouble. Ignoring Mum and Dad's warnings, I'd not told college about my project. Mainly because I knew they'd try and ban it before it had even begun.

"I'm sure," I said, brandishing the pie. "Anyway, Teddy needs to let it go." I held it up and FemSoc went totally nuts, high on group hysteria. I squinted back at the boys – they were so close to the college doors that if I didn't go now, I'd lose them.

Now or never. Let it go, or fight fire with pie.

Sensing my hesitation, Amber slapped me on the back.

"Go get 'em, Lottie," she said, encouragingly.

So I ran, and I did.

sixteen

I felt distinctly more stupid sitting in my English lesson alone, covered in lipstick. No one from FemSoc was in my class. And Will had film studies with Evie and Oli first thing, so I didn't even have him.

It was just me, sitting in a roomful of people, holding a horn, with lipstick all over my face.

To be fair, I didn't get a huge amount of stares. People at college were…used to me. After the college jukebox thing last year, Evie, Amber and I had been labelled *those crazy feminist girls*, which we took as a huge compliment…when we weren't alone in lessons.

I pulled out my textbook as we waited for our teacher, Mrs Roslyn, to arrive, and read through my essay notes. If I was likely to not get an A in any subject, it would be English lit. I wasn't very good at just examining other people's writing without going off on my own tangents. But Dad had told me Cambridge like it if you do "traditional" subjects, so I sucked it up. And used it as a bartering point to get out of doing my extra A level. I'd only just got away with doing art, but I pleaded needing a "creative outlet".

A girl I vaguely knew, Jenny, who I was quite sure didn't like me, leaned over and asked me, "Umm, Lottie. Why do you have lipstick all over your face?"

"I do?" I cracked up laughing while she stared at me like I really was mad. All the adrenalin of throwing the pie was soaking through me, making me feel light-headed. I hadn't even paused to see Teddy's reaction. I'd just flung it in his direction and run to class – Evie chasing after me singing "We Could Have Been Anything That We Wanted To Be" from *Bugsy Malone*.

"Sorry." I snorted myself out. "It's for a project I'm doing. For FemSoc."

Jenny nodded, like it all made sense now. "Riiiiight."

I beamed at her. "You're welcome to join us. You know that, right?"

Maybe I imagined it, but she pulled her chair a little bit further back.

"Yep. I know."

I'd invited her to join many a time, but Jenny was…well it was hard to find a way of describing her without me having to honk a horn at myself…but she was a girl's girl. All pink and make-up and posting Disney stuff on her profile pages. Not that those girls can't be feminists – but, umm… well Jenny hadn't always said nice things about me in the toilets. I'd overheard her calling me "an attention seeker" once while I was peeing.

I leaned back in my chair and tried to make my breath catch up with the rest of me. I focused on copying a technique Evie had taught me once that helped her when her OCD "came out to play" as she described it. In for five, out for seven...in for five...out for seven... I wonder if the pie actually hit Teddy? In for five, out for seven... I hope it did... in for five, out for seven, in for five, out for seven... My heart had just about returned to normal when Mrs Roslyn strode in, carrying a stack of poetry books in a wobbly pile.

"Hi, everyone, sorry I'm a bit late." She passed out the books. "I had to make two trips to the storeroom for these."

I studied the front of the book. Last week we'd been given Philip Larkin. And two weeks before that Walt Whitman...

I was all alone in this class... Everyone would stare... I didn't want to honk the horn but...but...oh no...this was going to be so embarrassing!

The loud quacking noise of my novelty horn vibrated off the walls of the English classroom.

I felt my face go bright red.

Mrs Roslyn spun, trying to find the source of the noise. So did the other twenty people in my classroom. They all turned to stare at me. I waved my horn sheepishly.

"Lottie, what on earth?"

I had to speak. I had to speak now before I lost my nerve. Come on, Lottie, it's okay. This is the first hurdle. The first time you're doing this by yourself. People will get used to it. They'll have to… Think of where male domination gets us… Think of Megan… Think of those men in the van…

"Umm, why aren't we studying any female poets?" I asked – my voice gave me away by shaking slightly.

"What? What are you talking about? Why do you have a horn?"

"That's neither here nor there," I found myself saying, even though I'd never used that phrase before. "But I've looked through our reading list for the whole A level course and, like, over eighty per cent of the books, plays and poems we have to study are written by men. Over eighty per cent… Don't you think that's a bit…well…sexist?"

At the word *sexist* I heard at least three separate groans, including from Jenny. As I said, after last year, I'd got a bit of a reputation.

"Lottie, you can't go around disrupting my class." Mrs Roslyn ignored my question to focus on my discipline. Just for once, I longed a bit for my posh old school. We were always encouraged to speak out there – to challenge what we were told. It was one of the things that made me think I wanted to get into Cambridge.

"I'm doing a project, for FemSoc," I said, holding up my horn with one hand, and pointing towards my war-painted face with the other. "Where I'm honking a horn" – and various other things – "whenever I see sexism."

Mrs Roslyn looked like she was trying very hard not to roll her eyes. "Are you now?"

"Yes. And, well, I know this isn't your fault, but this reading list is total bullshit."

There was a hum of oooohs at my swear. I hadn't meant to. But eighty per cent! Come on! For the national curriculum! What was wrong with women's writing? It's not like they hadn't written a lot. Was it not smart enough? Unless the woman had been dead for over two hundred years? Are books not essay-worthy if a vagina sat under the writing desk? What's that telling us, hey? That women's voices, what women have to say, the words they want to leave behind – that they're only twenty per cent important?

I didn't realize I was saying this out loud. Loudly. I also didn't realize I was standing up until Mrs Roslyn told me to sit down.

"Don't you agree it's wrong?" I pulled my chair in – wanting her to understand…to be on my side. Because otherwise – judging by the expressions on the faces around me – I looked beyond nuts, like *let's-put-her-in-a-straitjacket-and-add-in-some-padded-walls crazy crazytown*.

Mrs Roslyn looked like she had no idea what to do – her mouth just opened and closed, like a fish.

"Well?" My heart thudded so loud in my chest, every single inch of my guts were tight.

She shook her head, then opened her book, like none of this had happened. "Now, if we all turn to page twelve you'll…"

I couldn't believe it! Was I invisible? I couldn't be invisible. Everyone was still giving me strange looks. I had lipstick all over my face, for Christ's sake! My inner uber-cringe morphed into anger. I watched Mrs Roslyn start reading the stupid poem written by a man, with his stupid privileged poetry penis, simmering and boiling. THIS – this was why I was doing the project. Yes, it was embarrassing, yes I felt stupid – but I'd just raised a perfectly valid point (*one I'd been sitting on for months come to think of it, ever since we got the extended reading list*) and, rather than talk about it, I'd just been ignored and silenced.

I scowled down at my page, biding my time…waiting… waiting…

Finally, Jenny put her hand up. Good old Jenny, though she didn't know it yet.

"Mrs Roslyn?" she asked…and before she could even ask her question, I'd got to my feet and honked my horn louder than ever before. There was no choice.

"LOTTIE, WHAT ON EARTH?"

I honked longer than was necessary. It really was spectacularly satisfying. Everyone turned to me in stunned horror.

"Your title," I said…knowing the moment I finished talking, I'd be chucked out of class… Maybe I should've warned college after all. "It's sexist," I stated, hearing the whole room breathe in sharply. Mrs Roslyn's face drew in on itself. "Why 'Mrs'?" I continued. "I mean your husband is born a Mr and lives his whole life as a Mr. But not you. No, you have to declare to everyone whether or not you're married. Society dictates that you have to become a

MRS now, instead of a miss. It's the twenty-first century and yet the first thing women are asked on any form is to define their marital status."

Silence. Silence before the storm.

Her face turned red. The class was more silent than prayer-time at church. Then, because I was still pissed off, I shrugged, smiled, and for laughs, honked my horn one more time.

The last toot of the horn did it...

The rage visibly seeped through every part of Mrs Roslyn's body. She shook...she opened her mouth...to explode at me...to send me out...to God knows what...

She took a big breath in... "Lottie."

I braced myself...

We were interrupted by a sharp rapping on the door. We all turned as one of the college secretaries strode in, smoothing down her cardigan with the self-consciousness of someone who has a whole room staring at her.

"Sorry to interrupt you, Mrs Roslyn... But we need Charlotte Thomas in the head teacher's office." She paused for impact, or maybe I imagined it. "As soon as possible."

seventeen

Teddy told on me. Of course he did. He stood – grinning –
outside the head teacher's office, leaning against the wall. I
noticed a tiny bit of cream on his neck which he'd obviously
missed in the clean-up. Good.

After being kept waiting for almost an hour, watching
Mrs Roslyn go in and out of the office to complain about
me, our joint meeting with Mr Packson didn't last very long.
All the trouble I was in quickly dispersed when I explained
Teddy had called us sluts. And we had the same *Oh dear, are
we really back here again?* talking-to we'd had so many times
last year.

"I can't believe you're not suspending her!" Teddy pulled
his collar up even more to try and assert himself. "I mean,
she threw a pie!"

Mr Packson sat back in his chair and put his fingertips
together. "Yes. But you verbally assaulted her. If I'm going to
start suspending people, then I'll have to suspend you both."

I held my breath, trying not to give myself away. My insides flashmobbed with nerves – suspension would ruin me. It would ruin my chances of Cambridge. Dad would go totally nuts.

Suspension wouldn't ruin Teddy… As far as I knew, his only upcoming life goal was a gap year in Thailand for some "tight poon" – as he'd so delightfully called it, loudly, in the college cafeteria. The Teddy I briefly knew would never have used the phrase "tight poon", though I guess I hadn't really known him very well. Especially as I never could've predicted his huge reaction to our break-up.

"Sir," I said, so much desperation shoved into that one syllable.

Teddy gave me a side-glance, and smirked. Mr Packson raised his hand to stop me, and I bit my lip. How could it have got this real and backlashy and scary in just one morning? And I still had a month to go… I watched him deliberate and prayed to Buddha, even though he's not a god and doesn't really do prayers. My only hope was that Mr Packson needed me as much as I needed him. It made the college look good, if they got students into Oxbridge. And I was one of just five in this year group with a shot. Finally he said, "I'm not going to suspend either of you."

I almost doubled over in relief.

"But you've got to stop antagonizing each other…"

Teddy and I gave each other a look. It was never going to happen. For some reason, he was never going to forgive me for breaking up with him…

"And, Lottie, violence is never the answer."

"It was hardly violence, it was a cream pie!" I blurted out.

"And it ruined my shirt!"

"You have eight million other Lacoste polo shirts exactly the same."

"STOP IT!" Mr Packson shouted. "If the two of you are ever in this room at the same time again, I really will suspend you both. Teddy, go to class. Lottie..." Uh-oh...he wasn't finished with me. "Stay here."

Teddy shot me a smug grin before sauntering out and I glared at him then stood up straighter for Mr Packson. I wasn't *so* scared now... I had Mr Packson in the palm of my hand. He was the one who let us start FemSoc and who organized all my extra A-level stuff. He was even the one who encouraged me to drop history.

But, right now, he was levelling me with a stare.

"What's going on, Lottie? A cream pie? I'm not even going to begin to understand. Are you trying to start a fastmobby, is that what they're called?"

"Do you mean 'flashmob'?"

"Never mind. And Mrs Roslyn just came in to say that you made personal comments about her in your lesson. About her title or something?"

"I have an explanation."

He leaned back further, a tiny smile at the very corners of his mouth. "Ahh, I thought you might."

So I twirled my hands and explained my project to him – the rules I'd come up with, why I started it, how long it was running for. His face slowly morphed from a wry smile, to disbelief, then horror. His grey hair got greyer, if possible. By the time I'd brought him up to speed on my cream-pie-ing of Teddy and honking of Mrs Roslyn he was actually standing up.

"Lottie, I can't allow you to do this at college."

I took a sharp breath in. "What do you mean?"

"I mean…Lottie…" He stumbled on his words and I knew then how freaked out he was. "FemSoc was one thing. That was hard enough to get through the college governors."

I crossed my arms. "It shouldn't be."

"Charlotte, you will not interrupt me."

Uh-oh, he'd called me Charlotte. I was in trouble. I nodded with subservience. I couldn't get suspended…

"Charlotte, you have to agree the college has been very" – he coughed – "accepting of your extra-curricular behaviours."

I wanted to interrupt again, but felt I couldn't. That I'd lose my shot at winning him over, and then I'd lose my shot at doing this in good faith. I was going to do it anyway, with or without his say-so, but it would really help my entire life if I didn't get suspended.

"But you can't physically attack other students. Especially not with…I mean…cream pies? This isn't *Bugsy Malone*!" I tried not to smile. "I'm sorry. I'm sure this project means a lot to you, but I absolutely cannot allow you to carry it out on college property."

"But what if I stop pie-ing people?"

"Charlotte, it's not just about the pie!" He raised his voice and I imagined my hair being blown back. "I mean, it goes without saying that the pies break college rules. But it's more than that… Do you not see how being this…pedantic… may upset people?"

I opened my mouth then closed it again – freaking out.

"Take poor Mrs Roslyn for instance. You have no right to go around attacking people…not teachers, not students."

"But I…I'm not attacking her! I'm attacking sexism!" I was flabbergasted. Flummoxed. Totally and utterly bamboozled. He sat down, in a way that suggested the conversation was over. But it couldn't be over. He hadn't even tried to understand. All the shit that happened in his very own college that had caused me to take such action. "I…" I stumbled again.

He looked up, like he was surprised I was still there. "That's all, Charlotte."

I'd lost him. I'd lost my chance. I needed to win this, but I'd used up so much of my energy already – with the humiliation in English, with the anger at Teddy, with being totally blanked at the bus stop. My inner fight was flagging at the worst possible time…

A loud knock at the door.

"Come in," the head teacher bellowed. The door swung open and we both turned to look.

Will stood there – his eyes shining bright behind his glasses. His arms crossed. He bowled through, pushing past the secretary who was trying to announce his arrival.

"What now?" Mr Packson asked, his voice sharp in response to Will's arrogance.

"Will," I said in wonder, at the same time the secretary said, "William Chaplain, he says he's Charlotte's partner in this project."

Will didn't even make eye-contact – he just strode up to the desk.

"You can't stop us from doing our project," he said. "Well, you can try. But you'll regret it."

Mr Packson peered down his nose through his glasses. "Excuse me?"

Will took another step forward. "I've rung the local newspaper. They're running a story on Lottie. Full page. She's being interviewed within a week. Just think what they'll make of it if the college isn't behind a campaign for basic human equality."

I stared at him in utter astonishment. The local paper? What? Since when? And how did he even know I was in here?

Will carried on, before Mr Packson had a chance to respond. "Think about it. Why is Lottie even compelled to do something like this? What's happened to her, as a student under your guardianship, that she's been forced to take such drastic action? She was verbally assaulted today. In broad daylight, on your grounds, and you do what? You give him a ticking-off and think that will solve it? I've got the entire thing on film. We're uploading it to our video channel tonight…"

Yikes – Will really did not come across as an anti-feminist

at all. There was no sarcastic drone in his voice like normal, no smugness – just passion and fire and, mmm, yummy yummy, but I couldn't really afford to get distracted by that just now.

"You have a choice, sir. You can either support Lottie on this, and come out as a college that doesn't tolerate sexism, one that instead champions students who fight for equality… or you can be the head teacher who lets girls be verbally abused on campus and tells them off when they complain."

Although he hadn't looked at me, I took a step forward so we stood side by side.

Mr Packson looked flummoxed. Totally and utterly bamboozled. I didn't dare say anything; I didn't dare breathe.

"Give me a minute, could you please?" He waved us away with his hand.

I didn't need to be told twice. I half-ran out the room. My body had had far too much adrenalin surging through it far too many times today. I sank onto the comfy sofa in the lobby area and splayed my legs out. I felt Will sink onto the cushion next to me.

I didn't turn to look at him, because I was feeling lots of conflicting things. But I said: "Wow, you really came across like you cared. If I didn't know better, I would say you were a right feminist."

"Good thing you know better then, hey?"

I could feel his smile. "So, why?"

"I've put a lot of work into this documentary already. I think I can use it as my big piece to get into film school.

I don't want it to fall apart on its first day."

I rolled my eyes, even though he couldn't see. "So, nothing to do with the greater good then? You just want to further your own career?"

He finally turned to me, making the tips of our knees touch. I overruled my natural instincts and moved my knees away.

"Hey, look, I never said I was against feminism. I just believe in equality for *everyone* and, well, logic and reason. I have to, I'm a documentary maker! I believe in finding the truth. And you're always going on about *this-sexist-thing-happened*, and *that-sexist-thing-happened*, but that's just you saying so. I'm more interested in seeing concrete evidence."

I crossed my arms. "So me telling you something isn't evidence? Women all routinely saying the same awful stuff happens to them isn't considered *evidence*?"

"It's not scientific and objective evidence, no."

"So if I told you I had a shower this morning, would you say I was lying? Would you want photographic evidence?"

Will grinned. "Well, yeah, of course I'd want photographic evidence of you in the shower." And I hit him.

"Ouch. Come on! You left that one wide open."

"You've basically just admitted to not believing an entire gender's experience," I said, aghast.

"I'm not saying I don't believe you!" He ran his hands through his hair. "I'm just saying, I'm a reasonable guy... and I respond better to reason. To stats. Not...anger."

I shook my head. "Oh, I'm sorry. Am I not responding

to a lifetime of repression in an appropriate way for you?"
I made my voice all sarcastic. "I'm sorry, how rude of me.
Next time I feel too scared to walk alone in case I'm fucking
raped, I'll make sure I tell you about it really politely, to
spare your feelings, and then I'll let you hook me up to a
freakin' polygraph test so you can check I'm not exaggerating
just for kicks. SORRY IF MY RESPONSE TO FEAR IS
UPSETTING YOU."

I yelled so loud the receptionist came out from around
the corner to tell us to shush.

"Hey," Will said, his face reddening. "I just saved your
arse in there."

I pulled a face. "You did not!"

"Did too. You were totally flailing."

"Well, it's tiring. Living with sexist bullshit every day. I
know you think I'm HALLUCINATING it all or something
– but there is a lot of it out there." I pulled my horn out of
my bag and honked it right in his face. He covered his ears
with his hands.

"What was that for?"

"You," I said. "Thinking you've come to 'rescue' me..."
I smiled. "I was doing fine by myself."

Which wasn't strictly true, but whatever. In a second,
he'd grabbed the horn off me.

"Oi, give me my sexism horn back."

He held it behind his back. "You can't honk it at me! I'm
part of the project!"

I went to snatch it, but he dodged. I clambered at him,

tugging at his jumper, and he continued to evade me. We were both giggling, out of breath… God it was fun flirting with someone who looked like him. But I couldn't, especially after all the exasperating things he'd just said… I pretended to give up and lay back in the squishy sofa.

"It's my project, Will. I said I'd call out everything I saw – and, while I appreciate your input today—"

"Input? I just saved the whole thing from tanking!"

I ignored him. "I'm not going to allow you to make yourself Switzerland in this battle. If you act all male-superior, I will honk my horn at you. And…if you continue to keep it from me…I will not think twice about pie-ing the crap out of you."

Will looked at me, amused, before slowly surrendering my horn.

"Well, it was worth a try."

"Have you thought about – I dunno – actually emotionally backing this project? Listening to what I'm saying, and thinking about why I'm saying it, rather than trying to make it into an intellectual discussion you can win? Try being on our side, rather than just shoving a lens in my face and making snide comments?"

He stretched his arms up, the bottom of his stripy jumper riding up as he did so.

"Why are you so obsessed with, like, winning me over to your side? Why do you care that I'm not totally behind it?"

I threw my hands up. "I don't know. Maybe because I'm trying to CHANGE THE WORLD, and it's fucking hard work and it would be nice if people agreed with the indisputable FACT that you are much more screwed in this universe if you identify as a girl, compared to if you identify as a boy – instead of arguing with me. And, maybe, just maybe, we could work TOGETHER to make things better for EVERYONE if only you'd stop being a pedantic butthead."

I waved my hands so aggressively that the horn flew across the waiting area. I sighed and went to pick it up.

"You just need to calm down a little." He said it so patronizingly, I could've killed him.

Instead I picked up the horn, ran back, put it as close to his ear as possible and honked it loud twice. The receptionist hushed me again, shooting me dagger stares.

"OUCH! Stop it. What was that for?!"

"You just told me to calm down. I wasn't being uncalm! I was just being a girl and sharing an opinion – that is NOT UNCALM…" Okay, maybe *now* I was uncalm… "You wouldn't have said that if I was a guy. If I was a guy, and I was just talking about something I believed in, just slightly louder than I usually talked, you wouldn't use the words 'calm down' to me. You only tell boys to calm down when they're pissed out of their heads and about to punch someone in the face and get everyone barred from the pub, but, no…girls, all we need to do is raise our voices slightly and have an opinion and then it's like CALM DOWN, YOU MAD COW!" I had an adrenalin re-surge. Just when I thought this project was silly, or over the top, or could potentially ruin all my life plans…I just reignited like one of those trick birthday candles that don't blow out.

Will didn't have a chance to respond – though it looked like he was gearing up for a fight. Half his mouth hung open, in stupored disbelief, the other half was in a snarl. But Mr Packson's door was suddenly flung open and he strode out, wringing his hands.

"Charlotte? William?"

We glared at each other then followed him back into his room. He walked behind his desk but didn't sit down. I bet he'd learned that on some kind of head teacher training day.

"I've been thinking…" He looked over the tops of our heads. Not a good sign. "And I've decided, Charlotte, you can continue with this project…" It was my turn for my mouth to drop open.

"Really? Thank you, sir…"

He held up his hand to indicate he wasn't finished. "With some adjustments, of course."

Will and I looked at each other.

"For one," he continued, "I can't believe I've got to say this, but no cream pies!"

"But…!"

"None, not on college property. If I see even a hint of squirty cream on these premises, I will suspend you instantly. And you know what that means."

I looked down, wanting to argue, knowing I couldn't. I knew… No Cambridge… Dad would go beyond nuts.

"And it's not just pies. You cannot physically touch a student in an aggressive way at all during this month…

143

I mean, you're not supposed to anyway. I will do what I can to support you, Charlotte. And I want you to write something for the college newspaper…" He turned to Will. "You can tell that to the local paper. And William? You are free to leave. I need a few words with Charlotte by herself."

Will stalked out – no doubt triumphantly thinking that he was responsible for the project being saved. But my relief overrode my annoyance.

The door shut behind him and Mr Packson beckoned for me to sit down.

"Take a seat, Lottie."

Well, at least I was back to being Lottie.

He sat down too, and surveyed me over his pen pot and framed photo of his toddler.

"What's going on, Lottie?" he asked. "You're a month away from your Cambridge interview. Why would you distract yourself with something so…" He ran his tongue under his bottom lip. "Time-consuming?"

"Because it's the right thing to do," I repeated. For, like, the millionth time in my life.

"Do your parents know? What's going on with this, I mean?"

I nodded.

"And I can guess how they're taking it…"

I nodded. Mr Packson and my parents had met a few times, always to discuss "my shining future". Dad had always been a bit like a pit bull terrier with him. He wasn't used to how they were treated compared to at my old school – where parents were treated like bosses of their own corporations, the children just an "asset". You could schedule a meeting with any teacher, any time, and they'd fall all over themselves to tell parents what they wanted to hear. When Mum and Dad first wanted to quiz Mr Packson about my Cambridge chances last year... Well Dad wasn't happy when he had to wait a week and a half for a free slot. He'd made his unhappiness known.

Mr Packson smiled – like knowing my parents disapproved made him like the idea all of a sudden. "Are you *sure* this isn't going to impact your studies?"

I nodded. "There's more to life than studying, anyway."

"Be careful, Lottie. You're playing with your future here. I know how much getting into Cambridge means to you and your family."

I sighed. "Yes, it does. But this project doesn't clash with my interview date. And, you know what?" I thought about Megan again. "Sometimes you need to be able to look at yourself in the mirror. I don't want to be a hypocrite..."

He did another small smile. I was SO his favourite student – even if I was also his most difficult.

"We need to talk ground rules though; I can't have you personally attacking the teachers."

I shook my head this time. "It doesn't work that way. I can't pick and choose."

He didn't lose his temper. He just sat back in his chair, like I was about to tell him a story. "How does it work then?"

So I explained it to him – the whole idea, all the rules,

I even told him about the van men and how I got the idea.

"Jesus, Lottie," he exclaimed, in the annoying disbelieving way men tend to have when you tell them such a thing.

"It's okay," I told him. "'I've still been walking that way and the van's gone. I'm hoping they maybe got fired or disciplined or whatever."

After I'd finished, he leaned back further – mulling it all over. I tried not to look at his bald patch too much – but everyone at college said it was shaped like a kidney bean, and it really, really was.

"So…" he said. "You have to call out every bit of sexism you see in some way, but you don't do each thing more than once?"

I nodded, still eyeing the bald patch. "You got it."

"So, those horrid builders, say. You wouldn't take them on again?"

I sort of shook my head. "I wouldn't take them on in particular… But if some other guy catcalled me, I'd still take *him* on – because it's a new person. And, if the same person did something ELSE sexist, then I'd holler too. But, other than that, once it's out and I've hollered, then that's that." I wasn't sure why I was suddenly using the word "hollered", but I liked how it sounded – like I had spunk. Which, let's face it, is a sexist word, but I bloody do.

"So Teddy and his mates aren't safe?"

"They're safe from cream pies. I've agreed to back down on the cream pies on college premises."

"That's very generous of you."

"I know."

"I still can't have you attacking the teachers personally though…" He had another think. "I know… Calling it out? What does it involve exactly?"

I shrugged. "It's different for different things, it's all a bit ad-hoc if I'm honest. But, generally, in some way or another, I have to make it clear to society or whatever, that it's sexist."

Mr Packson was grinning. "Would telling the head teacher of your college make it clear enough? If he promised to listen and take it in?"

I could see where this was going… I narrowed my eyes. God, he was clever. Though I needed to compromise somewhere. I couldn't get suspended – we both knew it.

"I guess…"

He leaned so far back in his chair that he put his feet up on the desk, and folded his hands behind his head.

"Well, go on then, Lottie. You have my full attention. Tell me every single sexist thing our staff does – let it out. I'm the head teacher and I'm going to totally acknowledge it."

I chewed my lip and wished Will was here to film it – though I suspected Mr Packson wouldn't be doing this if he knew it was going onto our channel.

I threw back my head in defeat.

"We're going to be here a long time."

"I've got time."

"All right then. Well, my philosophy teacher, he always picks boys to answer questions over girls. I counted it once, it's like at least a 70:30 boy to girl ratio…"

eighteen

There was no greater sight than that of twenty FemSoc members honking their horns in the college cafeteria.

As yet another sexist rock song came on the jukebox, we all stopped our meeting, jumped on our chairs and started honking for all we were worth. Amber seemed to be getting into it more than anybody. She jumped up on the table, her face red with excitement, and yelled, "WOMEN ARE NOT BITCHES!"

Most of the cafeteria (Teddy's mates) were booing us and deliberately putting sexist songs on the jukebox just to enjoy the drama, fifteen per cent were ignoring us, and ten per cent kept coming over to ask what we were doing, listening to us explain it, then saying, "Cool."

All I cared about was that ten per cent.

Teddy was sat right next to the jukebox, giving me evils. Which was nothing new. I felt a surge of frustration. I really, really hadn't done anything WRONG to him. We'd dated,

I'd realized he wasn't for me. I'd told him, nicely, as soon as I'd figured that out. Why was he still SO angry?

Will was filming everything – albeit with a scowl on his bespectacled face. We'd had yet another fight after I emerged triumphantly from Mr Packson's office.

"You should have let me film Mr Packson," he said. "I can't believe you let all that footage go to waste!"

"I'll explain it all in my video diary tonight," I promised, trying to calm him. "Plus, I told you, I don't think he would've agreed to it if you were shoving a camera in his face."

After we'd suitably rejected the current song choice, we clambered back into our uncomfortable metal chairs and resumed our meeting.

Evie opened a bag of cheesy Doritos and passed them round the circle. I noticed her helping herself to a small pile before passing them on and my tummy twisted for her. She wouldn't eat from the bag once it had gone round the whole circle. It made me sad, even if she was so much better than she used to be.

Megan sat next to me, sketching as I spoke.

"So, you were explaining why you're still wearing make-up," one of our members, Georgina, prompted.

I nodded and tried to regain my trail of thought…it had been interrupted a LOT by all the misogynistic rock.

"Yes, I was. Because I thought that SOMEBODY…" I glared at Will. He glared back, but still kept filming. "…might ask. And I was right. I *have* decided to still wear my usual make-up for the duration of this project…but it's not been a decision I've made lightly," I said, as people started whispering. "I wanted to chat today about cognitive dissonance – have any of you heard of it?"

Everyone shook their heads. Evie shook hers especially hard. "You're obsessed with hard words," she called over the table, and everyone laughed.

"I know, I know, I know…I'll try and explain it as quickly as I can. Basically cognitive dissonance is just a posh term for having two personal beliefs at the same time that contradict each other."

There was quiet. The last chorus of the rock song was fading, so I knew I didn't have long. Especially as Teddy and the rest of His Lot were gathered around the jukebox now – pumping twenty pence pieces in and looking over with glee. I continued.

"So an example is loving cute baby pig pictures on Instagram but then still eating bacon…or…umm… I dunno, really rushing and getting stressed about arriving in time for a yoga class."

Amber butted in. "So, it's like hypocrisy?"

I nodded. "Yeah…I guess. And, I mean, everyone is guilty of it. No one is perfect. However, I was thinking about how cognitive dissonance works in feminism…"

The song ended and almost instantly some new song, "Pimp My Hoes", started playing. I mean…really? I hadn't even realized we had that song on the shitty jukebox yet, it was only just on the radio.

Teddy and his mates cheered – "This one's for you lezzas!"

Teddy called through his hands – getting about twelve pats on the back from the ladz.

Me, Evie and Amber found each other's eyes over the table, rolled them, then got up again. The rest of FemSoc followed and we blasted our horns. This seemed to make Teddy and his mates even happier.

This really wasn't how I wanted it to go – boys like Teddy enjoying it, using it to wind me up. But then, what did I expect?

I got down ungracefully and made my way over. Teddy saw me coming and puffed his chest out even more. The others all started wolf-whistling. My skin prickled... The horn in my hand... I was so desperate to throw it at his fat arrogant head... But I'd promised Mr Packson no more violence.

"You know using 'lezzas' as an insult is, like, the most backward messed-up insult ever?" I said, rage flowing through me. At them. At myself, for letting them get to me.

Teddy shrugged. "I just call it how I see it."

I narrowed my eyes. "Me too. And you're a disgusting pig-headed RUNT. Now, why don't you all just run along, or I'll tell Mr Packson about your disgusting homophobia?"

I stormed back to my table with jeers like "Oooh, she's going to tell on us" and "Ooooh, someone's on the blob" following me. I heard female laughter too, and saw Jenny and some of her friends giggling at me from the sidelines. I flipped Teddy my middle finger but kept walking. FemSoc crowded around, offering me words of encouragement.

"Did you actually just call him a runt?" Evie asked, patting my back. "That's my new favourite insult ever."

Will peered over the top of his lens. "I got all that on camera."

I smiled at everyone, accepting their commiseration, or whatever it was. It made me feel slightly better, but my stomach was still tangled into an impenetrable ball and the anger had a side order of exhaustion about it. What was I doing? Why was I putting myself through this?

And it was only my first day...

I sat back, grabbed a handful of crisps and chowed them down with half a bottle of Diet Coke. "So..." I clapped my hands like nothing had happened. "Cognitive dissonance." The others quietened, apart from the crunch of crisps. "As I was saying, I was thinking about how it relates to feminism, and how it will impact my project. I think one of the hardest things about being a feminist is cognitive dissonance. Your heart knows better...but, like, we've been so brainwashed into a certain way of being that it's almost impossible NOT to be a hypocrite. Like, knowing your weight shouldn't matter, but also really wanting to be thin...thinner than your friends probably. Or, like, I know that all the fairy-tale love stories we're told about Prince Charmings sweeping us off our feet are dangerous bullshit... I want to be a strong, independent woman with a good career and I don't want my happiness to depend on some bloke on a pony rescuing me—"

"That would be amazing," Amber interrupted. "If it was

an actual pony. How naff would a prince look on an actual pony? His feet scraping along the ground?"

Evie giggled. "A Shetland pony?"

"Even better!"

I paused to let everyone giggle, and took another sip of my Coke.

"But…"I continued, "I also *really* like watching that sort of film. Total cognitive dissonance! PLUS, sometimes, occasionally – well, more than occasionally – I dream of that sort of thing happening to me. Some gorgeous guy just rocking up and I fall totally in love with him and never have to worry about anything ever again…"

I looked over at Will, who was STILL filming. He must have had, like, ten battery packs in his pocket. He caught my eye, raised his eyebrows and I felt myself redden. It was MUCH harder talking about this sort of stuff with a boy there. It made even me feel shy about being brutally honest. I could kind of see the point of keeping these conversations females-only. No boys had expressed an interest in joining FemSoc anyway, despite all our best recruitment efforts…

"I know it's totally bullshit, but I do kind of fantasize about it…" Will raised his eyebrows again but I ignored him. "So, you see, I'm a total hypocrite, as Amber says."

Amber grinned – like she didn't mind at all that I was a huge hypocrite. Megan had been doodling next to me and I looked at her sketch of a Disney princess, carrying a briefcase and wearing power specs. "That's really good," I muttered.

She went red. "Thanks."

Another FemSoc member, Jess, put her hand up. "So you're not allowed to watch romcoms for a month?"

I shook my head. "Well, they've got better ones now with strong female leads that may pass the Bechdel test, but I won't be able to watch anything where it's just a really clichéd female whose only storyline is whether or not she'll find love."

Another member put her hand up. "So, why is make-up okay then? I mean, no offence, but you wear a lot of it…"

I smiled. Because I did. I really did. My face was essentially always half eyeliner. The girl asking, Sylvia, was a useful member of FemSoc, in that she had really strong beliefs but was totally different from me, Evie and Amber. Much more old-skool hardcore feminist. We had to calm down her *men-are-all-arseholes-who-should-be-burned* monologues quite often, and she'd threatened to start a new group as sometimes she lost her temper with us, and told us we were too soft.

"So…make-up, yes…" I nodded at her. "I had a long think about whether I can be a feminist and still wear make-up. I mean, you could argue we wear it just to make us more attractive to guys."

Sylvia nodded furiously.

"I mean, I really enjoy wearing it, but if it's just there to oppress me, then I guess I'm a hypocrite… But then I realized that I don't *feel* oppressed wearing make-up. In fact, I find wearing it quite liberating. It's a way of expressing myself, of being creative. Actually, I feel sorry for boys who don't feel they can wear it. And, most importantly, if all boys died tomorrow—"

"We can but hope," said Sylvia. A few of the group laughed. I didn't.

"Hey, Sylvia, don't make me honk my horn at you," I warned and she scowled. "But, yes…if they all died tomorrow, well, you know what? I would still wear it! It may have initially been invented for some screwed-up reason, but now I feel it's mine to reclaim. The same with skirts and dresses – again I feel sorry for boys that they feel they can only wear trousers…"

"I think their societal perks more than make up for it," Sylvia interrupted again. "You know…being paid more, getting to run most of the country and major corporations… having privilege shovelled onto them from the day they're out of the womb."

I saw a couple of people roll their eyes and knew I had to wrap things up. "I don't *feel* like a hypocrite when I wear make-up," I continued. "Therefore I'm going to continue to wear it." I paused…really wishing Will wasn't here for this next bit…especially with his camera running. "Hair removal on the other hand…"

All the girls laughed.

"No, Lottie? You're going to stop shaving?"

I nodded, glowing redder and redder. "I can confirm that I'm going to stop shaving my bodily hair growths."

"Everything?" Will's voice called out over his lens cap.

There was so much innuendo in that one word and he knew it – he stared right at me, a playful smile on his face. The glorious sexy bastard that I was quickly finding out he was.

I nodded again. "Everything." And I fixed him with such a Lottie-special stare that it was his turn to blush.

"I think this is one of the things I'm most scared of, especially because of my moustache." The table laughed; at least two girls butted in with, "Oh, Lottie, you don't have a moustache!"

"I know I don't," I laughed back. "Because I wax it! But I don't feel liberated waxing it, not like with make-up. I'm not waxing it to express myself – the same with leg hair and armpit hair. I'm doing it out of pure fear. Because I know I'd basically be shunned if I didn't. That's not a liberated place to be in. Imagine if right now, I raised my arms to reveal a huge, hairy bush in my armpit."

At least three girls shuddered. Even Amber said, "Eww."

"You see! I think it's disgusting too. But I also know that it's totally natural for women to have body hair. It's just society has decided it's gross – and we should all look like prepubescent plastic hairless Barbies. And, judging by the sheer extortionate cost of replacement razor blades, there's probably a capitalist agenda behind that too."

"A what now?" someone asked. I tried not to sigh.

"To make money," I explained. "Anyway, I have total cognitive dissonance about body hair, so if I'm going to do this properly...I have to stop shaving..." I still felt sick at the thought. "Luckily, what with it being winter and all, you'll probably not notice my legs. But in a week and a half's time, you should all start a Lottie's moustache watch..."

And, just as they all leaned in closer, without even knowing they were doing it, to inspect my mutant upper lip...I was saved by the jukebox. A ferocious cheer erupted from Teddy and his mates and one of Rihanna's less...er... liberated songs boomed through the college speakers.

We all got up on our chairs.

nineteen

I was exhausted beyond exhausted when I got home.
Philosophy had been a nightmare – because every
philosopher ever had exterior genitalia. And I'd forgotten to
tell Mr Packson that in our get-it-all-out-the-way meeting.
Art had been an equal fiasco – though at least I had Amber
and Megan in my class. Word had got round pretty fast in
college about what I was doing.

"She hates men," I heard a girl whisper, as I was mixing
up my paints.

"It's the Lottie Show again," her friend giggled, before
Amber stood up, loomed right behind them and said, "Can
I help you?"

It made it worse that it was girls saying it.

I rattled my key in my front door when I got home –
having to do the jiggle-dance I always had to do to stop it
from sticking. The waft of cooking hit me as I stepped over
the threshold and fiddled my way out of the beaded curtain.

"Lottie, is that you?"

I picked my way through the piles of laundry Mum had folded on the living room floor and went into the kitchen. She was stirring a pot of something that smelled fantastic. Mum went through vegan "phases" – usually if someone came and did a talk at her centre. I was always very happy to eat dead bits of animals, but vegan cooking was pretty awesome too. Especially when Mum ground up all the spices herself in the pestle and mortar.

"Hi," I breathed, leaning against the door frame to stop myself drooping. All I wanted was to flop upstairs, but my family has this thing about always acknowledging each other when we get home.

She stirred her saucepan once more then clanged a lid down. "Hello, sweetie. How was your day? You didn't trip over the laundry, did you? I'm about to take it upstairs."

"It was fine." I took in the laundry and the cooking and the sparkling surfaces of the kitchen that were always like that because Mum always did them. And did another sigh... I was so exhausted, and yet...here, still, the world was calling. "I started my project today."

Mum wiped her hands on her apron and her face pulled together in concern. "How did it go?"

I nodded. "Fine, I guess... Mr Packson gave me the go-ahead."

"That's a relief. And all your classes went okay too?"

I thought of the humiliation of being dragged out of English – and all the other horrors of the day.

"Yeah, they went fine."

"Any coursework?"

"Of course."

"Well, as long as this thing doesn't interfere."

I was going to delay bringing it up. I was going to break my own rules. But her saying that got my heckles up. So I just came out and said, "Why do you do all the cooking?"

Mum looked at her bubbling pot, confused. "What do you mean?"

I ignored her. "And the laundry, and most of the cleaning. Why is it always you?"

I'd never really thought about it. But, now, with my ultimate feminism searchlight on full-beam, I was seeing everything everywhere. Mum did basically *all* the household chores. Well, the ones I wasn't roped into doing – which was usually taking out the bins and stacking the dishwasher. She almost always cooked, she did the laundry, she hoovered, she chucked bleach around our two bathrooms, she washed up all the glass recycling ready to go in the special green bins at the end of the drive, she picked up the stray mugs and crumby plates that inevitably get scattered around a house and returned them to the kitchen... She did it all. All Dad did was cut the grass really. And you only need to do that like twice a year, right? I'd never noticed it before. Now it seemed glaringly obvious.

Mum went on the defensive, even though I was on her side. "Well, your dad has work to do." She stirred the pot even though it didn't need stirring.

"But you work too!"

"Yes, but my job's just a bit of a side job."

Was it? She worked hard, Mum. She had to do Saturdays as that was when most of her clients were off work. And I remember her job kept us all going financially a few years ago when Dad was made redundant. It was six months before he got the professor job. I don't like to think about that time. Dad went…dark. He sat in the house way too much. He even started watching *University Challenge* reruns on TV in jogging bottoms, where, usually, he only ever read big heavy hardback books in his special chair.

"I don't think it's fair," I continued, shrugging.

I jumped when Mum clattered her spoon down hard. "For Christ's sake, Charlotte. Do not go dragging me into this project of yours. We're being understanding enough as it is."

I dropped my mouth open. "But it's *not* fair. Dad should do more around the house!"

"Oh yes? How about you? Maybe instead of fussing, you could help me carry the laundry up to your room? YOUR laundry, I may add?"

I shook my head. "That's not what this is about." Though I felt guilty for not taking my laundry up. Or, like, doing it, ever.

"Your father does LOADS," Mum insisted. "Please don't bring us into this…thing of yours."

"I can't help it," I said, honestly.

"Well try." She picked up the spoon again and turned back.

Taking the hint, I slinked out – picking up my pile of clean clothes on my way up the stairs.

I couldn't concentrate on coursework. I turned my music up loud to try and drown out the carousel of stuff whirring around my head.

The humiliation of my English lesson…the anger at Teddy, the boys he hung around with, and those girls in my art class…the annoying stirring I got when I thought about meeting Will's eye in the cafeteria…Mum's face…Mum's anger. I was supposed to be sketching some still life for art, and I had all the fruit set up. But I'd not really got around to actually drawing it and it was starting to go a bit puffy. This wasn't like me. I took homework very seriously – I always did it straight away. The overly sweet smell emanating from the carefully arranged bowl of oranges suggested otherwise.

I didn't like it when I saw moral gaps in my own parents…

I'd grown up thinking they were so wise. Led mostly by Mum, we'd spent most of my childhood summers trekking around amazing countries, learning about balance and breathing and "Energy" – capitalized and put within speechmarks – and all the other superior *what-life-is-all-about* stuff. But I was starting to see cracks. Hypocrisies. Cognitive dissonances, I guess. I was an only child. I was all they had. Their one shot at raising a human – and stuff like "balance" and "values" were starting to get chucked out the ethical window. I'd never even considered feminism and how that related to them either… Until today. Now I saw my entire childhood flash back really fast, and memories popped out, tapping me on the head, yelling, *Lottie, come on, remember this? It will ruin your day even more, and you're deffo in that kind of mood!*

Memories like...whenever the cricket was on, which was a lot, Dad wouldn't even let us talk in the house – and Mum, even though she'd be knackered from fitting in her work around looking after me, would have to take me swimming. "That's just the way your dad is with the cricket," she'd say, like that made it okay... And how, whenever they had friends over, even supposedly "enlightened" friends from the centre, Mum would exhaust herself, running around, asking people what drinks they'd like, making sure all the food was coming out on time, whirling and twirling, while Dad just chatted and laughed with everyone, and didn't even say thank you or help with the washing-up afterwards, but declared himself exhausted and took me up to bed... How we all sat around the table and talked about Dad's job and what was going on with it all the time... but never really Mum's. And if she started sharing a story about an interesting client, I could see him glaze over and not quite take it in... Plus I'd never once seen him clean the toilet...

Could it be that my forward-thinking parents, the ones who tell me to reach for the stars and mend the world and believe in equality for all, my parents who flipped an actual coin to decide whose surname I'd take to make it fair, despite all that...could they be in an unequal relationship?

My phone beeped, and I jumped at it. Grateful for the

distraction, any distraction, from all the treacle-like thoughts my brain was determined to wade through.

It was Evie.

You okay, Lottie Bottie? You kicked extreme ass today. But that usually means a day has been hard. Call me anytime. E x x

A hint of a smile made its way onto my face. It spread wider when my phone beeped again. Amber.

I think I've got repetitive strain injury from honking my horn too much. You are my hero, Lottie. Now will you please come over and massage my achy palm?

As the light faded into blackness outside my window, I messaged them back and forth. I heard Dad come in. Mum called me for dinner. I ate in silence, listening to Dad blah on about some academic paper he was trying to get published, staring down at my plate.

I was less than twenty-four hours in, and my spirit was waning.

Back in my room, I tried to catch up on the work I'd missed from my day off with Megan. Eventually I heard my parents' getting-ready-for-bed noises – the click of the bathroom light, the thud of their bedroom door, a low murmur of voices, then silence.

I'd sketched approximately half an orange.

With a heart so heavy I was surprised it wasn't pushing down on my bladder and making me wee, I picked up the little flip-cam Will had lent me, turned the lens on myself, and started to talk...

twenty

It was shopping day.

I'd made it through five whole days at college. I'd been evicted from one philosophy lesson, verbally assaulted twice, had three more meetings with Mr Packson ("Lottie, I thought you wouldn't cause trouble in lessons any more? It's not your philosophy teacher's fault that the textbook refers to God as a 'He'"), and probably had about four thousand insults hurled behind my back. I got stares wherever I went – when I bought chips, when I went from lesson to lesson, as I walked into my art class with Amber and everyone went quiet, like they'd just been talking about me...

And I'd got a B in my still-life painting. Never, ever, in the history of ever had I ever got a B. I'd almost had heart palpitations. You can't get Bs and get into Cambridge. You may as well get Us.

Not your best work, my teacher had scribbled at the bottom in red pen. Followed by three giant question marks.

I snapped my sketchpad shut the moment I saw it, like that could contain the B and make it not spread elsewhere.

If it wasn't for Amber, Evie, Megan and the rest of FemSoc – flanking me, cheering me on, putting up posters whenever they got ripped down – I don't know what I would've done.

And now it was Saturday – precious restful Saturday – and I had to go shopping. But not until Will and I had sorted the edits of the first week's videos.

He looked quite scared when he arrived, like they all do. Mum's habit of "cleansing auras" tends to wig people out.

"Lottie," she called. "Your friend is here."

I pushed past the curtain and waved him up – not talking to Mum. We'd had another argument the previous night. About the B, because I'd stupidly told them… Dad had proper shouted at me.

It was very strange – seeing Will in my home. He juxtaposed perfectly with the surroundings – his hipster cool clashing with the wind chimes and the crystals decorating every flat surface. Amber and Evie had got used to mine by now, so it was almost new, watching someone see the sheer weirdness of my house for the first time.

Indeed, Will's eyebrows were raised mighty high, his smug smile pulling upwards.

I didn't say hello or offer him a drink – I just turned back up the stairs, knowing he had no choice but to follow me.

Will did a proper inspection of my room before he sat down. He stood still, taking it all in, then walked over to my chest of drawers, examining all my framed photos. My favourite was one taken at the beginning of last year, at this awful gig me and the girls went to at a church hall. We were all wearing black and holding ourselves up through laughter – none of us quite looking into the camera. Will picked that one up, his eyes examining it under the thick frame of his glasses.

I flopped onto my bed, waiting for him to stop nosing. Eventually he perched next to me – no nerves about it, like some boys have when you're both sitting on a bed.

"Your mum's interesting," he said, still scanning the room. "Did she cleanse your aura?"

"Is that what that was? Yeah, I guess she did."

"I'm not sure what good it will do you," I said. "Some auras just can't get clean…"

He laughed at that – a short burst of it, like he hadn't meant it. "I have an incurable aura?"

I giggled too. "A herpes aura."

"That's disgusting."

"You're telling me."

The laughter defused the tension in the room. The tension I couldn't explain. Well, I could… It was sexual tension. I'd experienced it enough with other people to know that's what it was. But it was the worst kind – the repressed kind. Because Will was an argumentative arse-end.

"So, I've got a first cut. You want to see?"

I bounced on the bed. "Yes!"

He reached into his bag and pulled out a proper posh

laptop – the new iWhatever by the looks of it. I wondered how he could've afforded it. He flipped open the screen and pulled up a page. I rolled onto my stomach to see better, my feet sticking up in the air.

"Wow, you've branded the whole channel." I pulled the laptop closer clumsily, making him sort of jump at me to stop me being too rough. All Megan's graphics littered the screen – it really, *really* looked wow.

"So this is the rough cut." He yanked the computer back, all protective. I smiled to myself. "I've made it private. I wanted to get your approval before making it live."

Will hit play, and I rested my hands under my chin to watch. He'd started it with a mini-cut of my first interview – explaining why I was doing it and what I hoped to achieve. I winced. My hair! Did it really look like that from that angle? I swear my nose wasn't so pointy usually. And my voice! Yikes! It was so deep! And I'd need proper enunciation lessons before I became an MP. But, as the interview faded into Will's montage of my first week of the project, my self-consciousness melted away. Wow. I saw his shots of me chucking the pie at the bus stop, grabbing members of FemSoc and laughing as I applied lipstick to their faces. He'd done a huge close-up on my face the moment Teddy and his ladz walked by and called us "sluts". He'd slowed it down – and my face, the way it reacted, was so much more poignant than any thoughts I'd actually had in the moment. The next shot was a long shot, of me running after him with a pie. It'd gone from totally cinematically dramatic to totally stupid within an instant and I howled out with laughter. A pie. I'd literally actually thrown a cream pie! The rest of the week flowed into a perfectly-edited montage and I found I couldn't not smile. Without being in my own brain, experiencing the embarrassment and dread, and having all the whispers behind my back edited out, this project looked totally ace. I came across totally ace! And, most importantly, so did my message. Most of it was me and the girls laughing. I wasn't coming across bitter or twisted or unreasonable. How it looked through Will's posh lens and triumphant soundtrack was *so* different to the shitty week I'd had.

When it went black, I turned to him. "You are annoyingly talented."

He did his wolf grin. "I'll take out the word 'annoyingly' and accept that compliment."

I rolled over so I was facing him, my face just…glowing with excitement.

"I mean, just…how?! How did you make it look that exciting? How did you make me come across so utterly kick-ass?"

"Well, that was the hardest bit."

I thumped him.

I reached forward and hit play again, re-watching it. Loving it more the second time around. After losing all my confidence this week, this video had returned it in spades. I felt strong again, like I was onto something…something that could really make people take notice and realize…

After the third watch, I rolled towards him again. We were

both on our stomachs now, the tips of our toes just touching. It made my feet itch in this really brilliant way, so much that I couldn't bear to move.

"You do know what you've done though?" I said. "You've made a brilliant piece of feminist propaganda here. Be careful, or people might think I'm winning you over."

He ran his hands through his hair and made a noise of exasperation. "I made a good film, that's all. I've tried to make it as objective as possible."

"You love feminism." I found myself poking him. Which wasn't wise. Especially as it made the tip of my finger fizzle in a gut-wrenching way.

"I don't. I told you, I'm a—"

"Yeah yeah yeah, yadda yadda yadda, Mr I Have To See Every Incidence Of Sexism Scientifically Proven Before I Deign To Care." I made my hand do the chit-chat thing. "God forbid you admit this project might actually be getting to you. Helping you change your mind."

He looked right at me. "People don't like feeling like you're trying to change their minds, you know that, right?" The way he stared made me feel all red, but I rolled my eyes in reply.

"Yep. I do know that. But what am I supposed to do? Just go, 'Oh well, people don't like having their beliefs challenged, I guess I'll just wait over there in the corner in case, by some miracle, they change their minds by themselves'? I've got to try."

Will's expression deepened for a moment, his eyebrows

arching up into…something…then the moment was lost and he smirked at me again. "You're certainly trying."

"What I'm hoping to do is catch the floaters," I said. "There's no point wasting my energy on people like you who just want to have an argument…"

Will opened his mouth to no doubt object and I batted him away.

"I know there's lots of people out there who just get this prickling feeling that something isn't right. They feel confused and…wrong…and confused about the wrong… and BAM, they see my kick-ass video and go 'FEMINISM – THAT'S WHAT I NEED. I NEED FEMINISM.'"

"You do know you sound like a terrorist recruiter?"

I did poke him then. And not because I fancied him but because he legitimately deserved the pokiest of pokes.

"You know what I think?" I said. "I think you only play devil's advocate all the time because it makes you infallible." Another poke – he tried to catch my wrist, that smile still on his face, but I pulled my hand back just in time. "But there's not much depth, Mr Deep Film-maker, to having nothing to believe in. And it's much easier to pick holes in other people's beliefs than identifying and fighting for your own."

His reply was dry, to make it clear nothing I'd said had gone in. "Are you finished?"

"I'm never finished."

"I'm starting to learn that. When are the others arriving anyway? Are you ready?"

172

I sighed and rolled off the bed onto my feet to get my bag sorted. "Yes, I'm ready…ish. They'll be here in a few minutes."

"Okay. I'll just put this live then. You all right with that?"

I shot him a smile as I checked my massive Operation Vagilante rucksack. "I am very all right with that."

There was five minutes of semi-contented silence – me pottering, him clicking away on his posh laptop. The doorbell still hadn't rung. I was a bit nervous. I was essentially going to almost-break the law a LOT in the next two hours. Technically, I'd only be breaking societal norms… but I was still terrified I'd get caught by a store detective or something. Plus I'd invited Megan, and I was worried about inviting her into the inner-sanctum of Spinster Clubness. Would it work? Would we gel?

"Right, it's all up." Will shut his laptop with a flourish and flopped back on the bed. Seeing him on my bed, my bed where lying-down things happen, made me feel all peculiar – so I sat all upright on my desk chair.

He stared up at the ceiling, then gave my room another once-over and said, "So, *this* is Lottie Thomas's bedroom?"

I felt all my prickles go up instantly. I reached into my bag, commandeered the largest horn, then pulled it out super quick and gave a long loud honk right in his ear.

"JESUS, LOTTIE, OWW, WHATDAFUCKAREYOUDOING?"

Satisfied, I calmly returned the horn to the depths of my bag of mischief. Will was clutching half his head.

"I've told you before. Just because you're my cameraman,"

I said, "doesn't mean you're immune from me."

"That really f-ing hurt, you…"

I whipped out the horn again. "Be careful, Will."

"You psycho…" he muttered, then ducked and missed my second blast.

"You are such a cock." I stood up, anger pulsing through my veins. "You know that, right? You know that everything about your personal brand is total and utter cock?"

"Jeez, I didn't even say anything!"

I levelled him with my eyes. "You said enough."

He'd implied it. That my bedroom was known about… that people had been here before… And I wasn't ashamed or embarrassed or any of the things girls are supposed to feel if boys get all judgy about the fact you may have – SHOCK HORROR – had and enjoyed sex with other people. But I was angry he'd brought it up. Because it was totally unremarkable and none of his business.

He held his hands up, like he was trying to make peace. "Look, sorry. I didn't mean it how you think I meant it." He seemed genuine, even quite mad at himself…

"Didn't you?"

"Well…I…" He trailed off, and did actually look very ashamed of himself. "It was just a joke."

"A sex-shaming joke."

"No! Lottie, I don't care what you do, who you sleep with. Honestly, it's your life. I totally mean that."

I crossed my arms. "Then why say anything…?" I added *YOU COCK* in my head.

"I actually don't know. To fill a silence, I guess."

"It's because you're a cock."

This time he smiled, and removed his hand from his damaged ear.

"You know what. Maybe I am. When I said that, I was being one. Sorry. Truly, I'm sorry."

I smiled too. "Repeat the following after me, and I'll let you come on the feminism shopping trip."

"You need to work more on your bribes."

"Repeat after me!"

"Okay okay." He held his hands up again.

"I, William," I prompted.

He bit his lip but relented. "I, William."

"Hereby declare."

"Hereby declare."

"That I am a massive cock."

A pause. A grin. Then... "That I am a massive cock."

"Which is very different from HAVING a massive cock."

A longer pause. "Which is very different from having a massive cock."

"And, in fact, me bringing up Lottie's sexual history is probably due to my insecurity that I don't have a massive cock."

"In fact, me...hang on! And, hey, isn't making a joke about the size of a boy's manhood slightly...dare I say it... sexist?"

We were both laughing now. I raised the horn over my head and honked it multiple times. He looked at me, and I looked at him. And this was usually the point where I'd kiss someone who looked at me like that, because I'm quite good at just kissing people when I feel like it. But I'd be a hypocrite to end all hypocrites if I let anyone as smug as Will be allowed the pleasure of kissing me during my feminist crusade.

The doorbell rang anyway, and we both looked up.

"That'll be the girls."

I raced downstairs to beat Mum to the door, and opened it to find Evie and Amber on my doorstep. Evie looked vaguely normal – though she was dressed entirely in grey. Amber, however, wore a giant fake nose with attached handlebar moustache, a mac, and when I greeted them, she opened up a big broadsheet newspaper to reveal she'd cut two eyeholes in it.

"I said *inconspicuous*," I said, rather than hello.

"I am!" Amber peered at me through her eyeholes. "I mean, look! I'm just reading the newspaper – nothing to see here!"

A thumping on the stairs behind me and Will had joined us.

"What the heck are you wearing?" He raised a camera to Amber's outfit.

Amber folded the newspaper and grinned from under her moustache. "Lottie said be inconspicuous."

Evie and I smiled at each other. "I think you've made yourself so inconspicuous that you're actually very conspicuous," I said.

Amber nodded furiously. "Exactly. The perfect double bluff!"

I couldn't help but laugh. "You will take it off, won't you?"

She crossed her arms and the newspaper scrunched up. "Maybe. Maybe not."

"We do honestly need to look under-the-radar today," I explained. "This is some hardcore civil disobedience. What if police speak to witnesses and they're able to say, 'She was five foot eleven, ginger, with a giant nose and moustache'?"

Amber grinned wider. "That's my point! I'll just whip off the nose and moustache and be safe from the law FOR EVER!"

"You're taking it off, right?"

She pouted. "Oh, all right!" She yanked off her facial appendages and opened up her mac...to reveal a neon T-shirt with *GIRLS JUST WANT TO HAVE FUN...DAMENTAL HUMAN RIGHTS* emblazoned across it. She took in our gasps of astonishment. "I've been waiting to do this all morning. I was so excited I forgot to eat breakfast."

I took in her T-shirt with stunned awe. "I am taking in your T-shirt with stunned awe."

"Isn't it amazing? Kyle sent it to me from America."

Evie stroked Amber's belly. "Seriously? Can we time-share your boyfriend, please? This is the best thing anyone has ever done, you know that, right?"

Will darted across me to film her, but said, "You can't wear that though, right? It will draw attention."

"Let me have my moment, Will," Amber barked. "I'm going to cover it with a jumper."

Will backed down, which shows the full force of Amber when she gets pissed off.

I was so busy asking Amber where Kyle got it from that I didn't hear Megan arrive. Not until she rang the doorbell. Even though the door was wide open and we were all standing right on the threshold.

"Umm, guys? I'm here?"

"Megan!" I turned and gave her a welcome hug. "Sorry, we were distracted by Amber's amazing T-shirt."

Amber pulled open her mac again to show it off.

"Oh, wow. Yeah, it's great." Megan kept pushing her hair back behind her ears. "I've brought that stuff you wanted, Lottie." She held out a plastic bag.

"You have? Oh my God, you're a legend." I looked inside, and my whole heart just filled up. "Megan, these are INCREDIBLE, thank you!" I pulled out all her paraphernalia and showed the others.

"Megan," Amber said. "I think I'm in love with you." And we all laughed. Megan's eyes were all shiny with light and fire. She went bright red.

Evie looked at her watch. "Are we ready to go? The shopping centre gets really busy after lunch."

I nodded. "I'm ready. Will, you got all your battery packs and unwelcome opinions?"

I watched him stifle a laugh. "I've got both."

"Right then," I said. "TO TOWN."

twenty-one

I made Will turn his electronic devices off, so we could gossip on the walk in.

"So, what's going on with you and Oli now?" I asked Evie, linking my arm with hers. "I saw you both staring at each other over the lunch table on Thursday, your lips all a-quiver with lust."

"Lottie!" she protested. "Nobody's lips ever quiver with lust."

"Mine do!" I shouted – then instantly felt weird that Will was listening. Especially after his bedroom comment earlier. As if he was a mind-reader, he said, "I'm going to walk ahead a bit. I...well...I'm feeling outnumbered."

"Told you," I stage-whispered to the girls. "He's scared of girls."

Will flipped me the finger and strode off in front of us. The playfulness of it gave me an unhelpful stirring.

Evie must be psychic because she proper whispered to me,

"I could ask you the same question. What's going on with you two? You're being all mean and sassy, like when you fancy people."

I made an *eww* disgusted face. "Are you kidding? Have you not heard him say the need for feminism is a figment of my imagination?"

"Hmm," she grumbled. But then stopped when Amber and Megan linked with us.

We walked for a few minutes, discussing boring coursework, then Evie said, "Oh, I've been meaning to tell you. Oli's having an eighteenth birthday party. Next weekend – at The Admiral. He says you're all invited." The excitement in her voice was thinly hidden.

Amber bumped her hip. "It all sounds like an elaborate ploy to pull you."

"Yeah." I swung her arm really hard. "I bet it's not even his birthday."

"Guys!" she protested. "It may all be an elaborate ploy to kiss some *other* girl."

"No chance," I said. "I see the way his basily eyes stare at you all basily."

"You two are so perfect for each other," Amber added.

Evie stuck her tongue out. "Jesus, Amber, Kyle has well and truly broken you, hasn't he? When did you get so romantic?"

"I'm scared for myself. Please don't tell anyone."

I wondered what it would take to *finally* get them together – if I could help engineer it somehow? Maybe if I dressed up as one of those cherubs from *Fantasia*, and brought them together by playing a flute?

"What the heck are you talking about?" Amber asked.

"Oh? Am I thinking out loud again?" I touched my throat.

Yep – I was.

Megan was all quiet and I felt bad for not including her in our banter.

"You coming then?" I asked her – examining her face, which was all of a sudden staring determinedly at the ground.

"Umm, yeah…maybe…" Another pause. She looked up. "Umm, who's going?" she asked Evie.

"Umm, Jane, Joel, I guess Will" – she made a face at his back, but he had his headphones on – "as they're in film together. Umm, most of our film class, I suppose. And then all the music tech people. Ethan…"

"The sex addict," Amber butted in, and we giggled. Evie had gone on a date with Ethan at the beginning of last year but he'd randomly got with someone else then told Evie it was because he was addicted to sex.

"Ethan's okay now!" she protested. "He's told me he's going to try not to have a girlfriend until he's twenty-two."

"Why twenty-two?" I asked.

Evie shrugged. "I don't know. He's not a normal person. Anyway, he'll be there, and the rest of The Imposters…" Evie trailed off just as Megan stiffened.

All of us pretended not to notice but she held herself like

someone had clamped down all her limbs with force. Max, her ex, was in The Imposters.

"I mean...they might not *all* come..." Evie stammered desperately, looking really guilty. Megan swallowed, saw our expressions, then struggled to smile.

"I'll see if I'm free," she said, all breezily, then gave us another *nothing's-wrong-here* smile. I wondered for the eight-millionth time what exactly had happened and why, if it was what we all thought it was, she wasn't going to the police. Why wasn't she talking about it? She needed to. She couldn't just keep it all locked up to sour inside of her.

An awkward silence descended and we pretended we didn't know why. Fortunately, Will saved us, taking off his headphones and turning round. He turned on his camera and pointed it towards my face.

Oh yes – the project – the never-ending project.

"We're here," he said.

And sure enough we were on the edge of our local shopping precinct. It was busier than normal for this time on a Saturday – the pre-Christmas shopping panic kicking in sooner every year.

"You ready, Lottie?"

I stared out at the pedestrianized concrete oblong of everyday suburban shiteness that was our local town. The usual gathering of parents with buggies, who sat on the benches near Primark, the posher mothers pushing their silver-spoon spawn around in Maclaren buggies, their arms straining under bags of shopping, the *Big Issue* lady who everyone at college did impressions of, the crowded entrance to the newish shopping centre that had a Nandos now. I looked at the shop windows, at the products on display. I looked at everything.

I saw at least eight sexist things.

I sighed. Already tired, but already excited about the fight I was about to fight. Though, if we escaped arrest today, it would be a miracle of the Feminism Gods. I just hoped, whatever happened, it wouldn't ruin my future…

"I'm ready."

twenty-two

Amber pulled out her home-made map.

"Dude," Evie said. "This looks just like the map Kevin makes in *Home Alone*."

"I know. I'm very talented."

I pointed my finger to the other side of town. "So," I said, my voice all authoritarian. "We're working in a criss-cross direction across town, to avoid capture by undesirables. We all need to be quick and efficient in our tasks – otherwise we *will* get caught."

Evie gulped – she wasn't the best rule-breaker. Though, because of her well-researched tweaks to today's schedule, we were unlikely to get arrested. Always get someone with OCD to help you be a criminal – they're good at thinking up worst possible outcomes.

Megan leaned over the map. "So, where we going first?"

Amber jabbed her finger onto a big red blob, showing off her chipped purple nail polish. "In the words of my hunky

American boyfriend" – she put on an accent – "first stop is the Drug Store."

Evie grabbed a horn, honked it, then sped across town. She sometimes took us by surprise like that – usually so well behaved and then KAPOW…totally brilliantly manic. We ran after her, Will on our tail, racing past the Saturday shoppers. We slowed as we got to the entrance and caught our breath. I looked in through the giant glass shop window with the pink frontage. It was pretty busy inside. A queue for the pharmacy stretched across most of the store.

"So," I said, in a stage whisper. "We better split up and enter in two groups. Shops always hate gangs of young people." I grinned. "They always assume we're up to no good."

We all raised our eyebrows at that.

"So – are you all aware of your mission?" They nodded. "Amber, you're going to cause a distraction. You still okay with that?"

She nodded. "I'm five foot eleven and ginger. I was BORN to make a distraction."

"Megan? Will can't have cameras on both of us, so are you okay filming Amber on your phone?"

"Er…okay." She looked unsure, scraping her hair back again.

"You don't have to be obvious," I reassured her. "She'll be causing a hold-up at the counter. Just pretend to be browsing near the till and point your phone at her discreetly."

Will's eyebrows danced all worriedly. "Have you ever filmed anything before?" he asked.

"Erm…no."

"Relax!" I interrupted. "Will, you can't be in two places at once. And it will look cool to have some mobile phone footage. It will make it all gonzo."

"All what-o?" everyone asked.

I sighed. "Never mind. Come on!" I pulled Will and Evie's arms to follow me. "Let's go."

We sauntered in as casually as we could, though I'd suddenly forgotten how a normal person walked.

"You're strutting," Will whispered from the side of his mouth, his camera held low so as not to get attention.

"I'm not!"

"Are."

"Not."

"Are."

"Not."

"Guys?" Evie interrupted. "Amber's about to make her distraction. We need to get on with it."

I peered over the top of a shelf and saw Amber approach the girl on the counter. She was carrying a pink box of ibuprofen – the ones they have for period pain.

"Excuse me," I heard Amber say, her voice much louder than normal (and it was pretty loud anyway). "I'm confused by this ibuprofen."

The girl looked Amber up and down, which happened to Amber a lot. "What is it?" she asked.

"Well" – Amber held out the box to show her – "it says here it's especially for period cramps. However, I was reading the label on the back – and the ingredients say it's just two hundred milligrams of ibuprofen…like all the other ibuprofens over there. But this one is more expensive and has fewer capsules. Why's that?"

GOD I LOVED HER. I wanted to stay watching her. The shop assistant already looked totally bewildered, reading the box herself. Agreeing. Then she picked up the shop phone and called someone over to help. We watched as a shop assistant lady put down the tubs of Vaseline she was rearranging and made her way to the counter. A queue had already built up around Amber, but she seemed oblivious. Only we knew she wasn't.

I wanted to watch. To see what she said. Because it was Amber and I knew she would be hilarious. But this time Will grabbed my arm – his touch jolting me back to my mission.

"Lottie, come on." I reluctantly turned away and scuttled after him and Evie into the Holiday Body aisle.

It was pretty empty, it being winter and all. I leaned right into Will's camera lens and did a big lion roar – which I've been told is surprisingly realistic.

"Right – cellulite cream," I snarled. "We're coming to get you."

Checking no one could see, Evie and I started picking up bottles of all the various anti-cellulite creams and cradling them under our armpits.

"What are you doing, Lottie?" Will asked me, all documentary-style.

"Hiding the cellulite creams."

"Behind the diarrhoea medicine!" Evie chuckled behind me.

We made our way to the Stomach Pain section – which was also, pretty empty.

"Why are you hiding the cellulite cream?" Will asked.

I pulled forward a line of diarrhoea recovery sachets, making room at the back, and planted four tubes of cream behind them. You could hardly see them there – it was brilliant.

I shot the camera a look – mid-mission. "Because," I said, "loads of women have cellulite. It exists for a biological reason. Women tend to store fat that way because of our hormones. Yet some smart-arse decided to give it a label and start telling us it was gross and we shouldn't have it. Basically, making ninety per cent of women feel insecure about their NORMAL bodies is just yet another way of controlling us, getting us to worry more about our thighs than the bigger things and feeling shit so we spend money on stuff we don't need, to prop up our capitalist society and the existing dynamics of power."

Evie popped up beside me. She'd already hidden all her creams behind some bottles of Rennie.

"In English, Lottie!" she demanded.

"Umm…" I tried again. "The invention of cellulite as something we should hate about ourselves and spend loads of money trying to get rid of is yet another thing that makes girls feel shitty about themselves."

"That's better," she and Will said at the same time.

I shoved the last few tubes behind some Gaviscon, shouted "Next mission!" and we scurried to the razor section. I took a peep over the shelves again, checking in on Amber. The queue was MASSIVE now and she was wavering. Her hair had grown in volume in the last two minutes – a sure sign of stress. Megan, I noticed, had put her hood up and had a pair of sunglasses on. I stifled a smile – she fitted in with us just perfectly.

"Quick," Will said. "We don't have much time."

I glanced back one last time at Amber.

"Can you ring it through and check?" she was yelling. "I mean, it just makes NO SENSE that something with the same ingredients, by the same brand, would have such a price difference just because the box is pink."

We slid to a halt at the shavers. There were customers there – a youngish couple, both staring intently at the men's razors, like his shave was an important joint decision or something.

Evie and I looked at each other helplessly. "What do we do?" she whispered.

I then overheard Amber raise her voice even louder. "NO I WILL NOT STEP TO ONE SIDE. YOU CAN'T CHARGE TWO POUNDS MORE FOR THE SAME THING JUST BECAUSE IT'S PINK."

We were almost out of time. But the sexism! The sexism of razors! It was there – and the rules of the project said I had to call it out. I plunged into my bag and pulled out the posters Megan had made.

"Let's just start in the ladies' section and see what happens," I whispered back. We ran-walked down the aisle and an explosion of pink and moisturizing strips and the word *GODDESS* engulfed us. The razors themselves dangled from the shelves – surrounded by photos of slender brown sausage legs on exotic beaches. When, usually, the achieved look is polka-dotted legs from where your fake tan has sunk into the hair holes, poking out from under a skirt that's really hard to pee in, at a shit, rainy barbecue in the park, where none of the guys let you cook anything. I thought of my own legs, hidden under my fifty-denier tights. They'd just got past the stubbly stage…but no one could see them… thankfully…oops…cognitive dissonance.

The couple were still lurking – with their weird unnatural interest in razors. We had to do this with them there.

"Ready?" Evie said.

"Ready."

I blobbed some superglue onto the laminated poster, spilling some onto my fingers which would be impossible to get off later.

Quick as I could, I stuck the poster so it dangled over most of the razors. The poster had a huge arrow, pointing left, towards the men's section.

IDENTICAL BUT CHEAPER RAZORS THAT WAY – JUST BE A MAN.

Megan had drawn a giant cartoon willy (complete with hairy balls) running away from a cartoon razor, with a speech bubble saying: *My pubes are cheaper than yours!*

Evie laughed when I stuck it up.

"It's disgusting and doesn't make much sense, but I love it," she said.

"It doesn't make *any* sense," Will said.

I heard Amber's call suddenly. "Abort mission. Abort, abort!"

And a whish of her red hair whizzed past us, towards the exit. I froze – looking around. The couple had disappeared, and a sales assistant lady was heading in our direction. The couple must've dobbed us in! The dobbers! I was so stunned I was internally using the word "dobbers" for the first time since primary school!

"RUN!" I yelled – way too loudly and thus drawing more attention to us. Will and Evie didn't need to be told – they were already running. The top of Megan's head flew past the shelf.

"WAIT," a voice called.

But we didn't wait. Within seconds we were out of the store, dodging slow shoppers, my toes thumping against the tops of my shoes – making our way to the dodgy fire escape Evie had picked as our first "safe house". I felt terrified, I felt strong, I felt alive… I was fighting. Again. It had been a hard week but I was still fighting…

twenty-three

Amber held out her overflowing wine glass and yelled: "I demand a toast!"

Evie and I looked at each other. Amber was pissed. She had a red-wine smile and her hair was drooping.

"To what?" I asked, louder than I thought. Maybe I was a bit drunk too.

"To not getting caught today!"

Will's own wine glass came veering into my hazy vision. "I'll drink to that," he said. "And, I now have enough video evidence to send you all down. You have to be nice to me for ever."

"I'll toast to this," I said.

"Me too," Evie said.

"Me three," Megan slurred. She was so tiny and slim I think the wine had made her ten times more wasted than the rest of us.

"Okay then." Amber's glass swayed mid-air, slopping

some down onto her hand. "Come on then – here's to NOT GETTING ARRESTED TODAY!"

"HERE'S TO NOT GETTING ARRESTED!" We all clinked in the middle, and yelling it made me realize just how relieved I was.

I leaned back in the big leather armchair and let the warmth of the wine flow through me – regenerating the parts of my body that had been sacrificed to adrenalin throughout the day. We'd managed to pull off the entire feminism shopping extravaganza without a hitch. At the clothes shop, Amber had started fake-crying in the changing rooms, yelling, "I CAN'T FIT EVEN MY CALF INTO THESE JEANS EVEN THOUGH THEY'RE A TWELVE. I'M A FAT COW." It'd been quite a beautiful moment actually. Almost all the female shoppers had flocked to her – telling her she wasn't fat, that the jeans were cut funny, cooing that she was beautiful. "THESE MIRRORS MAKE ME NOTICE CELLULITE I'VE NEVER NOTICED BEFORE," she'd continued wailing, while Megan and Evie filmed it all on their phones.

Meanwhile, I'd pulled out the Special T-Shirts Megan had made, and Will and I had dashed from skinny mannequin to skinny mannequin – shoving them over their heads. They were branded with #Vagilante and said things like: *I'm too thin to menstruate.* We were just getting noticed when we'd sped off to the toy shop. While surrounded by neon plastic bleeping things, we'd swapped the sign over the *Toys for Boys* aisle with the *Toys for Girls* one – so the boys' section was full of dolls, and the girls' was full of Lego and pirates. Then – *finally* – we'd finished up at the bookshop, inserting Post-its into the books we found most offensive. I slipped some Post-its into the latest novel by a famous male author, known for his "smart romantic comedies" that always won loads of awards, saying: *If a woman had written this, it would be called chick lit and win nothing.* We also hit the children's books – particularly the activity books. There was a display of colouring-in books – one was called *The Beautiful Picture Book for Girls* and the other *The Brave Picture Book for Boys.* Lots of Post-its went on there (*Boys can be beautiful too! Girls can be brave too!* And, the old favourite for good luck, *Gender is a social construct*). Now, exhausted, we'd crashed into a pub Will knew about that didn't ID. It was a proper old man's pub – all burny fire in the corner and old leather chairs and shaggy dogs lying with their heads between their paws.

Though Will had confused all of us by ordering two bottles of Merlot.

"No one our age is supposed to drink Merlot," Evie said. "I don't even know what Merlot is. But I know I'm too young to be drinking it."

But two bottles had become four bottles and we'd warmed to the taste of red wine. It was cold outside and it got dark so quickly. The wine just felt right in my stomach as I stared out into the blackness and wondered how we'd managed to get away with everything.

"So, Will," Amber said, her voice all loud from drunk.

"How have you found it spending the week with feminist freedom fighters?"

He eyed her over his glass, taking in her red-wine smile. He seemed very sober, even though he'd had the same amount as us.

"I've got good footage today, that's all that matters."

"Yeah but..." Amber swirled her glass in the air. "Aren't we showing you things to think about? Changing your mind a little bit? Just a little?"

"No," he answered simply.

"How not? With everything Lottie's pointing out?"

"Don't bother," I called over the table.

Will shot me a look that I couldn't figure out. He picked up his glass, all sophisticated, sipping it like a proper grown-up, and turned to Amber again.

"Why do you care that I don't agree with you? Why are all of you obsessed with getting me to agree with you?"

"Why aren't you answering my question?"

He shrugged – took another sip.

Evie answered for him. "He doesn't like having opinions other people have, do you, Will?"

He raised one eyebrow, but tauntingly didn't reply. We all just glared at him, distracted only by Megan's head falling down onto the table.

"I hate men," she declared, slurring her words messily. "You're all shits, you know that? You're all UTTER SHITS." She leaned back, and I saw her eyes fall back into her head.

Yikes – she was proper wasted.

Amber put an arm around her, trying to hush her and stop us getting noticed. Megan buried her face into Amber's shoulder and surprised us all by breaking into sobs. Her cries came from a place deep inside of her – the kind of hollow sobs that have been suppressed for too long. None of us knew what to do. Amber pulled Megan gently to her feet, and they disappeared into the ladies' loos.

Some of the old regulars were looking at us.

Will wrinkled his nose. "What was all that about?"

"I don't know," I lied.

Will crossed his arms. "She can't go around making generalizations like that anyway. You should honk your horn! Isn't it sexist for her to say all men are shits?"

"SHUT UP, WILL," Evie and I said at the same time.

He crossed his arms tighter and leaned back in his chair. "Oh, I see. One rule for boys, another totally different rule for girls."

"SHUT UP, WILL," we both said again.

"Christ," I said. "For once, will you stop trying to win the debating Olympics? Have you even thought what might cause Megan to say something like that?"

"Hypocrisy? Reverse sexism?" The way he tilted his head implied maybe the wine had got to him too, but I didn't care.

"Not now, okay." And I stood up and followed Amber and Megan into the loos – leaving Evie to tend to his poor ego.

* * *

I heard the wails before I pushed open the door. Inside, I saw Amber perched on the loo, Megan's head lolling into her shoulder, crying down her front. Amber was stroking her hair, shushing in her ear, trying to calm her down. She looked up when I blasted in and nodded me forward.

"Megan?" I cooed, kneeling down on the grimy floor. "Megan, what's wrong, honey?"

She shook her head into Amber. "Nothing. I'm fine."

Another sob signalled that she was quite the opposite.

"Megan, what is it? You can tell us. We're here for you." I stroked her back, while Amber stroked her hair.

"Everything's just so messed up," she croaked. "I'm so messed up. I don't know who I am any more… I… I…"

"Is it…?" I was about to ask about Max but Amber shot me a warning glance. "The wine?" I changed tack, making frantic eyebrow motions back at Amber. Why shouldn't we prompt her to talk about it?

Megan lifted her hair and I almost flinched. Her eyes were red raw from crying, her make-up everywhere. She looked so…lost. Like her entire being was a puzzle and she couldn't fit the pieces together.

"I'm sorry," she said. "I'm ruining everything. I'm sorry. I'm such an idiot, I'm such a stupid idiot."

"There's nothing to be sorry for," I cooed.

"Yes, there is. I've ruined your day… I've ruined everything… I ruin everything. No one will believe me if…if…"

My heart started beating really quickly. "If what?" I shot Amber another look.

Megan stared right into me, her eyes streaming… She opened her mouth, and I knew then…she was going to tell us, and we could tell her it was okay, that we believed her, that we'd help her go to the police, that we understood.

"I…I…I'm going to be sick."

Like a pro, Amber swung Megan's head around so she was face-down in the loo. Just in time too. We sat on the floor, rubbing her back as she retched up over and over.

"How much wine did she have?" I asked Amber. "She's wasted!"

"I'm not sure. But before you came in, she was saying she'd not had any breakfast or lunch. She said she didn't 'deserve to eat'…"

"That's worrying."

"That is totally worrying."

Another loud retch and a splashing noise.

"She needs to talk to someone," I whispered more urgently. But Amber, again, gave me a look that made my arm hairs stand on end.

"She just needs to do whatever she needs to do in her own time."

"She should go to the police."

Amber properly rolled her eyes at that, stabbing through my feelings. "Honestly, Lottie. We don't even know it's a police issue. And what you want to do isn't always what's right for everyone, you know?"

My face burned red, my throat stuck together. Amber never told me off! We never snapped at each other. And it hurt so much I almost wanted to push Megan's head out the loo so I could take a turn retching into it.

I didn't reply. I was too stunned. Too stinging.

We stayed with Megan, not talking. I was too upset to talk – upset at Amber, at what had happened with Megan... I'd thought maybe today – her joining us – would help...

Evie came in to check on us. "Will's said sorry," she said. "Though he prefixed it with 'I don't know why I'm apologizing but...'" She wrinkled her nose. "Anyway, he's offered to help us take her back."

Megan had stopped vomiting and was now just howling into the toilet bowl, wailing, "I'm sorry, I'm sorry," over and over.

"Megan?" Amber asked, her voice all soft. "You think you're okay to get up?"

"I'm so sorry. I didn't mean it...so sorry...ruined everything..."

"It's okay, you don't need to worry. Can you get up?"

With aid, Megan stumbled to her feet, her jeans splattered with toilet flush and God knows what else.

"I'll go get Will ready," Evie said, as Amber and I propped Megan up between us.

"Do you know where she lives?" I asked Amber, breaking our uncomfortable silence.

"I think she's near me," Amber mumbled, refusing to make eye-contact. "We sometimes bump into each other on the walk into college. But I'm not entirely sure."

"Megan?" I adjusted my weight so I could hold her up better. "Can you tell us your address?"

"Beech Drive," she muttered into her chest, her hair falling all over her face.

"Yep, that's near me," Amber said. "Come on, Megs, we're going."

Evie pummelled through the doors again to tell us Will had found a back entrance. "Everyone's less likely to see us." I thanked Will silently in my mind.

He arrived at the toilet threshold, and took her off us, putting Megan's arms around his neck and talking to her. "Hey, Megan, it's Will. Yes…I know…I'm an arsehole… yep…a giant one… shall we just go out and get some air? I don't know about you, but I'm boiling in this pub."

"Sorry, sorry, I'm so sorry."

"Nothing to be sorry about. Look, here's the door, shall we go through it then?"

Just as I was marvelling at his total personality transplant into "caring individual", Evie nudged me. "We need to get the bags."

"You're very good at thinking of everything," I said.

She tapped the side of her head and smiled. "Comes with the territory."

We left them with the task of getting Megan out unnoticed, and returned to our table to collect up bags, coats, scarves and all the other bundles of paraphernalia you need when you go on an activist mission during winter. Looking at the table I felt really sad and sobered up. It had been our celebration table – our triumph table. But all the euphoria had dribbled out. I began picking stuff up, swinging three backpacks across my shoulders.

Did you really think shoving a few hilarious T-shirts on underweight mannequins would help Megan? I thought to myself. Did you honestly think pasting a few Post-its in a book would stop awful stuff happening? You're deluded, Lottie.

"You all right?" Evie asked – I'd frozen mid tidy-up.

"I'm fine."

"You're not though." You couldn't get any hidden emotions past Evie, she snuffled them out like an emotion truffle-pig.

I gave her a small smile. "But I will be."

Evie picked up the glasses and took them to the bar, where the barman nodded thanks. I marvelled at her – holding them between her fingers without even going to wash her hands afterwards. What a difference a year (and meds and intensive therapy) could make.

"Evie?" I asked, as we picked up the final scarves draped around the chairs.

"Yes?"

"When you...got sick...you know? Last year?"

"Did I?" She laughed, and I laughed too. She'd been so undeniably sick it was...well...undeniable. She'd even ended up on a psychiatric ward.

"You may not remember it." I smiled. "A minor blip."

"Oh yes, that one. What about it?"

My face fell serious for a moment. "When you thought about everything you needed to get over to feel...well... well again...did it all seem too much?"

Evie sat down on the seat suddenly, folding the scarf she'd been holding. I hoped it was okay I was asking her about it.

"Oh yeah," she said without pausing. "It definitely felt too much. Thus the whole...like...freefall-into-madness thing."

I smiled sadly. "What happened to make you feel it was worth trying to fight?" I asked, choosing my words carefully. "What made you think it had...a point, I guess?"

She folded the scarf smaller and I wondered if I was going to piss off both my best friends in one evening. "I didn't," she answered simply. "For a long time I didn't feel there was any point in trying to get better, I was so convinced I never would be better. It seemed too huge, too insurmountable. But then, Sarah – you met Sarah, right?"

I nodded. Sarah was Evie's CBT therapist and the one who invited Amber and me to visit her in hospital.

"Well, Sarah said something one day. She said, 'You may as well try, Evie. It can't hurt.' And I realized she was right. Yes, trying was exhausting and hard and meant doing everything I didn't want to do and it seemed horribly pointless putting myself through all that if I didn't believe it would make any difference. But then, actually, I wouldn't know if I didn't try. So I started trying. And, yes, for ages it felt useless. But then, day by day, I noticed a few things began to give..."

I perched on the side of the chair, knowing we shouldn't take much longer. It was cold out, and it looked like Amber and Will had successfully manhandled Megan out of the pub.

"Are you having a crisis or something?" she asked, nudging me with her butt. "Is All Powerful Lottie having a blip?"

I shrugged. "Maybe. I don't know. It's just – what Megan's going through is so huge, and so awful, and she won't even talk about it. And I thought today would help but…what's a few hidden tubes of cellulite cream against that?" I found my voice catching and I felt even madder at myself. My tears weren't appropriate here, this wasn't my drama. It was Megan's and I felt like I was thieving it. But I couldn't help it. I felt helpless and distraught by what she was going through. By the fact loads of girls have shitty things happen to them and don't tell a soul.

"Do you remember, earlier this year, when you made us read *The Female Eunuch* for the Spinster Club?" Evie asked.

I nodded.

"Well, I have to admit, I didn't finish it all. It was HARD, Lottie. I only have a few GCSEs, remember? But anyway the bits I read and could understand were really good. And there was this one quote I kept coming back to. Especially when Teddy and his mates were so horrid to us about the jukebox thing. I can't remember the quote verbatim, but it said something about how society can't be changed in a lifetime. That so many people who fight for what's right won't see the results of their efforts before they die."

"Great – thanks, that's a cheerful thought," I laughed.

"I've not finished," Evie said. "But it says, you've still got to believe you're making a difference and place your hope in it. And think about it – think of all the great freedom fighters we've had, and how they never got to see how monumental they were. Martin Luther King, Mary Wollstonecraft, Emmeline Pankhurst… They'd be delighted if they could see how things are now. How much the fires they lit have spread."

"They'd also be depressed at all the work left to do."

"God, you're grumpy today!" Evie stood up. "That too. But they did change things. They had hope and belief they would, and they did. And have you thought, maybe all the things we fight against – people like you, me, and FemSoc and all the FemSocs around the country – that maybe we won't see the change straight away, or at all? But we will have left ripples and some people somewhere in the future will be glad for our ripples and inspired to make their own."

I felt warm for the first time since Megan left the table. "Why are you so wise?" I asked her, looking up in awe.

"Years and years of therapy."

twenty-four

It took quite some time to get Megan home.

She was exceedingly drunk, even after all the vomming. I was still bewildered as to how she'd managed it without our noticing.

"I'm sorry, I'm so sorry," she repeated into Will's shoulder.

Will – to give him credit – essentially carried her home, telling her it was fine, even getting her to laugh at herself through the sobs.

Amber and I didn't talk the whole way back. Tension crackled between us and, after initially feeling upset about it, now I felt mad. Why was she being so aggressive?

It was Amber who rang Megan's doorbell and explained everything to her parents while the rest of us shivered around the corner. I peered through a hedge and watched the porch of Megan's house get flooded with orange light as the front door opened. It made Amber's ginger hair look even more ginger. Megan's mum – from what I could see – didn't even look shocked. She just nodded while I watched Amber explain, and then reached out and took Megan's hand tenderly – bringing her in for a hug. Amber waved, then the door closed and she walked back towards us.

"How did it go?" I asked.

Amber, infuriatingly, just nodded and said, "Fine." Not offering up any more explanation. Well, I wasn't going to ask for one.

Evie's head was tennis-ing from me to her, her to me, chewing her lip – knowing something was up.

"Well, I'm just round the corner." Amber stretched her arms up. "See you guys at college on Monday?"

I nodded, Evie did too. Will coughed, to remind us he was there maybe.

"You've got your interview with the local paper on Monday after school," he reminded me.

"That's so cool." Evie's voice was a bit too cheery to compensate for all The Atmosphere.

"Hopefully…" I said. Amber didn't say anything. Seriously – what had I done?

"Well, good work today, chaps," Evie said – still trying to be chipper. "I better get back though. You know what Mum's like…"

We all waved and dispersed. Will actually lived quite near me and headed off in the direction I was supposed to, but I felt like being alone, so I walked the wrong way for a while. My chat with Evie had lightened me a little, but I still felt weird and lost and overwhelmed and totally confused about Amber.

I knew I should message her. Get it all out. Make it better. But I was too exhausted. The day's activities – the adrenalin, the week I'd had – it just sort of piled on top of me, making me too weak for any kind of conflict. Even healthy *let's-get-it-out-in-the-open* conflict.

I walked with my arms crossed – keeping my eyes down to avoid any sexism I might inadvertently see. No energy for that either.

Mum and Dad weren't in when I got home. A scribbled note from Mum told me she was at the centre and Dad was at the pub with friends. It was only early evening but it felt later. The night was already black, everyone's curtains closed.

I had so much coursework to do, but I didn't do any of it.

I really should've sent Amber a message but I didn't.

I fired one off to Megan.

Hey, you were so much help today, thank you! Hope your head is all right tomorrow x

A gloom seeped through me – one I wasn't used to. I'm not a sad person. I'm usually upbeat and perky. But this new gloom found me and infiltrated its way through my nervous system, shutting everything down.

Was today worth it? Would it make a difference? Why didn't I have any energy to mend things with Amber? And, at the back of everything, the biggest nagging gloom. Was I choosing The Project over the rest of my life? And if so, what did that mean? Cambridge and getting into it felt so far away in that moment – like a tiny speck on a horizon filled with this project and what it meant and how much energy it was taking from me. Energy that I knew, ideally, I should be saving for Cambridge, saving for my future, giving myself a chance to get into a position where I could really change things.

When my phone buzzed, I jumped on it. Hoping it was Amber – hoping she was making the first move, hoping she had the energy to do what I didn't.

It wasn't Amber.

It was Will.

The footage from today is incredible!

And a tiny speck of gold sparked in amongst the gloom.

I grinned before hitting reply.

WEEK TWO

twenty-five

The local news reporter wasn't how I expected him to be at all.

I'm not sure what I was expecting – but when this young guy, with Prince Charming hair and a cheap shiny suit turned up – I was suitably surprised.

"Hi, Charlie, is it?" He shook my hand aggressively, squeezing so tight the veins bulged out a little.

"Umm, Lottie."

"Oh yeah, of course." He made no eye-contact, giving me no confidence that he'd heard my correction. He looked over my head at Will. "And this must be your partner in crime, am I right?"

Will reached out and shook his hand. "Will," he introduced himself. "Thanks for coming."

We beckoned him over to the tables we'd set up in the library. I'd agreed it with Mr Packson. The interview would take place at college, as that would be the best place for photos. Also, it gave *"Dan, I'm Dan, great to meet you"* a chance to get some quotes from the college too. The library was empty, college hours over. A hard day at college over. Megan was pretending nothing had ever happened involving wine or crying. Whenever I tried to bring it up she lurched into an unrelated conversation, or pulled out a new design idea. Amber was still frosty as hell with me, and it made me frosty in return. Why was she choosing the hardest month of my life to suddenly make some kind of point about my personality? Evie – stuck in the middle – had spent the day navigating between us both. Keeping up a hubbub of pointless conversation, making us sit with Jane and Joel, so the extra company could defuse the crackling atmosphere. It was useful. But all I really secretly wanted was for her to whisper over to me, "Amber's being an unreasonable cow, don't worry, you're my favourite."

But she didn't.

It hadn't helped my mood that Teddy and his mates had come in wearing matching T-shirts with *MENIMIST* emblazoned across them. Or how loudly some girls in the canteen had laughed at them, giving me horrible looks when I honked my horn, and muttering loudly, "She's pathetic."

So that had been today. Now the journalist was settling himself down across the table. I could smell soured coffee on his breath. He pulled out an old-skool ringbound notebook, flipped it open, took the biro out from behind his ear and levelled me with a smile with underhints of lots of things…

"So, Charlie."

"Lottie."

"Yes, of course, sorry. So, Lottie, what gave you the idea to start such an…interesting campaign?"

I suddenly felt nervous. Everything I said was going to be recorded and used, and surrounded by text I didn't write and couldn't control. I had to make every word count.

I ran my hands through my hair, levelled him with my best Lottie stare – the one I knew had people eating out of my hands – and said, "Because I couldn't take it any more."

His pen started moving across his notebook. "Take what?"

"Any of it. All of it."

"I see… All of what?"

I took a deep breath and I began to tell him everything. Right from the beginning. But not the van men beginning – the real beginning. I told him about how my auntie on Dad's side always bought me dresses for my birthday – when I hated wearing them as a kid. How I was told I had to wear them, to be polite, and I wasn't allowed to run around and play football with my cousins. How my dad's family still can't get over the horror that Mum and I don't have his surname – thinking Mum somehow tricked him into this, rather than it being their joint decision. I told him how, before I'd even left primary school, I'd get vans honking me when I walked the short journey home because I got boobs early. I told him how ashamed I felt when my body hair appeared – how I knew, without even discussing it, that I needed to get rid of it. I told him how, literally every summer, I feel sick about showing off my body, as it will never be good enough. I told him about how, at my old school, one lunchtime when it was raining, all the boys lined all the girls up in order of who had the nicest arse and none of us even thought to complain about it. That everyone is surprised that I'm smart, because I'm pretty, and you can't be both without people distrusting you. I told him how I'm regularly called a slut and a whore because I've had more than one boyfriend – while, if I was a guy, I'd be a legend or a pro. I told him how I never feel safe walking alone. How at least once a day, I have a conversation where a guy's eyes wander to my chest and it makes me feel dirty. I talked and talked and talked and he scribbled and scribbled and scribbled.

Eventually I ran out, and I said, "And I've been lucky, I live in this country. I've had a relatively undramatic upbringing. Think how much worse it is for other girls… So, one day, I just knew I couldn't take any more. I had to do…something. And making all this stuff just…more visible, so everyone who tries to ignore it can't ignore it any more, is doing something."

There was a pause while he caught up his shorthand – weird symbols appearing over his notepad.

"Yes, right…wonderful…" he murmured, noting it all down. Then he looked up and grinned. "That was all brilliant, Charlie…"

"Lottie," Will corrected him this time.

"Yes…brilliant… I mean, I only have three hundred and fifty words to play with, but that was very…colourful."

I could feel that he didn't get it then and panic set in. He was a journalist, and he didn't get it. I had to make him understand… I had to get through somehow.

"What's it like, being a journalist?" I asked him and he looked up, surprised.

"Aren't I the one who's supposed to be asking the questions?" His grin was quite smarmy.

"I guess. I just wondered. It sounds like such a cool job…"

Will made eyebrows at me, obviously thinking I was off topic. But I wasn't. I was winning him over – I was good at winning people over. And I needed this disinterested man to be on my side.

"It can be cool. It can be a lot of hard work."

"What's your career aim?" I crossed and uncrossed my legs – leaning forward with apparent interest. "Like, do you always want to work at the *Gazette*?" I wrinkled my nose to show how distasteful I thought the whole thing was – though, secretly, I've always loved our local paper. There's such a charm to it. I always skim through it over breakfast when Mum and Dad leave it out – laughing at the crappy stories like cats being rescued from burning fish and chip shops, residents posing with their arms out in anguish at all the potholes. I felt a mixture of relief that we lived somewhere so safe and undramatic, and yet also stifled and stale that we lived somewhere where literally nothing happened.

"Umm, no. Not for ever," Dan admitted, mirroring my body language, which everyone knows means you're winning. "I want to work on the nationals."

An ambition. I could work with this.

I shrugged. "So why don't you?"

He laughed then. "It's not that easy, is it?"

"Why not?"

He leaned back in his chair, stretching his arms up to reveal small sweat patches. He'd apparently forgotten quite quickly it was supposed to be him interviewing me. It must get boring though, always being the one asking the questions, never the one answering them.

"Well, it's very competitive," he said. "They want you to do shift work. But the pay's terrible, and they start you on nights. But, like, the only way to get up to London is by train and, of course, they don't run through the night. So you have to live in London really." He sniffed hard. "And, yeah, well, I can't afford to live in London on the terrible pay… I did a few shifts for a national the other month. I slept on a mate's floor, under the dining table. Used my annual leave from the paper as well. Caned it hard… When a job came up I was certain it was mine but…"

"But…" I leaned forward and opened my mouth just a little, ignoring Will who seemed bewildered and annoyed.

"But, well it went to this guy whose uncle worked there. Can you believe it? Of course I could. It's very elitist you see, journalism. Everyone helping the same people up, you know? The person who got it had been working there for free for seven months. Seven months! He could afford to work for free that long. He stayed in his uncle's house, rent free of course."

I blew up my fringe. "That's so unfair." I sounded suitably outraged. To be fair, I *was* suitably outraged. Though I couldn't help but bitterly think, I bet it's even harder to get a job in the nationals if you're a woman.

"Yes. Totally unfair. But what can you do?" He looked less smarmy and more sad by the second. This was my moment...to make him realize we were the same really... just with different aims.

"You can fight," I said. "You can stand up to it, call it out. Say it's wrong."

Dan looked genuinely confused by the notion. "What? I couldn't. I'd never work again. I'd screw up my future."

I moved my own body away now – playing the space between us. I looked out the window, stuck out my bottom lip. "I'm worried I'm already screwing up my future by doing this project. I don't have time for coursework. My grades are suffering." They were...they really, really were...I couldn't even think about it, it made me feel so ill. I'd got another B that morning. It was one mark off an A but still... "Lots of people at college are taking the piss out of me. I'm supposed to be preparing for my Cambridge interview but I don't have any time for that either... But if there's something not right in the world, you have to fight. Otherwise, what? You're just saying it's okay that this happens..." I looked back at him, right into his tired-looking watery eyes. "It's really wrong what happened to you," I said, so sincerely, so heartfelt. "I'm so sorry."

twenty-six

"Jeez, Lottie. You had that man literally eating out the palm of your hand," Will said. "Well, not literally, but still."

We were walking towards town in a triumphant splendour of adrenalin. The rest of the interview had been a breeze. And when Will said our first video had over two thousand views already, Dan practically exploded.

"Wow, this is a real story," he said, scrolling through Will's laptop.

"You sound surprised." I laughed. He didn't need to know most of the hits probably came from people at college watching it to take the piss out of me or leave hilarious comments. I'd had to report one already.

Lottie takes it up the arse. A rumour that Teddy had started last year that refused to die. Or maybe he was the one who posted it.

"It was great to meet you, Lottie. Really great." Dan had shaken my hand and got my name right and actually seemed genuinely keyed up by the story.

I didn't think I would be called Charlie again…

"How did you do it?" Will said, still in awe of me. I think he was starting to realize he'd underestimated me…

I shrugged, like it was nothing, even though my insides were doing the funky chicken.

"With activism you've got to connect with people on an emotional level – make them feel like we're all in this together. I just got him to realize he feels like I feel, just maybe about a different thing…"

I looked up at Will, who was still staring at me all agog. So much so that he stumbled over a small fallen branch.

I grinned. "This is why I can't win you over," I said. "You're too logical and scientific in how you think. You don't have any emotional level for me to connect with."

"Hey!"

"It's true! The only way I could convince someone like you that feminism is important and you should believe in it, is if I made a completely watertight logical argument…and even then…you'd find some minor issues with the method in which the data was collected or something and jump on that so you could feel all superior criticizing my efforts rather than focusing on the feelings – the desperation, the violence, the helplessness, the just…wrongness of it all."

Will went quiet, kicking some leaves up, not looking at me any more. He muttered something.

"What's that? The rest of the class can't hear you."

Despite himself, he smiled, though he still didn't look at me.

"I said," he said louder, "there's nothing wrong with being logical."

"No, not always." I paused. "But I don't think you realize how upsetting it is when you feel someone's devaluing your experience. Look how angry me, Evie and Amber get at you. Do you ever think why? Do you ever think how it must feel to have horrible things you've seen or experienced judged and questioned by someone? Like it's our responsibility to convince you we're not lying, rather than yours just to believe us? Also" – I paused for breath – "logic is shit for social change. Look at climate change, for example. There's so much scientific evidence that we're destroying the planet – but nobody gives a damn until you shove a sad-looking polar bear on a tiny sheet of ice with a text-in number in front of them. Or imagine if Martin Luther King had stood up and started a speech with, 'I have a…really good piece of data here that proves racism is A Thing.'"

Will stayed quiet, and I let the triumph of the interview spill over into triumph that his silence might mean that I'd got through to him… God, I was smart sometimes. I know you're not supposed to say that about yourself, but I really am freaking superbly smart a lot of the time.

"I don't mean to upset you with all my questions," Will said, after a moment or two, his chin tucked down in what I was choosing to see as defeat. "I've told you, I'm a documentary maker. Do you not sometimes consider that it's my job to poke the nest? To get the best reaction out of you?"

"But you do it so gleefully!"

And he laughed. "I can't deny that's true."

"Where we headed anyway?" I asked, realizing I hadn't really been noticing our route.

Will gave me another reluctant grin. "I was going to take us out for dinner. To celebrate. But now you're being so difficult, I'm not sure if I will."

"You're taking me out for dinner?"

"Relax. It's just Pizza Express."

"I can't relax when I know dough balls are a possibility."

He kept smiling. "You like dough balls?"

"If that's an innuendo, it's a very bad and cringe one."

"It was a simple question, Lottie. Not everything has to be dirty."

We'd arrived outside the town's Pizza Express now, the basily aroma of pizza wafting out to us whenever the door opened to let stressed-looking families out. Our eyes met each other and we laughed. Him playing me, me playing him… Just like that he'd got our power dynamic back onto an even keel. I resentfully respected him for it.

"I can't let you pay for dinner," I said. "The project…"

"Lottie, this isn't a date." He said it simply, but it still felt harsh.

Why wasn't it a date? I instantly thought. Don't you want it to be a date? I gently stamped on one of my feet to jolt myself out of my pathetic girl spiral.

"It's two colleagues celebrating a good day at work," he explained. "If it *was* a date, no, you couldn't let me pay by the way. I find that such bullshit! The amount of times I've gone out with girls to eat, and they just stare at me vacantly when the bill comes."

I nodded. I agreed. It was inexcusable, really. You can't go around expecting gender equality one minute and then expect boys to pay for everything. My go-to rule on dates was always, always, to offer, then negotiate it between you. You buy this one, I'll buy the next one. Even when I was dating Posh Tim last year, who was infinitely richer than me.

"Fine then," I said, "if it's not a date, you can SO pay. I'm getting double dough balls."

Will bit his lip, resisting the urge to make another crap joke.

"I could never date anyone who gets double dough balls."

"Well. I'd never date anyone who is so insecure about their own balls that they can't handle being around double helpings of the dough variety."

I opened the door for him like a gentleman, and gestured him through. He got the joke, and curtsied.

"Oi. I'm not insecure about my balls!"

And we had dinner.

twenty-seven

"I still can't believe you ate two helpings of dough balls." Will surveyed the array of empty plates between us.

"Don't forget the two extra bowls of garlic butter," I added, sticking my stomach out and stroking it like a pregnant person. I turned sideways in my seat to show Will my food baby. "It's yours," I said, all dramatically. "And I'm going to call it Quentin."

Will arched his eyebrows at my expanding stomach.

"That is quite an accomplishment."

I pushed my stomach out further. "I know. I grow the best food baby out of all my friends."

His eyebrows went up further, if possible.

"You actually had a competition?"

I thought back to last February, when it had rained constantly for twenty days. Bored witless, Evie, Amber and I had challenged ourselves to eat a baked camembert each to see who made the biggest food baby.

"Oh yes. Evie and Amber made me a medal." Out of a Mini Babybel…and I'd eaten it. And made myself sick…

His nose pulled up. "How attractive."

"I don't care about being attractive."

"Every girl cares a little bit, even feminists. Cognitive dissonance, but still."

I thought about what he'd said as I looked around the restaurant, touched that he'd remembered my speech. Everyone's cutlery clink-clanked off the high ceilings, mixed with the screams of a tantruming toddler the other side of us.

"I guess I do," I said. "But not like in a *change-who-I-am* way. I mean, how exhausting would that be? Having to pretend you're someone you're not all the time – to be a persona. It must be so hard. I mean…like you…"

"Yeah." Will nodded, looking bored, though I was beginning to realize bored was just his resting face. He sat up. "Hang on! I don't pretend to be someone I'm not."

I picked up my glass of wine and took a deep sip. "Don't you?"

"Of course I don't!"

"But you must spend so long crafting your facial hair that way."

Will's hand went up to his immaculate mini-beard thing.

"And, like, don't you ever feel like watching a shitty movie, just sometimes? Because it's relaxing?"

He crossed his arms. "Define what constitutes a shitty movie."

"I dunno. One of those comedies where everyone poos themselves on a stag do. Or when ten cars crash into each other."

"I'd rather die."

"So you genuinely like watching what? Important Oscar-winning films with loads of boring talking and acting? All the time? For fun?"

"Yes, Lottie, I do."

"But you're not, like, actually this cocky, are you? Like, underneath it all you're desperately insecure and cling to your veneer of superiority like a safety blanket because you're scared, if you reveal the real you, everyone will hate it?"

He burst out laughing. "I am NOT superior."

"You are. You SO are." I drained my wine glass, letting its warm fuzziness make me feel all warm and fuzzy… and fuzzy…I'd had two large glasses…Will was paying. "You think you're better than everyone. You think you're better than feminism!" I gave him my best look over the rim of the glass.

"Just because people don't agree with you, doesn't mean they think they're superior."

I put my glass down, a bit too loudly. "But I still don't understand how you can NOT agree with feminism! After everything you saw me do last week."

He ran his hands through his hair. "Honestly, we're going to have this conversation again?"

I scrunched up my napkin in my hand. "I just don't get it.

I don't get you. You seem so smart…" I trailed off. And that's when I realized, Will *was* smart. He wasn't only an incredible documentary maker, but you could tell he was a deep thinker, and he was witty, and quick, and the sort of person I was quite sure gets As and Bs in his exams. How could someone that smart not agree with me? About something so undeniably right? Especially when they were so good-looking? I realized I didn't want to have this argument either. I was enjoying the meal, the wine, the glow in my tummy from the interview going well. The fact that I'd had enough wine to not be worrying about why Amber was inexplicably mad at me. To not be worrying about Megan and how lost she seemed. To not be worrying about my project – though, actually, I wasn't ever supposed to let that slip. So I admitted defeat and changed the subject.

"What got you into films then?" I asked, thinking, really, I hadn't ever asked him about himself. It was always him asking me questions, with that bloody lens shoved in my face. "Evie said it was Tim Burton who got her into films."

Will literally shuddered. "Ergh, that is *so* Evie."

"You are SO SUPERIOR!"

He smiled wolfishly. Like a sexy wolf. God, wolves really are quite sexy, aren't they, if you come to think of it? Or is that a weird thought to have?

"That one, I faked," he said. "I actually like Tim Burton."

"Oh my God, the boy can make a joke."

He smiled again.

"So, why are you into films?"

He leaned back in his chair as he spoke – telling me about getting his first camera when he was young. ("God, do you remember when you actually put things in a DVD player?") How all he wanted for his birthday was the newest equipment. He told me how he watched every single documentary on TV. ("The Attenboroughs, all the Panoramas, even those awful ones where they send cameramen to follow teenagers on their first holidays to Magaluf.") His favourite film-maker was this German guy who made this one documentary about a man who lived with grizzly bears until he got eaten by one.

"Please don't call him a 'German guy'," Will said, when I explained Evie liked the same person.

"Superior."

And he laughed.

Will relaxed when he talked about film. After a while his voice lost its authoritarian tone and his real enthusiasm came through. He looked all boylike, his eyes sparkly beneath his glasses. His forehead stopped wrinkling in disapproval at everyone around him.

We were having the most lovely time, until the bill arrived.

The young waiter plopped it on the table, right in front of Will, without even giving me a glance. Will reached for it, but I grabbed his hand, stopping him.

"Excuse me," I said loudly, to the back of the waiter who was already walking off.

Will twigged. "Lottie, don't. Come on, have a night off."

"The patriarchy never has a night off."

The waiter spun on his feet. "Is there a problem?" he asked, smiling, like nothing would ever be a problem if he just kept smiling like that.

I pointed to the small silver plate in front of Will. "I am capable of paying a bill," I said. "My vagina doesn't prohibit me from paying for my own dough balls."

It wasn't really necessary to use the word "vagina" – I winced the moment it came out. Will had turned bright red, his neck sinking into the starched collar of his posh shirt.

"I'm sorry, madam," the waiter said. "If you're paying…" He pushed the plate over to me.

"I'm not paying. He is." I gestured to the dying Will.

The guy's face scrunched up. "Then I don't see the problem."

I gritted my teeth – feeling guilty for Will, but a project was a project. A promise was a promise.

"The problem is…" I hated myself as the words came out. God it sounded petty…it *was* petty…but it was still sexism. "Is that you shouldn't just assume the boy is paying the bill. And also, while you're here…" Why was I still talking? I was definitely still talking. "When you brought the wine out to taste, why did you offer it to him? And not me? Do seventeen-year-old boys know more about wine than seventeen-year-old girls? Oh, yes, that's right…" I found myself smiling crazily. Will had turned fully red – there wasn't a single part of his face that wasn't totally tomato. "We're not eighteen… Soz."

I shrugged, keeping the manic grin across my face.

"I'll...umm..." The waiter looked completely broken. Not, like, emotionally broken – but just confused broken. "I'll get the manager."

I found myself waving my finger at him – okay, so two large glasses of wine was definitely my limit. "You do that."

The second he'd stridden off towards the kitchen, still shaking his head in bafflement, I leaned across the table.

"We need to go. Now."

Will was shaking his head, cringe bleeding all over his facial expressions. "Lottie, like, really?" His voice was shaking. "There was no need. It was just a bill. He was just nearer my side of the table..."

"There IS a need. But you can yell at me once we're outside. Come on now, GO."

I looked behind me – we didn't have long. I wasn't sure if you could get arrested for drinking underage, or if it was just the restaurant that got into trouble. I didn't particularly want to find out though.

Will's eyes were all wide as he fumbled with his many bags of camera equipment.

"Will, just dump some money on the table and run!"

He scrambled in his pocket, yanked out a few notes, flung them hysterically onto the silver plate I'd found so offensive, and then took off in front of me. I flung my own bag over my shoulder and ran after him, ignoring the tables of people who gawped at us, forkfuls of pizza paused mid-air on the journey to their mouths. Just as I pushed against the big glass door, I turned and saw the waiter and some other guy in a suit stride out of the kitchen. They saw our empty table and looked up.

"Hey," the waiter yelled, walking faster.

"Will – run!" And with my heart going absolutely berserk, I threw myself after him, the door slamming behind me. The cold winter air hit my lungs as my boots thudded heavily on the concrete. We sprinted past other restaurants and past the giant Starbucks, and then Will dived left into a little alleyway that took us into the car park of the local Waitrose. It was pretty quiet as it was a Monday night but there were enough parked cars to provide cover. We ran across it, my lungs gasping for air. Then Will ducked down behind a parked Range Rover and pulled me down with him.

There was silence, apart from the gasping sound of us regaining our breath. We peered out, waiting for the police, or an angry crowd with torches and pitchforks. Neither arrived.

After five minutes, we both leaned back against the car, breathing in a more measured way. I'd stopped wheezing, for instance. Which was good. Because I'd never wheezed before.

I turned to Will, who was still flattened against the car like he was about to get shot.

"So…" I tried to keep my voice light, knowing he was pissed off. "That was a new experience. Shall we go for dinner again next week?"

His eyebrows furrowed and his voice came out super strained.

"There was absolutely no need for any of that," he managed to say.

"Ahh, come on. It was fun."

He shot me a glance. A glance that said *none of that was fun.*

"What was I supposed to do? Ignore the rules of my project just because you were paying for two batches of dough balls?"

He stood up suddenly, his camera bags clashing against each other, and started walking away. I watched him for a second – stunned – then chased after him.

"Hey, what's your problem?"

He didn't answer me – just kept on striding.

"Come on, Will. What did you want me to do? Just leave it?"

He stopped and flung himself round. "Yes! That's exactly what I wanted you to do!"

"But…the project…" I didn't understand. It wasn't like he was new to the idea. He'd been filming it for over a week.

"It was just one stupid little thing," he said. "I mean…it's just a bill. It's just someone on minimum wage, putting a bill slightly more in front of me than in front of you… There was no need. NO NEED…for… Argh… God, that was so embarrassing. YOU are so embarrassing."

I stopped walking, tears prickling in my eyes almost instantly. I blinked them back, using them, turning them to anger…I was practised at that.

"No, YOU'RE EMBARRASSING," I screamed after him, my voice echoing around the mostly-empty car park. "You're more than happy to hide behind a camera when I'm putting myself out there, totally humiliating myself EVERY DAY for a good cause. But THE MOMENT you have to go through even a HINT of what I've been through this past week…" I started walking again, catching him up… "No, you totally wig out like a fucking…" I couldn't think of a word, I was too furious… "Fucking…GIRL…" I found myself shouting. Then I stopped walking. Will picked up on it too.

He turned, his smug little face still all red.

"Oh, that's great. That's just great. Are you going to custard pie yourself?" he asked. He was so jeery, we needed a new word for jeery…maybe jeery actually is a new word…

"Oh NOW you agree there's sexism? When I say something sexist that helps you win an argument? WHAT A SURPRISE."

I wasn't sure where all this anger was coming from, but it was coming from somewhere and there was a lot of it.

"It was just one bill!" Will shouted. "A tiny little bill!"

"It's never a tiny anything!" I yelled back. "That's the whole point! That's why we're here. That's why we're doing this. That's why we – annoyingly – have to spend all this fucking awful time together! Because it's NEVER JUST A BILL. It's the whole thing… It's invisible…it's lots of little things…and they make the big bad things happen…and…"

"Well, if you hate spending time with me so much, then I'm out," he shouted. "You need me more than I need you."

Panic. Panic set in. He couldn't be out… We needed a cameraman…argh…argh…

"Oh, will you get over yourself?" I screamed. Because screaming abuse at him was so likely to make him stay. "The one moment you had to participate, about something as 'silly' as a bill, you said it yourself, and you're out?" I started clapping. Because sarcastic applause was CERTAINLY going to make him stay. "Well done, Mr Neutral. Why not go film some dying people in a war and not do anything about it? And get annoyed when they bleed on you?"

He shook his head slowly. "You're crazy."

"You're an arrogant prick."

"You're a man-hating bitch."

We stood facing each other – his face orange under the car park's lights. I hated him so much. Everything about his smug...superior...passive...*nonsense*... I hated him, hated him...

Will kissed me.

One second we were glaring each other down, the next he'd grabbed my face, pulled me to him and kissed me – the force of it sending his glasses askew.

And, bollocks, it was a good kiss. A great kiss. All hungry and clutchy and everything I really annoyingly wanted because my hormones apparently didn't give a flying fuck about the patriarchy...but this guy had just called me a bitch!

I pushed him off. Yes, after maybe two minutes of solid tonguing. But I eventually pushed him off, so hard he flew backwards.

"You do NOT call me a bitch and then think you can

kiss me!" I wiped my mouth, knowing I was just on the brink of crying.

"You called me an arrogant prick!" He stumbled backwards, not missing a beat. He'd managed to go from fighting, to kissing, and cruise-controlled right back into fighting again.

"Because you are one!" I yelled.

"Yes well…" And I dared him to say it…to say I was a bitch again. I waited. He clenched his fists – to withhold his anger, or sexual tension or whatever…but when he opened his mouth, he said, "I'm out… This whole thing…it's ridiculous… I'm out."

Will walked away – all his bags jiggling. I stood and watched him turn black then orange, black then orange, as he strode in and out of the lighting.

Did I call after him? He'd called me a bitch…

I touched my lips – where he'd so recently been.

I didn't call after him.

I cried on a bench at the bus stop, then rang Mum and asked her to pick me up.

twenty-eight

She came in her old beat-up Volvo, bundled in about ten thousand shawls for the cold. I was sitting on the low wall outside the supermarket – the worst of the tears passed now. But somehow just seeing Mum sent me over the edge again.

She pulled up, her worried face peering at me through the windscreen. I waved feebly and clambered into the passenger seat.

The warmth of the car radiator hit me, making me realize how cold I'd got. Sitting there. Crying. Watching my breath crystallize and float off into the dark.

"Oh, Lottie, honey. What's wrong? You never cry!"

I snuffled and held out my hands to thaw them.

"Thanks for picking me up. I know it's not far to walk, but it's cold, and dark."

"It's fine, sweetie." She patted my shoulder, then shifted the car into gear. I leaned my head against the window, watching the stars blur by. I was so confused by everything that had happened in the last hour. Why did doing the right thing feel so wrong? And the wrong thing feel so right?

"I'm okay…" I said, into the window. "It's just…this project…" I regretted saying it the moment I did. My parents were looking for any reason to stop me. They still hadn't recovered from that B, and, to be fair, their worries seemed valid. Look at tonight for example. Usually on a Monday I'd be doing coursework until nine and then reading extra books until bed. Instead I'd charmed a journalist, charmed Will, pissed off Will, done a runner at Pizza Express, kissed Will, had a fight with Will and cried in a car park.

Shit like that does not get you into university, especially a university like Cambridge.

Mum surprised me by not jumping down my throat – she must've just had a reiki or something. "Aww, poppet, I'm sorry. It must be really hard. What happened?"

"It's just…like…really exhausting. And Amber's mad at me for some reason…"

"Really? That's not like you two."

"I know. But she is. And then there's this boy…"

"Uh-oh…" Mum said, laughing. "There's always a boy with you."

"Hey, that's not true." Was it? I didn't always have "a boy"…did I? Oh God…maybe I did… "It's not like that," I protested. Well it hadn't been like that…maybe it was now. "It's that boy Will who was over, the one who's doing all the filming." I paused, not wanting to relive it. "We got into a fight. He's quit the project."

Mum's eyes widened as she indicated left. "That seems a bit dramatic of him. What happened?"

I let myself smile. "I called him an arrogant prick."

Mum's eyes got wider, not in a good way. "Is this the boy you've been complaining about? The one who won't use the word feminist?"

I nodded, my head bashing into the window.

"Well do you really think screaming at him is going to help him come round?"

My mouth dropped open. "But he shouldn't need help coming round!"

"Maybe not… But has anyone ever changed your mind by yelling angrily into your face?"

I sulked for the rest of the short journey home. I wasn't the type of person to yell angrily in people's faces. I wasn't. I was funny and charming and threw cream pies! That is totally cute! And also, what's wrong with being angry anyway? If something is WRONG – isn't angry the only appropriate response? The only normal one? I mean, YES, I'd agreed to make this project funny rather than angry – but I couldn't not be angry. Why should I have to hide my anger to make people like Will feel more comfortable?

I wanted to call the girls. To let it out. To have them reassure me. That I'm right. That it's fine. That I'm charming. But I didn't even know how to approach Amber. She'd NEVER frozen me out before.

When we got in, I thought that because Mum had been nice in the car, I'd be let off the hook.

I was wrong.

Dad was sitting at the kitchen table, reading the newspaper. He lowered it when I came in to drink some water to counteract the two glasses of wine.

"Charlotte," he said, rather than hello. "Your mum and I are very worried. Your interview is coming up and you've hardly seemed to do any work."

Mum entered behind me, removing her several shawls and coming to my rescue. "She's upset, Ben. She's had a fight with a friend."

"With the girls?" Dad put his paper down.

"With this guy," I said. "He's not my friend."

"Oh. Another guy…"

"What is *that* supposed to mean?" I demanded, just as Mum kicked in.

"Come on, you two, let's all get on. It's getting late."

"THIS IS STUPID." I stormed up to my room – which is quite hard when you get tangled in beaded curtains. I slammed the door behind me for added impact, flung myself onto my bed, and tried to cry again.

Why was EVERYONE against me at the moment? I was trying to do a good thing! And yet people were acting like I was wandering round literally peeing on them. Maybe I should do that? It would make a point. I'm not sure what the point would be though.

Reasonable Lottie, who was dwelling somewhere very hidden in me, tried to throw up some things to think about. Like, yes, I had called Will an arrogant prick…and that wasn't very nice. Maybe screaming into people's faces wasn't the best tactic… But I was too emotional to let myself think about that. Mum thudded on the door, calling through the wood, telling me Dad wanted me to come down for a peppermint tea and a "reasonable chat about everything".

I called back that if he was so worried he could come and say so himself – rather than sending his wife as his slave.

She went away after that.

I pulled out my phone. Wanting so much to call the girls, to have them make things better. But somehow, without realizing it, I'd done something wrong with them too. Well, with Amber. And I didn't want Evie to feel stuck in the middle.

Will was out of the project…

I'd kissed him…

What were we going to do without a cameraman?

I stared out of the window for a long time, making those weird half-noises you make when you're on the verge of crying but haven't quite got the gusto to really go for it.

Then, I did the only thing I could do.

I pulled out my phone again, flipped it onto camera mode and told the lens everything that had happened that day.

Because if I didn't continue with this freaking project, what was all this for?

twenty-nine

Dad's words must've got through to me somehow. I woke in the middle of the night, drenched with sweat and panicking about university and exams. I'd done no work over the weekend, none that evening, spending every spare moment on the project instead.

The blob that was Cambridge seemed even further away on the horizon and I needed to run after it and catch up. I couldn't throw this opportunity away. Even though I was shattered and burned-out, I had to try and not let myself down. I had to dedicate some time to thinking about the future rather than getting lost in the now. Try to play the long game *and* the short game at the same time.

The next day I buried myself in the library. I didn't want to see any sexism. I didn't want to see Will. I didn't want to honk a damn horn and have everyone look at me like I was a freak. I didn't want to face Amber.

Plus, I had so much work to do. So much, so much work.

I was so behind I even skipped my philosophy lesson to catch up on my essay. I fired off a message to Jane, asking her to take notes, and holed up in the silent area. They had these little cubbyhole desks with segregated wood partitions on each side. I draped my multiple scarves over them, making it into my own den, and got to work.

After a solid hour and a half of writing, I stretched my legs and amused myself by changing the label over the "History" section to "Herstory". I took a photo and uploaded it to our Instagram account, using #Vagilante. Then I returned to work.

More time passed. I missed English too – but the tide of work was ebbing, and I thought maybe – just maybe – I'd be able to make my art class that afternoon.

Where I'd have to see Amber…

I pummelled through lunch, ignoring my grumbling stomach. I couldn't face the cafeteria anyway. I couldn't face the jukebox, and Teddy baiting me, and everyone always looking at me, and Teddy always glaring at me and, and… Oww, I was really hungry when…a sharp tapping on my shoulder broke me out of my trance.

I jerked up. It was Evie.

It must've started raining outside because she was wearing her cute yellow mac I'm always jealous of – it was dripping with water.

"I have come to rescue you from yourself," she whispered wisely. "And I've brought cheesy crackers to tempt you away."

She rustled a pack of Mini Cheddars under my nose and my stomach lurched.

"Thanks, but I've got so much to do." I went to take the Cheddars, but she pulled them away. I turned and followed them, like a donkey following a carrot.

"Nah ahh," Evie cooed, in an annoying voice. "In order to get these Cheddars, you have to join me and Amber for an three pound all-day breakfast at the cafe."

"Amber wants to meet me at the cafe?" I tried to keep my voice from sounding too hopeful, but I failed spectacularly. Evie's face flashed with something…a slight twitch of her eyebrow – enough to let me know that Amber *didn't* want to meet me at the cafe. My stomach twisted with pain and hunger.

"She's coming." Evie paused… "I tempted her with Wotsits."

I nodded sadly. "There isn't much Amber wouldn't do for a Wotsit. Evie," I asked, "why is she mad at me?"

Evie pulled down my scarves, dismantling my little hide-from-the-world cubbyhole. She even started putting my folders into my bag for me.

"God knows," she said. "But us not hanging out together isn't normal. Plus, because you've effectively gone into hiding, I've had to deal with the Vagilante fallout all alone this morning. And let's just say there's more supportive people to have around than Jane and bloody Joel when Teddy and the whole rugby team are on Operation Gentleman."

I helped pick my stuff up and wrinkled my nose.

"What's Operation Gentleman?"

"Their new idea to piss you off. The gist of it, I think, is to act like proper old-fashioned gentlemen, to make some half-baked point about how all feminists are evil. And how it will be the death of chivalry or whatever. I'm not sure. Anyway, I tried explaining to them that I'm not the one doing the project, I am just a friend and helpful hornblower. But that didn't stop them stalking me around college all morning – opening every door for me, and taking out every chair for me. Saying 'after you' ten million times and then guffawing like a sty full of pigs. Teddy's even wearing a top hat, for God's sake."

I swung my now-packed bag over my shoulder. "So, they're like, killing us with good manners?"

"Basically, yeah."

"God – what pricks."

"I know. They followed me here. They're waiting outside the library doors."

I shook my head. The severity of Teddy's hatred… But I didn't feel like worrying about that right now. Not with everything going down with Amber.

I could see Teddy and his scrum of mates through the glass of the library doors, and sighed. I went to push through the doors, but Teddy grabbed one and flung it open for me. He bent down and gestured with a flourish of his hand, like we were in the olden days.

"After you, madam," he said, with hysterical laughter behind him. Though, because it was the rugby ladz, it was more grunty huh-huh-huh than high-pitched giggles.

I rolled my eyes. "What's going on, Teddy?"

"Nothing. I'm just being a GENTLEMAN. You know? Why? Is that sexist? You going to honk your horn at just good old-fashioned manners now?"

I chewed my lip – weighing up what to do. Was this sexist? He was doing it to bait me, for my feminist project, which was definitely sexist… But you could argue it was just good manners – which is what he was counting on.

I didn't have the strength for this. I took a breath and walked past him, but very deliberately stepped on his toe as I did.

"Oi, you little…"

I sped off – Evie at my side.

"Amber's meeting us at the cafe," she puffed.

"Cool," I answered, my stomach lurching.

We skidded through the slippery corridor and squealed when we stepped out into the rain.

Amber sat stirring sugar into a blue mug of tea. The mugs here always looked dirty. Grease always seemed to cling to them no matter how much they were washed.

Evie and I had unsuccessfully shared her umbrella on the walk over. She was so short that rain had kept flying sideways into her, and she'd grumbled and complained the whole way. "Lower, Lottie! It's my umbrella."

"Sorry, I can't hear you down there."

But the laughing stopped the instant I shook my hair out

and spotted my ginger friend. She smiled shyly, waving hello. All awkward.

I hated that it was awkward.

Evie and I dripped onto the welcome mat for a moment, letting the worst of it seep out. I examined Amber in that time. Her hair had doubled in size from the rain, but she still looked so cool, as usual. Her art book was propped open, one shoulder of her dungarees hung loose. She was getting a lot of glances from all the cafe's usual suspects but, as always, she didn't notice. Amber always thought people stared at her because she was so tall – but it was more than that. The way she held herself, especially since the summer and meeting Kyle, she was the very definition of striking.

I felt a sudden swell of love for her, and hoped that whatever I'd done, I could undo it.

We sploshed over, leaving wet footprints behind us. I sat furthest away, hardly looking up. Evie took over being the one in charge, which was quite a rare opportunity for her.

"Have you ordered?" Evie asked, looking at Amber's mug.

She shook her head, her lips on the rim of the cup to stay warm. "Just tea. I was waiting for you."

I made my voice more enthusiastic than normal. "I wonder what we'll order?"

Both of them giggled – Evie more so than Amber. We always ordered the same thing – the three pound all-day breakfast. It was one of the first things we'd done when we all met last year and the habit just stuck. Yes, the cutlery was as plastic as the eggs – but the portions were huge and they did add mustard to the rubbery eggs which made them taste amazing.

The waitress, an old lady with greying hair and a grease-splodged pink T-shirt, came over, smiling hello. We were regulars.

"What can I get you, girls?" she asked, notebook poised. "It's really coming down out there."

Evie and I both ordered tea, and we all requested the breakfast deal.

"Always the same, always the same," she laughed, writing it down.

None of us spoke while we waited for the tea.

None of us spoke when the mugs arrived.

We all blew on our drinks and sipped. Blew and sipped. Blew and sipped. I really did think I was going to cry again.

Then Evie said, "Okay then, girls, before we get distracted by the meat – what the HECK is going on between you two?"

Amber and I looked at each other. I widened my eyes, in what I hoped was an innocent, open way.

"I honestly don't know," I said. Honestly.

Amber met my gaze. "You don't?"

"Well, no. Otherwise I would have apologized, obviously."

I took a big gulp of my tea that was far too hot. My tongue protested, but I stayed quiet and waited for her to let it out.

Amber picked up her mug, didn't sip from it, put it down again. "Ahh, okay then," she eventually said, pushing her bushy hair off her face. "I'm angry with you about how you handled Saturday."

"What about Saturday?" I played dumb, but I reckoned I knew what she meant now. Everything had been fine until we got to the pub.

"The Megan thing. You were...well...you came on way too strong in the toilets, Lottie."

"I did?" I didn't think I had.

"You really did. I was practically wincing."

What had I said? I tried to remember. I wanted her to tell someone – that was all. But that was a totally normal and appropriate thing to want.

"I was just trying to help."

Amber crossed her arms. "Yeah, I get that. But you come on a bit much sometimes, you know?"

"Obviously I don't."

Even though I wanted us to be friends, I still felt all prickly. There's something about people decimating your character – even if it's just the tiniest bit – that puts you on edge.

"Don't be pissy with me."

"You're the one being pissy with me. You've not spoken to me in days!" I said.

"I needed to cool down."

"From what?" My voice was louder. I didn't mean it to be – but it was definitely louder.

"From you."

I found myself standing up, and Evie was suddenly up

too – waving her hands and saying, "Hey hey hey hey."

The food arrived then and we sat back down. Three plates of grease, sausages, beans, grease, eggs, bacon, grease, and some dubious looking tomatoes were shoved unceremoniously in front of us, along with a silver holder of white toast triangles. I grabbed a slice and took a bite. I really was hungry...

Nobody said anything until Evie did. She'd separated out all the food on her plate, so none of it touched. And she'd asked for hers without beans. I wasn't sure whether to bring it up. I probably should, as she didn't usually do this and you had to keep an eye out for new bad habits of hers, but I couldn't face starting a row with her too.

"Amber?" she said, her voice all soothing. "What are you hoping to get out of this conversation?"

Amber's face was all red, blending into her hair. I suddenly didn't like her – just a flash, but a big one. And it made me scared and sad. Why was she being like this? She was staring at me too – neither of us really eating, half my toast in crumbs down my jumper. I widened my eyes again.

Then the spell broke and she threw her head back. "Argh, Lottie. Stop puppy-dog-eyeing me! You're so hard to stay mad at!"

When her head came back, she was smiling.

"I'm not puppy-dog-eyeing. Okay, maybe I am a bit. But I still don't get what I did!"

Evie took both our hands, like she was marrying us.

"Why don't you take it in turns to speak? Lottie, really try

248

and listen to what Amber's saying. And then, Amber, you need to hear Lottie's side too."

We all giggled at the awkwardness. "You sound like frickin' Kevin," Amber complained. Kevin was Amber's stepdad who lived in an American summer camp with Amber's mum. He was a very cheesy American counsellor type. "The next thing you're going to do is get out a Speaking Rock."

Evie speared her sausage with a fork. "We can have a speaking sausage? You're only allowed to talk when you're holding the sausage?"

"But you won't eat it after that," I protested, not if we'd touched it.

"Oh yeah, screw that." Evie took a bite of her sausage. "Just – go on – be adults. Take it in turns to speak."

I looked over at Amber, bracing myself for the personality assassination. I honestly didn't think I had the strength to hear it. I felt so droopy and crumbled.

"This is weird," Amber started, not looking at me. Then she looked up, blushing still. "Okay, Lottie. I'm sorry I've been avoiding you but…well…the Megan thing really got to me. I think sometimes you only see the world in terms of what *you* would do in a given situation…"

I opened my mouth to object, but Evie took my hand and squeezed it to stop me.

"And you forget how strong you are. Not everyone is as strong as you, Lotts. And your way isn't always the right way. It's only the right way for you – does that make sense?"

I didn't nod or shake my head. A million comebacks

flashed right up in my brain – but if I said them, I'd only start another row.

I didn't have the energy to row.

"I know you think Megan should tell someone, even just us, properly about whatever has happened. But it's her choice what she does. And actually, I feel like it's quite anti-feminist that you're pushing her into a certain 'way' of behaving."

I bit my lip. This wasn't fair. None of this was fair. And I had no idea where it was coming from.

There was a silence, while I gripped Evie's hand. Amber coughed, looked embarrassed, and said, "Okay, so I'm done talking now, Drill Sergeant."

"All right…so…" Evie took another bite of her sausage. I'd hardly eaten my food – it was probably getting cold. I felt sick. "Lottie Bottie?" Evie said. "It's your turn."

Half of me wanted to just placate Amber, to smooth over this fight so I wouldn't have to worry about it any more. The other half wanted to demolish her own personality – give HER a little lecture on everything that's wrong with HER… see how she liked it.

Do I roll over or do I fight? With one of my best friends?

I chose a fifty-fifty response.

"I'm sorry, Amber, but I don't agree," I said, forcing myself to look at her. She didn't seem surprised though. "Megan's seriously upset about something and I think it's really important that she tells someone about it. I'm not trying to frogmarch her to the police or anything – but, like, the other night, to me, that was a cry for help. You don't ignore those."

"I didn't ignore—" she started, but Evie shushed her.

"Come on, Lottie's talking. And I've eaten the speaking sausage."

"Thanks, Evie."

The whole thing felt so forced, and I couldn't believe it had come to this. I couldn't even remember what I'd said in the pub toilets the other night. I certainly hadn't grabbed Megan in a headlock and shouted in her face... Not like Amber was making out.

"I really don't think I came on that strong," I continued. "I'm not going to force her to do anything – but I am going to encourage her to open up."

Amber opened her mouth to protest and I lost it then. Totally lost it. I burst into sobs – startling everyone. The rest of the cafe gaped at us. I was so exhausted, so fed up with having to keep it together. I seemed to be making an enemy of almost everyone at college, I couldn't make enemies of my best friends too.

"Can we please not fight?" I begged. "I honestly think it's so unfair, SO UNFAIR, that you're being so harsh with me. I haven't done anything wrong. And I've got enough on, Amber! This project – it's already killing me and I'm hardly halfway through..."

As I wiped away tears, I saw both Evie and Amber goggle at me – their mouths open. I don't tend to cry a huge amount, so I guess it's always a shock when I totally freefall.

"What?" Amber said. "But you seem fine."

I shook my head miserably. "I'm not fine. It's horrid. It's okay when you guys are there, and the rest of the FemSoc girls. But I have to do a lot of it by myself, in class, with everyone staring at me. Everyone's rolling their eyes, like I'm nuts. And it's exhausting – there are so many bad things! I can't relax for a second. And I know I can't let anything pass, because everyone's looking at me, waiting for me to slip up, secretly hoping I'll fail so they can all jump on it and demolish me…" I thought of last night, and a big tsunami of extra crying hit me. "And now Will's dropped out, so we don't even have a cameraman."

Their open mouths fell opener.

"What?" Amber said. "He's dropped out? Why?"

Evie was shaking her head. "That's so typical of him," she muttered.

I nodded. "He quit last night… We went out for dinner, to celebrate the newspaper interview…then…we kissed… and now he's quit."

Their mouths were like giant holes in their faces now.

"You kissed him?" Amber said.

"Why?" Evie asked. "I mean, like, why? It's Will."

I shook my head into my hands, pressing my palms into my eyes to stop the crying. I felt so weak and stupid and miserable.

"I don't know. It just happened! You know I've got a soft spot for dramatic liaisons. All this stress must've caused a relapse." I looked up, right at Amber. "I'm not that strong,

Amber. I'm not… I thought maybe I was but this thing is cracking me up. So please don't start a fight with me, not now, not until this month is over. I'll lay off Megan. I don't agree with you, but I'll back off…"

Amber was smiling. Then she wasn't on the other side of the table any more. She was hugging me, getting her scarf in my fried egg.

"Oh, Lottie, you stupid thing. Why didn't you tell us you were finding it so hard?"

I squeezed her back in relief, in huge seeping blisters of relief. We hadn't sorted it, but maybe, just maybe, we could park it for now.

"I didn't realize until last night…then everything went wrong…"

Evie's arms were crossed. "I still can't believe you kissed Will!"

"Yes, I know. I'm a traitor."

"No wonder he was in such a foul mood in film studies this morning."

"He was?" Annoyingly I wanted to know. Some part of me inside stood on hind legs, panting for more knowledge. I pulled a face, trying to suppress it. Damnit – that meant I liked him. What was WRONG with me?

"Yes. Even more so than usual. Like, I know he's attractive and everything, Lottie. But seriously, do you think it's a good idea to be with someone like him? With all you're going through?"

"Yes, no! I know! Look, I'm not proud of myself, okay?

You know what I can get like. Anyway, if it's any consolation, I pushed him off and called him a prick – does that help?"

The two of them grinned. "Mildly. Kissing him though… I thought you had better taste," Amber said.

"Oi!" I bashed her with my elbow. "Does lecturing me on my taste in boys mean we've made up?"

She pretended to think about it, putting a finger to her chin, then grinned and hugged me again.

"You've got to tell us when you're hurting," she said. Which I took as a yes.

"That's the point I'm trying to make about Megan," I whispered, into Amber's bag. She went a bit stiff, then softened again. I knew then we were okay. The relief flowed through me like hot rain and – for the first time since the weekend – I felt like I had a scrap of fight left in me.

Evie, never wanting to be left out, joined in the hug. We split apart and returned to our breakfasts. My hunger had returned with a vengeance worthy of the Old Testament and I shovelled the almost-cold meat into my mouth with a lot of happiness.

Evie took a sip of tea. "Lottie," she said gently. "If this project is upsetting you – you don't have to continue it, you know?"

"Yes." Amber nodded. "We'll have your back – no matter what you decide."

"It's not like we have a cameraman any more, anyway," Evie added.

I put my knife and fork down, wiping my mouth with the

flimsy paper napkin. "I can't, you guys. We've come so far... it's going to be in this week's newspaper, for God's sake."

"So?" Evie shrugged. "It's not worth wrecking your health over."

I chewed the inside of my lip. "Other feminists have put up with a lot worse," I said. "Like the suffragettes – they got force-fed and jailed..."

And, in the end, it had all been worth it. This had to be worth it. It had to be. And now my friends were back on my side, I had the strength again. Strength to keep going.

"I'm fine, girls, seriously," I said. "We can just record things ourselves on our phones. Screw Will...I can do this. It's only two and a half more weeks. Just, can you both promise not to get mad at me? At least until this is over? I can't do this without you."

Evie squeezed my hand again, smiling all warmly, to promise she wouldn't.

Amber, however, was examining the bottle of ketchup.

"Amber?" I prompted. "Are we okay?"

She pulled a face. "Yes, well, I thought we were. But, Lottie, you've gone and nabbed all the ketchup!"

The rest of breakfast-lunch was good – well, after I'd gone up and asked for more ketchup. As we stood to pay though, I noticed the table by the front door. It was littered with tabloid newspapers – the cafe left them there each morning, for customers to read while they were eating.

Today's were typically terrible. Giant boobs on at least two front pages, under the pretence of news. I opened one up, and saw a barely-clothed woman practically on every page.

The girls halted when they saw what I was looking at.

There went the nice breakfast routine.

We didn't need to speak, they knew what I had to do. My stomach twisted in on its greasy contents...protesting... *Don't complain here, I like it so much when you come here.*

But a deal was a deal was a deal.

Amber shook my shoulder in a comforting way.

"We've got your back, Lotts. Even if they won't let us come here again – do what you need to do. We're here."

I let out a deep sigh, hugged them both.

Then I took the papers up to the nice old lady at the counter to complain about them.

thirty

The week went by easier with my two spinster pals by my side. And Megan was really starting to come out of her shell too. Our rule to only call out everything once made college less horrible. By the end of the second week, I'd pretty much honked my horn at every song on the jukebox, started rows with every teacher and, well, had more than a few run-ins with Teddy. He kept up the Gentleman flashmob for two whole days, until Megan had the genius idea of sneakily putting pink glitter in his top hat.

Will avoided me the entire week. I hardly saw him. Just a flash of his glasses one lunchtime, but by the time I looked properly, I could only see the back of his head slinking down the corridor.

I wasn't sure how I felt about what had happened. Gutted we'd lost such a good cameraman, but Megan had a surprisingly good eye. Especially when we spent one boring lunch hour at the newsagent having a honk-a-thon as we went through all the women's magazines.

"Look at this." Megan pointed at one particularly bad weekly glossy, with her phone in the other hand. "They have an actual article here about this new eating disorder they've invented called 'Health-orexia'. Because, you know, punning on anorexia is totally fine. Anyway, they've said how awful it is, and how this one woman actually died... but look..." She flipped the page. "Next page...look at this fashion shoot. YOU COULD FIT A THIRD LEG IN THE GAP BETWEEN THIS MODEL'S LEGS!? How is that not totally promoting eating disorders? What hypocrites!"

"Hello, Megan," I said pointedly, blown back by the volume of her voice. Usually she half-whispered stuff.

She laughed and covered her mouth, blushing. "I'm sorry. You're rubbing off on me."

"Don't apologize." I was so happy to see her like this. "And you're right about the magazine." I honked my horn and then apologized to Mr Keats, the shop owner, who I'd explained my project to. "It's like, dudes, pick a side. You can't be both!"

And we'd laughed, and my stomach had felt warm, with a new friend being made.

On Friday, things felt different.

The moment I walked into college, I felt eyes on me. Many of them. And people had mostly stopped staring after week one.

Evie and Amber both had first period free so I'd had to walk in alone. Which is normally fine, when people aren't staring at me.

What had happened now? What was wrong now? My world-weariness was back in an instant. I just wanted the weekend to come so I could hide – apart from going to Oli's party.

It didn't take me long to find the posters.

I'd forgotten the local newspaper came out on Fridays.

By the looks of the crappy photocopy tacked on the college corridor, good old Dan had given my story an entire page. But that was all I could really tell, as the rest of the photocopy had been altered by "hilarious" graffiti. The photo of me had a moustache and devil horns added – because Teddy *(it soooo had to be Teddy)* had the creativity of a shrew.

The headline had been pasted over too, with the "hilarious" alternative *LOCAL MAN-HATER SHAGS CATS*.

You know, actually? I had to admit that was pretty witty for Teddy.

I ripped the paper down off the wall. But, looking down the corridor, there were loads more. My heart just sort of… died then. It felt like it missed a few beats, and I wanted to lean against the wall and maybe cry. Because, you know what? I'd never been in a paper before. And yes it was only the crappy local, but now my first memory of this would always be that it was Photoshopped to make me look like an idiot and taped all over college.

I walked to my philosophy class – ripping each one down as I passed it, trying to ignore the looks, the whispers, the giggles. When I pushed through the door, Jane and Joel looked up – all pretending they didn't know. Jane smiled and beckoned me over, and I smiled and sat next to them.

"You all right, Cat Shagger?" Joel asked, just as Jane went, "Joel!"

He grinned and leaned back to retie his long ponytail. I grinned back.

"I'm good. Just…erm…sore…those cats can be really scratchy when they're in the mood."

A few people behind me laughed, alerting me to the fact that the whole class had been listening in and knew everything. I plonked out my books, and kept myself to myself through the lesson. When the bell came, I went to seek Evie and Amber.

They were at our usual table with Oli, who'd moved his chair closer than necessary to Evie's. I waved at them, and they all waved back – Evie the most enthusiastically. She stood up, and waved something over her head.

It was the newspaper.

"You're famous!"

I signalled I'd seen her, then quickly grabbed a Coke from the machine. Lots of people were still looking at me. Some random yelled "CAT SHAGGER!" across the room and a wave of laughter rippled towards me. I felt a bit sick.

I took a deep slurp, the sugar and caffeine hitting my bloodstream, then sauntered over like nothing was wrong.

Evie was practically jumping up and down. "Lottie, you're famous! You're in the paper! I've never known anyone in the paper."

"Yep, and I'm apparently a cat shagger," I replied.

"What? Was it you that guy just yelled at?" Evie asked.

"Have you not seen these?" I reached into my bag and took out the collection I'd ripped down.

Amber grabbed one. "Oh my God, no! Who would do this? I bet it was Teddy, that little runt…"

I nodded sadly. "It was definitely Teddy. It's a miracle you guys haven't seen them. I only managed to de-poster the old building."

Oli coughed – his face turning pink. "Umm, I took these down this morning." He reached into his backpack, removing a hefty wedge of posters.

I picked one up. "You ripped these down for me?"

Oli turned red, and coughed again into his hand. "Yeah, well, they were all over the art block on my way to graphics this morning. And, well, I didn't think it was very nice, so I took them down and…phmfft—"

I was hugging Oli. I was already round the table, hugging him tight. He was pretty slender, so I'm quite sure I was hurting him.

"Thank you SO MUCH," I said, finally letting him go.

He'd now turned purple, and when I risked a glance at Evie she was staring right at him, all sorts of longing and goo in her eyeballs. I could totally see what she saw in him. He just radiated goodness – and yes, though it shouldn't matter, he was very good-looking. All cheekbones and angles and green eyes – I mean who really has green eyes in real life? Oli did! He was too…tame for my liking, but I wished I could shove them together. Evie was definitely "well" enough for a relationship now, I reckoned – whatever "well" means. And Oli seemed much better too. I made it my secret mission to ensure they pulled at his upcoming party.

"It's okay," he stuttered. "Any time…I think it's cool, what you're doing."

That prompted Evie to get excited again. "Lottie, have you not seen the real newspaper story?"

I shook my head, taking another sip of my Coke and slumping in one of the uncomfortable canteen chairs.

"It's really good! Like, *really* good. I don't know what you said to that journalist, but he's not stitched you up ONCE."

She dumped the paper in front of me, open to the page I was on. I was on page three – THREE! I looked good in the photo – that was the first thing I noticed because…well… cognitive dissonance. I was holding up one of Megan's amazing posters, and doing the "WE CAN DO IT" pose, from that Rosie the Riveter poster.

The headline was huge, and said: *TOP STUDENT TURNS FEMINIST FREEDOM FIGHTER*, and a smaller headline underneath read, *Schoolgirl Lottie spends a month fighting sexism to highlight how unequal our town is.*

"Woah," I said, "this is awesome."

I was just about to start reading the actual article when two people arrived at our table. One very excited Megan: "Have you seen? My poster? They've used my poster!"

The other was – unexpectedly – Will.

He sat down next to me, all wound up, radiating energy. "Lottie, have you seen the coverage? It's brilliant! Even more so than I thought it would be."

I raised an eyebrow and gave him A Look.

"Umm, Will, aren't you supposed to be avoiding me?"

He shrugged it off, fumbling to get out his camera. My stomach did all sorts of things it shouldn't. The fact he smelled incredible didn't help matters.

"I was," he said, into his camera. "But I'm not any more."

Evie was smiling. "Couldn't keep away from the glory, could we?"

Will ignored her, and began setting up.

"What are you doing?" I peered at the paper to see what had actually been written about me.

"I want to get a shot of you reading the news story for the first time."

"Right…" Even though it wasn't very feminist, I started combing my hair with my fingers for the camera. "So, you're back in then?"

"Yep," he answered, like there was no arguing about it.

"So, are you going to apologize then?"

He looked up at me – right into me. And the intensity of his eyes made my stomach have further quivers. Just a hint of his arrogant grin played on his top lip.

"Are you?"

God, he was good at this! At challenging me, at making me want to do things, despite all my moral objections. Why was power, and people not giving in to you, so annoyingly attractive?

I shook my head stubbornly, and he proper smiled then – like he didn't expect anything less.

"Well then, me neither. Now, come on, let's try to get this in one take."

I'd forgotten, briefly, why we were all here, what this was all about. But I was snapped back to the present by Amber coughing violently and saying, "Sorry, excuse me, I'm just allergic to all the sexual tension in here."

I scowled at her. Will's smirk grew smirkier. Evie pushed the paper towards me. "Go on then, read it! It's great!"

Aware that Will's camera was now running, I gingerly picked up the local newspaper and began to read aloud. "A determined schoolgirl has launched a month-long project, promising to call out every single incident of sexism she sees," I began. I looked up. "That's an okay start, isn't it? Though I'm not sure why he's calling me a schoolgirl? I, like, turn eighteen in a month...anyway..." I turned back to it. "Pretty Charlotte Thomas says she hopes her Vagilante campaign will inspire a new generation of feminists, highlighting just how much girls have to put up with in today's society." I slammed the paper down. "Pretty?!" I shouted. "Why the fuck has he mentioned that I'm pretty? What's that got to do with ANYTHING?"

Will's voice came out from behind his lens. "You're going to complain about the sexism in a complimentary article about you tackling sexism?"

I slammed the newspaper down again. "Too right I am! What the hell? Seriously?" I looked at it again, found another problematic sentence and jabbed my finger at it. "Oh my God, look here." I went to read again, this time putting on a silly voice. "'Lottie, who says she's currently single...' WHAT? Why has he even mentioned that I'm single?" I was turning red with pure rage. This was ridiculous. I kept rereading it to check I wasn't hallucinating due to too much Coke. I scanned the rest of the piece. There was good stuff, stuff I probably should've been really chuffed with – he'd spelled my name right, he'd put a full link to our channel and hashtag, he'd even written a breakout box detailing the history of feminism! And yet, yet, sexist words kept peppering all this good work. I looked right into the lens. "This is really disappointing."

"Most people would be pleased with that sort of coverage, Lottie."

"I get that," I said. "But do you not see how it's ruined? It's like he listened to everything I said and then totally ignored the thing I'm fighting against! Did he think just because he's given my cause all this positive publicity that it's okay to make judgements on my appearance? To tell everyone I don't have a boyfriend? Would I have been put on such a prominent page if I had a face like a baboon's arse with explosive diarrhoea?" Evie winced at that description.

"Or would they have shoved me at the back with the announcements? If I was fat would I have even been put in the paper at all?"

Evie grabbed the paper back and checked the copy herself.

"Oh God, you're right. Sorry, I didn't read it properly. I just got so excited that you were in the paper."

I dug out one of Teddy's doctored versions and held it up to the camera. "At least it's nicer than this one, that's been plastered all over college."

Will's camera clattered to the table. "What the heck is this?" He stared at it like it was contaminated.

"You mean you've not seen them?" I tried to keep my voice chirpy, though, to be honest, just a glance at one made me want to go to bed for a very long time.

"Who did this?" The veins on his annoyingly fit forehead were bulging, as were the veins on his annoyingly strong-looking clenched fists.

I shrugged, pretending it was nothing.

"Who do you think?"

"Have you told Mr Packson?"

"No, not yet."

Amber was scrutinizing it now, her eyebrows drawn together. "How does one even go about shagging a cat? I mean, I don't know if it's humanly possible."

And with that awful mental image in mind, we started to laugh at the ridiculousness of it. I looked at them all, Megan still saying, "Well, I'm sorry, but I'm pretty chuffed my poster is in the paper." Evie and Oli pretending they weren't looking at each other. Amber sketching a speech bubble onto Teddy's doctored posters that said, *How does one even shag a cat?* And, Will, who'd picked up his camera and put it away – and was just giving me this look. Unashamedly. Like he liked me. Like the being angry at me part was over.

With all of them around me, my team, my crew, the pain from that morning lessened. I knew it would come back. But, for now, we just all laughed. And I felt like I could get through the afternoon – which was a start...

thirty-one

We got ready for Oli's party at Amber's house.

"Now…" I sat Evie down so I could apply her eyeliner for her. "Here's what you need to do. You get there, tell him his birthday present is outside, take him down an alleyway, then shove your tongue into his mouth."

She winced so much she messed up the perfect cat-flick I'd created.

"Lottie, no! I am more romantic than you."

"Megan? What do you think?"

I heard her giggle behind me. "I think only you could have the confidence to pull that off."

I grinned, and licked the end of a cotton bud to wipe off the wonky bit. "How is that not romantic anyway?" I asked Evie.

She eyed the cotton bud. "Please don't put your spit on my face."

"Oops, sorry, I forgot." I went and got a fresh one, dipping it carefully into eye-make-up remover this time.

Evie saw the guilt on my face. "Sorry. I just…you know…" She looked up at Megan, who was suitably confused. "Oh, I have OCD," she explained. "I'm all right, but I'm not the biggest fan of germs."

"A year ago I would've loved to have heard that," Evie said, smiling beneath me, the brave wonderful guru that she is. "But I'm getting better at being open about it."

"To be honest," I butted in. "I don't think people *without* OCD fancy my gob on their face."

Megan winked. "Will does."

I wiped up the smudge and climbed off Evie to get mascara. My heart did this annoying flutter when Megan mentioned his name but I pushed it back where it came from. It was nice to have Megan here – she'd agreed to come after I'd found out The Imposters had a gig somewhere else that night.

"I think Will would snog himself if he could." He definitely would as well. In fact, I was sure he'd kissed himself in the mirror at least once. He'd actually been round mine till late the previous night. The newspaper article had got him super excited, and he'd wanted to edit my response to it right away. We'd spent the night sprawled on our stomachs – refreshing the newspaper's website. My story, by ten p.m., had become their most viewed article.

"This is the start, Lottie," Will'd kept saying. "This is the start."

Hits on our channel had doubled too, and kept climbing. By the time it got to midnight we were practically asleep, in semi-spoons on my bed, lazily refreshing the counter. We hadn't kissed again. But we also hadn't had another fight…

I hadn't looked at the views today though. I honestly, really, wanted a day off. I'd hardly left the house all day, sleeping in late, and then trying to get all my art coursework done to keep Dad off my back. I'd pulled a few late nights and he'd noticed the light on under my door when he got up to go to the loo once. There'd been another Talk.

"Will would definitely snog himself…" Evie paused. "I bet he's tried to suck himself off," she added thoughtfully.

My mouth dropped open.

"Evie!"

She looked up, all innocent. "What?"

"It's just…I never…" Rude things didn't come out of Evie's mouth, like, ever. She was insanely well-mannered, and hardly ever swore.

"Megan, did this just happen? Did you just hear what I heard?"

Megan had actually put her hairbrush down in shock. "I heard."

"What? He blatantly has!" Evie protested.

I dropped the mascara. "We need to tell Amber about this. Instantly." I climbed off her lap and went for the bedroom door.

"You can't!" Evie called after me. "She's videotiming with Kyle."

"He needs to know this too."

I bashed out of Amber's door and followed her voice to her dad's bedroom. He and Amber's stepmum were both out, and had taken her bratty little brother with them.

I heard an American accent floating through the door and smashed through it excitedly.

"Guess what!" I announced to the back of Amber's head. "Evie just said something DIRTY!"

"Hang on," Amber said. I took that as an invitation to come crashing alongside her, and waved madly into her computer.

"HI, KYLE. YOU'RE LOOKING VERY AMERICAN TODAY!"

There was an exceedingly good-looking boy on Amber's screen – all white teeth and strong of jaw. Kyle – who was used to me invading their private video conversations by now – smiled, showing off more white teeth and waved.

"Well, hello, Lottie."

"CAN I TELL YOU WHAT RUDE THING EVIE SAID?"

At that, Megan and Evie appeared at the door. Megan holding herself up against the door frame with laughter, Evie with only one eye done. "Hey, it wasn't THAT rude."

Amber and Kyle managed to share a look between them, even while thousands of miles apart.

"What did she say?" Amber pulled them both in so Kyle could see them too.

I could see Evie turning bright red on the tiny square of us at the bottom of the screen. "She said Will was so in love with himself, she thinks he's probably tried to give himself oral sex." I waited for a reaction. When I didn't get enough of one, I yelled, "SHE USED THE PHRASE – SUCKING HIMSELF OFF."

"What?" both Kyle and Amber said at the same time.

"Have you been drinking?" Kyle asked.

Evie nodded, all ashamed of herself. "Just some wine… and well…some more wine."

We'd shared three bottles between us getting dressed. It was mostly, well, entirely, my fault. I'd stolen them off my parents, from their huge store under the kitchen sink, and had had almost a whole bottle to myself.

Kyle's all-American smile beamed at us through the internet connection. God, Amber was lucky. Okay, so her gorgeous hunk of a boyfriend lived thousands of miles away, but he was still one gorgeous hunk of a boyfriend. "You wasters," he laughed. Then he spotted Megan, who was barely in the frame in the corner. "You must be Megan," he boomed in his deep voice. "Amber's been telling me all about you."

"Hi." Megan blushed instantly, as Kyle really did have that effect on people. "Nice to meet you. Does this count as meeting you?"

"I think so. How d'ya do?"

Amber snorted. "Kyle, you really do say the most American things sometimes."

"What?" He lifted up his arms and I tried not to look because you shouldn't really fancy your friend's boyfriends

272

if you can possibly help it. "Who's Will anyway, Lottie?"

"Lottie's new conquest," Amber answered. "He's the cameraman for this project I was telling you about."

Kyle nodded. "Oh yeah, Lottie. Amber said. That sounds awesome."

Did I mention Amber's gorgeous hunk of a boyfriend is a gorgeous FEMINIST hunk of a boyfriend?

"THANK YOU," I yelled. Because I always get a bit excited in the presence of Kyle. "And Will is NOT my conquest."

"He so is," Amber said.

"Definitely is," Evie agreed.

"Completely is," Megan added.

"He's not!" Though part of me liked them ribbing me about him, it made everything more real. But it couldn't be real. He was *so* argumentative.

Kyle looked unconvinced. "I think the lady doth protest too much," he said, in the worst British accent the world has ever known.

"Kyle!" Amber waved her finger at the screen. "We've had words about that accent."

Evie, Megan and I eventually decided to leave them and returned to preening ourselves. Amber, when in America, had been educated by Kyle in the wonders of country music and had brought back loads of new bands for us to listen to. We were currently obsessed with one in particular called the Dixie Chicks and played one of their albums for Megan. Though they had this one song called "Goodbye Earl" where they murder their mate's abusive husband that I skipped past. We flicked our hair, and poured more wine and sang along at the tops of our voices.

I was quite drunk.

I don't drink to get drunk usually. Evie, and particularly Amber, were way worse than me. I usually only had two, to feel all warm and buzzy, but then would get excited by whatever was happening and forget to drink any more. But everything had been so nuts – I just wanted to forget and be in the present, to have fun to…whoops, I'd just knocked Amber's precious face powder onto the carpet with my arse.

"Shit," I stumbled about, trying to get all the powdery bits back in.

Evie was at my side. "She's going to kill you!" She and Megan bent down to help me. "This is the pricey one, the only shade pale enough to match her face."

"Shut up and help me hide the stain with a cushion."

It was easy enough, hiding stains in Amber's room – this stain just blended into all the other pre-existing stains. Amber was famously a slob – her room always decorated with half-eaten sandwiches, drying plates of oil paints, empty crisp wrappers. We'd just scattered a scatter cushion over it when Amber emerged, her eyes all pink.

"You okay?" I stood up to hug her, feeling guilty about the powder, though not guilty enough to tell her.

"Yeah," she said, her voice a bit snotty. "It's just…well… shitty…I miss him."

"It must be so difficult. I miss his arms already and I only saw them a few minutes ago."

Amber pulled back, grinning. I mentioned Kyle's arms a lot. To be honest, they were A-MAZ-ING. "Honk yourself, you perve."

"Argh, okay then." I dug around in my bag to pull out my trusty horn. I tripped over a pile of clothes as I tooted it, yelling, "Men shouldn't be objectified either, not even with arms like Kyle's."

We all laughed. Amber picked up the wine bottle, complained at how little was left, and emptied the rest of it into the plastic beakers she'd brought up from the kitchen. She drained hers and wiped her mouth.

"Have you seen how many hits the videos are getting? I was just telling Kyle, and we checked. Lottie, it's well over ten thousand."

My small intestine twisted in on itself. Though maybe it was my large, I had no clue which intestine was where. This was a good thing! A Good Thing. So why did I feel only dread?

"Really?" I feigned interest. "Do you have any more wine?"

Amber's face screwed up. "Aren't you excited? I mean, this is good news! The word is getting out there."

I nodded vigorously. It made my head swim. "Yeah, it's great. I just fancy a night off, you know?"

Evie, who was moussing her hair upside-down in a doomed attempt to give it more volume, whipped her head back up. "I thought the whole point is there is no night off?"

I nodded again. Oww. Whoosh whoosh whoosh.

"I know. I get that. If I see anything, I'll call it. That's the point. But, like, I also want to have fun, you know? Hey! You know what we've not done in ages?"

"What?" Megan asked, as Amber and Evie shot each other a look – one that probably suggested they were worried about me, but I'd forgotten the thought the moment I'd started having it…

"Just hung out and *not* talked about feminism." I was gabbling. "Let's do that soon! Just, you know? Chill out. Eat some cheeeeeeese."

"But, Lottie, the whole point of this project is we talk about feminism," Amber said. She and Evie were DEFINITELY giving each other a look now. Megan looked a bit lost, her expression the one you get when you realize you're not as close to a group of people as they are to each other.

"Yeah, well…it would be nice to, you know? Just have a night off…nothing…forget it…Amber, do you have any wine?"

I wasn't sure what I was saying. What I was doing. Amber, maybe reluctantly, I couldn't tell, went and stole some cherry brandy from the back of her dad's drinks cabinet. And I had two shots. Maybe three…well four…when the others weren't looking. Are you supposed to do brandy in shots? I just felt…tired…of feminism. I know. If you're tired of feminism, you're tired of life – or maybe that's just London? And I never thought I would be. I always had such a fire in my belly – burning burning burning, oww, well,

maybe that particular part of my stomach was the brandy…
but now I just wanted to not care. I had feminism fatigue.
Hey – that's cool! Alliteration! I freaking LOVE alliteration.
And, oh, where are my shoes? Is it really time to leave
already? God, it's cold outside. Good thing I'm forced to
wear these thick tights – to cover up my hairy legs.

They were so hairy already.

I was already a hairy person, even before I stopped taking
off all my hair. Shaving off…

Though I waxed my lip. You needed wax for that.

"Lottie? LOTTIE?" I was tap tap tap-dancing my way to
the party – to keep warm – and also – because if you're
looking at your tap-dancing feet, you can't see any sexism to
honk a horn at.

"Yep," I answered Amber's voice. It sounded like Amber's
voice. Still looking at my tap-dancing toes.

"I said, can we just stop at Megan's house here? She
forgot her phone. Is that okay?" She was in front of me, in
my tap-dancing path, looking at me. A warning in her eyes?
Maybe, it was Megan. We hadn't agreed on what to do about
Megan.

Though – awful as it was – tonight I didn't want to make
Megan do anything. That would require effort, caring –
things I didn't have the energy for. Not today, not now.
Too tired.

We waited while Megan dashed into her house,
apologizing. "Sorry, I left it to charge and forgot to bring
it out."

I still can't believe Teddy made those posters...

"I think she's quite wasted," I heard Evie whisper.

"I CAN HEAR YOU."

"All right then." Evie stopped whispering. "Lottie Bottie, you are superiorly drunk."

"I'm not drunk, you're drunk."

"That is the most typical drunk-person thing to say ever."

"You would know, drunky."

"Oh God." Evie sighed, then she looked past my face. "Did you get it, Megan?"

Megan's face was there – attached to Megan's body, because that's what faces and bodies do.

"MEGAN!" I ran at her, with my arms open. Slamming into her for a hug.

We all got in a line to walk.

Walking is hard.

My entire mouth tasted of slightly-off cherries.

"She needs some water when we get there," Amber was saying.

"You can bring the horse to water, but you can't make it drink!" I yelled, laughing at myself, slapping my thigh, which is actually quite hard, to be honest, if you're standing up and walking at the same time.

We were at the pub now. It was bright. It was noisy. It was packed.

We squeezed through people to get to the back room. Oli had hired the back room. That was SO Oli. He was so organized like that.

"I hope he's okay," Evie whispered to me, forgetting that, yes, well, I was probably too drunk to be confided in right now. "I mean, Lottie, he didn't leave the house for a year. A year! Now look at this. I'm so proud of him!"

And there was such love there. In her voice. It was subtle and soft, but, oh, the love. It oozed out of her and it was so pure that I welled up. Because I'd never been in love, not really. I'd been in lust a lot. But love…the way Evie was talking…I wanted it. I wanted to feel like that…

I was clasping her face. She didn't seem that happy about it. I was doing it anyway.

"Evie, schonestly, you gots to schtell him how you sfeel." Why was my voice coming out like that? That's not how my voice usually came out.

Evie's clamped-in face stared up at me. "Oh God, Lottie. Let's get you some crisps."

"I like crisps."

I liked the idea of crisps so much that I let go of her face.

She looked waaaay more grateful than she should. I wasn't clamping it that hard. Just a minor clamp.

People were greeting us – Jane, Joel, Ethan – God, Ethan was funny. Oli was making a beeline for us. Not us, Evie. Amber was at my side. Megan was saying something. But I kept just saying, "Crisps crisps crisps, let's all get some crisps."

The bar was so crowded – three deep. I couldn't wait that long for crisps.

"AMBER, I CAN'T WAIT THAT LONG FOR CRISPS."

She was sighing. Looking worried. Looking annoyed.

"How are you so wasted? What is going on? I leave you in my room for ten minutes…"

The crowd moved forward. Was there a band playing? The music was loud. So many people. So many people in the way of my crisps.

And then a smell. A good smell.

Expensive aftershave smell.

The sort of expensive that means you can also afford lots of camera equipment.

Will. Will's face. Saying hello. Talking to Amber rather than me.

"What's wrong with her?" he was saying, looking concerned. His eyebrows all up behind his glasses.

God, I liked his glasses.

"Will," Amber was saying. "Your feminist is broken."

thirty-two

He took me to a tiny room behind the bar.

He bought salt and vinegar crisps.

Everyone knows they're the best crisps.

"This is ridiculous," I kept saying, crisps in my mouth. "I'm not drunk. I just really need some crisps."

"Lottie, you do realize it's not even eight o'clock?"

"You're lying. It's way too dark to not be later than that."

"It's winter, Lottie. The sun sets at, like, five."

This wasn't a room – more a cupboard. There was even a mop. And boxes upon boxes of crisps – all stacked on top of each other.

Light came blasting into our cupboard, with the large silhouette of Amber. This made me greatly happy.

"AMBER," I yelled across the tiny room. "I'VE FOUND THE CRISPS!"

"Holy Jesus, she is beyond wasted," Amber replied, not to me, but to Will. She then dropped to her knees to study me.

"Lotts? How much cherry brandy did you have?"

I did? Cherry?

Oh yes. Ouch. It burned. But in a nice way.

"MORE THAN YOU." This was hilarious. I started laughing.

Cherry. Cherries were hilarious.

Will and Amber were looking at each other.

"I think she needs to go home," Amber said, biting her lip.

What? No?

"Agreed. But it's only, like, eight."

"Lottie?" They both turned to me. "We think you need to go home."

"No YOU need to go home." I tried to stand up, but my centre of gravity shifted and I found myself sprawled on the ground, everything hurting.

"My ankle! It hurts."

More muttering above me. "I would take her. But Megan's ex-boyfriend has just turned up. He wasn't supposed to be here and she's burst into tears and run into the loo…" That was Amber talking…about Megan. Max was here? Max wasn't supposed to be here?

Megan!

I tried to stand.

"I can help her!" I fell over again. "Let me talk to her, I can help her!"

They were ignoring me. "Jane's looking after her at the moment, but things are…complicated…I need to be with her…could you…would you mind?"

"I can take her home."

NO – not Will. Not him walking me home. I didn't want to go home. I'd just got to the party! But then…then… bed…lovely bed with no one looking at me and judging me and waiting for me to slip up and thinking I'm crazy and taking the piss out of me and saying I'm an attention seeker…and…yeah…home…that would do nicely.

I heard Amber hesitate. "She's very drunk. You won't…"

Another pause. By this point, I'd managed to get up onto all fours, and was now teetering on the brink of standing up.

"I won't what?" Will said, his voice super pissed off. "Take advantage? Is that what you're hinting at? For fuck's sake! Who do you think I am?"

"I'm sorry, but I don't know you very well."

"Not all boys are effing rapists. God, you girls! Give us some credit. And you wonder why I don't take your side."

I carefully stood up straight. I was up! Uppity up!

"VOILA!" I announced, breaking their argument. What was it about anyway? I couldn't remember. I stood up for – oooh, let's say three seconds, and then, like the leaning tower of Pizza, I fell to the floor again.

"You're okay taking her then? Sorry. For what I said. It's just, well…look at her…I'm worried."

"I'LL BE FINE JUST HERE," I was yelling.

"She's a funny drunk," Amber was saying. "She'll be okay. You'll have plenty of time to come back afterwards."

I was being lifted now, and the strong scent of Will's aftershave overwhelmed me. His arms felt strong, lifting me onto my feet like I was a rag doll.

"You all right, Lottie? I'm going to take you home."

Vaguely remember walking back through the pub.

Vaguely remember saying, "Thank you so much for coming, thank you thank you, it means the world to have you here," to people as I passed.

Maybe there were looks. I can't remember.

I was used to looks by now.

Vaguely remember, through the crowd, seeing Evie and Oli. They stood, their noses almost touching, both smiling slowly at one another. It was like someone had taken a photo of them, and everything around them had gone hazy.

They were so in love.

Something had happened.

And I felt just this incredible warmth in my belly with happiness for her, mixed with a terrible sadness for myself that I wasn't touching noses with someone...and I also felt suddenly very ill indeed and the back of my throat tasted like sour cherry...

Outside. I was outside now.

God, it was cold.

Will guided me, leading me off the road and back onto the pavement. I didn't feel ashamed, I was having quite a good time actually. I hadn't seen one incident of sexism...

Hang on...

Will was walking me home.

That was sexist. Damnit! Would it never just go away?

I stopped in my tracks, making him collide with me.

"You can't walk me home." I crossed my arms around

myself, stumbling as he wasn't holding me up any more.

"What? What are you talking about? Come on."

"No." I stood stubbornly, like a donkey. And no one can move a donkey once they've decided they want to stay put awhile. "It's against the rules."

"What rules?"

I couldn't really make out his face, everything was too blurry. Half of it was orange from the streetlight and it reminded me of the other night, in the car park, how we'd kissed.

It had been a good kiss.

But there was no time for that.

"The project," I said. "This is sexist!" Half-arsed fuzzy thoughts belly-flopped into my hazy brain. "I mean, why is it safe for men to walk around in the dark, but not women? It's a way of controlling us! Of keeping us indoors, of hiding us away. We're told we always need to get home safe, we're told not to walk alone, we're told not to make ourselves vulnerable... We're always so scared of being attacked, being raped – when really, we're statistically much more likely to get raped in our own houses so it's all a FACADE. YOU CAN'T CONTROL ME!" Not sure why I was suddenly yelling, but I was. "I have to walk home alone. It's in the rules."

Will shook his head.

"Screw the rules, Lottie. You're wasted. I'm taking you home. It's nothing to do with you being a girl, it's all to do with you being twatted. You can give the project a rest for tonight anyway."

Tears sprang up in my throat. "But I can't," I whimpered.

"That's the whole point."

Will wasn't moving, and I wasn't going to slip up. Nah ah. No-sir-ee mister. I was COMMITTED to this. I would be INFALLIBLE. I...I...I know...I'll do a runner.

And suddenly I was running, past Will, past the row of shops that was our mediocre town...run run run...all alone...all independent...I was sticking to this project...I'm not sexist...I can get home by myself...oww my ankle... keep going...God, it's quite scary doing this, isn't it? I hope I don't get murdered...hang on...no...that's just the patriarchy talking...but jeez it's dark and...and...

"Lottie, wait up, you pain in the arse!"

I looked over my shoulder. Will was chasing me – his striped shirt flapping behind his skinny frame. He was faster than me. Less drunk.

I was very aware I was drunk.

"No no no no," I yelled behind me. "You can't catch me..."

I was laughing, laughing as I ran...Will catching me up...but I didn't look back...

"Lottie, you're a total loon," I heard him gasping.

Maybe I was. But I hadn't caved, and he didn't catch me up. Not completely. Eventually we found a rhythm. Me stumbling about, dropping things out of my bag, Will running five metres behind me, cursing under his breath and picking up all the debris I left in my wake. My purse... my phone...my special eyeliner...and soon it became a game – both of us gasping with laughter...

Will followed me all the way home.

thirty-three

Sleeeep.

Lovely sleep.

Lots of lovely sleep.

And it's so comfy here and dark and warm and nice nice snuggles. Yes, my pillow smells all stale and strange for some reason, but let's turn it over now and go back to sleep.

Sleeeep.

thirty-four

I woke to a sharp knocking at the door.

"Huh?" I lifted my head, all disorientated. Oick. That hurt. Why?

Hang on...

Last night. Hazy last night. It all came crashing back to me, like someone pouring an ice bucket of water over my head.

Ooooh, that would be quite nice right now actually. Ouch.

Another rap at the door. I tried to call "Come in", but it came out like a groan.

"Lottie! We're coming in!"

It was Amber and Evie's voices. What were they doing here this early? I hadn't been that bad, had I?

I mean, yes, I'd had to leave a party before nine o'clock in the evening, but everyone has had to do that at one time or another.

The door opened and there stood my two best friends – looking surprisingly perky and yet quite worried at the same time. Amber held up a two-litre bottle of Coke – making her the best human being that's remotely possible.

"Lottie?" They peered at me, all grossed out. I hadn't even lifted my head from the pillow. I was just staring at them, all lying down in the smelly dark, like when Jane Eyre's mate dies at the beginning of the book. "Your mum sent us up. She didn't say you were still asleep."

They stepped over the threshold and I tried to scrabble myself into an upright position, rubbing my eyes. Feeling sleepy and disorientated and, yes, well, bloody hungover too. My mouth made itself extra dry at the sight of the Coke.

"That better be for me." I reached for it, like a frail old person who's been found lost in the bush. "What are you guys doing up so early?"

They shared another look of all meaningful meaning, then turned back to me.

"Umm, Lottie," Evie said slowly. "It's gone one in the afternoon."

What? How?

"It's not nice to tell lies, Evie," I said to her.

Her eyebrows furrowed. "Have you been asleep? Like, all this time? And I'm sorry, but can I open a window? No offence, but it stinks in here."

I shook my head in bafflement as Evie desperately stepped on me through the duvet to get to my window. She threw the curtains back, letting in bright winter sunshine and I cowered back as my eyes adjusted. While Evie opened all my windows, Amber busied herself with going downstairs and getting three plastic cups for the precious Coke. When she came up, I'd finally managed to get myself upright, though I was still holding a hand up to my eyes to protect them from the sun. Evie had done a quick grossness sweep of my room – piling bits of my stuff into the corner, making the air clean – though I think it was more for her benefit than mine. I was counting the hours I must've been asleep. I was unconscious by, like, nine.

Nine, twelve hours until another nine...ten..eleven... twelve...one...SIXTEEN HOURS. I'd been asleep for sixteen hours! And it wasn't even like when I've been drunk before, and you wake up dying at 5 a.m., have to drink ten glasses of water, do an almighty pee, whimper and take aspirin for a few hours and only THEN go back to sleep.

Oooh, wee. I really needed a wee.

I rolled out of bed. Literally rolled, onto the carpet and then tried to push myself up from there. Which wasn't the smartest of ideas because the floor is lower than the bed was.

"Hang on," I told my friends, who were staring at me like I was a circus freak. "I just need to wee and de-ming. Then you can tell me why you're here."

Because I hadn't really thought why they might be here.

I peed, splashed water on my face, smelled my hairy armpit, winced, and decided to have a super-quick shower so Evie didn't relapse from the sheer grossness of me.

Ten minutes later, I felt vaguely more normal – though still totally spaced out from all the sleep. I came back to my room with a towel wrapped around my head.

Biscuits had been acquired. Lottie and Evie sat cross-legged on my bed, sharing custard creams and Coke.

I smiled and went to sit with them. Amber handed me a glass of Coke and I took it thankfully, picking up a biscuit in my other hand.

"So?" I asked, spraying crumbs all over the bed. "What's up? Why are you here? Do we need to do FemSoc planning or something?"

They shared yet another look and then Amber put her half-eaten biscuit down and I knew something serious had happened.

My eyes widened – shit. What could it be? Was it Megan? I had weird rehashed half-memories from the night before. Amber saying something about Max turning up...was she okay?

"What? What is it?"

Evie answered. "Lottie, we're worried about you," she said simply.

What? Why?

I closed my eyes to take in what she'd said.

They were worried about me.

THEY were worried about ME?

It was never that way around. I was the sorted one, the groovy one, the sunny one. I was never the one other people worried about. I was applying to Cambridge. I was going to change the world. I was always absolutely-fine-thank-you-very-much-how-are-you?

Evie launched in, filling the silence, "Don't take this the wrong way. It's just because we care. But, Lottie, you seem quite different this week, and we think this project must be catching up on you. And it would be weird if it didn't catch up on you – what with Teddy being the way he is, and all the stress you have about university, and Megan – we're all worried about Megan."

"How was she last night?" I interrupted. I didn't like hearing what she was saying. I didn't like thinking it was me she was talking about.

I was Charlotte Thomas. I was a fighter. I was strong. I didn't take any shit…

Amber answered, her biscuit left discarded half-eaten on my duvet. "She's okay…well…as okay as you can be, considering what we think might've happened. She sort of lost it a bit last night when Max turned up… Their gig slot got changed so they dropped in to say hi to Oli. I thought it was going to be a major drama. But she just, like, vanished into the loos for ten minutes, crying hysterically. Then when she came back it was like nothing was wrong. She was totally fine the rest of the night…although she did majorly keep her distance from him." Amber looked down at her biscuit. "You're right, by the way, about her. I think she needs to talk to someone. I just don't know who it needs to be. Like, we don't know her that well yet… But I think she lost a lot of friends in the break-up from Max, we might be all she has... We walked home together..."

It was Evie's turn to interrupt. "But we're not here to talk about that. Not right now. Lottie, we're here to talk about you. What's going on? Why did you get so wasted?"

I shrugged. "I'm fine. I just probably needed to eat more dinner beforehand or whatever."

"Don't lie to us," Evie scolded. "It's us, come on. What's going on with you?"

And the sympathy and honesty in their eyes made me wilt... I flopped back onto the bed – rerunning through the whole evening, which, admittedly, didn't take too long.

"I dunno what happened," I said. "I guess I'm just...so tired. Of all the bad stuff I'm having to constantly monitor and call people out on, because I know everyone is just waiting for me to slip up. It's just, like, all merging into one, you know? Don't tell anyone, please don't tell anyone, but I feel like I care less, rather than care more. Does that make sense? Like, I'm not angry any more, I'm just knackered and can't be bothered." A lone tear escaped my eye and slid down my cheek before I had time to wipe it away unseen. "And I'm fed up with everyone at college looking at me like I'm a pain in the arse, like I'm not fun any more – I'm just this angry shouty thing..." I trailed off. Feeling like the universe's biggest traitor to feminism everywhere. But also...also...so relieved to have said it that half of my tummy relaxed.

I looked up at Evie and Amber – waiting for the judgemental looks, the disappointed drop of their bottom lips.

But I'm stupid, because they're amazing, so of course they just looked worried and each took a hand.

Evie's eyes were all open and earnest. "Oh, Lottie! We were researching it online this morning, what's been going on with you. We think what you're feeling is an actual thing."

"What do you mean, a thing?"

Amber nodded, her bushy hair thudding side to side. "There's a word for it. It's called Activism Burnout. You've just described all the symptoms."

I tried to understand what they were saying... It sounds up myself, but it wasn't usually this way round with me and them. I was always the teacher... Now I felt broken and they were stepping up.

"So other people feel like this?" I asked slowly.

They both nodded. "Yes! There's even, like, special psychotherapists who are also campaigners who treat full-time activists to stop them going cuckoo," Evie said.

"Do you really think I've gone cuckoo?" I gasped.

I was fine. Totally fine.

Evie – the experienced expert in the ins and outs of "going cuckoo" – very tactfully said, "We think you may be on the edge...which is why we've come round."

"To tell you that you can stop," Amber added. "That we will still be your friends and we will still love you if you decide enough is enough and calm this project down."

My mouth fell open in utter horror. "Stop? No, I can't stop."

"You can," Evie said. "The world won't end. I promise you.

I've been convinced the world would end many a time, but the world has this irritating habit of continuation…"

The thought of bowing out… No no no. My brain just rejected it straight away.

"No," I said, very determinedly. "I'm not giving up. I'm in this for the long haul."

"Even if it's impacting your mental health?" Amber asked.

It wasn't. Well, it was. But it wasn't.

"I'm fine," I insisted. Which wasn't true but it wasn't untrue. If I couldn't last for two more weeks, what did that say about me? Especially about everything I wanted to do with my life, everything I needed to change. I could not be one of those people who break quickly. I couldn't, I couldn't. "Look, I know I'm not acting fine, and maybe I'm not TOTALLY fine – but who is? Yes, okay, so I'm tired and scared and angry, but at least I'm doing something about it. I was tired and scared and angry before I started this thing – that was why I started it. It's hard – it's been much harder than I thought, and I'm terrified that we're only halfway through – but I'll be fine. This is like my salvation, you know?" I smiled. "Caring too much is what's breaking me, but it's also what's mending me, if that makes any sense?"

Both of them were smiling – maybe I'd convinced them. Maybe I'd even convinced myself.

"Good," Amber said. "But if you have a wobble like last night, ANY wobbles at all, you are to call us, okay? We are here for you…especially now…" She turned to Evie. "Shall we show her?" she asked.

I lurched forward. "Show me what?"

Evie nodded, a grim look on her face, though with hints of a smile underneath. Something was up – but what was it? Evie reached into her coat pocket and got out her phone.

"What is it?" I pressed.

"It's your video channel," she said… She pulled up the channel homepage on her screen. "It's umm…taken off… I think the newspaper story has spread."

She turned her phone to me and I took it with shaky hands. I blinked. I blinked again.

"Umm, girls?" I said. "Since when did this have over one hundred thousand views?"

Amber was wringing her hands. "Since yesterday. Have you turned on your phone yet? I think you'll have some missed calls. It's…well…this thing. It's all over the internet."

I dived for my phone on my bedside table. The battery had gone, so I plugged it in, waiting for it to load. The moment I pushed the on button, it lit up like a pinball machine – buzzing crazily in my hands.

Missed call. Voicemail. Missed call. Message. Missed call.

"Guys, my phone is possessed." I looked at it in horror.

"Yes, well, some of those missed calls are from us – asking how the hell you are," Evie said. "Thanks for turning your phone off."

"The battery died," I answered, dialling my voicemail. "Who are all these from anyway?" I pressed #1 for loudspeaker and we all put our heads together to listen.

"Hi, is this Charlotte Thomas's number?" A sharp voice cut through the stifled air of my bedroom. "My name's Clare, I'm a reporter for *The Guardian*. It would be great if you could ring me when you get this message…"

"Oh my God!" I dropped my phone onto the duvet. "OH MY GOD OH MY GOD OH MY GOD." But I had no time to properly react before my phone clicked onto another message.

"Hello, Charlotte Thomas? This is Stanley calling from *The Mirror*. We would love to talk to your about your project, give me a call back on…"

"Hello? Charlotte? Jack here, from *The Sun*. Do give us a call back. We can pay you."

"Hello? Charlotte Thomas? My name's Nora from the BBC…"

Evie, Amber and I just looked at each other – not saying anything – our eyes all bulgy.

"Have you looked on your Twitter?" Evie eventually said.

"No." I grabbed my phone again and pulled it up. My notifications showed over a hundred messages. Never in my life had my notifications been even in double digits. I only ever really got replies from Evie and Lottie and the rest of FemSoc – usually with links to sleepy pandas or whatever. Apart from that one time when Caitlin Moran replied to me and we'd all run around Evie's bedroom screaming.

All of them were basically the same thing.

@LottieIsAlwaysRight Hey, can you follow me back please? I'm a reporter and would love to DM you about your project.

"Guys?" I looked up at my friends. "What's happening?"

Evie took my phone, staring at it like she'd never seen Twitter in her entire life.

"Lottie?" she said. "Are you sure you're not burning out? Because I think you've just set a lot of things on fire."

WEEK THREE

thirty-five

We were on a train to London.

"I can't believe I'm missing another day of college," I said, as we whooshed past fields full of cows. "I've got a Cambridge interview prep session tomorrow and I've not done any of the reading."

Amber stretched back and put her legs up on the empty chair opposite. "You are almost as relaxed about Cambridge as Evie and I are about university. Which would be fine, except IT'S CAMBRIDGE."

"I'm not relaxed, I'm just distracted," I argued. "And you guys are allowed to be relaxed. Your applications aren't due till after Christmas. I guess, if I don't get in, I'll hopefully get into one of my backup options. Maybe…" Or maybe I'll mess up my exams so much I won't get in anywhere.

None of us spoke about uni much – I think all of us were a little bit in denial about being separated. Well, I was the most in denial. Amber and Evie were both staying local –

Amber planned to do her art foundation year, and Evie wanted to stay at home and commute to the nearby university Dad worked at "just in case of a relapse". I was the only one being separated really, and the thought made me almost hope I messed up my interview so I wouldn't have to leave them.

"I'm nervous," I told the girls…plus Will, who was reading the newspaper. "Evie. Please tell me the story of you and Oli getting together again to take my mind off it."

Evie raised an eyebrow. "Again? Seriously?"

"Yes please. I need happiness to hold onto, to help me forget the fact that I'm about to humiliate myself in front of the whole country."

Amber tried to help me breathe. I hadn't even realized my hand was flapping until she caught it.

"You'll be fine," she said. "You're Lottie. You're frustratingly charismatic, even on no sleep. Everyone will love you."

I looked right into Will's ever-present lens. He'd closed his paper and started filming again. "What do you think?" I asked him, through the eye of the camera.

The camera wobbled in a nod. "You're going to be fine. You've totally got this."

My tummy wasn't just in knots, it was in those kinds of never-ending knots you get when all your necklaces decide to orgy in your make-up bag during a flight to a holiday somewhere. Sweat dripped off me, despite it being, like, minus two outside. The cows in the fields flashing past us were so cold they were huddled together like penguins, and yet the sweat still came. My heart felt like it was everywhere else in my body apart from where your heart is supposed to be.

"Evie!" I demanded. "Take it from the top!"

She sighed and started telling the story again. I relaxed as I let the now-familiar words roll over me and started to smile, watching the countryside roll on by in a blur as we chugged our way towards the capital.

After Amber and Evie told me that Operation Vagilante had exploded, we'd spent a good hour panicking about what to do. We'd then rung Will, who'd run over in Sunday jogging bottoms and made me confused by how good he looked all sweaty. Will had been amazing. Within twenty minutes he'd worked through all the calls, telling me which ones were and weren't good opportunities. "Don't ring back that one, they'll just want you to take your clothes off."

"What, even with my hairy legs and moustache?"

"Umm…actually…"

He came more alive than I'd ever seen him. There was this manic energy to him – rather than the sloth-like arrogant judginess of a demeanour I was used to. It suited him. Plus, he'd wasted no time in making Evie and Amber wet themselves by recollecting how I'd run away from him ("like some pissed-up feminist gingerbread man") the night before. After another hour, and many, many phone calls, I had a "publicity schedule" for the following day. We'd picked one pre-recorded TV slot that would go out that evening, one "major broadsheet" and one "tabloid with a heart".

"Let the others fight over the scraps," Will had said, like that made *any* sense. When he'd eventually left – leaving me quivering with dread, nerves, enthusiasm and lust – the three of us were able to catch up on normal girl things. Like Evie and Oli FINALLY getting together!

Evie not-very-reluctantly told the story again to us and some nosy people in our carriage. Almost as soon as we'd arrived at the party (and I'd already been decanted to the storeroom to eat crisps and sober up), Oli had taken her by the hand, led her away just the two of them and said, "I don't want to ruin my night by spending all of it kicking myself for not having the courage to do this," and THEN HE'D JUST KISSED HER. Like a fucking movie star! Now they were instantly together. Because, well, we'd all known they'd been effectively together the past year, since she'd got better (and he'd got better too). And they'd finally allowed themselves to embrace the inevitable.

Evie couldn't stop smiling and it took me away from my insane fear and insane jealousy. Her phone also wouldn't stop going off – with sweet messages from him. The retelling of their romantic bliss took most of the forty-minute journey to London Victoria. Megan messaged, to ask how it was going. We'd invited her along but she had a presentation she had to do for sociology and promised to try and cover for us attendance-wise. Amber was on the thinnest of margins still, and I knew I'd struggle to catch up on yet another day's missed work. Cambridge and the interview was just this blob of hardness in my guts that I kept trying to pretend wasn't there. But I had a training session the next day with Mr Packson to help me prepare, and I hoped that would be enough to pull me up to speed.

"Hoped" isn't a strong enough word sometimes…

When the train eventually groaned itself in, we collected up all the mess we'd made and emerged out of the ticket barriers into the packed arrivals hall. The others ushered me to the Tube, a coat pulled up around my head like I was a celebrity. "Just keep your eyes on the ground," Will instructed. "There are too many armed anti-terrorist police around for you to go berserk with a horn right now."

When we got to the Tube, the police presence decreased and I abandoned my coat enclosure. According to the electronic sign, there was only one minute until the next train. I looked down the stretch of Tube platform. Advertising billboards were everywhere.

"Amber," I said urgently. "Sharpie."

After a quick rummage in her bag, a pen was in my hand.

"Just keep it casual," I said to them. "We don't want the cameras to pick up on what we're doing."

A distant rumble signalled the train arriving, so I worked fast. A weight-loss advert for Christmas got a scribble of *You're lovely the way you are*. A poster for a new Christmas film called *Miss Claus* – depicting some blonde Photoshopped actress leaning over in a tight sexy Santa suit, with loads of minimally-dressed female elves behind her – well, that got a scribble too. I drew a messy speech bubble coming out of Miss Claus's mouth that said, "*All I want for Christmas is equal pay for female actresses in Hollywood.*"

"*Voilà*," I said, just as the rumble of the train turned into a roar.

Evie and Amber applauded politely, while Will got some quick close-ups of my handiwork. The Tube doors opened and people poured out onto us. We waited till it had emptied somewhat and clambered on.

"Where are we going?" I asked, as we sat down on the brightly-patterned seats.

"Umm, Oxford Circus, I think." Will strained his neck to look at the sign.

At Green Park, some guy got into our carriage and sat next to Evie, even though there was lots of room elsewhere. He was chewing gum, wearing some shiny suit, and without even clocking our existence, he stretched his legs right out – like he was sacrificing his crotch to the gods or something. Evie's legs instantly squished against mine as she readjusted to make room.

She looked at me.

I looked at her.

I turned to Will.

"Your camera on?"

He nodded, that same hint of a smile on his face that I'd interpreted to mean he was resenting my awesome.

I got up and lost my footing a bit as the Tube jolted. Then I walked past Evie and sat on the other side of shiny-suit man.

I yawned, all dramatically, and aggressively opened my legs as wide as my skinny jeans allowed. My legs were so wide my hip joints actually cried out in a *Lottie, we don't bend that far* way. I had the force of momentum on my side and knocked his leg out of the way, like we were playing French Bowls or something. Just to up the ante a bit, I let out a huge manly groan – all primal.

Shiny Suit looked at my incoming legs in utter shock – his eyebrows drawing up into his gelled hair, his bottom lip falling ever so slightly open.

I bet no girl had ever fought him for leg-space in his life.

We caught eyes and I nodded at him. But not normally. All lad-like, *we're all blokes here*. A macho nod.

"It's nice, isn't it?" I grunted. "Feeling like you deserve all this space?"

I could feel the seats shaking with the girls' muffled laughter.

Shiny Suit did not know what to do with himself. But he drew his legs closer together.

I used the opportunity to spread mine wider.

I was relying heavily on the fact that people in London are willing to accept just about any kind of weird or rude behaviour, just as long as they aren't late for work.

So far, it was working. Shiny Suit looked horrified, and yet he said nothing.

"This is so great, isn't it?" I said. "Really airs out your bits?"

A large snort came from Amber's direction.

Shiny Suit's eyes opened wider, but still he said nothing. The Tube slowed. "This is our stop," Will called.

I closed my legs and stood up, staring the man down, who was determinedly looking everywhere but at me. Evie and Amber could hardly stand, they were laughing so hard.

The doors beeped and slid open, revealing a huddle of people waiting to clamber on board.

"Lottie," Will warned.

I leaned over and said very calmly and politely to the man, "Maybe be a bit more mindful about how far you spread your legs, mate." God knows why I'd just used the word "mate". Acting male was rubbing off on me very quickly.

I didn't wait to see the look on his face before I turned and jumped down onto the platform, the girls and I holding each other up, we were so hysterical.

We emerged onto the polluted, crammed bustle of Oxford Street – inhaling the fumes of about ten million buses.

We were discussing the Tube episode with Will. Who was playing devil's advocate, as per bloody usual.

"I'm just saying," he said, "I'm not sure it's a sexist thing. I mean, it's uncomfortable having...you know..."

"A penis?" I provided, and felt a surge of joy when he blushed slightly.

"Yes," he confirmed. "And balls..." It was my turn to go red. "I sit like that all the time! It's uncomfortable having to keep your legs closed."

Amber rolled her eyes at him as we dodged past the scrum of girls clamouring to get into the flagship Topshop.

"Yes, well, do you think it's comfortable for girls to be constantly squished up against the wall just so you can air your balls? Is your comfort more important than ours? Evie, where are we going?"

Evie, who was on smartphone-map duty, poked at her phone, looking lost.

"Erm – maybe that way?" She pointed up a side street. We took her uncertain words as gospel and followed the direction of her finger.

"That's not what I'm saying," Will continued. "You're muddling up my words. As usual. I'm just saying I don't think it's deliberate. It's just, like, what guys do for comfort. It's not intentional."

We'd just passed three gorgeous-looking coffee places in a row but I resisted the urge to go in. Coffee always made me over the top, and I was fizzing inside enough as it was. In fact, my stomach felt pretty determined to empty itself and I hoped there would be a loo at the BBC studios.

I was going to argue back, but decided to save my energy for the interview. With a nod of my head, I let Amber at him instead.

"It doesn't matter that it's not intentional," Amber ranted, her hands up in the air with anguish. "This is the whole point…"

And her rant took us all the way – including a wrong turn and a backtrack – to the BBC Broadcasting House.

We all stopped and looked up at it – causing at least four annoyed business-type people to thump into us and tut.

I felt so ill.

It was huge. The building stretched upwards in a giant horseshoe – gleaming all green and curvy and important-looking.

"Woah," Will said. So stunned the argument ended. "Lottie, this is the real deal."

Then, without making any big drama about it, he took my hand – entwining his fingers with mine. The touch shot electrical currents all up my arm, sending tingles to everything. My heart began beating even faster than it already had been.

To distract myself, I reached out and took Amber's hand. She looked at it, smiled, then she reached out and took Evie's.

We all stood there, in a line, staring up up up at a place that had the power to tell so many more people than our tiny town what we believed in and why it was right.

"I'm going to mess this up," I said, my voice catching in my throat. Fear rendering my vocal chords useless, which is very un-bloody-helpful when you've got a day full of interviews in front of you.

"No, you're not," they all said, at exactly the same time, like magic.

thirty-six

"How much make-up do you use on the male presenters?" I asked the make-up artist.

"Umm, they still get a bit of powder but that's about it," she answered, scraping my long dark hair back into a headband.

"Then that's all I want. A bit of powder."

She furrowed her eyebrows. "You sure? I'm booked in to do you for forty minutes."

"I'm sure. Just top my face up with powder then we're good to go."

She picked up a teeny tiny brush and sucked on the end of it, which didn't seem very professional to me.

"Your left eyeliner flick is wonky," she pointed out.

"It will be fine," I reassured her.

I'd done my own make-up that morning and was determined to stay looking like me. Not some professionally-coiffed version of whatever the media wants a young feminist to look like. Also, I needed a lot of attitude and eyeliner – to look like Lottie. The few times Mum and Dad had made me groom properly for a wedding or something, it was always terrifying to look at myself. I'm pretty – the sort of pretty that feels unfair. Like I've lucked out too much. If I didn't backcomb my hair and shovel eyeliner on, I looked so symmetrical and as-girls-are-told-they-should-look that even *I* hated me. I did not want that version of me all over the papers and TV. I didn't want to be a "pretty" feminist. I didn't want to make it that easy for them.

I'd been to the toilet twice, and still felt like I had another four trips in me. Getting inside the BBC had been like entering a spaceship. Glass walls grew up to higher than I could tilt my head back. We'd had to give our names at this ginormous desk, sign in, get given special visitor IDs and wait for "Jane" from "Hospitality" to let us through the security doors.

Shortly after, I was separated from my friends.

"Girls, Will, come with me. You can see Charlotte afterwards. We've given you front row seats."

"What? They can't come with me?"

We'd hugged ferociously, and I'd welled up – like we were saying goodbye for ever.

"You're going to be amazing," Evie whispered, with me and Amber in a headlock of a hug.

"You will," Amber promised.

I held onto their words like they were precious pearls. But backstage, all alone, I felt them roll out of my hands and get lost in the corridor.

Will had given me a stiff hug goodbye, and I'd hung on longer than was probably appropriate. "You'll be fine," he'd said into my ear, making all the hairs on my neck stand up. "Just be the annoyingly intelligent, charming, rampant feminist that I know you are."

And I'd clung even tighter, and made myself very confused about something that had nothing to do with the fact I was about to go on national television.

Now I was being powdered and told I wasn't going to meet the presenters until the moment of the actual interview. Some lady dressed all in black explained what questions they were going to ask. She'd clapped me on the back when I'd explained my project and said, "Brilliant, I wish I'd had the guts to be you at school," which filled me with a temporary glow that everything might be okay after all.

But now, with a bored make-up artist sitting on the chair in front of me, I was beginning to lose faith.

"So, why you here today?" She began the laborious process of putting all her brushes and pots back into her giant case.

"They're, umm…I've been doing a project," I said. "A project about feminism. And, well, our hits are almost at one hundred and fifty thousand."

The lady – through my haze of nerves I vaguely remembered her telling me her name was Gill – carried on packing up her stuff.

"I'm not a feminist," she said. Just like that – straight out there with it.

"Oh, can I ask why not?"

She glanced up, but looking at me differently, like suddenly it wasn't so friendly any more.

"Because don't all feminists hate men?" she said. "I don't hate men. I love them! I love my boyfriend, I love my dad—"

I interrupted her. "Feminism isn't about hating men. It's not about that at all. It's just about equal rights."

She didn't look like she was listening, or maybe she was listening but not taking it in. She was very trendy – with a pierced eyebrow and tattoos all up her arm. "I guess I just don't feel the need for it, you know? But good luck with your interview."

I looked at this woman. This perfectly nice woman who also happened to perfectly disagree with everything I was about to go on TV to say. And I knew there'd be others like her out there. And they might not be as polite. And they'd be watching and disagreeing and thinking I was disgusting or wrong or messed-up or lonely or mentally ill or bitter or a slut or a prude or a killjoy or a whinge-bag or a bra-burner or a yeller or a lesbian or a man-hater or an attention-seeker or maybe just even a teenager. Either way, whichever bullshit label they wanted to give me, they were going to stick it on me. I wasn't in my nice little Spinster Club bubble any more – where the only people who didn't agree with me were a spurned rugby player, girls like Jenny, and some arrogant cameraman who really needed to stop being so annoyingly attractive. I was about to walk onto a stage, in front of a camera that would transmit the very essence of what I believed as a human person all around the country to other human persons who might just think I was an uptight idiot.

I wasn't sure I was ready for that.

To be judged. Tested. Held up as a shining beacon of what I cared about the most.

What if I screwed it up? What if I didn't make sense?

"Oooh, love, we need to touch up your powder already, you're dripping."

The lovely-but-unfeminist make-up lady came at me with a poufy brush, dabbing my damp forehead. The edges of my vision vanished.

"Are you okay? Hang on, help! I think she's going to…"

Everything went black – just like they tell you it does when you faint.

thirty-seven

The producer, Chloe, was awfully nice about it.

"Happens all the time," she said, handing me a glass of water. She'd come all the way out of her important room to check I was okay.

"I don't usually...do that."

She smiled a warm smile. "You don't normally go on national television."

"Oh don't remind me, you're making it worse."

She laughed as she scribbled something down on her clipboard. She was cool-looking, wearing jeans and Converse, with a big woolly jumper.

I was beginning to get the feeling back in my fingers. My breathing was returning. Though my body was still acutely aware it was about to get shoved in front of a camera while I ripped open my soul and bled all over the purple sofa.

Did souls bleed actually?

And if they do, what colour is the blood?

Hang on, that's not a helpful thought right now.

"Thank you for being so nice about it," I told her.

The warmth of her smile radiated off me so much I could almost have got a tan.

"You think you're going to be okay to go on? We need you in ten minutes."

Ten minutes. Ten of the Queen's minutes. Hang on, was it just pounds the Queen had? Oh dear, fuzzy brain. Candyfloss brain. This would not do. I couldn't expect to be prime minister if I went totally goo-goo the moment I got any publicity.

"I'll be fine," I said, sounding just about as confident as I was – which wasn't much.

"Good. I'm really excited to watch your piece, Lottie." She took my glass away from me and put it down on a table. I hadn't noticed it shaking in my fingers. "I'm the one who suggested we book you. I love your project. God, I wish I'd had your guts when I was your age."

I looked up at her slowly. "You...you do?"

She nodded. "Girl, you're fearless."

I was?

"You're just what we need. I'm so glad you're doing what you're doing."

Her smile was tanning my insides now – my intestines would need aftersun, she'd made me feel so warm, and strong and, more importantly...right.

"Thank you," I squeaked.

"Now, you ready to meet Jordan and Sue?"

Jordan Gold and Sue Phillips were the presenters. I'd watched them countless times through my TV – they were always on in the background of my life. Jordan was famously a "silver fox" – everyone always commented on his shiny grey hair. Sue couldn't get mentioned in any newspaper without the word "curves" being used. She was the body shape tabloid newspapers always dragged out as "healthy" or "pro real-women" – like maintaining a double-D chest with a tiny waist didn't take a considerable number of eating restrictions and trips down the gym…

Uh-oh…I was going to have to say a lot of things they wouldn't like.

Just as I was taking another quick desperate gasp of air, Chloe reached over and squeezed my hand, like we were the best of friends.

She lowered her voice to a whisper.

"Make sure you bring up the age gap," she hissed. "Jordan has never co-presented with any woman less than ten years younger than him."

It was all I needed to hear to know I was going to be just fine.

"And we're filming in five, four, three…two…" The producer didn't say the word "one". He just pointed at us, and a bright red light came on.

I was sitting on the sofa, opposite Jordan and Sue, who grinned inanely at me. The lights were so bright I couldn't see the audience – worse than that, I couldn't see Evie and Amber in the audience.

I was alone. I was sweating.

This was happening.

Jordan and Sue turned their perma-grinned faces to the cameraman and started talking, all smooth, like they'd done it a million times before, because they had.

"Now, we have a special guest with us today on the show." Sue's boobs were trying to break free from her tight wrap dress. "Charlotte Thomas's video channel has been rocketing in hits this week due to a very interesting project she's started."

"Yes," Jordan said, taking his turn on the autocue. There was a proper autocue, and me, MY NAME, was on the autocue. Somehow I had ended up on an autocue? "She decided that for a month she would call out every instance of sexism she saw – no matter how small…"

I couldn't really hear them properly. Time was slowing to sludge. Nothing seemed real. Was this real? I pinched my hand. It hurt. It was real.

Jordan finally turned to me. Yikes, his teeth were white. I was almost blinded by them. They looked just regular white whenever I watched him on the TV, but here, in real life, especially under all these hot lights, they glowed so brightly we could use them to help land planes, or stand him at the top of a lighthouse and get him to help steer ships away from the rocks and…and… Oh shit, Lottie, he's asking you a question and there's a national television

319

camera pointing at you and you can't stop thinking about his teeth.

"So, Charlotte," he said, already laughing. "I guess, if you want to be true to this project, you're going to have to tell us what you've already noticed here that's sexist?" He laughed again then, all fake and *yeah-let's-see-you-try*.

Sue tittered too. "Yes, let's get that bit out of the way, shall we? Then we can get to talking about what led you to take such drastic action."

I froze up. I couldn't say, could I?

I had to say – that was the point. That was always going to be the point.

The lights were so hot, my skin so slick. I could feel sweat powering through the thick layer of powder on my forehead, damp patches erupting beneath my newly hairy armpits.

"I…I…"

I stammered. I never stammer. I'm always about the words, the attention, teaching, preaching…

"Go on," Jordan said. "You don't have to be afraid of us. We can take it."

Could he?

I thought of Evie and Amber in the audience. I thought of Megan at college, spending every day trying not to bump into Max for whatever reason she was too scared to tell us. I thought of all the girls watching, who may've been waiting for someone like me to say things they'd always thought but had never been able to put into words. I thought of women being spoken over in meetings. I thought of girls not being able to walk to school without being leered at. I thought of girls who didn't get the chance to go to school at all...

So my mouth opened and I found myself saying:

"Well, for one, Jordan... Why are your female co-presenters always at least ten years younger than you, and never the other way round?"

thirty-eight

The pop and instant fizz of a champagne bottle opening.

Oh my lordy, Mum and Dad were actually drinking.

Dad expertly caught the stream of bubbles in the glass and poured it in, quickly swapping it for another glass as it got full.

Mum was still hugging me. So tight I couldn't breathe.

"My baby. On the telly. I'm so proud of you, Lottie."

I sank into her, so tired. So very tired. I'd been running on past-empty since we'd all collapsed on the train back from London. We'd gone straight from the studio to the newspaper office, then an interview, then a photoshoot where they asked me get out my hairy legs, then another office, then another studio.

I'd told the story of the van men sexually harassing me so many times I'd started to doubt it was real.

I'd been asked if I was single, and then had to point out

how sexist that was, so many times I wanted to stab things into people's eyeballs.

"Don't be proud yet," I said. "They may have cut me."

"Well you'd better not have missed a full day of college to get cut." Dad was half smiling, half meaning it.

"NONSENSE!" Amber appeared in a blur of excitable gingerness. She picked up some full glasses of champagne, holding as many as she could between her fingers, and turned to go back to the living room. "I watched it all. You were uncuttable… Though they may have to bleep out some of your swears."

Mum pulled away and held me at arm's length. "Lottie, no! You didn't swear on national television, did you?"

I gave her my puppy-dog eyes. "Only a few times. It just slipped out."

Dad was already popping another bottle of champagne – they really did have a stockpile under the sink.

"We didn't raise you to talk like that, Lottie," he said, heaving with disapproval.

I stuck my tongue out at them. "Your daughter is on national TV this evening, talking about inspiring positive social change. Do you really have to find the one bad thing to latch onto right now?"

Dad smiled, and I knew I'd got him.

"Help me carry these out to the others."

Our living room was pretty crowded – every available flat surface covered with Megan, Evie, and some other FemSoc bottoms. Oh, and Will, of course. Who'd been a delight all day, but went all weird and moody and sulky on the train journey home and wasn't really talking. Him and my dad instantly clicked though – as superior-intellectual types tended to do – and he'd mostly been following him around, asking him lots of questions about academia.

Megan was with Amber, both of their long bodies sprawled out on our dated rag rug. Evie had invited Oli. They sat smushed together on one of our old armchairs, hardly able to keep their hands off each other. Not in a lusty way, more an intense hand-holding and can't-stop-looking-at-you-like-I-can't-believe-my-luck way that made me feel a pang inside. A few other members of FemSoc were scattered here and there – plus Jane, who was latching onto me because she didn't really know the others.

My piece would be beamed around the country at 7.30 p.m.

The next day, I'd appear in two national newspapers...and then maybe more than that if all the others copied the story.

Somehow I had made all this happen.

I dispensed more champagne. It was 7.25. We'd already screamed and whooped when Jordan and Sue had mentioned me in the "coming up" section.

Megan twisted round, beaming. "Mr Packson lost his nut when you guys all didn't come into college today."

I tried to hush her with my eyes, but Mum had already heard.

"Oh no, Lottie! You didn't tell the college you were off?" Megan's eyes widened with apology but I shook my head in reassurance.

"There wasn't time," I said. "Plus, I have practically one hundred per cent attendance. One day off won't hurt. Especially as I was nice about college in one of my interviews."

"Still though, Lottie," Dad butted in, from his place on the superiority sofa with Will. "It isn't a good time."

I felt myself flush red. Did we need to do this now? With, like, six of my friends listening in?

"I'm more than aware that it isn't a good time," I said slowly, trying to keep my temper. "But this is something I had to do."

"AHHHH!" We were interrupted by Evie squealing. "Lottie!"

I whipped round to the screen and there, there I was. The whole room erupted into high-pitched squeals even dogs would have had trouble hearing.

Every organ in my body stood to attention and I felt like I was hovering above myself somehow.

"Lottie, it's you, it's you!" Amber yelled.

My first thought was, *Jeez, that eyeliner flick really is a bit wonky*, which wasn't really the point. I looked a bit dazed, as I waited for them to introduce me. Then Jordan and Sue turned to ask me their first question… Uh-oh…would they cut it? Would they include the bit where I called out Jordan and the age difference?

But when on-screen Lottie opened her mouth to talk, I saw something take over. My face suddenly relaxed, my posture became all confident, I…just…lit up… I mean,

I knew exactly what I was about to say, I'd lived it only hours ago, but I still craned forward to see it better.

I'm sorry. I don't mean to sound up myself. But I was electric!

The whole room gasped as I made my first quip about the age gap.

"Lottie, you didn't," Mum sighed. "Oh, look at his face! He doesn't know what to do with you."

"They kept it in!" Amber sang. "They ruddy kept it in. I love them!"

I could barely hear what was going on, what with the whooping, and everyone piling onto me to hug me and tell me how awesome I was. But Jordan's mouth was wide open on the screen, looking stunned that I'd gone there, and Sue was pissing herself laughing.

"Shh," Evie yelled. "We're missing it."

We quietened and tried to return our attention to the screen, but it all seemed so odd and was all going so fast. I glugged back my champagne, then reached over to the spare bottle by Dad, pouring myself another glass and glugging back some more.

We were already past their reaction to my age-difference question – Sue laughing and saying, "It's so true!" – and they were both grinning, loving me. It was obvious now that the hosts loved me, though I couldn't tell at the time.

Electric Lottie was now telling them about how she got the idea for the project – so electric. So dazzly and electric. Then I mentioned Evie and Amber, our Spinster Club, and all three of us screamed and jumped on each other. Then I brought up FemSoc and EVERYONE screamed again. Finally, they started asking about all my videos, and Electric Lottie started to talk about Will.

It was very clear Electric Lottie liked Will a lot.

My face visibly softened on the screen, and then tried to harden again. But I couldn't keep it up, and I gooed out again.

"He does film studies at our college," Electric Lottie said. "And he's been amazing. You need to keep an eye on that one. And he's been pretty tolerant considering he's been hanging around me in a permanent state of anger for two weeks."

The hosts laughed. "And so he should be!" Sue said, smoothing down an invisible crease in her tight dress. "You're doing all this for a good cause."

I was nodding. "I am. He…he… Well, I couldn't have done it without him."

Oh no. I was falling for him. Electric, on-TV Lottie and here-on-the-sofa Lottie was falling for him. Bollocks bollocks shitty bollocks.

Could anyone else tell?

I tried to look over without him noticing – suddenly all shy. With a side glance I chanced it, and his eyes met mine. Will was watching me – very carefully, very intensely. Could he tell? It was so obvious. But was that just me?

Electric Lottie had begun talking about something else but Now Lottie still stared at Will. And Will stared back. I couldn't take my eyes off him. I felt vulnerable and freaked out and also just…okay, slap me…mesmerized by how he was looking at me and what I thought it meant. He squinted, just slightly, and tilted his head with a tiny smile – one that asked, *What are we doing, Lottie?*

Then he turned back to the screen, and the moment was gone.

Dazed, I followed his lead and tried to watch the historical moment of me being on television for the first time in my life. But I wasn't following any of what I was saying.

Why do I like him? I can't like him. Does he like me? He can't like me. We argue too much. He won't openly use the word "feminist"… What's wrong with me? Why is my heart ignoring my incredibly-clever-maybe-going-to-Cambridge head? There was a gut pull, deep inside of me. An instinct.

Will is not what he seems.

He is better.

You know he is better.

Loud cheers and applause and everyone jumped onto me, marking the end of my TV debut. Dad and Mum were first in there, squeezing me into them.

"You were brilliant. So concise, so likeable. We're so proud!"

Megan beamed at me, happier than I'd ever seen her. "Lottie, that was awesome! You're going to have recruited about ten million new FemSoc members."

Amber had the channel up on her phone. "Oh my God, guys. We've had an extra ten thousand hits just since you were on."

Evie managed to leave Oli's side and, because there was no room left to hug my body, crawled on her belly and hugged my leg.

"You were awesome! You were already awesome when I watched it the first time. But it plays back even more awesomely."

Congratulations and cheering and more champagne being popped and Mum and Dad looking like they'd never, never be prouder – though of course they would be if I got into Cambridge – and hugs and songs and all linking arms and whooping them up in the air and where was Will? Where had he gone? Did I need to talk to him?

And, when I eventually broke free, he'd left.

thirty-nine

I woke late. My tongue fuzzy and my head heavy from last night's champagne.

Ouch. Bollocks. Ouch. I looked at my phone – I had less than half an hour before I needed to be at college for my special Cambridge training session.

Ouch. Bollocks. Ouch.

There was no time to wash my hair, so I scraped it back into a bun and dedicated the rest of my short amount of time to shoving on eyeliner and demolishing a banana. Then I flew out the door, in a whirlwind of bag and sheets of paper and clattering, glad Mum and Dad were already at work so they couldn't tell me off for being late.

I ran to college – head down, to avoid any new bus posters or other sexist items I really didn't have the time to object to.

Then I remembered…

I was in the national papers this morning…

Me. My face. My story…

But all I had time for was a quick pause and a moment to think how delightfully mad that was before I had to carry on running again.

Also, my thoughts were filled with other confusing things. I liked Will. Somehow, despite all my resistance. I really liked Will. He'd vanished last night in a way that suggested he'd sensed that I liked him.

And running away from it told me everything I needed to know.

But enough. The bell was ringing and I was still five minutes away from class on the wrong side of campus and HELLO – Cambridge interview. This was everything I was working towards, this was everything I wanted…I think.

I would not let a fit guy in spectacles, and the fact I was now a TV sensation, ruin that.

Everyone whispered as I pushed through other late students in the halls – some familiarish faces yelling, "I saw you on the telly!" and, "You were great!" I smiled but carried on dashing to class, trying to ignore the not-so-nice looks I was also getting. Finally, when I'd run to the point of hardly breathing, sweat all over my face, removing half my winter clothes as the blasting heat from the radiators hit my damp body, I got to the classroom and bashed through the door.

The quietness of the room hit me like several brick walls compared to my inner stressing.

"Welcome, Lottie," said Mr Packson in a deadpan voice. "You're late. So you're not getting into Cambridge."

He turned to the other four people in the room. Three boys I didn't know and a girl I vaguely recognized from my economics class. "It goes without saying that, if you turn up late to your interview, you're not going to make the best of impressions. Leave plenty of time. You and your parents may even want to stay overnight in a hotel beforehand to save worries about traffic on the motorway."

"Sorry," I panted. "I overslept."

"At least come up with a lie, Lottie," he laughed, gesturing to an empty chair which I fell into gratefully. "And I can't wait to hear why you weren't at college yesterday but we can discuss that afterwards."

His laughter had stopped and he'd got his very best angry face out of the cupboard. Uh-oh. He was mad. Quick, Lottie, throw him.

I looked right at him. "I was on the television," I said. "I bunked off because I was invited to go on television." Then I beamed at him, and he grinned back quickly, despite himself, before fixing me with another glare. The others stared or glared at me. I couldn't figure out which. I took my water bottle out and sucked on it hard while Mr Packson brought the attention back to him.

"Right" – he clapped his hands – "the interview process. Now, you've probably heard rumours about how hard it is. And sorry, folks, but those rumours are true. That's why we're here…"

* * *

Half an hour later and my brain was melting as I tried to keep all the new information in. Mr Packson had done a lecture, then made us practise our questions and answers on each other, and now he was giving us his final top tips.

It was going to be hard.

I'd always known it was going to be hard, but I'd just sort of assumed it would be fine, that I'd be able to handle it. I mean, I always got top marks.

But, as Mr Packson kept pointing out, we'd be up against all the other brightest students from all the other schools in the country. Essentially, at Cambridge I wouldn't be bright. I'd be average.

I wasn't sure how I felt about that…

I couldn't not get in. I couldn't, Mum and Dad would go nuts. And it was what I wanted, wasn't it? It was what we'd always had planned. I'd worked so hard, and yes, I'd let things slide these past two weeks or so, but I was well over halfway through this project now. And it would all be finished by the time I had to put on my best posh weird suit thing Mum had bought especially and go charm my way in.

The girl, who I'd learned was called Agatha, put her hand up. "So you're saying that some of them may ask us questions that they KNOW we don't know the answers to, like, deliberately?"

Mr Packson nodded. "Yes, to try and throw you. To see how you're able to think analytically, even without all the facts."

I put my hand up.

"Yes, Lottie?"

"That's not very nice of them."

I could see him struggle not to smile again. "This isn't about being nice, Lottie. This is about getting into one of the most prestigious academic institutions in the world."

"No excuse for bad manners."

He put his hands to the pressure points at the side of his eyes.

"What are we going to do with you?" I beamed harder and he carried on. "They will, potentially, ask you very obscure questions on things you're unlikely to know about. Last year, a student of ours wanting to read English Literature got asked about Sigmund Freud's early works, which is obviously a totally different subject. Your correct response to these questions?" He clapped his hands. "Be honest. Say very simply, 'I don't know' first. Cover yourself, don't try and blag it, that's what they're looking out for. Then try and answer the question based on lateral thinking. They're not always expecting you to have the answers, they just want to see what skills you have to figure things out. So this student said, 'I don't know', but then went on to hazard a pretty good guess based on the small amount she did know about Freud."

I put my hand up again.

"Yes, Lottie?" he asked wearily.

"So they deliberately ask us questions they know we don't know, to try and get us to admit to them we don't know the answer?"

"Umm…yes."

I pulled a face. "What bell-ends."

The other four looked at me like I'd just blasphemed. Even Mr Packson looked like he'd had enough.

"Lottie, let's have a chat at the end of this session, shall we?"

After a few more practice rounds, everyone else collected up their stuff and left. The bell hadn't rung yet, we'd finished about ten minutes early. My mouth was still dry from a slight hangover and I'd already downed all my water. By the look of Mr Packson's face though, I wasn't going to be allowed to go refill my bottle any time soon.

"Take a seat, Lottie." He pulled a chair up to his desk.

I slumped down and fixed him with my best look. "I'm sorry about yesterday. I got all the calls from the media on Sunday, I didn't have time to ring the office…" I trailed off when he put his hand up.

"We'll get to that later. Let's just start with how today's session went." He rustled some papers, then put them down and fixed me with a very steady stare.

"What about it?"

"It's your attitude, Lottie. Umm…well…are you sure you *want* to get into Cambridge?"

I found myself nodding before I'd even let the question sink in, such was my instinct to say yes.

"Of course I do! Why?"

It was everything – it opened the doors. The doors I needed to smash through – to get to the places, the places where you were in a position to change things…

"It's just – well – these places. Cambridge…Oxford… They're very well-established…establishments, I guess, for want of a better word. They're incredible places to study, don't get me wrong, but there can be some people there with a snobby attitude…and I guess I'm worried. Well, Lottie, come on…" He was smiling. "You're not very good at sucking up when you need to, are you?"

I stayed quiet for a moment, so I could digest what he'd said.

"You think I won't get in?"

He didn't say "yes" straight away, and my heart picked up its pace. No no no no. I had to get in, I had to, I had to. It was the plan. It had been ingrained in me for so long that I didn't even know what the alternative was.

"Well, you know your grades are excellent. Your extra-curricular activities…they won't be put off by FemSoc, I don't think… As long as you don't rant at them in the interview. And you've obviously won all those prizes…"

I blushed. Not many people knew that. But when I was at my old posh school I'd been entered into all sorts of competitions – essay-writing ones, maths ones… I always won… I had the trophies stashed somewhere in my room in a box… I just didn't like telling anybody, in case they thought I was full of it.

"But they won't like it if you go off-piste in Cambridge

interviews. You've got to play the game, Lottie. And I'm not sure, when pressed, if you're capable of that. Once you're in, great. I'm sure they'll celebrate that critical mind of yours. But will you be able to hold your tongue to get in? You know what I mean?"

I could feel the pulse in my neck thud all bulgily, *thud thud thud*, as the blood thumped around my body in panic.

Was he right? If I got a stuffy person and a stupid question, could I let it go? I mean, I'd left my old school and it was plenty like that.

All I'd ever known, all I'd ever been told by my parents, was that going to Cambridge or Oxford sorted you out for life. Yeah, there were exceptions, but everyone knew it opened the doors. It wasn't just about the prestige of the degree – it was the mates you made when you were there, those bonds. Inevitably this bunch of people would grow up and get jobs in all sorts of important places, and you'd all got drunk together in first year and pissed in a punting boat, or whatever it is you do to bond. Those friendships – they changed things.

I wanted those doors opened for me.

Not just for me. I wanted to smash through them, so I could leave them open. To let other people in after me.

Yes – maybe I sound like a wannabe feminist superhero. I guess maybe it was my ego at play a bit. I'm self aware enough to know I've got a hefty ego on me, and you can't feel much better about yourself than when you're changing the world...

"Are you okay?" Mr Packson said, and I realized I hadn't replied.

I picked at a piece of skin that had come loose around my thumb, digging my fingernail into it, trying to rip it.

"Is Cambridge…sexist?" I asked in a very small voice. "Am I… Is it…likely something sexist will happen in my interview?"

Mr Packson's face darkened. "I'd like to say no. Cambridge has a women's officer, they're pretty vocal. And King's College, where you've applied, is very progressive. Cambridge even started running consent workshops for Freshers, did you see? It was on the news a year or two ago?"

I nodded, remembering seeing it.

"But…" he continued, running his hands through the little hair he had left. "Those are the students – they're much more with the times. You may find, on your interview…the board that are talking to you…well…as I said…they're unlikely to appreciate you being a maverick. Yes, it may be only men who interview you. There are more male professors than female professors, I'm afraid."

I opened my mouth, but said nothing. I closed it again.

Mr Packson tried to smile. "I saw you in the paper this morning." His voice was softer.

"I've not seen it yet. I overslept. We were celebrating… being on TV yesterday."

"Yes. Everyone was talking about it in the staffroom. They said you did well."

I couldn't help but fill up with pride then.

"This project though. Does it run into the date of your interview?"

I shook my head. "No. It's the week after."

I could see he was visibly relieved. "Ahh, well, maybe it will be okay then."

All my thoughts were crowding in on my brain, bashing and pushing into one another. Trying to get my attention.

"I'm not going to stop calling out things that are wrong the moment this project is finished," I said.

We were startled by the bell ringing. It was always so shrill. I had art with Amber and Megan next. The bell jogged Mr Packson into action and he started collecting up his papers.

"I know, Lottie," he said. "But maybe this one day, this one interview... Perhaps you could let it slide? Pick your battles, you know?"

That's what I'd planned to do. But hearing him say it out loud made me feel all peculiar, like I'd suddenly eaten something funny.

"We'll see."

forty

I hadn't looked at my phone since I'd woken up and when I glanced at it on my way to art, I had about ten billion notifications. Just as I was about to start opening them, I spotted Amber down the corridor.

"Lottie!" She waved. Her face was…odd… Pinched, but with a smile. "You're here! I've been messaging you."

We caught up with each other and walked to class in step.

"So? Have you seen the news stories?" she asked.

I shook my head. "No! I drank too much bloody champagne and overslept. What are they like? Is it all good?"

Amber hesitated before she nodded, moving out the way for a group of stoners heading in our direction. One of them, Guy, the druggie prick who'd messed Evie around last year, turned as I stood aside to let them pass.

"WOAH – YOU'RE THE GIRL FROM THE TV!" One of his mates pointed at me like I was some kind of exhibit.

Guy – who I'd hung around with for a LOT of last year because of Evie – laughed in my face. "Watch out, dudes, it's the FemiNAZI," he said, like we were strangers. They all creased up and made the Hitler salute.

"Grow up," I told them, pushing past.

It didn't bother me, much. Well – it's not every day people compare you to Hitler but, umm, still.

"What is it, Amber?" I said, when they were behind us. "You hesitated. Are the newspaper stories bad?"

We'd vetted the journalists so carefully, and they'd seemed really on my side yesterday. I mean, yes, they were still journalists…but…

She smiled. "The stories were fine, you came across all smart and awesome as always." Amber pushed through the double doors of our art room with her back and I followed her in. We walked over to our usual spot.

Megan was already sitting down, paintbrush in hand.

"All right? How's the hangover, Lottie?"

"Hey, Megs. It's okay actually. Apart from Amber here is freaking me out a little."

Amber crashed into her seat. "It's fine. It's nothing."

"So why is your worried face out?" I sat down on my chair, avoiding looking at my canvas. Our topic for this term was "Passion", and I'd been attempting to make a photomontage/painting/3D thingy of all the women in history I admired. But, right now, it was only half-done and looked a mess.

Amber paused.

"Tell me…"

"It's just… Have you seen your phone? Have you been on our channel?"

"Not yet. I overslept and then I had this meeting… But it's been buzzing like crazy…why?"

"It's just…well… I guess I can show you."

Megan and I raised our eyebrows at each other in a *what's-up-with-her?* way, while Amber got out her phone and pulled up the news stories. Saffron, our teacher, was late as usual. I leaned over eagerly, trying to see what they'd done, the headlines they'd used for me, whether my hair looked okay.

"Ohhh, it looks GOOD!" Megan squealed, looking over my shoulder. And my tummy started to fizz. It did look pretty good…

"Yeah, I told you. The stories are FAB. It's just well… I guess it starts with the comments." Amber scrolled down to the bottom of the story, and I saw there were over two thousand comments.

"Oh my God, two THOUSAND? Don't people have better things to do?" I joked, but I felt instantly sick with apprehension. Comments sections under news stories weren't good – especially comments under news stories about feminism. Sure enough, looking over Amber's shoulder, the top one read:

What about men's rights? Does this silly teenager even think about those? We have less access to our children, our life expectancy is lower. But no, let's just focus all our attention on WOMEN – because that's equality, right?

It wasn't even that bad. It was to be expected…but still the fizzing in my stomach soured and white hot anger coursed through me instead.

"Has he not read what I said?" My fists clenched in on themselves. "Did he ignore the bits where I said about how sexism impacts all genders? Did he not watch the video where I had a go at people using the phrase 'man up'?"

Amber winced behind her mass of hair.

"Hang on," I said, butting her shoulder out of the way. "What's that say?" I read it out loud. *This comment has been removed because it breaks moderating guidelines.* And there's another one. And another… Why are they all being removed?"

I was starting to guess though. Things had to be quite nasty to get removed by a newspaper's moderating team… The fizz that had become anger now morphed into anxiety. My guts had no idea what to do next.

"I, umm…well… Your story's getting a lot of attention – which is great!" Megan said, but the brightness in her voice was so forced I'm surprised she didn't snap an artery.

"The downside is," Amber finished for her, "umm…as a side effect, you've drawn out some trolls."

Trolls.

My phone.

I dived into my coat pocket and got it out, bringing up my accounts. I had more notifications than could even work on the counter. My vision went hazy. Maybe they'd be nice things? Maybe maybe…

I clicked on my notification page, and straight away my hand went to my mouth.

U R a slut bitch. Hope u burn.

Angry bitches like u deserve 2 get raped. Watch your back.

You gonna hollar when Im raping u whore?

Amber was looking over my shoulder now – she gripped me tight.

"Lottie…oh Lottie…it's stupid. Just ignore it."

I was scrolling madly, hardly able to hear her. All my senses were on alert – the room seemed bigger, the noises of students seemed louder, my ears hurt, my eyes hurt. I kept scrolling.

Amber gripped tighter. "Lottie, stop looking at them."

Bitch I know where u live. Watch it.

"Can they really know where I live?" I asked, somewhat desperately. "They didn't put my address in the story."

"LOTTIE!" Amber actually grabbed me and shook me. "You need to stop looking at it. Turn your phone off!"

"She's right," Megan said. "This is just what happens when a feminism story gets in the news. I mean, it's horrible, don't get me wrong. But it's normal. None of these comments mean anything! They're just trying to silence you because you're standing up for something good."

Their words floated above me, not quite landing. Then they sank in, and I felt so terrified about what I needed to do next that I almost forgot to breathe.

"Lottie? Lottie? You're not talking. You're never not talking!" Amber said.

"Guys?" I looked up at them, tears in my eyes. My hands shook on my phone. "I can't ignore it – it's sexism." I gasped for breath, looking at the door, our teacher still AWOL. "I have to reply to them, I have to call them out. It's the rules of the project…"

Amber's eyes widened. "Lottie, no! You'll make it so much worse."

"She's right," Megan said. "This is surely outside the project remit. Don't feed the trolls, remember? It's what everyone says."

I ignored them and looked down at my phone again. I'd already received ten more notifications. Only two of them said nice stuff. The others were horrific. I hit *reply* to one and began punching in some words.

"Lottie, what are you doing?"

"What do you think I'm doing? What's the battery like on your phones? Megan, can you film me replying to them? Otherwise Will will get annoyed."

They looked at me like I'd gone completely bonkers. Maybe I had. But I'd made a promise to myself and I was in the newspaper because of it. I couldn't turn back on it now.

You are a sexist pig.

I hit send.

Could they really find my house? Was I really in danger?

I copied and pasted what I'd just written and fired it off to the other people threatening me. Bish bash bosh.

"Look!" I pointed at my phone. "Some people are favouriting my reply!"

"Lottie…" Amber's eyes were filled with tears. "Please, stop."

"You know what?" I asked, feeling full of energy, feeling on edge, feeling mad… "I don't think I have time for classes today. Not if I have to reply to all this scum…"

"Please, Lottie. Come on, let's talk about this."

"Lottie, you can't let them get to you," Megan said.

"I may just skip today and go home. This is going to be a full-time job," I replied, mostly to myself.

"You bunked off yesterday. Lottie, stop hitting reply! This won't help anything."

"I DON'T HAVE ANY CHOICE!" I yelled and the art room fell silent, as the whole class turned to look at me. One girl, this snotty girl we'd never liked, stage-whispered in her friend's ear, "Oh, look, it's the attention seeker again. Pathetic much?"

Attention seeker?

My phone was vibrating so hard it was making my hand itchy and hot.

I wasn't an attention seeker. I was just trying to do a

had been compromised.

Still I pressed refresh.

Ctrl + C of my *you're a sexist pig* response.

Ctrl + V.

Over and over.

It was making them worse.

My phone was buzzing so hard it had fallen off my desk several times.

Initially most of the messages were from Amber and Evie, asking if I was okay.

I'd fired back, *No, but I want to be alone right now. And I don't mean that in an overrule-me-and-turn-up-anyway kind of way. I love you both. I'm fine.*

I so wasn't fine.

Some of the buzzing came from calls from journalists, answerphone messages from journalists, a few FemSoc people asking if I was okay…the rest were from my notifications.

The abuse. So much abuse.

I'd been pinged a link to more news stories – new ones about me, stories about how I was personally responding to every single bit of abuse. This, of course, made everything get even more out of control. My battery died, my phone stayed on the floor. Mum and Dad – oblivious to everything because they had no interest in social media – just thought I was working – they were delighted.

When would this stop? When could I stop?

At least ten different people had told me they wanted to kill me today.

And I'd had to reply to them.

A loud knock at my door.

"I told you, I'm working! And I'm not hungry."

The squeak of the door opening.

"Then don't eat me."

And, for some reason, the sound of Will's voice just broke me. I didn't acknowledge him, I didn't say hi. I just slumped over onto the desk and started wailing. It was a new realm of crying for me. My throat was making noises I didn't even know were possible. Will was at my side instantly, a hand resting uncertainly on my shoulder. I choked and rasped and gasped for air in big gulping sobs. Will waited, his hand shaking on my juddering body, not saying anything. But he was there. Silent, but there. Like he knew I needed to cry myself out.

Which, in time, I did.

Slowly, I raised my head, taking him in, giving him a small watery smile. He didn't look like his usual self – his normally perfectly-quiffed hair was all stood on end, like he'd been raking his hands through it, deep circles under his eyes even his thick frames couldn't hide. Yet when he smiled back, that underlying self-confidence shone through. Dented, but still there.

"I've never had a girl cry so hard when I enter their bedroom before," he said. "Usually they're much more enthusiastic."

My watery smile diminished and I pointed to my sodden face. "Trust you to think this is all about you."

Will looked at my screen. Another fifty-six alerts had cropped up during my crying spell.

"I know this isn't about me."

Instinctively, I went to click on the little fifty-six number icon, which had just transformed into fifty-eight. But Will's hand shot out and grabbed mine – pushing it away.

"No, Lottie, come on."

The feel of his hand on mine… It sent sparks exploding off inside of me…even with all this going on. I tried to push him away though, to click, to carry on with this job, but he held me tighter.

"I've got to!" I said. "The project!"

"I don't give a flying fuck about the project right now, Lottie," he said. "Come on, away from the computer."

With a big swoop of his arms, he'd pulled me up and was carrying me over to my bed. He plopped me down with a thud and I just bounced to a stop and curled up in a ball.

"Where are Evie and Amber?" he asked, his voice soft, worried. I curled up further.

"I told them not to come, I told them I was fine."

"And they believed you?" He sat gingerly on the end of my bed.

I couldn't stop thinking – there must be more messages by now. Were these ones going to be nastier? Were these ones going to be from more dangerous people? Why did everyone keep reposting me? They were making it worse. It kept spreading, like a demented virus…

"They know when to leave me alone." I gave him a very

pointed look, even though, really, I was relieved he was there. Relieved and other more confusing emotions.

"You need to stop replying," he said simply.

"I can't."

"You can."

"I'll be a hypocrite then. It's just what they're waiting for."

"Who's they?"

"The people. The ones waiting for me to fail."

"Are you doing this for them though, Lottie? I thought you were doing this for you?"

I uncurled myself and sat up so I could study him. I must look a mess, my eyeliner all cried off and the bits of it that weren't, all over my face. My hair matted with drying tears.

"Of course I'm doing it for me, but..."

"But what?" He shrugged all dramatically. "You also want to torture yourself by engaging with those low-life pond scum who probably only share one brain cell between them? You do know some of those messages are illegal, right? You need to tell the police."

I ignored most of what he'd said. "I'm supposed to be doing this to try and change people's minds," I said, my voice all high-pitched with the effort of not crying.

"And you are! There are so many good messages coming through on our channel. You're reaching people, Lottie. But, with reach, you touch the bad with the good. You're never going to change some people's minds. You need to protect yourself from these arsewipes..." Even in all my pain,

I smiled at the word "arsewipes"... "Stop replying, save your energy. There's still a week and a half left..."

He nervously, well, nervously for Will, reached out and tucked a bit of hair behind my ear. Not so much in a sexy way, but a tender way. I found myself leaning my cheek into his hand, and more electric shocks jolted through my face – and, by the looks of it, up his arm. He almost pulled back, I saw him start to...then he relaxed and held my cheek.

I closed my eyes, kept them closed for a moment. Opened them. Looked right into his.

"I'm not changing *your* mind," I reminded him and I went to refresh again.

Will grabbed me, stopping me. He took both my wrists, pulling me round to look at him. Our faces were almost touching. I stared straight at him – angry, so angry. After everything he'd seen, he still...

"Lottie," he said, his face so intense I almost needed to look away. "You changed my mind ages ago."

"I what?"

He broke into the most cocky smile. "In fact, I think you changed my mind the first day I met you."

I slowly shook my head side to side, not hearing properly. "What? But you've been such a..."

"Arsewipe?"

I nodded. "Well, you've disagreed with everything I've said."

"I know I have...look..." He was still clasping my hands tight. I leaned forward – not quite understanding my reaction. I was broken, I was so tired, I didn't like this boy... Well, I wasn't supposed to like this boy... "I'm...I don't know...I don't like admitting I'm wrong, okay? I don't like losing arguments. I kind of dig my heels in to save face...Plus, well, the more I wound you up, the better you got... It really did help the project, I like to think..."

I was smiling. With everything that was happening, I was somehow smiling. Because Will. Because the words that were coming out of Will's mouth.

"Will?" I asked slowly...biting my lip to stop my smile. Our foreheads were touching. "Are you trying to tell me you're a feminist?"

"Don't tell anyone, will you?"

Our lips were together. Our hands went from holding each other to wrapping around each other's bodies.

I wanted this. I so wanted this. I needed this.

All the shit from today, all the messages, all the scared I was feeling was drowned out by how good his tongue felt in my mouth, how every part of my body felt pressed up against him. We fell backwards onto my bed, our legs entwining, Will's hands all over my body. Three weeks I'd held off kissing him properly. Three whole weeks. If you knew anything about me, you'd know I don't wait three weeks to kiss people I want to kiss. And my body was making up for it now.

Will, of course, was a brilliant kisser. I knew he would be, of course he would be. My mouth couldn't leave his, I couldn't get close enough to him. Raw primal lust streamed through me and I welcomed it. I was back, Lottie was back. I leaned up, still kissing him, and began to undo the buttons on his chequered shirt.

He pulled away. Reluctantly, I could see. But his lips left mine and I raised an eyebrow.

"Will? Why are we stopping?"

"You're upset," he pointed out. "I can't…when you're upset."

I rolled my eyes. There was no way I didn't want this. Every bit of my body and my brain wanted this. Yes maybe you think that's weird and I was vulnerable or whatever, but all I knew was that I needed him. And it didn't feel like for a screwed-up reason.

"Will," I said, "I'm doing a project where I call out sexism. Remember? You're filming it? Do you really think it would be in line with that if I let you take advantage of me right now?"

I reached to kiss him again. He was reluctant initially, shaking his head but not actually taking his lips away. I took that as a sign and climbed onto his lap. He started kissing my chest then, moaning into my skin. I leaned my head back, soaking it up.

Will – he was what I thought he was. I was right. He *was* good. I knew it…and, oh God, that felt good.

We fell sideways, only breaking contact so I could run and lock my door. My top was off. Will's was almost totally unbuttoned. I reached out, touching his lean chest. More kissing and clothes falling off and him muttering that I was beautiful and me closing my eyes and enjoying every moment, every word, every touch, every taste.

He was digging in his bag for his wallet, producing the foil wrapper of a condom. I kissed his naked shoulder as he put it on. So impatient. By the way his hands shook, I knew he was as impatient as I was.

Then it was on and we fell back again. His mouth on my mouth – feeling him against me. The sweet anticipation of the connection growing in me. I wiggled upwards, to angle myself. Not wanting to wait any more.

Then his mouth was away from my mouth and he was raised on his elbows – inches from it happening.

I didn't want it to stop. I looked up at him, an impatient smile on my face, making my eyes all puppy-like. God, the way he was staring at me. I could get drunk on it for ever. Will. Nice Will. Fit nice Will. Fit nice feminist Will.

His mouth was by my ear, gently biting it, then whispering. "So, Miss Feminism. How do we do this in a way that passes your project guidelines?"

Ahh, that's why he was stopping. His voice was so sexy, every part of me quivered. His eyebrows were cocked in his natural, arrogant way – all my insides dissolved.

I grinned at him. "Well," I said, pretending to think it through. "I guess, in order to stick to the rulebook, I'm going to have to go on top, and I'm going to have to…you know…?" I raised my eyebrows back and his smile stretched further. "Do you think you can manage that?"

I was already climbing onto him.

"You know what?" he replied, staring at me in the sort of way you should never ever forget. "I think I can manage that just fine."

forty-two

Afterwards, I shoved on some clothes and dashed downstairs to tell my parents we were working on an edit together. If they suspected anything, they certainly kept it to themselves. They congratulated me for the millionth time for the newspaper stories – Dad was even cutting them out to put in a scrapbook. They obviously hadn't seen the online version...or the new stories, the ones about me versus abuse. For a moment I was grateful my dad was such an academic above-all-that-social-media-stuff dinosaur.

I busied myself with making toast and peanut butter and pouring glasses of milk before returning to my room.

We did it again, after we'd eaten the toast. This time was slower, but no less urgent. Will had obviously had practice and knew what he was doing. My match, almost...

I put some music on to muffle any non-homework-sounding noises.

I felt high on lust. It was always like this with me. I would be okay about a guy, feeling all in control about it. But the moment I slept with them, some part of me would just be unleashed.

We lay, knackered, in bed – Will tracing his finger up my arm, making my skin tingle, listening to the music.

"That whole thing about you changing your mind better not have been a line to get me into bed."

He raised his eyebrows. "Like you needed a line."

I pushed him. "Shut up."

"Do you really think I'd lie about something that important to get laid?" he asked, shifting his weight so he was propped up on his elbows above me. He grinned. "I don't have trouble getting laid, Lottie."

I rolled my eyes at him. "Calm down, Casanova. You are the most arrogant person I've ever met, you know that, right?"

"That's funny…" He reached out and ever-so-gently stroked my face. "I could say the same thing about you."

"I'm not arrogant!"

"You SO are."

Before I could protest, his mouth was on mine and we kissed ravenously, me pulling him properly onto me. Just as we were about to embark on lucky third time, there was a crash at my bedroom door, a gasp, and we both turned in horror to see a disgusted-looking Amber and Evie standing in the threshold. Mum must've let them in and I didn't hear the door knock because of the music. Amber was carrying a bag of cheesy tortilla chips, Evie holding a jar of salsa and a giant bar of Dairy Milk.

"Oh my God, guys!" I dived under the covers, pushing Will off me, wiggling into my jeans. "What are you doing here?"

"Sorry, we're going, we're sorry."

"Just give us a minute," I said, from beneath my duvet.

Will was under the covers too, grappling with his shirt buttons. Even in the darkness, I could see he was bright red.

A minute later and we were suitably less naked. There was a knock on the door.

"Come in," I called, and the girls reappeared.

"I think I need more therapy," Evie said. "I'll need more therapy to recover from that image than I've ever needed for my anxiety issues."

Amber's mouth was wide open. "My eyes hurt. I'm going to see that horrific image whenever I close them for the rest of time."

"This room smells of things I don't want to think about," Evie said. "I'm opening a window."

"Guys," I said, all breezily, like they hadn't just seen my nipples, "what are you doing here?"

I chanced a glance back at Will. He'd plastered his stupid smug smile over his face, trying to brazen it out. But his glasses were wonky and my heart did this weird...thing...

"We came to see if you were okay," Evie said. "Especially when your phone went to answerphone."

She was still looking from me, to Will, back to me.

"Lottie?" Amber asked. "Can we chat to you privately for a sec?"

I looked at Will, who only shrugged, like nothing had happened at all in the last two hours. "I've got some editing to do anyway." He pulled his computer out of his bag on the floor, as Evie and Amber pushed me into the bathroom.

Amber sat me on the edge of the bath. "Lottie, what the hell?"

"Will?!" Evie said. "We sort of hate Will, don't we?"

"I know, I know," I pleaded with them. "It only just happened."

"What's going on?" Amber demanded. "He's not used the fact you're all vulnerable today to get into your knickers, has he?" She straightened up, her fists clenched and I reached to calm her.

"No, he hasn't taken advantage! Girls, come on! You know me better than that."

"You've had a rough day," Evie pointed out.

Even in her interrogation mode, I could see her eyes darting around the bathroom, looking for dirt or germs or whatever it is she worries about. I didn't live in the cleanest house, to be fair. And Mum and Dad used herbal cleaning products that didn't seem to do much.

"Yes, I have," I admitted, and it all came rushing back with the full force of its horror. "But...well... I like him, guys. This hasn't come out of nowhere."

Evie perched very nervously on the bath next to me. "How can you like him? He doesn't even agree with the project."

"He said he does agree. He was just too..."

"Prickish?" Amber supplied, crossing her arms.

"Proud," I corrected her, very defensive of Will all of a sudden. Damn hormones that got released when I slept with people. Or maybe it was nothing to do with hormones and everything to do with what Will was like in bed…and that he was nice! Feminist nice!

I could see Evie already wavering – she saw the best in everyone, that girl.

"Is that what he said?" she asked. "He's actually believed in this thing the entire time?"

I nodded. "That's what he said… That he was won over from the start, but just too proud to admit it. It was only after we'd had that conversation that the whole sex thing happened. I can't go around breaking the rules of my own project."

Amber's arms were still crossed. "How do you know it isn't just a line?"

I shrugged. "I don't. But it didn't feel like a line. I know he's said some douchey stuff…" Amber's face went even more self-righteous. God she was annoying sometimes. She's the one who ran off across America with a dude she hardly knew. "But I think maybe it's, I dunno…from a place of insecurity maybe…"

Amber interrupted me. "Will? Insecure?"

I laughed. "Okay, maybe that's not the right word… He's not a dickhead though. I don't think this is just a sex thing…" And the moment it was out of my mouth I knew it was true. Will and I were going to argue, a lot. We were going to be fiery, a lot. We were going to play each other, a lot. We were definitely going to have sex, a lot. But, just from this one afternoon, I felt something had clicked a little.

I thought maybe we were going to fall for each other… a lot.

"So can you just trust my choices?" I pleaded. "I've got enough to worry about today."

It all came whooshing back again, full-throttle, and I put my head into my hands and found myself crying. The happiness from my mini sex-break truly dispersed into fear and misery of what would be lurking on my computer when I went back into my bedroom.

The girls kicked into action, saying sorry, patting my back.

"We trust you." Evie gave me an extra pat. "I think maybe I'm just still in shock. I mean…Will… But still…you've had a bogus day. I think we need to talk about what's going on."

A half-formed sob echoed out of my mouth, so loud I was nervous Mum and Dad would hear. I felt overwhelmed by how much more I needed to do, the replies I still needed to write – the trouble they'd cause. They'd just keep coming. The hatred and the threats and the fear and the arguing and all I had tried to do was stick up for something.

"Let's go back to your room," Amber suggested. "Dare I say it, see what Will thinks."

They collected me up – somehow I'd got a bath towel draped around me, but I kept it there, nestling my face into it.

"He says I need to stop replying," I said, my hands shaking

as I wrapped the towel-shawl further around myself.

"For the first and only time in the universe, I'm inclined to agree with him," said Amber.

We pushed back into my room and there was Will, glasses straight, tapping on his computer like none of his body parts had been in none of my body parts in the last hour. The coolness of it made my stomach squirm in a way that made me nervous…

"We're back," Evie declared. "We've decided we're not going to throw you out the window."

Will leaned back in my office chair. "I'm delighted to hear it."

Amber gave him a glare – still not quite trusting him, I could tell. Then she said, "Lottie told us you think she should stop replying to all the sexist trolls."

He nodded slowly, weighing up what he was thinking. "I did. I think she should go to the police too."

I shook my head. "No, and no. I can't give up now, not when everyone else is waiting for me to mess up. And the police won't take it seriously. They'll just say it's all my fault or something."

I fell back on the bed, the smell of Will and I wafting up as I did. I giggled. I felt mad, terrified, unhinged.

The girls sat on my carpet – giving my bed a wide berth. I kept trying to look at Will, to try and figure out how he was feeling…what it all meant. Half of me was scared for my life and my general sanity. The other half was worried he wasn't going to message me tonight, or say it was all too complicated.

God, I was pathetic. I would blow my horn at myself if I had the energy.

"Lottie…" Evie's voice was soft, the kind I imagine people use when they're negotiating with kidnappers. "If you keep replying it won't stop. It won't go away. It's not achieving anything. It's just making you upset."

"But it's sexism! I have to point it out. That's the—"

"I know, that's the whole point. But you also need to pick your battles, Lottie. You won't win here. You're just going to break yourself, use up all your energy on fights where you have no chance of coming out on top. You will not change these idiots' minds. They are the bad dudes who are on the wrong side of history. We'll go 'I can't believe that happened' in fifty years' time when it's turned into a movie or something, in utter wonder that humans can be such twats."

I smiled sadly. "But the point isn't to win. It's just to make people aware…"

"Which you've done. You're all over the papers, Lottie." Will butted in now. He stood up and came over to the bed, taking my hand.

The relief I felt, with him taking my hand. What it meant. He stared right at me – all his defences gone. There was just sincere care there. Yikes, what had happened to Will? I'd broken him!

"Just send out one last response, saying something like, *Everyone who's sending me hate is a sexist pillock who deserves to be shat on by a giant bird with diarrhoea—*"

"That's an odd metaphor," Amber interrupted and Will laughed.

Will laughed?!

I'd definitely broken Will.

"Well, you'll think of something better than that," he said. "But you get the gist. Then close your account, stop the reposts and reblogs from spreading… It will cool down quickly then."

I kept shaking my head. "I can't. It's giving up."

"It's not. It's looking after yourself," Evie said.

I started crying again, and Will clasped my hands tighter – his fingers entwining with mine.

"I can't…I can't…"

"Nothing is worth you sacrificing your mental health," Evie said, her voice all therapy.

"But women did so much more and endured so much more," I protested. "The suffragettes let people force feed them, lots of feminists around the world are laying down their lives. I mean, look what happened to Malala! And what? Me? I give up the moment someone says something mean to me on the internet?"

I sounded so pathetic. So, so pathetic.

How was I this pathetic? I was *supposed* to want to be prime minister.

And yet, the thought of those replies, sending them out, seeing what came back. My skin went hot, my breathing went…

I was giving up.

I was going to give up.

Because I wasn't strong. I wasn't a fighter. At the first sign of it getting hard I was going to roll over and give up.

They had silenced me. Just like they wanted to.

I was weak...

I cried on them for a long time. Cried so much that I didn't even have an appetite for the chips and salsa, which shows how broken I was.

Seriously...

But, in time, they won me round. And at about ten, just as Mum and Dad were making cooing noises outside in the hallway about it being "college tomorrow", Will filmed me typing out my final catch-all response. While crying.

"Do we really need to show me crying?" I asked.

"Yes." He nodded.

"But they'll know that they got to me."

"No," Amber scolded. "It will just show you're an actual person having a completely legitimate reaction."

"Me crying will just make them send more hate," I pointed out. It was true.

They all knew it was true.

Will was clicking about, doing stuff I didn't understand.

"We're turning off comments on the videos. You're temporarily closing your accounts. Yeah, they'll still say stuff, but the important thing is, you won't see it... Woah...hang on..." He stared at the screen with his eyes practically bulging.

"What is it?" I asked. "Is it bad? What are people saying now?"

"It's not bad, Lottie. It's…" He turned around in my spinny chair and shook his head.

"What is it?" we all yelled.

"It's our channel," he said… "It's just passed one million views."

forty-three

I eventually fell into bed in a confused stupor, trying to make sense of the good and bad things.

GOOD THING – you've had over ONE MILLION views!

BAD THING – at least ten people have promised to rape and/or murder you.

GOOD THING – Will! You had mindblowing sex with Will.

GOOD THING – and he's already sent you a message saying he had an amazing night and that he's proud of you...

BAD THING – amongst all the death-threat business,

you've missed yet another day of college before your Cambridge interview.

GOOD THING – your friends will always be there for you.

BAD THING – you gave up. You're too weak, you messed up.

I scrabbled around in the covers, opening my window, shutting my window, staring out of my window to check a potential murderer wasn't hiding in the bushes.

I cried. I remembered things with Will... I smiled...

I cried...I smiled...I cried...I smiled... One million views...

When I finally found sleep, I was smiling.

forty-four

I slept heavily and, when I woke, I felt lighter. Just knowing no one could send me anything else did help…

Hang on, why was it still dark?

Hang on, why was my phone ringing?

I reached for it in the darkness, grabbing at where it was charging at the wall.

6.30 a.m. What? It was the middle of the night!

And it was Will's number?

My tummy melted, replaced straight away by nerves.

People don't ring in the middle of the night (well, before 7 a.m.) unless something bad has happened. I slid the screen up to answer.

"Are you dead?" I joked, my voice husky from not being used yet.

Will's voice was not jokey in reply. "Have you been online yet today?"

All my hairs stood up instinctively. Something was wrong. Something else had happened.

"It's not even today yet," I joked again, lamely. "Why are you up so early?"

"Lottie…" He took a deep breath and I knew my instincts were right. It was the sort of breath you take before delivering bad news.

"What is it?"

A pause. A pause so pregnant it was going to give birth already.

"It's Teddy, he's done something… Lottie? Lottie?"

I didn't need him to tell me anything else. He'd given me the only word I needed. Will gabbled at the end of the phone, all flustered, anger lacing every word. I couldn't tell if it was at me yet, or Teddy.

"There were journalists hanging around at college yesterday. I didn't want to tell you, as you were already so upset…I…I…I didn't think anyone would talk to them anyway. We told people not to."

I slowly rolled onto my stomach, pulling the laptop down in front of me, starting it up as he carried on ranting. I typed Teddy's name into Google then clicked on *News*.

My hand went to my mouth.

It was a trashy tabloid site, but still a national newspaper. There, there was his sorrowful-looking face. Next to a huge headline that read, *FEMINIST TEEN'S BLACK WIDOW PAST*.

I gasped in actual horror.

"Lottie?" Will's voice was frantic on the phone. "Lottie, are you there?"

I was reading the story under my breath.

"*Teen feminazi, Charlotte Thomas, has become a viral sensation this past week with her month-long video project to call out sexism. But, according to her devastated ex-boyfriend, gender equality isn't something she takes into the bedroom...*"

This. This was awful.

"Lottie? Lottie?"

I dropped my phone, ran to the bathroom, stubbing my toe in the dark and vomited into the toilet. I stayed there for a while, clenching the sides of the toilet bowl.

Teddy...

How could he? How could he? How could he...

I hadn't even read most of the story yet.

Mum and Dad were making waking-up noises in their bedroom and I stumbled past them, croaking, "Good morning," so they wouldn't suspect anything, back into my room, shutting the door behind me. My phone was glowing. My call with Will had rung off, but he'd tried ringing back four times.

I couldn't talk to him.

Not yet.

Maybe not ever.

I brushed a tear from my face and forced myself to sit upright at my desk with the laptop, thinking maybe if I tried to view this professionally, I wouldn't get so upset. I wiggled the mouse to activate the screen, and there was my face again. Teddy had obviously given them one of the photos he'd taken last year. There weren't many, we had hardly dated. But there was that one day when we'd gone to

Brighton and shivered by the sea all day in the non-existent winter sun. He'd taken a few selfies of us on his phone… Here they were. The sea and Brighton pier in the background. They'd picked a bad one of me, my eyes squinting from the wind, my hair all over my face. Teddy looked nice though. My insides froze with hatred.

I dragged my attention away from the photo and started reading the story again.

Edward Burrington, eighteen, says he dated the notorious Charlotte last year before he heard about her man-eating reputation.

"Once we got together, everyone told me what a slut she was," he said. "I didn't believe them at first. I was in love. I wish I had listened to them now."

I was shaking my head.

Slut. I was being called a slut in a national newspaper.

A fresh wave of nausea hit me, tears pouring down my cheeks. My phone kept buzzing but I ignored it. I knew I should stop reading, but I couldn't. It was like I was in full-on self-flagellation mode.

So I scrolled down.

But soon after saucy Charlotte had taken Edward's virginity, she lost interest and cruelly dumped him.

"I was heartbroken," Teddy told us. "I honestly thought we were soulmates."

No you didn't, Teddy, I thought. *Nobody would treat someone the way you've treated me this year if they thought that.*

"When people came to comfort me, they told me this is what she does. She has sex with boys and then dumps them afterwards. It's a feminism thing. She says the only way to beat men is to behave like one."

Where was he getting this from??? How? How was this thing printed? They hadn't even rung me to listen to my side of the story!

They were still giving Teddy column space.

"This stupid project of hers, she says it's all about equality, but really she's one of those man-haters. This is all about revenge for her. She's a black widow spider. She's dangerous."

I didn't read any more.

I was too stunned to cry properly. I just stared at the screen, shaking my head.

Mum called through the door. "Lottie? You've not gone back to sleep, have you? You've got college soon."

"I'm up," I called back, my voice cracking.

There was no way I was going to college. Not with this, not with lies about my sex life splashed all over the papers and everyone reading it. The way Teddy would look at me all triumphantly – revenge for something wrong I did to him that he'd totally imagined.

And I'd only just got through yesterday…

Oh God – Will would read this! Of course he had already – he was the one who'd phoned me about it. What must he think?

What must anyone think?

I'd always tried not to care before. That's how you give away your power, by caring what other people think. As long as nobody thought I was a nasty person, I didn't worry about the rest. I mean, why bother? You couldn't control it anyway.

But this had broken that.

I knew I wasn't a slut… Was I?

And it's a totally horrid word anyway, that I'm totally against. I'm against the whole concept. A slut isn't even a real thing – it's just a thing society has made up, an imaginary noun used to shame and control women. If I'd read this story and it wasn't about me, I would've been publicly declaring how awful it was.

It *was* about me though.

And now, now…everyone thinks I'm a slut…

I lay my head on my hands, collapsed forward and really started to cry then. The sobs heaving up out of my back – my phone still ringing like crazy.

Was it Will? Probably. Pretending this hadn't altered how he thought of me. Probably thinking how quick I'd been to have sex with him, multiple times, the day before.

Probably thinking that's a pretty slutty thing to do.

Or it would be Amber and Evie. Caring, always caring. But whatever they said or did, it couldn't take any of this away. Not even with a lifetime supply of cheesy snacks.

Mum called through my door again and I started. College. I was supposed to be going to college.

No way in hell. But they couldn't know that. They'd been clucking a lot about this Cambridge interview, saying how important it was I knew the syllabus inside and out. In amongst all my public glory (and shaming that they didn't know about) they were still making sure I kept my eyes on the prize.

I wondered if Cambridge would read this.

Then I laughed through my tears. No chance. At least their intellectual snobbery would stop them ever reading this paper.

I began getting dressed, wiping the tears from my eyes the moment they fell, hoping my face would clear up enough before I went downstairs so my parents couldn't see I'd been crying.

There was another thing to think about.

What had just happened. This. Teddy. That whole mess.

It was sexism.

A tiny sliver of my brain that wasn't in total free fall could identify that.

And, if it was sexism, that meant I needed to call it out.

Which was exactly what they wanted me to do.

Enough...

I didn't have the strength.

I was broken. I was willing to admit that I, Lottie the unbreakable, was totally and completely annihilated.

I wasn't going to call this out.

I was going to hide.

I'd been silenced.

And you know what? I was relieved.

forty-five

My parents didn't suspect anything through breakfast, and I was out the door before them anyway.

I wasn't going to college. Nope. I didn't have whatever insane mental strength you would need to go into college the day you're publicly shamed for being a girl and having sex with more than one person. I'd turned my phone off too and left it in my bedroom.

Yes, I was sure Evie and Amber would be worried, but I was so humiliated I couldn't even face having that conversation with them now.

Will might be worried. Or he might worry I'm a black widow slut…

It annoyed me how much I cared what he must think.

It was a cold and damp morning, the wind swirling my hair around my face. I walked without much clue where I was going, just as long as it wasn't in the direction of college. I passed a new sexist poster at the bus stop.

I didn't do anything.

I was done. I was spent. I'd given it everything and all it had done was bite me so much in the arse, I was surprised I had any arse left – just a hole that poo fell out of.

That's really gross, Lottie.

I found myself climbing Dovelands Hill, the spot where me and my other spinsters had first made friends. It took up most of my energy, my breath frosting as it left my mouth in rapid sobby heaves. I collapsed on the bench at the top and surveyed the landscape below me, my teeth chattering from the chill.

I was lost.

I wasn't usually able to admit that, but then, there, alone, I could.

I'd tried to do something good and now I was being publicly shamed. The sheer unfairness of it hit me in waves of fury and I screamed out over the view – scattering some birds from the trees.

Why wasn't Teddy being publicly shamed for doing this to me?

I was innocent. The only thing I was guilty of was not liking him as much as he wanted me to. Of maybe taking too long to figure that out. I'd broken up with him with respect and care.

Now he was calling me a nasty slut in the national press, ruining my reputation, and I couldn't do anything. Well, I could do something. I could fight back… I was supposed to fight back. But I had no fight left in me.

I thought of how it had all started – with those two men in the van. How strong I'd felt when I'd taken them on.

But it wasn't worth this. The fight wasn't worth how I felt right now. Damaged, ashamed.

Humiliated…

Maybe this is why people don't bother changing anything. It's not just having your hope crushed in the palm of society's hand, but having your spirit crushed too. Your sanity questioned.

Am I crazy?

Is this really a problem?

Is it really worth all this to try and fix it?

Especially when it's likely this won't fix it?

I started to cry again – tears jumping off my face like paratroopers. Really depressed ones.

I thought I was strong but I'm not.

I thought I could change things but I can't.

I thought I didn't care what anyone thought, but I do.

Maybe I should just roll over. Shut up. Calm down. Zip it. Stop whinging. Cease and desist.

Maybe I should just look out for me, put me at the top of the pyramid. Focus on revision, focus on Cambridge. Get in, get a brilliant job, earn loads of money, drop some pound coins into a collection tin when I passed to ease the guilt that I was letting the universe eat itself but it's okay because look at this lovely new lipstick I've bought.

It would be easy.

It would be nice.

I wasn't going to change anything anyway.

I stayed up there until I couldn't feel my limbs from the cold – I'd gone past the point of numb. I was just going to stop the project. Not announce it or anything. Just stop posting videos, stay offline...go back to college maybe in a few days' time...with a hammer to smash in Teddy's skull...no...not murder. Murder bad.

It was so cold my brain was broken.

The house was empty when I let myself in. Dad off teaching people stuff they'd never need to know, not really. Mum rubbing the physical knots out of people that life had given them.

I turned on the TV. I hadn't watched any really since I'd started this thing. It was impossible. Like, every single panel show was just always men men men men, and one token woman who always gave themselves a hernia trying to be heard over all their verbal dick-measuring.

I didn't have to worry about that now.

I stayed away from news channels, just in case I was on them, and settled into some show where they make over your house while you're out swimming or whatever.

"That's shit wallpaper," I told the television.

"That's a shit chair."

"That's a shit painting."

I didn't stop watching it though. In fact, the only break I had was to go into the kitchen and open a bag of grated cheese – shoving fistfuls of it into my face.

"That's a shit pair of curtains."

It worked to some degree. My brain was only replaying back Teddy's words every 2.5 seconds, instead of every 0.5 seconds.

I must've slumped into some kind of daytime TV coma, because when the doorbell went, I jumped, my heart pounding like a gunshot had been fired.

Doorbell. People.

I stayed where I was.

The doorbell rang again.

I stayed where I was.

Knocking.

I stayed where I was...

Then. "Lottie? Are you in? It's Megan."

Megan?

I found myself standing up.

I couldn't face the girls, or Will. But somehow Megan, I could answer my door to her. She stood on my step sheepishly, hopping from one foot to the other. She wore a sad smile that instantly confirmed she'd heard or seen the newspaper story.

"Can I come in?"

I didn't say anything. I hadn't spoken all day, other than to tell the interior designers on the TV they were shit.

"I have a present for you," she said, in a bargaining voice. She reached into her nice leather satchel I'd always lusted after and pulled out a T-shirt. "I made it today." She held it out so I could read it. It was crumpled, but it had a unicorn on it, with a speech bubble that said in big neon letters:

SLUTS AREN'T REAL.

A small smile played on my lips.

"Am I allowed in?"

I took the T-shirt, holding it up. She'd made it herself, I could tell her style anywhere, but it looked so professional. You could sell it in a shop. I let her in and followed her through to the living room.

"Do you want a drink?"

"A cup of tea would be nice. It's freezing outside."

She sat on the sofa, all birdlike. I left her there and went to make the drinks quickly, then brought them back.

Megan's presence didn't fill much of a room. She was small and dainty and unassuming and always covered her hands with the sleeves of her jumper. Her fragile energy somehow calmed me. She wasn't going to give me fighting talk, or lie about it all being okay. I needed that right now.

"I almost didn't recognize you without your eyeliner," she commented, thanking me as she took the mug of tea.

"I don't even recognize me without eyeliner."

She smiled. "Are you okay?"

I shook my head.

"I'm sorry for what Teddy did. If it helps any, I heard he's been suspended. He may even get expelled."

It didn't help any. It didn't help at all.

I took a sip of my tea, saying nothing. Looking everywhere but at her, in case I saw more sympathy on her face.

"Evie and Lottie said they tried to come round earlier but no one answered."

384

"I went out."

"They're trying again soon. They've sent me first."

She'd been sent? That wasn't a surprise really.

"Will was looking rather desperate today at college too. He said you've turned your phone off."

Will… My heart did little confused leaps.

I didn't know what to say. So I took another sip of tea and said, "I'm stopping the project."

"Lottie, no!" Megan's energy shifted right away. She was on the sofa, then she was next to me, grabbing my arm urgently. "You can't."

I shook my head. "I'm sorry. You've been great, and so helpful… But I can't do this any more. I…I'm…I'm not brave enough."

I started to cry again, with the shame of admitting it out loud.

Megan didn't comfort me though.

She made an annoyed tut and went, "Oh really, Lottie? For fuck's sake. What's bravery got to do with it?"

I looked up. Surprised at her sudden lack of sympathy.

"I don't have the strength!" I tried to explain. "Everyone's saying how strong I am all the time, but I'm not. I thought I was, but I'm not."

Megan shook her head. "Jeez, what are you even saying? What sort of sociopath would you be if this didn't upset you, Lottie? You're not GOD…even if you act like it sometimes."

"I was under the false impression you were here to be

nice," I said, still stunned. Though her harshness had kicked me out of my stupor.

"I was. Until you said you were quitting this project. Lottie" – her voice did soften then – "I've found these past few weeks really…helpful." A long pause. She was going to tell me, oh God, I hoped I handled it right. "Look, I know you and Amber and Evie know something happened with me and Max, that you've probably guessed the truth."

I stayed still, to keep her talking. She wasn't getting upset or emotional or anything though; it wasn't how I'd pictured it. Though it was weird I'd pictured this moment at all.

"And…well…I've found it useful to have something to focus on – to feel like I'm doing something about it… Don't stop, Lottie. I know what it feels like to think you're not brave or strong enough, believe me. But you are helping people. And surely that gives you some strength?"

I picked my words carefully. This wasn't about me any more, this was about her.

"Megan. Do you think you need to tell someone what happened?"

She looked up at me, still no emotion. Still no crying. Whereas I was still crying. Because actually, what Megan was surely going through required more strength and more courage than what I was doing. And if she could even get out of bed most days, that was quite something.

"I've told my mum." My mouth dropped open. "We're dealing with it."

Dealing with it by telling the police? Dealing with it by

getting Max prosecuted? Dealing with it by going to counselling?

But Megan didn't say anything else. She just met my eyes, and hers were fiery. Daring me to ask her more questions. Daring me to judge how she was dealing with this. And I realized that I shouldn't judge her. That I *had* been judging her. For not fighting the fight that I would've fought. When I have no idea what sort of fight I'd be capable of fighting if that happened to me anyway.

So I just said, "I'm so sorry something bad happened to you. If I can do anything…"

A small smile. "You can not quit this project."

I gave her a small tearful smile back. "I'm not sure I can do that."

"Why not? What's the worst that can happen? Hasn't it happened already? Look, Lottie" – her eyes watered a little – "horrid things happen, but you *can* get through them. Believe me."

"I'll always believe you."

She smiled, wiped away a tear before it began, ignored my interruption. "So why stop? You've taught me to fight, Lottie. Maybe not in the way you want me to. But I still feel I'm fighting. You've pulled me into it. Now it's my turn to pull you back into it."

I was crying harder. We were both crying harder. My heart ached for her. I wanted to take it all away – take her pain away.

"Why did you start this whole thing anyway?" she asked,

wiping her nose on her hand. "Can you remember? I know you say it was those men in the van. But what was the feeling? Remembering may help…"

I bit my lip, trying to sift through my memories. It had been the men who harassed me, but it had also been Mike stealing my line and the first FemSoc meeting and…and… my philosophy homework. I'd totally forgotten about that homework. Which wasn't great, as it was my Cambridge interview in two weeks' time. I remembered that train careering down the tracks – two horrible consequences. Me deciding that avoiding one horrible consequence is never worth allowing another to happen.

I didn't want to be the person who flicked the switch.

But that was different, that was about saving other people, not saving me.

"Do you think it's harder," I asked her, sipping my tea, "to stick up for other people, or to stick up for yourself?"

"Is that why you did it? To stick up for other people?"

I nodded. "I think so… Like what happened with you." She stiffened but didn't stop me. "Maybe, I dunno…I can find my strength when I'm battling for someone else, when I'm not, like, the victim…" I wished I hadn't just used the word victim, I hated it so much, but Megan didn't seem to mind. How was she so calm? If I was her, I would be screaming from the rooftops, I'd be yelling from the wings of aeroplanes I'd hired out.

Actually…would I?

I wasn't sticking up for myself today. Not now it was me

hurting, me burning, me turning into ash.

"I know I've already said it, but I'm so sorry about what happened to you," I blurted out, almost wanting to cover my mouth afterwards.

But Megan, calm, calm Megan just said, "I'm so sorry about what's happened to you, too."

"But what's happening to me is so silly…compared with…"

She shook her head. "It's not silly. It's serious. That's why we're all worried. Anyway, you shouldn't compare these things. You can't put different measurements on pain. Isn't that what your whole project is about?"

I nodded – wondering how she was so wise this afternoon. She was right. All of it was bad. What had happened to Megan, what Teddy had done to me, girls walking down the street and being told they have nice tits, pills costing that bit more money just because they're pink, boys knowing it's more socially acceptable to punch someone in the face than to cry silently in their bedrooms, toddler girls being told they're pretty, toddler boys being told they're brave. Pink and blue. Trousers and skirts. Rape culture and glass ceilings. A skeletal model sauntering down a catwalk, a lonely girl being called fat on the internet.

It was all harmful. And you can't measure harm. It's unquantifiable, like love. Like fear.

I'd done this because *all* of it was wrong, and yet it was always being dealt with separately. Cut up into segments, everyone arguing about whose segment was the most worthy.

Fighting any harm is worthy.

And as Megan and I finished drinking our tea, I realized it takes a great deal more courage to fight for yourself than to fight for others. To confront your own pain, rather than everyone else's. My body felt covered in scars. These last couple of weeks had been cut after cut after cut and I was battered, bruised, damaged, and on my way to broken. If I didn't find the strength to fight now, I'd never find it.

The doorbell rang, jolting Megan and me out of our chat. She looked sheepish again.

"That will be the others. I was given an hour's head start."

"You mean Lottie and Evie?"

"Yes, them. And…well…"

She got up and answered the door, even though this wasn't her house. I followed, puzzled, embarrassed, not really wanting even Lottie and Evie to see me without eyeliner on.

The door flung out into the wind…into the two dozen people standing on my doorstep.

I gasped.

Evie and Lottie were at the front, of course. Looking worried, but also excited. Like they'd just cooked up some excellent plan. Behind them stood all of FemSoc, beaming at me like they'd never been so proud of anyone in their whole lives. And it wasn't just FemSoc there. Jane, Joel, Mike from my philosophy class, Oli, Ethan, so many of them.

And there, at the back, was Will. Straining forward to see me…

"What the hell? What are you all doing here?" I covered

my tear-stained make-up-free face as much as I could with my hands.

Amber and Evie stepped forward.

"Letting you know that you don't have to get through this alone."

I flung myself at them, hugging them so hard. Crying again. Always with the crying these days. Everyone clapped.

"Thank you," I said, as we released hugs. Then, to the others, "Come in. I don't know how you're going to fit in my living room, but we can try."

I watched as two dozen people attempted to get through Mum's beaded curtain. They sat everywhere – on all the seats, on the floor, on the coffee table, some were even halfway up the stairs.

"Umm…I don't know what to feed you all."

Evie and Amber held up bulging carrier bags. "Sorted!" they yelled. Evie began unpacking. They laid out at least ten types of cheese first, then a trillion packages of crackers.

"You brought cheese?" I still wasn't sure if this was all real.

"Oh yeah," Evie said, like it was totally normal to be unpacking three slabs of brie from a shopping bag at 3 p.m. on a Wednesday afternoon. "A Spinster Club always needs its cheesy snacks."

"Spinster Club…?"

I looked around at everyone. They were still smiling at me, some chatting amongst themselves, others clapping me on the back and saying, "Teddy is an arsehole."

Spinster Club was just for me, Amber and Evie. It was always just the three of us.

Then I looked at Megan, who was handing out more slut T-shirts that she must've made that morning. And at Jane, and even Joel, handing round paper plates with cheese on them. And Will, who hadn't spoken to me yet, but who was setting up his tripod in the corner. When we caught eyes, he gave me such a small but loaded smile that I felt my insides glow...

These people were all spinsters too. I saw that now. And they were here because I needed them.

"Yep," Amber said, loud enough for everyone to hear. "We've officially opened the club out to new members."

"We've started a rota for who buys the cheesy snacks," Evie explained.

"I...I..." I was filling up again. I'd been through so many emotions in one day. Happiness wasn't one I was expecting. No part of my body was prepared for it. So I found myself slinking into business mode.

"So, what's on the agenda?" I asked, reaching out for the brie. "Seeing as you've obviously shoved through a new membership rule without me, I'm assuming you've made an agenda without me too."

"Too right," Amber said.

"We've got them here." Evie handed out sheets to everyone, and people took them through mouthfuls of cheese and crackers, spilling crumbs all over the carpet. I reached for one, but Evie snatched it back.

"You don't get one."

I scrunched my nose up. "Why not?"

"Because it's a surprise. It was Will's idea." Will nodded at me again from his tripod area. "All you need to do is sit down, eat some cheese, and please, for the love of God, put some eyeliner on because you're scaring me."

And for the first time that day, I laughed. Something I'd never have thought possible when I got the phone call that morning.

I did what she said.

forty-six

It took a few more minutes of paper rustling, and someone asking where the toilet was, and arguing over who'd eaten the last Dairylea Dunker, before we were settled enough to begin.

Evie stood up first, crunching a cracker under her foot by accident.

She was so poised in front of the crowd – so different from the Evie who'd wobbled with nerves at the FemSoc meeting she'd led only weeks ago. She was being strong for me – because I needed other people's strength right now.

"Thank you for coming, all you new Spinsters, you," she started. "Amber will be giving you your membership cards as soon as she gets round to drawing them." Amber saluted. "We're here today because recently one of our founding members has come under attack..." Everyone turned to look at me, and I felt myself go hot. "As you know, Lottie's been running a very important project, for a very important reason, and it's gone further than we could've ever hoped. But as a result of all this craziness, well…it's dragged the arsewipes out from their hidey-holes and now they're hurting our friend."

I was so red I was quite sure I was beyond a red colour. What's next after red? Puce?

Amber stood. "We're scared all this is going to stop Lottie from continuing, and none of us could blame her for that. But in order to help her decide what's right, we've been rounding up all the good things that have happened from the success of this project. So Lottie can focus on the good, just for a little bit, instead of the bad."

Huh? Good things? What good things?

Will stepped out from behind the camera now – his eyes never leaving mine.

"When you hung up the phone this morning," he said, putting himself in front of his lens for the first time, "I started going through all the comments. Not just on your personal pages, but at the bottom of the news stories too. I'm not going to lie, Lottie." He stared at me with real pain in his eyes. "It wasn't all nice. But there was a lot of good stuff in there too. A lot. A hell of a lot. There are loads of people fighting your corner out there right now. Not just in this room, but all over."

"What?" I asked, but Amber stood again before I could continue.

"Right, guys…" She pointed to Jane. "You first, Jane."

"Go first with what?" I asked, just as Jane got up to stand, rustling her agenda.

"Shh, Lottie. Just listen," hissed Amber.

Jane self-consciously pulled down her jumper and began to read. "This girl makes me feel less crazy," she read, her eyes on the paper. "Thank you so much, Charlotte. I've always felt like I'm alone by being upset about all this, but now I know the world is what's mad, not me." Jane sat down again.

"What was that?" I asked.

Amber ignored me again, and pointed at Joel. "You. Next."

Joel, who'd always been too cool for anything, rolled his eyes, but he did stand up, playing with his ponytail with his spare hand.

"This girl ROCKS," he said, reading from the page. "If everyone did what Charlotte is doing, we'd have gender equality within a year." He made the metal sign at me with his fingers and sat back down. Still stunned, I made it back.

"Next," Amber commanded.

Sylvia jumped to her feet. "Charlotte, you're an inspiration. I'm going to try and start a Feminist Society in my school now because of you. First stop – WHY CAN'T WE WEAR TROUSERS?"

I'd begun to cry. Again. Evie and Amber stood by my side, rubbing my back.

One by one my friends stood up and read something out. Some were funny, some were painful, one mentioned abuse from a boyfriend and Megan quietly got up and went to the bathroom. I was a mess by the end, a weeping incoherent mess.

I couldn't believe I'd reached that many people. All the good I'd somehow managed – whilst throwing custard pies at rugby players and being publicly outed as a slut.

Fighting for something you believe in isn't easy. If you hit a sore spot, people are going to swipe at you, gripe at you, try to undermine you, infuriate you, try to shut you up and put you back in your box. I was starting to learn that was a sign you were asking the right questions, picking the right scabs. And though it's easy to lose yourself along the way, and start focusing on all the people who don't want things to change – for whatever broken, messed-up reasons of their own – you can easily find your way back. By listening to the people giving you a hand up. To the people who have your back. To the people who don't think you're a raving lunatic. Let them be your mirror – not the haters. Let them give you the strength to get the job done.

When the circle had finished, when I was an utter mess, when all the cheese had been devoured…Will came over, stepping over everyone's legs and kissed me gently on the forehead. The combination of the intimacy of it and publicness of it crumbled me further.

"So," he said, loud enough for everyone to hear, yet it still felt like an intimate whisper. "Are you going to see this thing through to the end?"

I looked at all their cheese-smeared faces. Faces of people who didn't need to be here. People who would've found it much easier to laugh at today's newspaper, discuss it behind my back, tell everyone I was an attention-seeking whore. But instead they chose to pile into my parent's hippified living room and use their energy on building me back up again – giving me the courage to carry on.

I smiled through my tears and nodded.

"This slut says yes."

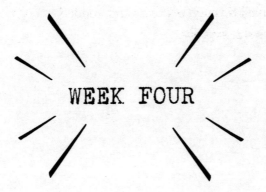

WEEK FOUR

forty-seven

Dad: "What do you mean, Lottie? *You're never going to stop this project?* What, ever? What about your Cambridge interview? You promised it was just for a month, Lottie...Lottie?"

Mum: "Lottie, this is your future. Your entire future. Do not throw it away."

Dad: "I didn't raise you to be like this. It's not just you who's worked hard for this, we all have. As a family. Don't be selfish, Charlotte. This is a huge opportunity. It will change your life."

Mr Packson: "Lottie, Cambridge will not take kindly to you pointing out every incidence of sexism you see in your interview...no...no...yes...yes, they are looking for independent thought...but not that kind of independent thought, Lottie...Lottie?"

Evie: "Maybe there won't be any sexism at Cambridge… What do you mean there's an annual jelly-wrestling competition? I mean, WHAT?"

Amber: "Fuck uni. Let's go travelling."

Mum: "Lottie, why didn't you tell me about this story in the paper? Lottie? Are you okay? This is terrible. Why didn't you tell us?"

Dad:…

Me: "The interview's tomorrow, Will. What do I do?"

Will: "Whatever you feel is right."

THE FUTURE

forty-eight

Here are the things I knew about Cambridge:

1. Their male students are statistically more likely to get first class degrees than their female students.
2. Around seventy-eight per cent of Cambridge professors are male.
3. Once every year, after exams, Magdalene College holds a jelly-wrestling event where female students in their bikinis grope each other and writhe around in jelly while hundreds of male students watch.
4. But they do have women-only colleges... Is that sexist? Or good?
5. They have a Women's Officer, who runs "Consent workshops" teaching freshers about the importance of sexual consent.

* * *

Mum and Dad insisted they came with me, though they wouldn't be allowed in. We drove in silence, tension crackling and fizzing between us in the car. There'd been arguments and more arguments. When Dad first found out about the newspaper story, his skin lost all its colour and he sat right down on the floor, looking sick. He didn't speak to me for the rest of the day. I couldn't tell if it was embarrassment, or sympathy. My auntie had gone absolutely nuts for one, ringing the house to say I'd shamed the whole family. Whatever it was, he came down to breakfast the next morning and started telling me off about the project, about Cambridge, about how I couldn't let one ruin the other.

"I don't want that either," I said. "But I want them to want me for me, not a toned-down Diet-Coke version of me."

It was a bright winter's day, the sun glowing in a way that made everything look a really stark yellow. We passed a *Welcome to Cambridge* sign and it was like driving into Hogsmeade. I'd seen photos on the internet, but it didn't prepare me for how pretty it was in real life. Fairy-tale-like buildings stretched up into the sky; there were actual cobbled streets, made from actual cobbles. And there were students everywhere, biking along in their winter coats, groups of them walking together, clutching coffees, carrying books, laughing.

I slunk down in my seat, feeling embarrassed that I was with my parents.

It was so beautiful. I closed my eyes and tried to picture myself there and it came easily. I had visions of myself running around, clutching one of those black flat-caps to my head, even though I think you only wear them when you graduate. I pictured the things I'd learn, the people I'd meet – the way I could grow and become the sort of person who'd go on to do great things. In my head, I looked happy, relaxed fulfilled…then I pictured some jelly-wrestling and the daydream was shattered.

I mean – jelly-wrestling!

My parents and I fought about where to park.

My parents and I fought about where to get lunch.

My parents and I fought when the waitress at lunch gave the bill to my dad and I called her out on it.

"Lottie, honestly. Please tell me you're not going to be like this in the interview."

"It's one day. Can't you hold it in for just one day?"

"When she gets back, I want you to apologize to that waitress."

"Lottie? Where are you going, Lottie?"

I screeched my chair back, grabbed my bag and dashed out of the cafe. I couldn't stand it. I was too nervous and scared and terrified and confused and nervous and…and…

I dodged down a few alleyways, until I was sure I'd lost them. Then, to stop them worrying – well, to minimally decrease their worrying – I sent them a message, saying:

> I just need some time to myself. I'll meet you outside
> the entrance to King's fifteen minutes before.

As I took off through the city, my head was spinning with all the thoughts. I felt giddy and not-with-it and all the other exact-opposite things of how you're supposed to feel before a Cambridge interview.

I navigated my way to King's College, using a mixture of my phone and the map that had been sent to me in the post. I had about half an hour.

I'd seen photos on the brochure, but when I arrived at King's, the scene still made me not inhale adequately for a good few seconds.

The college was beautiful. A manicured stretch of grass was surrounded by the most stunning grey-brick ye-olde buildings that seemed to just murmur secrets and knowledge and distinction. The famous spire of the chapel seared into the bright blue sky, like it was an arrowhead guiding me there.

It was just about warm enough to take my coat off and use it as a protective cushion from the stone wall outside. I sat myself down, the interview pack perched on my lap to signal to people that I sort of belonged here, for today at least.

I would only belong here if I got in…

A group of students walked by, clutching folders and laughing as they made their way to a lecture. They looked so happy, so proud of themselves, so…I dunno…part of a community.

Recently, I'd started to think more about what it would be like when Amber, Evie and I all went our separate ways at the end of the school year. It made me feel so ill I tried not to dwell on it. It was inevitable though. Time would rip us apart, float us on different gusts of wind, grow us up, make us have separate experiences, and we'd have to cling on and hope we didn't grow apart as well as into grown-ups.

I would have to make new friends, wherever I was, wherever I ended up. And, looking at the passing group, I really felt they were the sort of people I could be friends with.

A girl had her arm slung around the others, and just as they passed, she said, "I know this vastly undermines everything he said and stood for but, man, Karl Marx did good beard."

Everyone laughed. I wanted to laugh – to be part of it – but I just smiled eagerly at them from my spot on the wall. The girl noticed, smiled, and slowed – letting the others go ahead. She pointed to my pack. "You here for an interview?" I nodded, delighted she was talking to me.

"You scared?" she asked. I could hardly see her features against the low sun.

"I made my parents stop on the motorway three times on the drive here," I answered. "It's only a two-hour drive."

She laughed again. "I was bricking it too," she said. "But it's not so bad. Don't believe the horror stories you hear."

Her mates dawdled, waiting for her, and she stepped away, towards them, into the shade. She was pretty, but not in a way that asked to be commented on. Bleached blonde hair, cut very short. Just a smudge of red lipstick, nothing else. I felt dorky in my suit.

"Do you like it here?" I asked, not wanting her to leave.

Her face broke into another natural smile, her lipstick spreading across her face.

"It's brilliant," she said. "It's so hard…but it's the best thing I've ever done. Though I think everyone says that about whatever uni they go to."

I could tell her attention was divided, but I chanced another question.

"I'm scared about behaving in the interview," I said. "I have a lot of…er…opinions."

She came and stood closer to me, looking over my shoulder at my brochure. "What you applying for?"

"Human, Social, and Political Science."

Her smile widened. "Just like me! Let me guess, you want to change the world?"

My blush answered her question and she laughed, just as her friends called, "Portia."

"Coming," she called behind her, and she took another step closer, so we were almost at eye level. "Well, if you're panicking, I guess it's worth telling you that you don't have to get in here to change the world…"

"But?" I prompted.

"But," she said, weighing up her words. "I'd be lying if I said it wasn't amazing here. It's just…" She looked back at her friends. "Something else, you know?"

I took in my ornate surroundings once more. "I know… Any last tips?" She was turning to go.

"Oh sure," she replied over her shoulder, as she walked away to her waiting friends. "The same as for everything in life, just be yourself."

I watched her walk away.

Just be yourself.

Everything in my life was supposed to have been leading up to this moment. So I could get in and that would take me to a different moment. Moment upon moment until eventually, in time, I could be in a position to change things.

Getting into a place like this changes things.

But, as I flipped through the brochure again, students grinning inanely at me from the pages as they studied on the lawn, or swaggered down stone corridors, I had a thought.

I had already started to change things.

My project had started something. It had sown seeds, it had reached people. It had lit fires, it had opened minds, changed opinions, raised eyebrows, started dialogues, poked bears, turned Will, helped Megan…

And I'd done all that without a fancy degree from a fancy place. I'd done all that without knowing the right people, saying the right things, moving in the right circles. I was Lottie, I was no one really. All I had was my voice, my anger, and the determination to voice my anger in the best way I knew how. And look what I'd done. With just that. Well, that, and the two best friends I could wish for by my side.

I didn't *need* to get in here...

I'd thought I might, but I didn't.

I could get wherever I wanted to go by myself. I could change things by myself. I'd proven that already.

I stood up, wiping my cold arse from where the damp of the stones had seeped through my coat.

And I decided.

I only wanted to go here if they wanted me for me. I only wanted to go here if they *got* me. I wouldn't try and tone myself down so I could get them.

I was ready.

forty-nine

Mum and Dad were already waiting outside – looking even more nervous than me. I expected a telling-off, but their faces softened when they saw me.

"Lottie!" Dad went to hug me. "We were worried you might not turn up."

"I'm here."

Mum suddenly looked teary. "Look, darling, about your project…"

I held up my hand. "Please, not here."

"I know, darling…" She took my hand. "I just want you to know. Well, we'll always love you, whatever you decide."

I looked at Dad. "You will?"

He nodded. "Yes, Lottie. Of course. But…well…" Mum must've given him a lecture, telling him to back off. "Just think about what the most important thing is," he continued, giving me a meaningful look, "in the long run."

I met his eyes. "I will."

* * *

They called me precisely on time.

Even with everything I'd just decided, I felt incredibly nervous. The full force of my panic hit me the moment my name was read out. My palms instantly slickened and I wobbled up to standing, giving a feeble smile to the lady holding the clipboard.

"That's me."

"Come with me, dear." She walked off down an ornate corridor and I followed her and her very yellow cardigan, past doors with signs on them asking for quiet.

"Here you go." She stopped outside a door and gestured for me to go in.

My hand quivered on the handle. I took a deep breath then, before I lost my nerve, I turned the knob.

The room was small, cosy. Books were everywhere – lining up ramshackle-like, right up to the ceiling.

And there, in two big leathery armchairs, with a small table separating them, two fellows sat.

Two male fellows.

Male.

Both of them.

They stood up, leaning over to shake my hand. One of them was older, with a limp handshake that felt very cold – "I'm Professor Brown." The other dude, younger, so young

414

he looked like he didn't need to shave very often, had a firm grip and a wide open smile.

"Charlotte Thomas, nice to meet you. Thank you for coming. Now please, do sit down."

I found myself sitting, playing with my hands, twisting them over in my lap.

"Now," Professor Brown said, "I'm just going to explain what's going to happen. We already have the written assessment you did as part of your application, so we'll talk about that. And we'll also talk about your personal statement and why you're applying here. It's a discussion really, rather than an interview. We want to hear more about what you think."

I think it's a shame you're both men.

I nodded. "Sounds swell."

SWELL? SWELL? LOTTIE, WHEN HAVE YOU EVER USED THE WORD SWELL BEFORE NOW?

Do I mention that they're both men? Is that sexist? Or just coincidence? Maybe there'll be two women in my next interview? They said there might be more than one. Do I ask? Do I bring it up? I knew I was supposed to, I knew what I'd decided, out there in the courtyard, less than half an hour ago, but I was still shaking for some reason.

"So…" the young man said. He'd told me his name. I couldn't remember it. Julian? "We were reading your personal statement, and it says here that you're interested in women's studies?"

Oh God, they were going straight for the feminism.

Out of all the things I'd written in that freaking statement, they were going for my Achilles' heel. Had they seen my campaign? Is that what they were hinting at?

"That you started a society of sorts at your college?"

I gulped, maybe I nodded. I wasn't sure. My head didn't feel connected to anything – certainly not my sweat-engulfed body.

"That's right."

"Well, as you know this course is called Human, Social, and Political Science, and we do discuss the role of women…"

Which is why I picked it.

"So, with that in mind," Julian continued, "our first question is – if you could, what would you do to try and eradicate gender inequality in society?"

My eyes widened.

I couldn't answer that without bringing everything up. Everything I'd done. Was that why they were asking me? And, if I was going to be true to my project, would they mind me asking them some very pressing questions myself?

I knew what they were looking for. Mr Packson had explained how they worked and I knew they wanted me to pull the question apart. To show my wider reading, to show how I could think rationally, to show I was capable of independent thought (as long as I was referencing a lot of published academics' independent thought).

They weren't asking this so I could tell them about my video channel.

But that was what I was doing to try and eradicate gender inequality. And I was proud of it. I was so, so proud of it.

"Charlotte?" the professor prompted, looking unimpressed.

I hadn't answered. I hadn't said one thing. I knew I was standing on the edge of something – that this was a moment in my life that would become a "before" and "after". I knew I wanted to leap off…but everything I'd ever been taught was to comply and behave in these sorts of situations.

"Sorry," I mumbled, trying to buy time to sort myself out. "I'm thinking."

It came out so much more aggressively than I'd hoped. Professor Brown raised an eyebrow. Julian was kinder about it.

"Maybe if you think out loud, Charlotte? Then we can see how you get to your answer?"

Oh no, I was choking. I was totally choking. And I hadn't brought up the fact they were both male yet…if I was going to… What was I going to do…? This was my last chance to decide. Be a drone? Be who they wanted me to be? Suck it up for a day? It's just one day! Learn how to pick my battles? Learn some fights aren't worth the sacrifice? That sometimes, just sometimes, it's okay to let things go? Especially if it's for a better outcome in the long run?

I still wasn't talking. It was getting awkward now. I probably had thirty seconds left before they wrote me off… The nerves got to her…such a shame… But I wasn't nervous about the thing they were assuming I was nervous about.

When you want to fight for what you believe in, you come across a lot of obstacles. People who don't agree with you, people who agree with you but only some bits, people who delight in ripping you down, people who are threatened by the strength of your belief.

But I was beginning to realize, the biggest hurdle to overcome was the hurdle of yourself.

Was I going to sabotage myself?

Or, actually, was I going to set myself free?

I remembered what Megan had said: *"Think back to the beginning, Lottie. What made you want to do this in the first place?"*

And I remembered the train, and the line, and flicking the switch. And that knowledge, deep inside of me, that I never wanted to be the one flicking it.

I wanted to be the sort of person who could face themselves in the mirror.

I wanted to be the sort of girl who knows you've got to pull out the bottom bricks of the pyramid, to topple the top ones.

I wanted to be the Lottie who inspired all those emails read out last week, by a roomful of all the best people I've ever met.

I wanted to change things on my own terms, to show that there's no right or wrong way to change the world. There's no entry test. You don't need to suck anything up. Pay any dues. Just you and your anger and your voice is enough. If you only have the courage to use it.

"Charlotte?"

I looked up, staring them straight in the eye. I opened my mouth to speak.

There is no going back – not once you've raised the veil, not once you've opened your eyes. You can't stuff it all back in a box, not once you've seen it. You can't pretend it's not there.

…So many people pretend it's not there.

I was not going to be one of those people.

"Well, the first thing I would do," I said, my voice so confident I didn't even recognize it, "is ask why it's two *men* interviewing me to get into the most prestigious institution in this country. And then…" I paused for breath…

"Then, I want to tell you why I'm asking that."

the end

a letter from holly

To my spinsters,

When I was twenty-five, I was sexually harassed on my way to work. In fact, what happens to Lottie at the opening of this book is essentially word-for-word what happened to me. I was going through A Very Bad Year, and something snapped in me that day. I knew I wanted it to stop. All of it. I didn't want any other girl to walk down the street and have that happen to them. That was the day I came up with the idea for this trilogy and the Spinster Club and Evie, Amber and Lottie.

Sometimes I want to thank those horrible, awful men in the van. As, really, they changed my life. Writing these books has changed me – they've helped me grow and learn and develop. What's been so amazing is seeing how you guys have responded to them too. Honestly, I could never have dreamed how funny, angry, strong, honest, brilliant and kick-ass my readers would turn out to be. Whenever you contact me to say you've started your own Spinster Club, or stood up to some sexist bullshit, or done a school assembly about International Women's Day – it warms my heart in such a deep way I can't even describe it.

Even with three whole books to explore feminism, I felt the spinsters and I have only exposed the tip of the iceberg that is inequality. I wasn't able to touch properly on feminism and how it relates to race, or disability, or sexuality, or gender identity, or class. Inequality is like a really shit onion, with layers upon layers of oppression pinning down different people in different ways. My experiences of being a woman will be different from yours. Lottie's, Amber's and Evie's experiences won't be entirely like yours. Also, if you're one of my awesome male readers, that doesn't mean you aren't also oppressed (and doesn't prohibit you from being a spinster either!).

I couldn't cover it all. But, what I hoped would happen with these books is that it would inspire you to fight for the change you want to see. To help you realize that, whoever you are, whatever you've experienced, whatever hardship you've faced, you have a voice and you are allowed to use it. Your voice counts. Your experience counts. Your anger counts. Together we can fight this. Together we are stronger. Together we can fight for a world that is healthier and happier for everyone in it.

I'm writing this on the first proper day of spring 2016, looking out at the daffodils. I don't know where you are as you're reading this. But wherever it is, I am reaching through my computer screen, and holding your hand through the pages of this book. I am travelling through time to tell you to GO FOR IT. I want to hear YOUR voice. I want to hear YOUR experience. What happens to you and what you go through matters. Your voice matters. I am passing on the torch. I want to see what fires you start (please, not literally, please always be safe). If these books have started a ripple in you, I want you to take that and make your own ripples.

It's not easy. Fighting for what is right rarely is. You will have days when you're too exhausted or angry to speak out. There will be times when it's not even safe to. Some days you'll get it wrong, or change your mind, or be a huge hunking hypocrite, and have people drag you across the coals for it. You'll come across people who are more pond-scum than people. You will find yourself defending your anger, defending your experience, practically daily – not just to The Man, but even to other feminists. Even, sometimes, to people you love and adore. But you're not alone. Find other people who get it. Start a Spinster Club. Find people who say "Me too", rather than denying your experience. They're out there. They care. They understand. If you look for them, you will find them. And it changes everything. It makes the fight so much easier.

Thank you so much for coming on this journey with me. I cannot wait to see what journeys you are yet to go on. The incredible things I believe you are going to achieve. And, of course, the cheesy snacks you are going to devour.

Spinsters – it's over to you.

TO BE A FEMINIST?

If you've been inspired by
Lottie's story and want to start
your own Spinster Club, here are
a few ideas...

Speak up!

Be the change you want to see. If you see something sexist, call it out if it's safe for you to do so. Ask questions, demand answers. If everyone did this, we'd get there so much quicker.

Check out Emma Watson's book club

Hermione *cough* I mean Emma Watson has started an online feminist book club, where you can read along with Hermione *cough* I mean Emma to grow your understanding of different feminist issues.

Help charities

Women's services are being cut hard and fast, and you can help raise money/volunteer for charities filling these gaps. Seek out charities that you feel passionate about – there's loads of great info online.

Start a Spinster Club

Honestly! Some of the best feminist campaigns have come out of girls just getting together and chatting about how WEIRD it is to be a girl. Book some time in every week with people you trust and feel comfortable around to just have a big natter. It's mad how inspired you feel afterwards.

And to get you started, check out…

Holly's
SPINSTER CLUB
book list

One of my favourite things about writing the Spinster Club trilogy is that I've been on my own feminist learning journey through writing the books. Here are my favourite books I've come across while doing my research.

1) HOW TO BE A WOMAN by Caitlin Moran
This half autobiography, half feminist manifesto literally changed my life. It was like my gateway drug into feminism.

2) MEN EXPLAIN THINGS TO ME by Rebecca Solnit
This collection of feminist essays will make you angry, very angry. But in a good way. A way that makes you want to turn all this new-found anger into ACTION.

3) EVERYDAY SEXISM by Laura Bates
This book, based on the game-changing blog of the same name, shoots dead any argument that feminism is no longer needed. A collection of the ridiculous/heartbreaking/head-bashing NONSENSE of the everyday sexism that girls and women face, every day.

4) I CALL MYSELF A FEMINIST: THE VIEW FROM TWENTY-FIVE WOMEN UNDER THIRTY

Something will appeal to everyone in this inspiring collection of young feminist essays. It's essentially a look at real-life Lotties, Evies and Ambers around the UK and all the kick-ass stuff they're doing. It also shines a light on some of the lesser-discussed parts of feminism, like experiences of trans women, Muslim women and loads of other brilliant voices. Perfect for dipping into.

5) WE SHOULD ALL BE FEMINISTS by Chimamanda Ngozi Adichie

Based on her incredible TEDx talk, this manifesto is incredibly short and yet incredibly powerful. It's a bit like doing a shot of hardcore feminism...in a good way.

SPINSTER CLUB
discussion points

So you've bought the cheesy snacks and got the girls on board. Here are some topics to get your feminist fires burning, inspired by Evie, Amber and Lottie's own Spinster Club discussions.

Name a film that passes the Bechdel test
To pass, a film has to have at least two women in it and they've got to have at least one conversation about something other than men.

Do you recognize any cognitive dissonances in yourself?
It's not always easy to uphold feminist ideals in the face of social norms. Where do you struggle the most?

Why have "spinster" and "feminist" become seen as offensive words?
The Spinster Club began because the girls wanted to reclaim the word spinster and make it mean something positive. But why was that even necessary?

The web can be seen as a negative place

where feminists are open to attack. But can
it be beneficial too?
Lottie discovers that when you fight for something you
believe in, "people are going to swipe at you". But do the
positives of online feminist communities outweigh the
negative comments?

Why does feminist behaviour in relationships
make people feel uncomfortable?
How can we get people to move past traditional gender
roles, like guys being expected to pay the bill on a date, or
girls feeling uncomfortable about asking guys out?

How can your class, race, religion,
sexuality, gender-identity and disability
impact your experience as a woman?
Lottie wants everyone to add to her feminist "duvet" of
different female experiences. How can feminist campaigns
include more diverse voices?

What made you realize you were a feminist?
For some people, a particular experience, book, or person
awakens them to feminist issues, just like Lottie's experience
with the van men prompted her campaign.

And finally, who can make the biggest food
baby?!
Bring on the cheese!

We'd love to hear about YOUR SPINSTER CLUBS, and your favourite moments from the SPINSTER CLUB trilogy. Join the conversation online and start sharing!

#SPINSTERCLUB

(Virtual cheesy snacks welcome...)

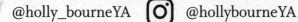 @holly_bourneYA @hollybourneYA

@Usborne @UsborneYA

 www.usborne.com/youngadult

usborneYAshelfies.tumblr.com

EXCITING NEWS!
The girls are back in a
SPINSTER CLUB
special

...AND A HAPPY NEW YEAR?

Find out what happens to Evie,
Amber and Lottie beyond college, beyond
the Spinster Club, as they reunite for an
epic party filled with New Year's
revelations...

Coming November 2016

ISBN 9781474927222